continued . . .

"Sure to please the fussiest of historical romance readers."
—*Romance Reviews Today*

"Anne Gracie does it again: *The Accidental Wedding* is funny, charming, and completely endearing . . . There are some authors I pick up when I just want some comfort at the end of a long day. Anne Gracie is one of them. Although the stories have their share of excitement, ultimately it's the love between the characters and the remarkably well-drawn relationships that pull me in and keep me in the story."—*Night Owl Reviews*

"A fairy tale any girl would love. Two people, likely to never know love, find each other to make the perfect match in this extraordinary love story. Anne Gracie's writing is historical romance at its best . . . Anne Gracie has created a story of Cinderella finding her prince and doing her best to give them the most perfect happily ever after . . . [It's] a delightful and fanciful novel that is charmingly romantic and sure to mesmerize you long after you've read it!"   —*The Season*

"Gracie has created some of the best heroines in romance fiction . . . Nobody is better than Anne Gracie at evoking tears and laughter within a single story."   —*The Romance Dish*

Praise for
To Catch a Bride

"Anne Gracie at her best, with a dark and irresistible hero, a rare and winsome heroine, and a ravishing romance. Catch a copy now! One of the best historical romances I've read in ages."   —Mary Jo Putney, *New York Times* bestselling author

"Swiftly moving . . . Appealing and unconventional . . . Will captivate readers."   —*RT Book Reviews* (4 stars)

"Threaded with charm and humor . . . [An] action-rich, emotionally compelling story . . . It is sure to entice readers."
—*Library Journal* (starred review)

"There is so much I liked about this one, it's hard to find a place to start."   —*All About Romance*

"It was loveable and laugh-out-loud, full of heart and of memorable and interesting characters."   —*Errant Dreams Reviews*

"A fascinating twist on the girl-in-disguise plot . . . With its wildly romantic last chapter, this novel is a great antidote to the end of the summer."
> —Eloisa James, *New York Times* bestselling author

"One of the difficulties of reviewing a favorite author is running out of superlatives. An Anne Gracie novel is guaranteed to have heart and soul, passion, action, and sprinkles of humor and fun."   —*Romance Reviews Today*

Praise for
His Captive Lady

"With tenderness, compassion, and a deep understanding of the era, Gracie touches readers on many levels with her remarkable characters and intense exploration of their deepest human needs. Gracie is a great storyteller."
> —*RT Book Reviews* (4½ stars, Top Pick)

"Once again, author Anne Gracie has proven what an exceptionally gifted author is all about . . . She gives life to unforgettable characters and brings her readers along for the ride in what has proven to be an exciting, fun, and heartfelt emotional journey. Absolutely one of the best romances I've read this year!"   —*CK²S Kwips and Kritiques*

"Anne Gracie has created a deeply emotional, at times heart-wrenching, journey for these two people who must learn to trust one another with their deepest feelings and darkest fears."
> —*Romance Novel TV*

"A winner . . . A charming, witty, and magical romance . . . Anne Gracie is a treasure."   —*Fresh Fiction*

continued . . .

Bride By Mistake

Anne Gracie

BERKLEY SENSATION, NEW YORK

THE BERKLEY PUBLISHING GROUP
Published by the Penguin Group
Penguin Group (USA) Inc.
375 Hudson Street, New York, New York 10014, USA
Penguin Group (Canada), 90 Eglinton Avenue East, Suite 700, Toronto, Ontario M4P 2Y3, Canada
(a division of Pearson Penguin Canada Inc.)
Penguin Books Ltd., 80 Strand, London WC2R 0RL, England
Penguin Group Ireland, 25 St. Stephen's Green, Dublin 2, Ireland (a division of Penguin Books Ltd.)
Penguin Group (Australia), 250 Camberwell Road, Camberwell, Victoria 3124, Australia
(a division of Pearson Australia Group Pty. Ltd.)
Penguin Books India Pvt. Ltd., 11 Community Centre, Panchsheel Park, New Delhi—110 017, India
Penguin Group (NZ), 67 Apollo Drive, Rosedale, Auckland 0632, New Zealand
(a division of Pearson New Zealand Ltd.)
Penguin Books (South Africa) (Pty.) Ltd., 24 Sturdee Avenue, Rosebank, Johannesburg 2196,
South Africa

Penguin Books Ltd., Registered Offices: 80 Strand, London WC2R 0RL, England

This is a work of fiction. Names, characters, places, and incidents either are the product of the author's imagination or are used fictitiously, and any resemblance to actual persons, living or dead, business establishments, events, or locales is entirely coincidental. The publisher does not have any control over and does not assume any responsibility for author or third-party websites or their content.

BRIDE BY MISTAKE

A Berkley Sensation Book / published by arrangement with the author

Printing History
Berkley Sensation mass-market edition / January 2012

Copyright © 2012 by Anne Gracie.
Cover art by Judy York.
Cover design by George Long.
Cover hand lettering by Ron Zinn.
Interior text design by Laura K. Corless.

ISBN: 978-0-425-24579-8

BERKLEY SENSATION®
Berkley Sensation Books are published by The Berkley Publishing Group,
a division of Penguin Group (USA) Inc.,
375 Hudson Street, New York, New York 10014.
BERKLEY SENSATION® is a registered trademark of Penguin Group (USA) Inc.
The "B" design is a trademark of Penguin Group (USA) Inc.

PRINTED IN THE UNITED STATES OF AMERICA

10 9 8 7 6 5 4 3 2 1

In memory of my beloved dog, Chloe,
who kept me company through
the writing of the last ten books.
A loving companion,
she found joy in the simplest of things.

One

❦

London 1819

"You're a madman, Ripton!"

Luke Ripton shrugged and gathered his reins. "The curricle can be repaired, Jarvis. At least your horses aren't injured."

"No thanks to you!" Jarvis snarled. "Passing me like that—you damned near grazed my wheels—"

"But I didn't," Luke coldly interrupted. The man drove like an over-anxious debutante. "There was no need to swerve so violently. You had only to hold your nerve."

"Nerve? I'll give you nerve." Jarvis started forward, only to be restrained by the friends who'd come to witness—and bet on—the race.

"Steady on, Jarvis. Lord Ripton won fair and square," said one of his friends.

"You were a fool to challenge him in the first place," said another, a little too drunk for tact. "Everyone knows Ripton don't care if he lives or dies. Makes him—*hic!*—unbeatable."

Luke tipped his hat to his still fuming opponent and drove away. Was it true? Did he care if he lived or died?

He considered the question as he drove back into town. It was not untrue, he decided as he turned into Upper Brook Street. He wasn't certain he deserved to live. He'd tempted fate often enough.

But fate, it seemed, had other plans for him.

The letter in his pocket confirmed it.

He pulled up outside his mother's town house. The house belonged to him, of course—it came with the title he'd inherited when his uncle and cousins had been drowned two years ago. But though Luke was fond of his mother and youngest sister, he preferred not to live with them. His mother had a tendency to fuss. Luke preferred his bachelor lodgings, a neat suite of rooms in Clarges Street, where nobody questioned his comings or goings.

"*T*hank God!" Lady Ripton exclaimed as Luke entered the drawing room. She rang for fresh tea and cakes.

He kissed the cheek she raised. "I'm not unduly late, am I?" She'd asked him to call on her in the morning. It was just before eleven.

"No, but I was worried about you, of course. These frightful races! I don't understand why—"

"—why impertinent busybodies bother you with things that are not your concern," Luke interrupted. He'd done his best to keep such activities from his mother, dammit.

"Not my concern? My son, my only son, risking his neck in the most reckless—"

"My neck is in perfect order, Mama. I apologize for any unnecessary worry," Luke said crisply. And when he found out who'd been passing tittle-tattle to his mother, he'd wring their *neck*. "Now, what was it you wanted to talk to me about?"

As if he didn't know. Molly's impending come-out was all his mother and sister talked of. Even though Luke had given her carte blanche to order whatever she liked, Mama still wanted him to approve all the arrangements—her way of reminding him he was head of the family. How she'd react if he ever actually made a suggestion of his own . . .

Mama had been a widow since Luke was a schoolboy and Molly a little girl. Luke had been away at war since he was eighteen, and Mama had managed to launch and successfully marry off Luke's two older sisters. She was accustomed to ruling the roost, though if anyone suggested as much, she would be horrified. It was a man's job to rule.

So each week they went through the ritual of Mama producing plans and expenditure and Luke approving.

He drank his tea and listened with half an ear. Today he was even less interested in her arrangements than usual. He had to tell her about the letter in his pocket.

She wasn't going to like it.

"Now, about the ball, I thought we'd invite forty to dine beforehand. Molly and I have compiled a list, but there's the question of who you would like us to invite. I don't mean dearest Rafe, Harry, or Gabe, and their wives, of course—naturally they are already on the list. Molly has never forgotten how, when she was still a little girl, all you boys promised to dance with her at her come-out. Thank God you all came back from the war."

Not all, Luke thought, but then his mother hadn't known Michael very well.

"Is there anyone special you'd like me to invite? Any special lady?" she said with delicate emphasis.

"Lady Gosforth?" he said, naming his friends' great aunt.

His mother slapped him lightly on the hand. "Do not be provoking, Luke. You know very well what I mean. It's two years since you came into your uncle's title, and it's high time you thought seriously about marriage."

Ah. His opening. Luke set down his teacup. "As to that, I have been thinking seriously about marriage." Damned seriously, in fact.

His mother leaned eagerly forward. "You have a bride in mind?"

"More than in mind; almost in hand, you might say." He

swallowed. It was harder than he'd thought to admit what he'd done.

"Almost in hand? I don't understand. You mean you're about to propose?"

"No. I'm married."

"*Married?*" Her teacup froze halfway to her mouth. Her wrist trembled and the cup dropped from suddenly nerveless fingers and clattered to the table, spilling tea over the delicate polished surface. His mother ignored it. There was a long silence, then she said in a voice that shook only a little, "You cannot be serious!"

"I am. Quite serious." He rose and went to the sherry decanter.

"But when did you marry? And who's the girl? And why, for God's sake, why?"

He poured her a glass of sherry and thought about how to present his marriage in the best possible light. It wasn't going to be easy. He wasn't sure there was a best light.

She took the glass in a distracted manner. "Don't tell me—she's some designing harpy who tricked you into—"

"Nothing of the sort!" he said firmly. "Do not take me for a fool, Mama. She is a lady, very respectable, very well born—"

"A widow," said his mother in a hollow voice.

"Far from it. She is young, the same age as Molly, not yet one-and-twenty."

His mother eyed him shrewdly, looking for the fly in the ointment. "What's her name? Who are her people?"

"Her name is Isabella Mercedes Sanchez y Vaillant, and she is the only daughter of the Conde de Castillejo."

His mother's elegant brows snapped together. "Foreigners?"

"Spanish aristocracy." It was a quiet reprimand.

"Refugees." She sighed. "I suppose she is desperately impoverished."

"On the contrary, she is an heiress. And she is not a refugee."

She frowned, looking puzzled. "I haven't heard of any Spanish heiresses visiting London. Where did you meet her?"

"In Spain, during the war."

"During the *war*?" His mother blinked. "So long ago? Then what has she been doing all this time?"

"Sewing samplers and doing her lessons, I imagine."

"Sewing—" She broke off, gave him a narrow look, then said with dignity, "This is no time for teasing, Luke. Why have I not met her? Met her parents? And why such a hole-in-the-corner wedd—"

"Her parents are dead. And you have not met her for the very good reason that she is still in Spain." And he wasn't teasing.

"In Spain?" She frowned. "But it's years since you were in Spain. I don't understand. How can you have married a girl who is still in Spain?"

Luke glanced away. "The marriage was some time ago."

She leaned forward, her face filled with foreboding. "How long ago?"

"In the spring of 1811."

She did the sums. "Eight years ago? When you were *nineteen*?" She stared, her brow crumpled with bewilderment. "And all this time you never thought to tell me? Why, Luke? Why?"

"It seemed the right thing to do at the time." It was the only explanation he was prepared to give.

Closing her eyes as if it was too much to bear, his mother leaned back in her chair and fanned herself, even though, being March, it wasn't the least bit warm.

"*Samplers?*" Her eyes flew open and she sat up with a jerk. "How old was this girl? In 1811, Molly was a child of—"

"Thirteen. And yes, Isabella was almost thirteen when I married her."

"You married a *child*?" she almost shrieked. "Oh, the scandal when this gets out!"

"I have no intention of letting it be known."

"But Luke . . . Thirteen! A mere child! How could you?" She looked at him with faint horror.

"Don't be ridiculous, Mama," he said with asperity. "Of

course I never touched her. What do you take me for?" And because he could still see the confusion and anxiety in his mother's eyes, he continued, "I married her to protect her, of course. And then I gave her into the care of her aunt, who is a nun."

His mother shook her head and said in a resigned voice, "Catholic as well. I might have known." She swirled her sherry pensively for a few moments, drained her glass, and said decisively, "We shall have it annulled."

"No, we shall not."

"But you were not yet one-and-twenty, not of legal age to marry without parental permission. And if the girl is untouched, an annulment is—"

"No."

"Of course you must. You simply apply to—"

"Mother."

She bit her lip and subsided.

Luke said, "I applied for an annulment. It was refused."

"On what grounds—"

"The marriage is legal, Mother," he said in a voice that brooked no argument. Luke had no intention of explaining to his mother or anyone else why an annulment was not possible.

She looked at him with dismay but read the resolution in his eyes. "So what will you do?"

"Honor the marriage, of course. I have no other option."

"And the girl?"

"She has no other option, either."

"So I collect, Luke, but what does she think? How does she feel?"

He gave her a blank look. "I have no idea. It doesn't matter what she thinks or feels—the marriage is legal and we're both stuck with it—and I hope I don't need to say, that's for your ears only, Mama."

"Of course," his mother murmured.

"The Spanish are used to arranged marriages; this will be no different. Besides, she's been raised in a convent."

His mother gave him a puzzled look. "What has that to do with it?"

"She'll have acquired the habit of obedience," Luke explained. "Nuns devote their lives to poverty, chastity, and obedience."

His mother blinked. "I see," she said faintly.

"So, that's that. I'll be off then." He stood to leave.

"Luke Ripton, do not dare step a foot out of this room until you have finished explaining."

Luke raised a brow. "I've told you everything you need to know."

His mother rolled her eyes. "How like a man."

It seemed to be some sort of accusation, though what else he could be like was beyond him. But clearly his mother felt the need to hash over the thing some more. Luke reluctantly sat down again.

"Why did you not tell me about your marriage before?"

"I thought it wouldn't matter." Thought he'd be dead. Or the marriage annulled.

"Not *matter*?" Her mouth gaped. His mother never gaped.

"It was wartime, Mama. Anything could happen. To her. To me." He shrugged. "But it didn't." She shut her mouth, then opened it, and he quickly added, "I made the necessary arrangements in the event of my death. Everyone taken care of; you had nothing to worry about."

She stared at him in silence. "Only the loss of my son."

He shrugged again. "But it didn't happen. As to how the *ton* will react to the news of my marriage, I plan to put it about that I'm traveling to Spain on some other purpose—"

"Visiting your Spanish properties? It's the only part of the estate you've neglected."

He stiffened, not liking the accusation, though it was true enough. He'd intended to sell off the Spanish properties, wanted nothing to do with them. He wanted no reminders of his time in Spain. He loathed the place. It made him feel ill just to contemplate returning there.

But fate had risen to bite him once more. The annulment had been denied and he had no option but to return to the country he'd sworn never to set foot in again. Stirring memories he'd tried so desperately to forget.

"Yes, the Spanish properties, if you like. And then I'll return with a Spanish bride on my arm."

"I suppose that will work," his mother agreed. "But oh, Luke, this makes me so sad. I've always hoped you'd find a lovely girl who'd—"

"A marriage of convenience will suit me very well," he said in a crisp voice. "Now, is there anything else you wish to know before I leave?" No point in letting his mother dwell on her dreams for him to make the kind of marriage she'd had with his father. They were her dreams, not Luke's.

His dreams . . . A sliver of ice slid down his spine. The less said of them the better.

"Is she pretty, at least?"

He thought of Isabella the last time he'd seen her, her face all bruised and swollen, all angles and that too-big nose, like a fierce little baby bird, new hatched and ugly. "She was barely thirteen, Mama. She'll have changed in eight years." He hoped so, at least.

His mother saw he'd avoided the question. "Will I like her?"

"I don't know," he said helplessly. "I knew her for barely a day, and it was under extraordinary circumstances. Who knows what she is like now? Now, I really must go—"

"One more thing."

He waited. There was a long silence. His mother shifted restlessly in her seat, twisting a handkerchief between her fingers. "Luke, I know you don't like to talk about . . . about . . . and I have respected your privacy, you know I have, but now I have to ask. Was this the thing that happened to you in Spain, the thing you will not talk of?"

He stiffened and looked away. "I don't know what you mean."

She said gently, "Just because you choose not to acknowledge it doesn't mean your mother can't see that something terrible happened to you in Spain."

"I went to war, Mother," he said in a hard voice. "War changes people."

"I know," she said softly. "I saw it in all you boys. You all came back changed. But with you, my dearest son, there was something more; something very personal that cut deeper."

He almost flinched at her choice of words. She could not know, he reminded himself. Nobody knew. He hadn't spoken of it to anyone, not even Rafe or Harry or Gabe.

"I've seen your friends recover, and settle down, one by one, but not you . . . Whatever it was, it still haunts you."

He forced a careless tone. "Well, whatever you imagine haunts me, it isn't this marriage. To be honest, I barely gave it a thought. She was just a young girl, Molly's age, who was in trouble, and by marrying her I was able to save her from a nasty fate. I thought we could get an annulment, but . . ." He spread his hands in a fatalistic gesture.

Before his mother could persist, he rose to his feet. "I've been in correspondence with Isabella's aunt—the nun, you will recall—and advised her I would collect Isabella at my earliest convenience. I leave tomorrow for Spain."

"Tomorrow?" She sat up, distracted as he knew she'd be. "But Molly's ball is in three weeks!"

"I'll be back in time for that," he assured her. "I promised Molly when I first went to war, and then again when I went to Waterloo, that I'd return to dance at her come-out. There's no danger I'll break my promise now. There's enough time to get to the Convent of the Angels and return. I'll inform Rafe and Harry of my plans, and they'll be on hand should you require any masculine advice or assistance."

His mother dismissed that with an impatient gesture. "And what if you're delayed?"

He placed a light kiss on her cheek. "I've survived everything that Boney could throw at me, Mama. What could possibly delay me now?"

*L*uke went directly from his mother's house to the Apocalypse Club in St. James. Established shortly after Waterloo, the club catered largely to young officers who'd served in the war. It was a small, discreet establishment, and Luke and his friends found it a convivial place. Contrary to the assumptions made by nonmembers, the one subject members almost never discussed was the war.

Tonight would be an exception.

Luke found Rafe and Harry in a private salon, lounging in overstuffed leather armchairs, sipping wine, boots stretched out toward the fire, the picture of masculine contentment.

How did they do it? Restlessness still gnawed at Luke's vitals, and it was years since the war had finished. Four long years.

Rafe rose to his feet. "About time you got here."

Harry drained his wineglass, gave Luke a friendly punch on the shoulder, and jerked his head toward the dining room. "Come on. The scent of steak and kidney pie has been calling to me for the last twenty minutes."

"No time for that," Luke said. "I'm off to Spain in the morning."

"*Spain?*" Both his friends looked at him in stupefaction.

"You swore you'd never set foot in Spain again," Rafe said.

Luke shrugged. "Needs must. Sit down and I'll fill you in," he said.

He told them the story, just the bare bones—the circumstances of the marriage was his business and Isabella's, and not even these, his closest friends, needed to know the sordid details.

"Married all this time?" Rafe was incredulous. "And never a word to any of us? I don't believe it." He sat back, his bright blue eyes boring into Luke.

"It's true," Luke told him. "I had a mission into the mountains and came across her on the way back to headquarters. It was"—he swallowed—"I married her for her own protection. It was—you know what can happen."

"You mean you were trapped into it? We were green boys back then."

Luke shook his head. "Not trapped at all. The marriage was my idea."

After a moment, Rafe asked, "So this Isabella, where is she now?"

"Where I left her. In the convent. In Spain."

"A *convent*?"

"Good God, she's not a nun, is she?" Harry said.

"No, she's damned well not a nun," Luke said irritably, fed up with questions, even though he knew they were perfectly natural. He'd had enough from his mother.

"Does your mother know?" Rafe began. "No, of course she doesn't, otherwise she wouldn't have spent the past couple of years flinging debutantes at your head." He shook his head. "Explains why, when you had your pick of the prettiest girls in the *ton*, you never gave any one of them a second look."

Luke grimaced. "I couldn't have married any of those girls. They were babies."

Rafe snorted. "As opposed to your mature thirteen-year-old bride."

"She was the same age as Molly, Rafe," Luke snapped. "Would *you* have left her unprotected in the mountains?"

Rafe had known Molly since Luke had brought him home as a lonely schoolboy. Chubby-cheeked toddler Molly had adored him on sight. Rafe shut his mouth.

"So why did you leave her in Spain?" Harry asked. "Why didn't you send her home to your mother?"

"Because it wasn't supposed to be a permanent marriage," Luke said, exasperated. "It was just a temporary measure. I—we thought the marriage could be annulled later. And besides—" He broke off.

Harry twirled his brandy slowly in his glass. "Besides, you thought you'd be killed before that happened." He glanced at Rafe. "We remember what you were like after Michael was killed."

The fire hissed and crackled in the grate.

"This was before Michael died," Luke said.

In the distance they could hear the clinking and clattering of crockery and silverware. Michael was the sunniest one of them all; bright, uncomplicated, the golden boy.

Luke forced his mind back to the present. "I told my mother about Isabella this evening. She's not very happy about me leaving the country so soon before Molly's come-out—"

"I'm not surprised—" Rafe began.

"—so I told her she could call on you for any advice or assistance she and Molly might need. Escorting them to balls and routs, shopping, that sort of thing."

Rafe struggled to hide an appalled look. "Er, delighted to assist Lady Ripton, of course."

Harry let out a crack of laughter. "Haven't you heard how delightful Rafe's found the preparations for Ayisha's first London season? Endless discussion of silks and laces and bonnets and the intricacies of female what-have-yous." He waved his hand to indicate reams of never-ending discussion. "Rafe, my lad, you'll be in your element."

Rafe sent Harry a black scowl. "You and Nell should never have introduced Ayisha to Lady Gosforth. The woman lives to shop! She has even infected my sensible Ayisha."

Harry chuckled. "Force of nature, Aunt Gosforth."

"Naturally I included you in the offer, Harry," Luke said smoothly. "You know how fond my mother is of you."

Harry's grin slipped. "Blast. You know I'm no good at all that society stuff."

"But you'll do it." It wasn't a question. He knew they would.

His friends sighed and nodded. Rafe refilled their glasses. "There'll be a deal of talk about this marriage, you know," he said. "Could get ugly. You know they're betting on who'll be married first, you or Marcus."

Luke grimaced. "I know. I want you to put it about that I've been called away to Spain on an urgent estate matter— my uncle owned vineyards in the south of Spain, if you recall. No mention of any bride; just estate business."

"Excellent notion," Rafe declared. "Then, when you return from Spain with a blushing bride on your arm, everyone thinks you two met, fell in love, and married in the space of a week or two."

"Let the *ton* gossip about the whirlwind romance." Harry nodded. "I'll drink to that."

They drank.

After a moment Rafe said, "You do know, I suppose, that if you bring a Spanish bride home, every eligible female in the *ton* will want to claw her eyes out. I hope she's ravishingly pretty."

Luke sipped his brandy. "She's not. But she's a brave little soul. She'll manage."

*L*uke's mother tossed and turned late into the night. Her son had always brought home strays and wounded creatures, from the first bird he found with a broken wing, to boys from school, like Harry and Gabe who had no family to go to, or Rafe whose father had no use for him and showed it.

It was one thing to love your son for his kindness to wounded creatures; it was quite another to see him bound to one in the shackles of marriage.

For the last four years she'd watched the young ladies of the *ton* simper and flirt and do all but throw themselves at Luke, seeing only his handsome face and, since his uncle died, his title. It hadn't worried her that Luke showed little interest. They were shallow creatures for the most part, not worthy of her beloved only son.

This year she was confident she'd found several very pretty girls with character, the type of girls who would love Luke for himself. She'd been looking forward to introducing them.

Now there was no point.

She reached for the hot milk she'd ordered, but it was cold now with a nasty skin. She pushed it away. Her bed felt colder and emptier than ever.

She'd never stopped missing Luke's father; never stopped reaching for him in the night and waking to find herself alone. The love of her life; she shouldn't complain. They'd had twenty of the happiest years together.

It was what she wanted for Luke, for all her children. A love to last a lifetime.

She pulled the covers around her and tried to sleep.

Luke and his friends had returned from the war heartsick and weary, yet imbued with a restlessness that caused them to perform feats of wild recklessness that were enough to make a mother's hair turn gray. Grayer.

Oh, Luke tried to hide them from her. He took care never to do anything in front of her that she might worry about, but still, she'd heard.

Luke's father had been just as wild as a young man, so she tried to be patient with her son and his friends. And when Luke and Rafe had those shocking curricle races, driving at those frightful speeds, she reminded herself to give thanks that at least they'd returned safely from the war. Even if they seemed bent on breaking their necks at home.

But one by one Luke's friends had married and, oh, it had done her heart good to see the lonely, unloved boys she'd once known grow to manhood and each fall in love with a woman who adored him in return. She'd watched as a deep inner certainty, a profound happiness, replaced their former restlessness.

She'd wanted desperately for her son to find the same.

But eight years ago one good deed had shackled him forever to a strange foreign girl; a girl who wanted to be married to Luke no more than he wanted her.

For her sake, and perhaps for the sake of this unknown girl, Luke had put the best possible face on it, but it was just like his racing. She knew he hadn't told her the whole story.

She had the deepest misgivings about this marriage.

Something dreadful had happened to Luke in Spain when he was a young lieutenant. His denial hadn't convinced her that it wasn't connected with this girl.

Her son was very good at hiding his feelings. Luke would make sure that no one—not his mother, nor his sisters, nor even his friends—would suspect a thing.

Gallant to the bone, he was, and proud, just like his father. He would rather die than let anyone know this foreign girl had—wittingly or unwittingly—trapped him in a loveless marriage. And that he was desperately unhappy.

Lady Ripton grieved.

Two

Spain 1811

The trouble, when it came, was not what Luke had expected. He'd been on the lookout for the enemy—the French—and also for Spanish *guerrilleros* and motley bandits, for the mountains harbored many, and sometimes he couldn't tell the difference. They were allies, the English and the *guerrilleros*, but a lone man on horseback was easy pickings for desperate men, and the mountains were full of desperate men.

This trouble was a scream quivering faintly on the wind. High and light. A woman, or a child.

Luke Ripton, newly commissioned lieutenant in His Majesty's Territorial Army, hesitated. It would not be the first time a woman had been used to bait a trap, but he'd fulfilled his mission. He carried no secret messages or gold on him now.

The scream came again, shrill and filled with real terror. Luke plunged his horse down the steep slope toward the sound, weaving through the pine and beech forest.

Through a gap in the trees he saw a stocky, thickset man hunched over a small, slender female. She was tied at hands and feet, but she writhed and bucked, struggling like a fish caught on a hook.

Luke drew his pistol, but he couldn't get a clear shot through the trees. Besides, he didn't want to hit the girl. He urged his horse toward them.

The man opened his breeches and threw himself roughly on her. The girl twisted and smashed her bound fists hard into the man's face. He yelled and fell back, cupping his face. His hands came away red. He grabbed her wrists and forced them back. She bit his hand, and he cursed and gave her a back-hander across the face.

Blood blossomed on her face, and she fell back, stunned, and the man threw himself again on her supine body.

Shouting, Luke leapt from his horse and raced toward them. It took an agonizingly long time. Intent on his prey, the attacker seemed not to hear.

With a roar of rage, Luke lunged across the last few yards, grabbed the man by the scruff of the neck, and hauled him bodily off the girl.

He went sprawling in the dust several feet away, rolled, and came up with a pistol in his hand, firing at Luke before he even got to his feet.

Sudden heat seared Luke's neck, as though a hot poker had been touched to his skin. The man rushed at him. Luke fired.

The man jerked and staggered back, as if hit, but remained on his feet. "The jewels are gone," he growled in a coarse dialect that Luke only just managed to follow. "And the girl is mine." He wore the ragged remains of a uniform. His nose was a mess of blood, and his cheeks were raked with fresh livid scratches.

Deserter, Luke thought. A man with nothing to lose.

"I don't care about any jewels," Luke said, speaking in Spanish. From the corner of his eye he could see the girl wrestling with the ties that bound her. "Just the girl."

"You want to die for the sake of this skinny bitch?" The man dragged his breeches up with one hand and glanced around the clearing.

Luke knew what he was thinking. One horse. One man. Excellent odds.

This man was older, tougher, meaner than Luke. And Luke's other pistol was in his saddlebag. But Luke didn't move. Standing between the man and the girl, he braced himself.

"So be it." The deserter dropped the spent pistol and produced a vicious-looking knife. He bared broken yellow teeth in a mirthless smile and hurled himself at Luke in a rush.

The blade flashed in the sunlight, and Luke responded instinctively, arching back. It missed him by a hairsbreadth.

Luke kicked the side of the man's knee hard as he passed. It should have broken the bastard's leg. It didn't.

He stumbled, staggered sideways, and slashed at Luke with the knife again.

Luke scooped a handful of dust, threw it in the man's face, and dived, chopping at the man's throat. He choked and stabbed the knife toward Luke's face.

Luke smashed his fist down on the man's wrist and grappled fiercely for control of the knife. They swayed, locked in desperate battle. The glittering blade inched toward Luke's throat. Luke forced it back, straining every sinew, the bones of his wrist feeling as though they would crack. The man's face was inches from his. He stank. His breath was hot and fetid.

Abruptly the deserter's grip loosened, as if he were beaten, then he gave a sudden twist and strove to thrust the blade in. Luke, alert to the trick, dropped his hip in an old wrestling move, threw his enemy off balance, and shoved back, hard.

In an instant it was all over: the knife slid in, neat as butter.

The man gasped and sagged slowly to the ground, spewing obscenities. His eyes were incredulous, disbelieving, even as the light faded from them. His body curled protectively around the blade, his own blade, lodged deeply in his gut.

Luke stepped away, his lungs burning. He watched for a moment, then turned his back on the dying man.

The girl saw him turn toward her, and wrestled more frantically than ever with her bindings. She was all dust and rags and nakedness, bony spine and skinny, scraped ribs.

"Don't be afraid," Luke said in Spanish. "No one will hurt you now, *señorita*."

She glanced at him over her shoulder, turning furious, terrified eyes on him, tearing at her bindings, even though they must be cutting into her flesh. Luke's heart twisted in his chest. She was barely out of childhood.

"Stop it, little one. You're only hurting yourself more." Luke pulled off his coat and dropped it over her nakedness. She hesitated, her golden eyes defiant and wary.

"That's right," Luke said gently. "I won't hurt you." He squatted down, pulled out his knife, and reached for her feet. Instantly her bound hands rose in desperate, defensive claws, their nails broken and bloody.

"Hush, *niña*. Don't be frightened," Luke said in the kind of voice he used on a skittish horse. "I'm just going to cut you free."

Her eyes flickered sideways, and he saw a bloodied rock lying beside her. He smiled. "So that's how you smashed that brute's nose. Clever girl. Now let's get you free." With calm, deliberate movements he cut the rags that tied her feet.

"Now, for your hands." Hesitantly she held them out to him, and he cut through the strip of cloth that bound her.

She wriggled into his coat, pulling it over her nakedness.

Her body was thin, unformed, and childish. Beneath the dust her skin was marred with darkening bruises, scrapes, cuts, and smears of bright, fresh blood. Her barely there breasts, her belly, and her thighs were scraped and smeared with blood.

Luke's heart clenched. Had he arrived too late?

She scrambled to her feet. Gripping the bloodied rock in a grubby fist, she buttoned his coat one-handed, her gaze darting between the still figure of her erstwhile attacker and Luke.

"He's dead," Luke said quietly. "I killed him. You are safe now, *niña*. It's all over."

Her eyes were huge and golden, like a fierce little hawk;

one side of her face was badly bruised and starting to swell. Her lips were split and still welling with slow blood.

She was heartbreakingly young, perhaps twelve or thirteen years old. The same age as his youngest sister, Molly. But there was a world of difference between his happy, sheltered little sister and this fierce, battered scrap.

Luke's throat burned. War was no place for little girls.

"You're safe now," he repeated, not knowing what else to say. He had no idea if she even understood him. She looked Spanish, but she might be Basque. Or even French, he supposed. She hadn't said a word so far.

In French he repeated that she was safe, and that he would not harm her. Her eyes flashed hatred at the sound of his French—she was Spanish, then—so he said, "I am English. I will not harm you." He knew no Basque, so he stuck to Spanish.

There was a long pause, then a violent shudder passed through her and she started to shiver.

Instinctively he reached out to hug her, but she flinched away, the rock raised and ready to strike.

He stepped back, holding his palms up. "Sorry. I simply meant to comfort you."

The golden eyes burned with doubt.

"You're the same age as my little sister," Luke said helplessly. He stared for a moment, silently cursing himself. Stupid thing to say. What would she care of his sister?

He was almost twenty years old, a man—an officer—and yet, for the first time in his life, he had no idea what to do.

He was no stranger to women, and having grown up with three sisters, he'd imagined he understood the female sex pretty well. But he'd never faced anything like this before.

He wished his mother was here. She'd know what to do with this girl, how to reassure her. He'd even welcome his bossy older sisters, Susan and Meg. They were both married, but not Molly. Not his baby sister, turning thirteen next month.

Please God Molly would never have to know such evil existed.

The young girl's legs were long and skinny and shockingly naked under his coat. With one hand, she tugged down the hem, still gripping the rock in her other hand.

Turning his back on her, Luke went to fetch her clothing, which was scattered about the clearing. He picked up a long skirt, part of a riding habit. It dangled in shreds from his hands. He found a short brown coat, beautifully made of good quality fabric. Now ruined. Every item of her clothing was shredded, unwearable. The swine must have cut every garment from her. But why cut it to shreds?

"You will find no jewels there," a hoarse little voice grated from behind him.

The jewels are gone.

"I know nothing about any jewels," Luke told her. "I simply wanted to return your clothing to you. Take my shirt. It's long—longer than that coat—and will cover you decently. It was clean on this morning." He pulled his shirt off over his head and tossed it to her.

She made no move to catch it. It fluttered to the ground at her feet. Her eyes burned.

She needed time to calm down. "Tend to yourself, *chiquita*." He nodded to where a small stream gurgled at the far corner of the clearing. "While you wash the blood and dust from your body, I will bury this swine. Then we shall talk."

He whistled, and in a moment his horse, Brutus, appeared. He kept a small spade in his pack—it was useful for fires and digging trenches around his tent on wet nights.

From the corner of his eye he saw the girl scoop up his shirt and bend over the man. Checking for herself that he really was dead, Luke supposed. He didn't blame her.

He found a gully on the opposite side of the clearing and began to enlarge it, digging a hole big enough to bury a man in. Not a man; a beast.

After a few minutes, he noticed the girl edging toward the stream, watching him all the time. Good. She would feel better when she was clean.

He scraped and dug until the sweat rolled down his body.

The thin mountain soil was hard and stony. A shallow grave was all this bastard deserved.

He paused for a moment, glad of his bare torso and the breeze that cooled him, and glanced toward the stream. She was taking a long time about that wash. She sat with her back to him, waist deep in the cold mountain stream, scrubbing herself vigorously.

A prickle of unease ran over him as he watched her, and without knowing quite why, he found himself quietly approaching the stream. His shirt and coat lay neatly folded on the riverbank, and beside them lay the deserter's wicked-looking knife, the blade now clean of all blood. Ye gods, she must have pulled it out of his body.

She was scrubbing herself with coarse river sand, grabbing handfuls of the rough substance and rubbing it into tender skin, hard.

"Stop it, *niña*! Stop it!" Luke took a step toward her, hesitated because she was naked, snatched up his shirt from the bank of the stream, and waded in, boots and all. Her fists flailed at him blindly, but he dropped his shirt over her head, wrapped the sleeves around her tightly, and lifted her from the water. And held on.

She fought him like a little wildcat, writhing, kicking, and trying to bite him, but he'd expected that, after seeing her under attack before, and he'd made sure to wrap his shirt around as much of her as he could in an attempt to swaddle her.

He simply held her tight, murmuring soothing words in a mixture of English and Spanish. Slowly his words penetrated her panic, and she seemed to realize he was making no attempt to hurt her. Gradually her struggles became less violent, and eventually they ceased.

His grip on her eased. She turned big golden brown eyes on him, glittering with exhaustion.

"You must not punish yourself, *niña*," he said softly. "It was not your fault. It was *not* your fault."

She stared into his eyes for a long moment.

"All trace of him is gone from you," Luke told her, hoping like hell it was true.

She bit her lip and looked away, then gave a long, shuddery sigh. And suddenly her desperate brittleness crumpled and she was a little girl, weeping inconsolably in his arms.

"Hush now, little one. It's all over," Luke murmured helplessly, over and over, rubbing a soothing hand over her back and wishing to hell there was another female here who would know what to do.

Female tears always unmanned him, and these were not even the easy tears he was used to from his sisters. Each sob came hard won, wrenched, scalding from her. The bony little body shuddered against him as she fought her tears.

He held her tight and made soothing sounds. After a while she gave a long, quivery sigh, stilled, and became quiet.

"Thank you, *señor*. I apologize for . . . my outburst," she said politely in a cold little best-manners-at-teatime voice that contrasted almost shockingly to her situation. "You may put me down now."

His coat lay bundled on a patch of soft grass next to the bank. Luke set her down beside it. "Stay there and rest," he told her. "Put the coat on to keep warm, and spread the shirt out to dry. It won't take long in the sun. I'll finish the grave."

He resumed digging. A little later he heard a sound and glanced up. His horse was grazing quietly on the soft grass near the stream. The girl approached Brutus, murmuring softly and holding out her hand as if there was food in it.

Brutus stretched his neck out curiously, then, as the girl came close, shook his head and trotted skittishly out of reach. Luke grinned and returned to his digging. That game could go on all day. Luke had trained his horse to come only to him.

Luke had nearly finished the grave when he heard a movement behind him and turned.

She wore his shirt. It hung to just below her knees, crumpled, still damp. She had long legs, skinny rather than slender, gawky like a newborn filly. Her small feet were bare and dusty. Her damp, dark hair was plaited tightly and inexpertly in a crooked coronet around her head.

He ached for her vulnerability. Over his shirt she wore his coat fastened tight to the throat. It was a short coat, cut to finish at his waist. On her it reached below her nonexistent hips. The shoulders bagged, and she'd rolled the sleeves back as best she could. A little girl playing dress-up.

Only the set look on her battered little face said otherwise.

Even without the marks and swellings from the brutal blows of her attacker, she was an odd-looking little thing; a mismatched collection of features with those big golden eyes, a mouth too wide for her face, a pointed chin, and the sort of strong, bold nose that was the legacy of some ancient Roman ancestor. With her crooked hairdo, split, swollen lips, a bruised cheek, and a rapidly blackening eye, she looked downright tragic, like something new-hatched and vulnerable fallen from its nest.

Luke had been rescuing fallen hatchlings and strays all his life.

"Feeling better now, little one?" he asked gently. The pinched face tightened. Stupid question—of course she wasn't. He gave her a reassuring smile and took a step toward her.

"Don't move, *señor*," she said and pointed a pistol at his heart.

The deserter's pistol. She must have hidden it in the folds of his coat. Spent, but she wouldn't know that. "Don't worry," he said. "I wouldn't hurt you for the world."

In answer she cocked the pistol. With casual expertise.

He raised his brows. "I see you have some familiarity with pistols. But that one isn't loaded."

"*Sí*, it is."

"No," he explained. "The ball was spent when he fired at me. See, he grazed my neck." He showed her the place that still burned.

"I know. I saw him shoot you. I reloaded the pistol."

"You *what*?"

She jerked her chin in the dead man's direction. "I took the shot and powder from him."

His jaw dropped.

"He is dead," she said defensively, as if he'd accused her of stealing.

"I know. I was just surprised that you know how to load a pistol."

She shrugged as if it was nothing special. "My father taught me to use a pistol when I was a child."

When I was a child. As if she were a child no longer.

"I must leave this place now," she said, darting a glance down the mountain. "Get your horse. I cannot catch him."

Luke smiled. "There's no hurry."

"*Sí*, there is." She hesitated, considered him for a moment, then explained. "There are men chasing me. If they catch me—" She swallowed and jerked her chin at the grave. "My cousin Ramón will do the same thing to me as that pig!"

"Your *cousin*?"

"*Sí*. Oh, he will marry me first, even though he hates me and he knows I hate him. He will say it is because he is a man of *honor*!" She spat out the word. "But the truth is, it is the only way he can get—" She broke off.

The jewels? Luke wondered. Was she some kind of heiress?

"And after he weds me, to make sure of me, he will . . . do *that*." There was a flat note of despair in her voice.

"No, he won't," Luke said firmly. "Not if I can help it."

"You will help me?" she said incredulously.

"I will." He laid his hand over his heart. "My word of honor as an English gentleman."

"English?" She narrowed her eyes. "You don't sound English."

Luke shrugged. He was dark haired, dark eyed, and spoke Spanish like a native. It was why he'd been sent on this mission. "Englishmen can speak Spanish, too."

She snorted. "Not like that. You sound nothing like an Englishman. That's an Andalusian accent."

She had a good ear. "I spent the summers of my childhood on a relative's property in Andalusia," he admitted. He and the younger of his two cousins had been sent there by his uncle, the Earl of Ripton, to learn the wine business. He'd loved Spain in those days.

She frowned, unconvinced. "You don't look English. Englishmen have red faces and blue eyes."

Luke smiled, amused, despite the situation. "Not all of us, I promise you. I truly am English. Lieutenant Luke Ripton, special dispatch rider under the command of General Sir Arthur Wellesley himself, at your service." He saluted.

The suspicious look didn't fade, nor did the pistol waver. "Say something in English, then."

"You're an extremely suspicious girl," he told her in English, "but I can't say I blame you, not after all you've been through." She didn't respond, and he felt a bit foolish.

"So, now I've told you my name," he resumed in Spanish. "What's yours?"

"Isabella," she said eventually.

"Well, Isabella, we'll leave this place soon, but first I must bury this fellow."

She muttered something in a low stream of angry-sounding Spanish.

"I know, but it must be done," he said firmly.

The next time he glanced up, she'd put the pistol away. She stood watching him, rocking slightly and hugging herself as if she were cold. It wasn't a cold day.

Finally the hole was big enough. Luke dusted off his hands—he had a few new blisters now—and dragged the body to the grave. He rolled it in.

"Now, a few words."

She gave him a burning look. "He deserves no words, nothing!"

Luke turned to the grave. "Lord, here lies a cur who, among other things, betrayed his country and brutally attacked a child. May he receive your divine judgment." He glanced at Isabella and added in English, "And may this courageous young girl receive your blessing and heal in body and spirit. Amen."

"Do you wish to say anything?" he asked her.

She came to the lip of the grave, peered in, muttered something angry that he didn't catch, spat into the grave, then crossed herself.

"Good." He began shoveling dirt into the hole and glanced at her as she stood, watching. "The sooner it is done, the quicker we leave."

She immediately kicked some dirt into the grave. Clumps of earth fell on the dead man's face. Her expression hardened. She kicked again and again.

Soon it was nothing but a long mound of dirt. "Now we stamp it down. Hard. Like this." Luke stamped down with his boot, and after a moment she stepped forward and gave a tentative stamp with a small, bare foot. It left a perfect imprint in the dark mountain earth. She stared at it for a moment, and her face quivered with some fleeting emotion.

She glanced up and saw him watching; then, with an air of defiance, she stamped again. And again. And again.

Like dancing on the grave, only angry, vengeful. It was probably the wrong thing entirely to do with her. Encouraging a very young lady to stamp on a grave in her bare feet was something he was pretty sure would horrify his mother, but his mother had never faced the kind of thing this girl had. Anger was better than self-blame. Anger scalded, then healed.

Finally it was done. In a few months the grass would obliterate all sign of what had happened here. All outward sign.

Luke went to the stream and washed the dirt from himself. He scooped the clear, cool water in his hands and drank.

Behind him he heard a click. A pistol being cocked. He turned and faced his fierce little hatchling chick.

"And now, *señor*, no more delays. Catch your horse. We must leave."

"Put that thing away. I don't respond to threats." He pulled out his penknife and began to clean his nails, whistling softly under his breath.

After a moment, she made a small frustrated sound, stamped her foot, then put the pistol carefully away. "There!"

He smiled, put his penknife back in his pocket, and, putting his fingers to his mouth, gave a shrill whistle. Brutus lifted his head and trotted toward them. "Can you ride?" Luke asked her.

"Since I could walk."

"Astride?"

She snorted. "Of course."

Interesting. Well-bred young ladies did not ride astride. She was a bundle of contradictions. Luke pulled a pair of cotton drawers from his saddlebag and handed them to her. "Put these on."

She gave him a dubious look.

"They're clean," he told her. "And they'll stop your thighs from chafing."

She pulled his drawers on, screwing her face up in irritation as she tried to find a way to make them stay up. Luke fished a length of twine from his saddlebag and handed it to her. She scowled as she knotted it around her waist. "I hope those pigs burn in hell for cutting up my clothes."

Luke frowned. "*Those* pigs? There was more than one?"

"*Sí.* Two of them. They knew my escort."

"Escort?"

She gave him a haughty look; some feat, given the state of her face. "Naturally my father sent an escort. And I would have brought my duenna, only Marta is too fat to ride. Papa sent three of his most trusted men: Esteban, Diego, and Javier. But that swine and his friend, they knew them. They had served with my father, too." She spat in the dust. Another thing a well-bred young lady would never do. "Deserters, but we did not know that at the time. They said Papa had sent them with a message, and when we stopped, suspecting nothing, they killed Esteban, Diego, and Javier." She gave him a guilty look. "At first I escaped—at the first shot Javier told me to flee—but my horse went lame and they caught me."

Luke scrutinized the clearing. There was no sign of any other man, dead or alive. "What happened to the second man?"

"They quarreled, and he ran off with my horse and all my belongings."

"You mean with the jewels?"

She rolled her eyes. "Not you, too. How often must I say there were *no jewels*! As if I would ride through bandit country carrying jewels! That's why my clothes are ruined. The fools thought I had jewels sewn into my clothes." She muttered something under her breath.

"Where did they get the idea?" Luke asked curiously. Her attacker had spoken very particularly about jewels, not money or other riches.

"Who knows where fools get such notions?" she said, but her gaze slipped sideways. She knew more than she was saying, but Luke just wanted to get the girl to safety and return to headquarters in good time, so he didn't pursue the question. She was welcome to her secrets.

She added impatiently, indicating her attire, "I have donned these barbarities, so can we leave now? Ramón will not be far behind me, and he rides with no care for his horse. I must get to the convent."

"Convent?" Luke swung onto his horse and held a hand down to help her mount.

"The Convent of the Broken Angel. Up there." She jerked her chin toward the mountains, then grasped his outstretched hand, placed a bare foot on his boot, and swung lithely up behind him. Without waiting, she thudded her dusty little heels into Brutus's flanks and they moved off.

Strangely, the higher into the mountains they went, the more he felt her tension rise. Her grip on him tightened, and her anxious craning around to look back the way they came became more frequent.

"So, the Convent of the Broken Angel, is it?" Luke said. "Interesting name."

"The proper name is Convent of the Angels, but since lightning struck one of the angels and broke its wings, everyone calls it the Convent of the Broken Angel."

"Are you intending to become a nun?"

She answered with a snort. "No. I go there on the instructions of my father. For safety . . . perhaps."

"Perhaps?"

"My aunt is there. A nun."

"I see. I gather she is not related to this Ramón."

"No, she is from a different side of the family—from the side of my father's mother."

"Then that should be all right," Luke said in vague reassurance.

There was a short silence, then Isabella added, "But I do not know her well. And nuns are sworn to practice *obedience*."

Luke's mouth twitched. "I gather you don't approve of obedience."

She sniffed. "It depends. I obey"—her voice wavered—"obeyed my father in all things. But my aunt, she is not the Mother Superior, and I do not know whose side the Mother Superior will take."

"In what way?"

"Now that Papa is . . . is dead, and Felipe, too, who was my father's heir and my betrothed, Ramón is the head of the family, and if he orders my aunt to give me to him . . . I do not know what the Mother Superior will do. These are dangerous times in Spain, and I do not know if the Mother Superior is with Papa's side of politics, or against it. And I am another mouth to feed. If she is not a patriot, or Ramón offers her money . . ."

There was much in what she said, Luke conceded. Spain was a country at war and split within by politics. But surely, if Ramón truly intended to force the child into marriage, no nun, no matter what her politics, would hand Isabella over to him.

"Nuns are also sworn to chastity," Luke reminded her. "Perhaps she will take your side."

"Perhaps," she echoed doubtfully. It was clear she had no confidence in that.

"If it was your father's dying wish that you go to the convent, his wish must be honored."

For a few moments she said nothing, then she said, so softly that he almost didn't catch it, "Perhaps."

A few minutes up the road they found the rest of her belongings scattered about. Luke stopped to let her go examine them in case there was something she could retrieve.

But there was nothing. Everything, even the saddle, had been shredded in the search for the elusive jewels. Once an exquisitely made piece, the carved and decorated lady's side-saddle was now a wreck. Luke could see where some kind of metal decoration—possibly silver—had been wrenched off and the stitching slashed apart. Nothing of value remained.

One thing was clear: all question of jewels aside, with clothing and a sidesaddle of the highest quality, Isabella must come of good family. It gave weight to the suggestion that she was an heiress.

She picked over her ruined belongings, then picked them up and threw them into the bushes. She turned to him and said, "Take me with you."

"What?" And then he realized she'd spoken in English. "You speak English?"

"Not well, but my mother was half English, and I understand everything." She brushed that aside and, gripping his stirrup, said in a rush, "Take me with you, to your army. I will be your servant, dress as a boy—I look like a boy, I know. I will cut off my hair, and nobody will know I am a girl. Please, I beg of you—"

"I can't do that." Luke cut her off gently. "It's impossible."

"But Ramón will come," she said in despair. "He will take me from the convent and . . . and . . ."

"I can't take you with me," Luke told her. "My life is too dangerous."

"And mine is not? Please, Lieutenant Ripton." She stared up at him in mute entreaty.

"No." Luke held out a hand to help her remount. It went very much against the grain not to help her, but it was quite impossible to smuggle her into camp as his servant. All he could do was to deliver her to the convent, to her aunt. Her father must have known what he was doing when he sent her there. Surely.

"Then I will stay here," she said, not moving.

"Here? In the mountains? Don't be ridiculous. You won't survive a week out here." He gestured to the rugged landscape.

"I can. I know how to live off the land. My father taught me how to be a *guerrillera.*" She gestured at the surroundings. "Better here in the mountains than in Ramón's hands. My father taught me to hunt and—"

"No. Now get on this horse," Luke ordered. "I promise you I will look after you. No one will take you; no one will force you."

Her eyes narrowed. "You promise?"

"On my honor as an English officer and a gentleman." What the hell was he doing, promising such a thing?

She gave him a long, searching look, then offered a satisfied nod and mounted up behind him. As they moved off, she laid her cheek against his back, and her skinny little arms wrapped trustfully around him.

Luke felt it with a sinking heart. What had he done? And how the hell was he going to keep his rash promise?

The answer came to him as they rode into a small village. The first building they saw was a little stone church. A priest stood by the doorway, his face toward them, as if expecting them.

It was Fate, thought Luke. Fate had looked after him so far in this war. He would trust it again.

"Isabella," he said. "I think I know of a way to save you from Ramón"

"How?"

"You will need to trust me. I promise you can, but you must do this of your own free will."

"Do what?" The voice was small but laced with hope. The weight of her expectation made him hesitate.

He dismounted and lifted Isabella down so he could talk to her face-to-face. She turned her bruised and battered little face up to his. "Do what?" The trust in her clear golden eyes was disturbing.

The enormity of what he was about to do flooded his consciousness. He was risking everything, his career, the respect of his peers . . . but he could not simply leave her to her fate.

He explained. "If I marry you, Ramón cannot."

Her eyes widened. "Marry *you*? You want me to marry you?"

He nodded. "Only if you want to." Luke swallowed, feeling the whole basis of his life slowly slipping away. What would his friends say? What would his mother say? He had no doubt what his commanding officer would say.

"Yes I will marry you, Lieutenant Ripton." She said it in a rush, as if she feared he would change his mind.

"It's just a device to stop Ramón," he warned her.

She nodded. "I understand. And afterward I will come and be your wife in the army."

"No, I told you, it's too dangerous."

"But—"

"Afterward you will go to the Convent of the Angels and live there until it is safe."

"But—"

"You will not be coming with me. You're not old enough to be married. This is only to keep you from Ramón, understand."

She nodded. "I understand." She glanced at the church. "We will do it here? Now?"

"If you want to."

"I do."

The priest took some convincing to marry them. He spoke to Isabella and Luke separately and together. Isabella's injuries worried him greatly, but she was fervent in her wish to be married, and she swore Luke had not harmed a hair on her head. On the contrary.

And in the end, it was wartime, and better a couple united in sin—even if one was a heathen Englishman—than another young Spanish girl debauched.

They repeated the sacred words, Isabella barefoot and dressed in Luke's shirt and drawers held up with string. Luke signed a series of documents, the priest witnessed them, and within the hour Luke and his child bride rode north to the Convent of the Angels, where he handed an exhausted young girl and a packet of documents over to her surprised aunt.

Isabella was safe.

Three

The Convent of the Broken Angel, Spain, 1819

"*I* don't want to die an old maid," the plaintive voice began.

Isabella Mercedes Sanchez y Vaillant, known to her schoolmates as Isabella Ripton, bent over her sewing, wishing she could block out the conversation to come. She knew it by heart. It was a daily ritual, as regular as any other ritual in the convent routine. She was fed up with most of them, but particularly so with this one. It did no good at all; only rubbed their noses in their own misery.

"And I don't want to become a nun."

Now Paloma would interject and say something about having faith and about what a lovely bride Dolores would make. Rubbing salt in the wounds, if only she realized it, but she never did. Paloma was as thickheaded as she was kindhearted.

Bella stabbed her needle through the worn white linen. She loathed sewing. She longed to get up and leave, but she was stuck there for at least another hour. She had a pile of worn-out sheets to sew, sides to middle, to give them another lease of life. Penance for something or other. Running. Or impiety, or something like that. For breathing, probably.

"You must have faith, Dolores," Paloma said gently. "Your father will send for you. I'm certain of it. Why would he not, such a beautiful bride you will make. Any man would be proud."

Bella gritted her teeth. It was nothing to do with Dolores's beauty or otherwise. It was about money. And family pride. It was the same reason all the girls were still stuck in the convent, long after their schooling was complete and years after the war was over.

Spain might be free of the French, they might have a Spanish king on the throne again, not Napoleon's puppet or his brother, but it was not the same country it had been before the war. Many great families were on the brink of ruin, some because they'd sided with the French and the Spanish traitors, others because they'd spent their fortunes funding a private army to fight a guerrilla war, and some because they had had their homes and estates—and therefore their means of earning a living—destroyed; part of the catastrophe of war.

The blue-blooded families of the girls who remained in the convent were too poor to afford a rich dowry for their daughters and too prideful to allow them to marry below their class. Not unless the prospective husband was of enormous wealth, and even then, some families refused to sully their ancient bloodlines with the blood of some jumped-up peasant.

Rather than let their daughters suffer such a fate, they'd left them to rot in a remote mountain convent: unwanted, forgotten, abandoned.

The sons of the nobility, of course, were snapping up as brides the daughters of these same wealthy, jumped-up peasants. Their blood was unfortunate, but the noble family name must not die out, and the bride's wealth would help rebuild the family fortunes.

Bella had explained this to Paloma a dozen times, but all Paloma did was smile and say, "We must all have faith."

She'd make a good nun, Isabella thought. Or a saint. St. Paloma of the missing dowry. Paloma's brother had gambled Paloma's dowry away, and now he was refusing to let her return home. Things were different since Papa died, he'd written. There was no appropriate husband for her, and she was better off in the convent, in the tranquil environment she was used to.

Bella picked up a well-worn bedsheet and ripped it savagely in half. Tranquil environment indeed! She'd love to lock Paloma's brother up here, to give him a taste of tranquil environment. Endless prayers, endlessly repeated dreary, pointless conversations, and endless, endless sewing.

She started stitching the two halves of the sheet together. Bella only ever did mending. The other girls and the nuns mostly did fine embroidery. The convent was famed for it. Bishops all across Spain, and even in Rome, wore vestments and used altar cloths embroidered here in this remote mountain convent.

Before King Ferdinand had been crowned, the girls had been mainly occupied in sewing their trousseaux. Now they worked almost wholly on altar cloths and vestments. Like the nuns.

Isabella's talents lay in other areas, Reverend Mother always said. The other girls thought she was just saying that, being Isabella's aunt, but Bella and Reverend Mother knew better.

"I wish I had your faith, Paloma," Dolores told her. "I think we'll all still be sitting here when we're old and wrinkled, snoring away the day like Sister Beatriz."

"Speak for yourself, Dolores," Alejandra snapped. "I, for one, will not be left rotting in a convent. Even now my father is in discussions with a noble family from Cabrera."

Dolores huffed and threaded her needle. "The only eligible man left in Cabrera—of noble blood, I mean—is the old *vizconde*, who is past sixty, twice widowed, and desperate to get an heir. If it is him your brother is courting, I pity you."

Alejandra shrugged. "I would rather wed an old man than be forced to become a nun." The girls glanced at Sister Beatriz, but the elderly nun snored gently on, oblivious. "Besides," Alejandra continued, "as my father said, he is rich, and old men die. Then I will be free to do as I want."

Another girl spoke up. "They say the old *vizconde* is poxed and that is why he could not get a son on either of his wives."

The girls exchanged glances.

"That cannot be true. My father would not marry me to a poxed man," Alejandra said into the silence. "He would not."

The others nodded, murmuring reassurance. But they had all heard the tales that lying with a virgin could cure a man of the pox . . .

"Papa would not do such a thing," Alejandra repeated. "He is too fond of me, I'm certain." But her confidence was clearly shaken, and it was more a prayer than a certainty.

It would be her father's decision and the *vizconde*'s, not hers. She was just a daughter, to be given where it would do her family the most good. And times in Spain these days were desperate.

"If he does, you must refuse," Bella told her.

"Refuse?" Alejandra gasped. "Disobey my *father*? Are you *mad*? I couldn't!"

"Why not?"

"Why not?" Alejandra repeated. "Because I couldn't." She added, after a moment, "I have never disobeyed him in anything. *Never*."

Bella knotted her thread. "Then it would be good for him to experience something new."

All the girls stared at her, shocked.

"How do you think he would react?" she asked Alejandra.

"He would kill me!" she said with a shudder.

"Kill you, or merely beat you?"

"Merely? He would thrash me to within an inch of my life!"

"One recovers from a beating. A poxed old *vizconde*, though . . ." Bella let that thought sink in. "Has your father ever beaten you before?"

"Never," Alejandra said proudly.

"Then why do you think he would beat you now?"

Alejandra looked surprised, then thoughtful. "It's my duty to my family to marry well."

"It's a father's duty to find you a decent husband," Bella countered.

Alejandra bit her lip. "I don't know . . . Papa would be so disappointed in me."

Bella snorted. "He will survive his disappointment. He might also come to respect you." She shrugged again. "It's not my business what you do, but if it was me, I'd refuse."

"Which is why you're always in trouble," Alejandra retorted.

Sister Beatriz snorted and sat up. "What's that? Tongues wagging? Sewing, girls! Sewing!" She clapped her hands in a brisk manner, and the girls bent over their sewing. Needles flashed in silence, and in a short while the elderly nun dozed off peacefully again.

"Isabella's husband might come for her soon," Paloma said on a bright, let's-change-the-subject note, and Bella groaned silently. She knew what would come next.

Alejandra gave a scornful snort. "Who, the imaginary one?"

"He's not imaginary, is he, Isabella?" Paloma turned to Bella.

Bella didn't answer. They'd been over this a hundred, a thousand times. At first she'd fought the accusation tooth and nail, but now, after all these years, she was half inclined to think she'd dreamed it, dreamed him. But Reverend Mother had the marriage papers in her desk, and his signature was on them, firm and black and clear. Lucien Alexander Ripton, Lieutenant.

"Of course he is," Alejandra insisted. "Her tall English lieutenant, with his broad shoulders and his so-beautiful face *just* like an angel!" she said in a mocking voice. "An *angel*, wed to *Isabella Ripton*?" All the girls laughed.

Bella doggedly sewed on. She understood why they pecked at her. She might attack someone, too, if she was about to be married to an old, poxed *vizconde*.

Besides, it was her own fault. She shouldn't have told them in the first place.

After the hasty marriage, Lieutenant Ripton and her aunt

had decided to place her in the convent under the name of Ripton, Bella taking his name in the manner of English wives instead of keeping her own name, as Spanish women did.

Her aunt had instructed Bella not to tell anyone she was married—not the Mother Superior of the time, nor the other nuns, nor any of the girls. Then, she said, if Cousin Ramón came looking for Isabella Mercedes Sanchez y Vaillant, daughter of the Conde de Castillejo, Mother Superior could truthfully tell him that no such girl was in the convent; only the sister of an English lieutenant.

It was strange, but exciting, having a new name.

And sure enough, Cousin Ramón *had* come, and Reverend Mother had assured him no girl of that name was in the convent. Sweet, elderly Reverend Mother, so patently truthful and innocent, and so obviously distressed by his tale of a young girl who'd fled her home to cross Spain in such terrible times—anything could have happened to her, the poor, young innocent. Dreadful, dreadful! She'd offered immediate prayers for the lost girl's safe recovery, and even Cousin Ramón had to believe her.

So at first, Isabella never told a soul she was married, and when the elderly Mother Superior died and Isabella's aunt took her place, Isabella's security was assured—as much as anyone's security could be in wartime.

But a few years later the fighting was over in Spain. Napoleon's puppet was ejected, and King Ferdinand was crowned king of Spain, and relatives turned up to collect this girl or that. The convent was full of talk of dowries and settlements, of betrothals arranged and marriages planned. The girls were abuzz with excitement and nerves and romantic speculation.

At almost sixteen, Isabella was still plagued by pimples and a flat chest, and when even the younger girls started to patronize and pity her, she could not bear it. In secret whispers in the dark one night, she'd confided in her friend, Mariana, about Lieutenant Ripton, her tall, dark Englishman, as beautiful as an angel, who'd killed a man to protect Isabella, and then married her to save her from her evil cousin Ramón.

Now the war was over, he would surely come for her and take her away to England.

But Mariana had whispered Isabella's secrets to another girl, and soon it was all through the convent, and of course, nobody had believed her. Skinny, plain Isabella Ripton, secretly married to a handsome Englishman? As if anyone would believe that.

Her name? Pshaw! So she had an English surname—many Spaniards had English surnames. It proved nothing.

"Has he seen a picture of you—a truthful one?"

"Why would he want to marry a girl who looks like a boy?"

"He knows what I look like. He *chose* me," Bella used to tell them proudly, hoping her pimples would be gone and her breasts would grow by the time he came for her. "Nobody had to arrange it."

"So you know nothing about him. For all you know of his family, he could be some peasant!"

"He was an officer, so of course he's not a peasant. And he's tall, strong, and fearless; the most beautiful man I ever saw in my life!"

"*Beautiful?*" The other girls laughed.

"Beautiful like an archangel," Bella insisted. "Beautiful and terrible. A warrior angel! Just wait till he comes. You will see."

And some girls would continue to scoff, and some would sigh and secretly envy her.

At night, in her small stone room on her hard, narrow bed, Bella would spin dreams of Lieutenant Ripton . . .

Lieutenant Ripton lay mortally wounded, and Isabella would find him and care for him, and he would be miraculously cured by her tender solicitude, and fall madly in love with her.

Lieutenant Ripton would be attacked by the enemy, and Bella would stand by him, and together they would fight them off, and as the enemy fled, he would turn to her and say, "Isabella, without you my life would be over. I love you."

Many and varied were the deeds of bravery and daring she

performed in her dreams, and at the end of each one, Lieutenant Ripton would say, "Isabella, I love you."

Lieutenant Ripton would know Isabella as nobody in the world would know her. And he would love her. Truly love her. And she would love him back with all her heart. And they would be happy forever and ever after.

Day after day, week after week, Bella had prayed for Lieutenant Ripton to come—even to write, but there was no word, no sign.

Still, she would rage and defend herself, defend him—he *was* as beautiful as an angel, he was busy fighting, he was a hero, he was too important to be able to come just now, but he would come for her, he *would*!

Gradually her skin cleared up. Her breasts remained disappointingly small, and she learned from a smuggled-in looking glass that she would never be a beauty, not even pretty. "Interesting" was the most charitable assessment of her features.

Still, Lieutenant Ripton did not come, and as the years passed, the dream of the handsome husband who would love her—*must* love her—slowly began to wither on the vine.

The truth was there, staring her in the face. Like the fathers and brothers of the other girls who remained in the convent, Lieutenant Ripton had taken her money and abandoned her. He was not much better than Ramón. He'd done it more kindly than Ramón, perhaps, but in the long run, the result was the same.

Some nights, lying in her hard, narrow bed, Bella secretly wept for her broken dreams. But tears did nothing, so she scrubbed them away. She would look up through her high, barred window and gaze at the stars outside.

There was a world out there, and she wanted to be part of it.

The other girls continued to taunt her, teasing her about her imaginary husband. And Bella still defended him, still stubbornly claimed there was an important reason why he couldn't come—one had one's pride, after all—but nobody believed her; not even Bella herself. It was a routine like everything that happened in the convent.

She said to Alejandra, "You could come with me, if you wanted."

"Come where?"

"I'm leaving the convent." Her announcement was followed by a stunned silence.

"Is he comi—" Paloma began.

"No. Nobody is coming for me, Paloma." Isabella glanced at Sister Beatriz, who was still asleep, and said in a lowered voice, "I'm leaving anyway."

"Reverend Mother won't allow it," Alejandra said.

Bella shrugged. "She can't stop me. I'm a married woman, and in two weeks I will be one-and-twenty." And if Reverend Mother tried to stop her, she'd go over the wall. It wasn't as if she hadn't done it before, and Reverend Mother knew it.

Alejandra sniffed. "I don't believe you. What will you do? How will you support yourself? Who will protect you? It's dangerous—"

"I will support myself," Bella said. "And I will protect myself. I won't stay here, waiting forever for someone to rescue me. Life isn't a fairy tale."

"Isabella Ripton," said a voice from the doorway.

All the girls jumped guiltily.

"Isabella," Sister Josefina repeated as she entered the door. She was the youngest and prettiest of the nuns, closest in age to the girls, merry and lively, but dedicated to her vocation. "Tidy yourself up. Your hair is a mess. Reverend Mother wants you to come to her office at once. You have a visitor!"

"A visitor? Who?" In eight years, Bella had never had a visitor. Not since Ramón had come looking for her, and failed to find her. And why would Ramón come back after all this time?

Sister Josefina smiled. "Can't you guess?"

Mystified, Bella shook her head.

"An Englishman."

Bella froze.

Sister Josefina nodded. "Tall, dark, and as beautiful as an archangel."

Bella couldn't move a muscle. She couldn't utter a word or even marshal a coherent thought.

"A very stern, very masculine archangel." Sister Josefina sighed. And a blush rose on her cheeks.

Lieutenant Ripton was *here*?

"Isabella?" Sister Josefina said.

Bella started. Everyone was staring at her. She pulled herself together. "I told you he'd come," she managed and moved toward the door.

"Tidy your hair," Sister Josefina reminded her, and Isabella started tucking in the errant strands that had come loose from her braid.

"Her hair?" Alejandra exclaimed. "You can't let her go dressed like that!"

"Like what?" Isabella glanced down at herself, puzzled. She looked the same as always; neater than usual, in fact. She smoothed her hair back.

"In those . . ."—Alejandra gestured—"those *convent* clothes! She hasn't seen her husband for eight years. She can't go to him in those!"

"Yes, she needs something pretty," Dolores agreed.

Bella looked down at her plain dark blue and gray dress. "I don't have anything pretty." She'd arrived at the convent with nothing, and the convent had dressed her ever since. The lack had never bothered her. Until now.

"No, but I do," said Alejandra. She turned to Sister Josefina. "Sister, let us dress Isabella nicely to meet her husband. Please, Sister, we won't take long."

"Yes, pleeeeease, Sister," the other girls joined in.

The young nun glanced from the girls' eager faces to Isabella standing there in her drab clothes. "Be quick then," she said. "Reverend Mother is waiting."

*L*uke sat across the desk from Isabella's aunt and willed himself not to fidget. She was now the Mother Superior and seemed in no hurry to move things along. He'd left his horses outside the convent in the care of a grubby urchin.

Times were still bad in Spain, and the mountains were no doubt still full of brigands. And most thieves started young.

"She won't be long, Lieutenant Ripton." Isabella's aunt had aged a good deal in the last years, Luke thought. Her face, under the severe nun's garb, was thinner, her pale ivory complexion drawn tight over high cheekbones and blurred with a web of fine lines. The war had not been easy on her.

"Lord Ripton," he corrected her. Her brows arched, and Luke explained. "I inherited the title from my uncle who was drowned in an unfortunate boating accident."

"I had not realized you were the heir to a . . . ?"

"Barony. I had no expectations of it, but my uncle's two sons drowned with him, and so the title and estates came to me."

"Estates?" she inquired delicately, a reminder that however the marriage had been made, any alliance was still about blood and wealth. She was still Isabella's aunt, after all.

Luke, however, had no intention of discussing it. "Suffice it to say I still have no need of Isabella's fortune. How is she?"

"Isabella is well. Grown up. In two weeks' time she will be twenty-one. She will, I am sure, be surprised to see you after all this time." Said with an edge of acid.

Her tone annoyed Luke. He pulled out the letter he had received and broached the matter bluntly. "This letter denies my application for annulment. It says, 'On information received by the Mother Superior of the Convent of the Angels.'" He slapped the letter on her desk. "Eight years ago you told me an annulment would be a straightforward arrangement."

She fixed him with a steady gaze. "I did not know then that Isabella was no longer a virgin."

Not a virgin? Damn. The bastard must have got to her after all. Luke had been sure he'd saved her in time. Apparently not. His brows snapped together as another thought occurred to him. "Don't tell me she—"

"No, there were no unfortunate consequences," Mother Superior said in an austere tone. "Isabella herself told me of the attack—she had nightmares afterward, you see. But what's done is done, and so . . ." She spread her thin-veined hands in a fatalistic gesture.

Luke nodded. "How did Isabella take the news?"

"Isabella is a lady by birth and training."

In other words, Isabella was resigned to her fate, as he was. So be it.

The Mother Superior steepled her hands and rested her chin on the points of her fingers, peering down her long nose at him. "What are your plans, Lord Ripton?"

"We leave immediately for England."

The elegant arched brows almost disappeared under the wimple. "Immediately?"

"Tomorrow morning," he amended. She would need to pack, he supposed. But the sooner he was gone from this accursed country, the happier he'd be.

The nun inclined her head graciously. "Then this will be Isabella's last night in the convent. We will hold a small farewell at dinner for her. You are, of course, invited."

Silence lapsed. Luke drummed his fingers lightly on the desk.

Mother Superior eyed his fingers contemplatively. Luke stopped drumming.

Where the devil was Isabella? She was taking her time.

Mother Superior began to tell him about the history of the convent and the story behind the broken angel. She eyed him thoughtfully when he shifted restlessly for the third time.

Sitting still was not Luke's forte. Nor were tales from a convent. At least not this kind.

The Mother Superior moved on to the subject of his bride. His *bride*.

"Isabella is a good girl, really. A little hotheaded and impulsive—her father was like that, too, as a boy. She will steady once she's given adult responsibilities. That's the trouble—she's not suited to convent life. She's not the contemplative sort."

Nor was Luke. His gaze wandered the room. Lord, but he would have gone mad cooped up in this place for eight years.

He recalled Isabella's sudden dread when he'd brought her here all those years ago. She'd panicked suddenly and begged him again not to leave her there, to take her with him. Of course, it was impossible.

He remembered her as a battered little scrap, all big eyes and questions, his little baby bird. Had she grown into a swan in the last eight years? A man could only hope.

Eight years . . . Where had they flown? He still couldn't believe she was now in truth going to be his wife. For the rest of their lives.

"And then there's her sewing." Reverend Mother paused, and Luke realized she was testing his concentration.

"Her sewing?" he prompted, trying to look interested. Where the devil had the girl got to? He wanted to get this over with, meet her, make the arrangements, and then leave this blasted country as quickly as possible. He found himself rubbing the spot just below his left shoulder and stopped.

"I do hope you are not expecting exquisite embroidery from your wife."

"Exquisite embroidery?" Luke repeated blankly.

"The convent is famous for its embroidery," she said with gentle reproof. "World famous." As if he should know who was whom in the world of embroidery.

"Congratulations," he said politely. Where was the chit? Dragging her heels?

Had she other plans? A marriage to some Spanish fellow, for instance.

No, she couldn't have met anyone stuck here in the mountain fastness with a bunch of nuns.

Although the Spanish did tend to arrange such things . . .

"Isabella, alas, was never able to acquire the skill of fine sewing."

"It's of no interest to me whether she can sew or not," he said bluntly. Right now he was wondering if she could walk. Where was she?

If he didn't know better, he might think he was nervous. But that was, of course, ridiculous. There was nothing to be nervous about. It was a done deal. They were married. No way out of it. Firmly leg-shackled.

If he was feeling mildly jumpy, it was nothing to do with meeting his wife after eight years, and everything to do with being in this blasted country again. He needed to leave. Immediately.

"It's to be hoped you will take an interest in what your wife does do well," she said severely. Luke was reminded of being back in the nursery. She went on. "Showing an interest in a woman's daily concerns is a way to strengthen a marriage. A neglected wife is an unhappy wife."

Bloody hell. He was being lectured on marriage by a *nun*.

"Isabella's taking rather a long time to get here," he observed coolly. "Is there a problem?"

She gave him a thoughtful look then reached for her little bell, but before she could ring it, there was a knock on the door.

Luke jumped as if it were a gunshot. He straightened his neckcloth, ran a hand over his chin, and smoothed back his hair.

"Enter," Reverend Mother said, and the heavy oaken door swung slowly open.

A small, thin girl in a fussy, frilly dress entered, her hair twirled into an elaborate nest of curls and draped with a lacy mantilla. Her face was made up, pale with some kind of powder, her lips brightly rouged into a tiny bow, her cheeks glowing with the same color. She curtsied and darted him a shy glance from huge golden eyes. He remembered those eyes. This, then, was his bride.

Luke politely rose to his feet, hoping his disappointment didn't show.

Four

❦

This, then, was her husband. Isabella tried not to stare.

He was even more beautiful than she remembered. Eight years ago she'd seen him with a child's eye, and he was her savior and, she had to admit, she'd confused him in her mind a little with the angel of the statue. She had, after all, only known him a day.

But she was a child no longer, and he was . . . he was breathtaking. Tall, dark, his skin burnished with the sun, a rich dark gold flush along his cheekbones, and such fine cheekbones they were. His nose was a strong, straight blade; his mouth, severe and beautiful. And his eyes, dark, so dark they looked black, but she knew from before they were the darkest blue she had ever seen. There was no sign of blue now.

All those nights dreaming of him . . . and now. He was not the same.

She remembered him as very tall and strong with a loose elegance of movement. Now he seemed bigger, more . . . solid, his shoulders broader, his chest deeper. A man, rather than a boy, with a soldier's bearing—no, a hunter's bearing. Alert, tense, wary.

She could see other changes in him, now that she looked. The brightness, the resilience of youth had been burned away, leaving the hardness of bone and bitter experience behind. And cynicism, she thought, looking at the hard, chiseled mouth.

The war had left none of them untouched.

Lieutenant Ripton might be as beautiful as an angel—a stern one, as Sister Josefina had said—but there was a darkness in those eyes of his that had nothing to do with any angel. Except a broken one.

His eyes, the eyes that had danced in her memory, now watched her with a flat, assessing look.

She swallowed and held her head higher, knowing what he would see in her, knowing they were ill-matched. The girls had done their best to make her look as beautiful as they could. It wasn't their fault she looked as she did. She knew she'd never make a beauty. She desperately wished she looked pretty for him.

But she could see in his eyes she didn't.

Dear God, but it was Mama and Papa again, Papa the handsome eagle soaring high and Mama the plain, dowdy little pigeon, bleeding with love for a husband who never looked twice at her.

Mama's words rose unbidden to her mind. *Guard your heart, my little one, for love is pain. Love is nothing but pain.*

Lieutenant Ripton was still the handsomest man she'd ever seen. Lord, but the girls were going to have to eat their words when they saw him.

And she was not her mother.

"Isabella, how do you do?" he said, and his voice was deep and, oh, she remembered it, remembered the way it shivered through her, even though he was talking to her now like a polite stranger.

She managed to return some sort of polite response—something inane, she was certain, but this was why children were drilled in good manners, she thought irrelevantly; so when they couldn't think what to say, the right thing popped out anyway.

He bowed and bent over her hand.

His hair was dark and thick and combed smooth and neat. She'd remembered it as constantly tousled, windblown. Now it was almost . . . regimented. She wanted to touch it, to run her fingers through it, to mess it up as it used to be. Reverend Mother would have had a fit.

It occurred to her that Lieutenant Ripton might not like it, either. There was no warmth in his eyes, the way she'd remembered. But perhaps he was nervous, too.

He pressed his lips to the back of Isabella's hand, a light, dry pressure that was over almost before she felt it. Hardly worthy of the name of a kiss.

Certainly not the kind of kiss she'd dreamed about all these years. It was more like a meeting of strangers than a glorious reunion. He hadn't even smiled at her.

She hadn't smiled at him, either, she told herself. It was nerves, just nerves.

Her eyes ran over him as he straightened, trying to drink in the changes, boy to man. He was a young man still, younger than she'd expected. He could not yet be thirty, she was sure. As a child, she'd thought him much older.

"How old are you?" she blurted.

"I beg your pardon?" he said, and at the same time she heard Reverend Mother sigh. Isabella Ripton, putting her foot in her mouth again.

Too bad, Isabella thought. She wanted to know, and it wasn't rude to ask. He was her husband. Her *husband*.

"How old are you?" She wanted to know everything about him.

"Twenty-eight." Just.

"So you were twenty when we married." Younger than she was now.

"Nineteen, actually. I turned twenty a few weeks later."

She nodded. That would account for the difference in him;

he'd been little more than a boy when they'd married, an impossibly beautiful stripling, full of the joy of life. Now he was a man, still impossibly handsome but with the weight of experience and the knowledge of war graven into him.

Her chest felt suddenly tight and full, as if her heart was swelling. This man, this stern, grave, handsome man, was going to be her husband. *Was* her husband.

Her girlhood dreams hadn't died after all, she realized shakily. They'd just grown a protective skin. Now he was here, tall, severe looking, and beautiful, examining her as closely as she was staring at him. A dozen memories of him were re-called to life by the solid reality of his presence.

She devoured him with her eyes. Lieutenant Ripton, her Lieutenant Ripton, was here, come for her at long last. He hadn't forgotten her. He was here.

"You're all grown up," he said, his gaze dark upon her, and she suddenly remembered his long, long eyelashes and how it wasn't fair that a man should have such lashes. They made her breathless, those lashes . . .

Her secret girlhood hopes and dreams stirred again within her, returning to life like flowers lain hidden and dormant through the bitter snows of winter, sprouting new, tender shoots, unfurling petals to the sun.

His dark gaze ran over her, taking her in as she'd taken him in. What was he thinking? Did he like what he saw? And what did he see?

She wished again she had a proper dress that fitted, one she liked instead of something fussy and elaborate, covered in frills. She'd had to wear one of Paloma's dresses; all the others were too short.

She tried to think of something to say, something clever or interesting, something to make this tall, grave man look at her, see *her*, not the silly dressed-up doll the girls had made of her.

"How was . . . How was your war?" she said, and she groaned inwardly at the gaucheness of the question. If only she could go back out and start this whole meeting over.

His gaze shifted, and he glanced toward the window to the

courtyard. "As you see, I survived." Suddenly there was a faint chill in the room.

So much for that topic, she thought. She should ask about his trip. People did when someone had made a long, arduous journey.

He really was a stranger. She'd been thinking she knew him because he'd lived in her dreams so long, but this man was not her handsome prince, the Lieutenant Ripton of her dreams. He was someone else, a cold, reserved stranger. She knew nothing about this Lieutenant Ripton. And he'd come to take her away.

"Why now?" The words popped out without thinking.

"Isa*bella*," Reverend Mother said in a repressive tone.

"I beg your pardon?" Lieutenant Ripton gave her a cool, steady look that was meant, she was suddenly sure, to make her retract the question, to change the subject.

The look annoyed her. Particularly coming from eyes with such long, beautiful lashes. Eyes like that had no business giving such cold glances.

She opened her mouth.

"Isabella, that's enough," Reverend Mother said in a warning voice, accompanied by her famous Quelling Stare. It usually reduced Isabella and every other girl in the convent to abashed silence.

But Isabella was a schoolgirl no longer. This was her husband, and she had a right to know why he'd left her in the convent for eight interminable years, and why, long after she'd given up all hope of seeing him again, he'd suddenly turned up.

"Why did you come for me now, Lieutenant Ripton?"

"Lieutenant Ripton no longer. I sold out of the army as a captain," he corrected her. "And the year before last, I inherited my uncle's title and estates and became Lord Ripton. Which means you are now Lady Ripton."

She turned the information over in her mind. It wasn't what she'd asked him. "Yet for the last eight years I've had no word from you. The war has been over for several years, so why wait until now to come for me?" Something to do with his title, perhaps? A service to the Crown? A wound that took some years to heal? Though he looked in perfect physical condition.

He frowned, as if her question didn't make sense. "Why now?" he repeated crisply. "Because I only just discovered the application for annulment was rejected."

The word hit her like a blow. "*Annulment?*"

"That's correct, *annulment*," he repeated, as if she were somehow slow of wit.

"You tried to annul the marriage? Our marriage? And you found you couldn't?"

"Correct." He gave her a searching look, and his frown deepened.

She stared at him. He was so matter-of-fact about it. The remnants of her dreams, newly wakened to life, curdled as she put it all together. "So you've come for me now because you have no other choice. Because you can't get out of the marriage and—oh!—of course, because you're Lord Ripton now, and you'll need a legitimate heir—correct?"

He stiffened and gave a short nod. "Yes, but—"

"And for a legitimate heir you need a wife, and you thought, oh yes, I had one of those eight years ago and I left her . . . Now where did I leave her? Oh yes, a convent, where she'd be in the care of nuns and no bother to anyone. And now, because you're *stuck* with me, you've come to fetch me like a parcel you set on a shelf and forgot—correct?"

Hot tears of bitter humiliation welled up behind her eyes. She squeezed them back down. She would rather die than let him see how badly he'd hurt her.

Or anyone else. Oh, how she'd boasted . . . The triumph with which she'd left the sewing room a few minutes ago. Her prince had finally come.

Because he'd tried to get rid of her and failed.

He was silent a long moment. "I can see you're upset, but—"

"Please excuse me. I feel . . . unwell." Clinging to the last remnants of her dignity, she hurried from the room.

* * *

*B*ella ran through the quiet corridors. Penance if she was caught running, but she didn't care. She wasn't a schoolgirl anymore. She had to get away, to think, to understand . . .

She headed for her favorite place, a tiny courtyard on the far side of the convent, shaded in summer, a pool of warm sunlight in winter. A place for contemplation, Reverend Mother had said when she'd found Bella there once.

She'd been in tears then, too. In trouble for fighting, defending the honor of her absent husband. His honor . . .

The thought brought a fresh spurt of angry, bitter tears as she flung herself onto the cold stone bench that had been witness to so much of her misery.

The other girls had been right all along. It had taken stupid, stubborn Bella Ripton eight long years to learn the truth they'd recognized from the start. He hadn't wanted her. He'd abandoned her to her fate. And he'd tried to annul their marriage, to erase all trace of it.

And failed.

She felt sick. Devastated. Furious. He thought he could just come and pick her up. Bella the Parcel. Stick her on a shelf until he remembered her.

Because he needed an heir.

Didn't need *her*, just a wife.

Didn't want *her,* just an heir.

All those years of worry on his behalf. What a *fool* she'd been.

She dashed scalding tears from her cheeks. Her fingers came away pink and streaky. Paloma's rouge. She pulled the handkerchief from the bodice of her dress and scrubbed at her face, trying to remove the rice powder and rouge. Why, oh, why had she let the girls dress her up like a stupid doll for him? She could have been dressed in a sack for all he cared.

Humiliation roiled in her gut like an angry snake. She felt ill. Such a fool she was, coming all dressed up, primed for a romantic reunion.

So many times she'd sat in this small, sunny courtyard, remembering her wedding day. To tell the truth, she didn't remember all that much about it, only standing in the little whitewashed village church with the priest saying the words, a mumble of Latin. She remembered holding Lieutenant Ripton's hand; it was so big and warm, and her hand so small and cold. It was cold in the church, and he'd rubbed his thumb lightly back and forth over her hand, a silent reassurance that everything would be all right, just as he'd promised her in the pine glade . . .

The priest asked a question, and just as Lieutenant Ripton answered, a beam of sun shone through the narrow windows of the tiny church and gilded his face, and he looked like an angel. He'd glanced down at Bella and smiled, just with his eyes, and she felt so safe, as if she'd been blessed.

She'd been so certain the golden beam of sunlight was a sign that her marriage had been blessed, that it was meant to be.

Stupid, dreamy fool . . .

When the others found out he'd tried to annul the marriage, how they'd pity her. She couldn't bear it.

There were whispers once, about someone's cousin whose marriage had been annulled because she didn't please her husband. The girl was returned home, shamed and disgraced.

How much worse to have had your husband try for an annulment and fail? All of the shame, and none of the comfort of escape. She'd become one of those stories that girls whispered about. Utter, public, never-ending mortification.

"Isabella?" Reverend Mother's voice came from the courtyard entrance.

Isabella hastily wiped her eyes and turned to face her, expecting a scold, but though it was Reverend Mother who came toward her, it was her aunt who held out loving, sympathetic arms, saying softly, "Oh, my dear." Isabella fell into them, sobbing afresh.

"My dear, I thought you knew," Reverend Mother said when Isabella had finally sobbed herself out. She handed Isabella a clean handkerchief. "Wipe your eyes and blow your nose."

"What do you mean, knew? How could I know?" Isabella blew her nose loudly.

"Lord Ripton was correct; annulment was the plan from the beginning."

"It *was*?" Isabella whispered.

Her aunt nodded. "I thought you knew." She gave her a compassionate hug. "But there was a lot for you to take in that day, I know, and you were still a child, so I suppose it's understandable that you didn't fully comprehend."

"But . . ." Isabella swallowed to remove the lump in her throat.

"Lord Ripton married you solely to protect you from a forced marriage to Ramón."

Isabella nodded. "I knew that. But the marriage was still real." Wasn't it?

"It was legal, of course, but at the time it was just a stratagem. His intention—*our* intention—was to have it annulled when you were twenty-one." She patted Isabella's hand. "He planned to set you free to make your own choice, my dear."

Bella sniffed. "Why didn't you warn me—you must have . . . Didn't you know how I feel—felt about him?"

A rueful expression crossed Reverend Mother's face. "I could see you had a schoolgirl crush—not surprising when a heroic young man rescues you, and such a handsome one, too. But I believed you'd grow out of it, and you did." She eyed Bella with a mixture of concern and doubt. "Didn't you?"

"Yes," Bella said dully. She did, she told herself. She felt nothing at all for him—now.

Humiliation twisted in her gut. How foolish, getting all upset about an arrangement that had been in place for eight years, only she'd been too stupid to remember it.

All the dreams, all the glorious romantic stories she'd told about her husband.

All stupid, vain, childish . . . lies.

She stared down at the worn stone cobbles of the courtyard and wished she could seep between the cracks and dissolve deep into the earth.

"In any case," Reverend Mother continued, "shortly after you came here I knew an annulment was not possible."

"How did you know?"

"My dear, you told me yourself of the . . . attack."

"Yes, but . . . but what has that to do with it? Was it because Lieutenant Ripton killed the man? Because he was a deserter and—"

"No, my dear, it was because the man . . . er . . . compromised your virginity and that is why no annulment could be granted."

"But Lieutenant Ripton didn't—"

"No, no, of course not. But after that, no other man— no gentleman, I mean—would be prepared to take you to wife."

Bella frowned. "Lieutenant Ripton is a gentleman."

"He is indeed, and now a titled one—you really must learn to call him Lord Ripton—and so we must be grateful for his forbearance in this matter."

Bella wove the handkerchief between her fingers. So now she must be *grateful* he was willing to overlook this terrible flaw in her—because he had no choice in the matter. Grateful that he'd come to collect this defective package that no other gentleman would want.

Grateful that she had no choice in the matter, that she must go with a man who clearly did not want her but was prepared to regard her with *forbearance*.

Foolish Isabella Ripton, dreaming of love when her lot was to be forbearance.

She twisted the handkerchief, tightening it around her fingers until it hurt. She would be just as trapped in an unwanted marriage as she had been by convent walls.

"Isabella? Do you understand what I am telling you?"

Bella nodded, as if reconciled, but her aunt wasn't deceived. "It is a good marriage," she insisted. "Lord Ripton is not of your father's rank, but he is a titled gentleman, a good man of good family, and his war service was very distinguished."

"How do you know about his war service?"

She snorted. "Did you imagine that I would make no inquiries about the man who married my niece?" She stood.

"For heaven's sake, Isabella, stop looking so tragic. You will live a rich and privileged life with a kind and handsome gentleman. You will go to elegant London parties and wear wonderful clothes. No other girl here has half as much to look forward to—and any one of them would take your place in an instant if she had the chance. Now pull yourself together. Lord Ripton is waiting to speak with you."

"*Now?*" Isabella's hands flew to her hair. She must make a terrible sight.

But nuns had no patience with vanity. "Yes, now. You've kept him waiting long enough."

*L*uke paced back and forth in the cloisters. He was considerably dismayed by Isabella's reaction. It was clear to him that she'd cherished . . . expectations of him. *Romantic* expectations.

Women often did that—took one look at his face and imagined he was someone else entirely, some blasted Byronic hero, to be sighed and swooned over. Spin fantasies about.

He was no fit subject for any young girl's fantasy.

He recalled the way her face had crumpled when she'd realized he'd tried to have the marriage annulled. He swore silently. A girl who'd lost both parents in a war, who'd fled her home in fear of a forced marriage to a despised cousin, who was brutally attacked on the road, and who was desperate enough to agree to a sham marriage to a stranger—how could such a girl cherish any kind of fairy-tale expectations, let alone eight years after the event?

Judging by her reaction, it seemed this one did. And Luke was going to have to deal with it.

It would be cruel to encourage any expectations she might have. The sooner she realized that this marriage would be a practical arrangement, the better. It might not have been what either of them planned, but with the right attitude they could make the best of the situation and forge a marriage of . . . of contentment.

With all that she'd experienced, she must surely realize—deep down—that it was better this way. That fantasies and romantic dreams were dangerous delusions, a trap for the unwary.

Life was grim, and looks could—and did—deceive. Bad things happened, even to people who didn't deserve it. Especially to people who didn't deserve it. She must know that.

And if she didn't, Luke would set her straight. Because life wasn't a fairy tale.

"Lord Ripton?"

Luke turned. "Reverend Mother?"

"Isabella is ready to talk to you now."

*H*e found her sitting on a stone bench in a small court-yard.

"I'm sorry you were upset," he told her. "I didn't realize you hadn't understood about the annulment. It wasn't a secret."

"I know," Isabella said in a small, stifled voice. Her face was turned away.

"It was no reflection on you."

"I know. Reverend Mother explained it to me."

Luke nodded. He felt awkward, because she was obviously still distressed, but he was determined to say his piece. "But just because it hasn't ended up the way we planned it doesn't mean it won't work out well in the end. As long as we know what to expect." He took a breath and added, "And what *not* to expect."

She said nothing, and taking her silence as assent, he continued. "For instance, it would be foolish for either of us to expect love of the sort that poets write about. Ours will not be that sort of marriage."

Still she said nothing.

"But I hope we will become friends," he said. "Marriage is a partnership, and if we work together we can have a life of . . ." He paused, searching for the right word. "A life of solid contentment, even happiness. Is that not a worthy goal?"

She didn't respond, and he touched her shoulder. It was rigid. "Isabella?"

She finally turned to face him, her eyes drowned and burning. Her elaborate hairstyle was a mess, and her painted face, a travesty. Strangely it recalled to him the bruised, battered face of the little girl he'd married, and without thinking he slipped a comforting arm around her shoulders. "There, there, my dear, it will not be so bad, I promise you. I'll take good care of you. You must not worry."

"I won't," she said stiffly, scrubbing at her cheeks. Her hands were slender, brown, and ringless. Luke fingered the ring in his pocket. His mother's ring. Despite her misgivings about the marriage, she'd asked him about a ring, and when he looked blank, she'd given him hers.

He took Isabella's hand. "I've brought you a wedding ring."

"But I still have the ring you gave me." She pulled it from the neck of her dress, his old signet ring tied onto a worn ribbon. He remembered now he'd given it to her when the priest has asked about a ring. It was too big for her then and still was now.

"This one will fit better."

"Do you want this one back?" Her fist closed possessively around his signet, giving him his answer.

"No, you keep it." He reached for her hand again and slipped the golden wedding ring onto her finger, and then, on impulse, he kissed the hollow of her palm.

She shivered and snatched her hand back. "You don't even know me."

"And yet we are married."

"Many marriages begin thus," said her aunt from the entrance to the courtyard. "Your own parents' marriage, for instance, Isabella."

"This is different," Isabella said.

"Indeed it is," Luke agreed. "It is our marriage, and we will make of it what we will." He patted her hand and left.

* * *

*I*sabella knuckled her eyes fiercely. He'd been so *kind*. So *understanding*.

She'd rather he'd *beaten* her. It would have been easier to bear than this . . .

Humiliation scalded her.

All her own fault. Because Isabella Ripton was stupid, stupid, stupid! Dreaming silly schoolgirl dreams instead of paying attention to what was really happening.

She wished he hadn't been so kind. It would have been so much easier if she could be angry with him, blame him. But he'd given her the protection of his name for the last eight years, and now it was time for her to pay that debt.

He'd offered her a life of security, of contentment, and Reverend Mother was right—it was more than that. She'd take her place in English society. She'd have pretty dresses and go to parties and . . .

She bit her lip. She didn't care about dresses and parties.

But that didn't matter, she told herself. It was wrong for her to be sitting here filled with self-pity because she was married to a kind and handsome man, when poor Alejandra might be forced to marry a horrid old poxed *vizconde*. And the others might never marry at all.

She was lucky. There were so many reasons why she should feel deliriously happy that Lord Ripton had come for her.

A single tear rolled slowly down her cheek. She dashed it away. She was her father's daughter and she would not weep over what could not be changed.

She was not a child anymore to rail at fate. She was a woman and she would make her own happiness.

*T*he small, scruffy boy appeared from nowhere again, as the convent gate shut firmly behind Luke. "You want your horses now, *señor*?"

Luke considered it. "How far is it to the village?"

"Just a few steps," the boy assured him.

"Is there an inn?"

The boy laughed heartily at the idea. "The nearest inn is more than ten miles away, *señor*. But if it is a drink you want . . . or a bed for the night?"

"A bed."

"Then you must stay at my home," the boy said. "I am Miguel Zabala, and I am the man of the family."

He was small and skinny and barely ten years old, but Luke didn't laugh. "Take me there and we'll see," Luke told him.

He soon learned Miguel's "few steps" were the estimate of a large-minded spirit, but Luke didn't mind the walk down a narrow, dusty track. The boy skipped along beside him, chattering incessantly, part travelogue of the places they could see from the road, and part his views on life and the various people he'd known.

Luke listened with half an ear.

Isabella's reaction to his arrival had been a little disturbing. It was clear to him that she wanted the marriage as little as he had. A situation that could not be allowed to continue.

His title hadn't impressed her in the least. Well, she was the daughter of a *conde*.

She'd seen through him at once. He did need an heir. There was no shame in that. It was his duty to his family name. Bearing an ancient name herself, she should understand that.

And if nothing else, duty would have been drummed into her at the convent. Particularly the wifely duties: to love, honor, and obey.

They were stuck with each other and would have to make the best of it. He needed to reconcile her to their situation, and quickly. He had no intention of putting up with tantrums from a reluctant bride.

His own attraction to her was lukewarm at best—not that she'd shown herself to advantage, with that ghastly old-fashioned dress with the frills and flounces, and that hairstyle, and the paint. But that didn't matter. He'd give her no cause to regret their marriage. He'd treat her well and be a faithful husband to her. And by the time children came along, they might even have found love of a sort. Many people did.

He thought of her odd golden brown eyes staring out from behind the powder and paint like an angry little hawk hidden in a posy. She might have changed out of all recognition, but those eyes of hers were exactly as he remembered, especially when they flashed with temper or were drowning with hurt.

The one part of her that was without artifice, reminding him of the brave little girl he'd married. Change was inevitable, he supposed, after eight years. He would have to get to know the young woman she'd become. And she would have to accustom herself to the man he'd become.

A new start for them both, to begin at dinner.

They rounded a rocky bluff, and a small village came into view: a handful of ragged-looking cottages huddled on the edge of the mountain. Not a prosperous place.

Miguel pointed to the smallest and meanest-looking house of all. "I will tell my mother you are coming," he said and ran ahead.

Luke resigned himself to a night spent in the company of bedbugs and fleas. He'd had worse during the war.

By the time Luke reached the cottage, the mother was waiting in the doorway. She was fairly young, not yet thirty. Two small children peered out shyly from behind her skirts. Miguel, with a freshly washed face, introduced them, then took Luke around the side of the house so he could see what good care he'd taken of Luke's horses.

They were tethered in a kind of open lean-to shed and had been given clean straw and water. The tack was hanging from nails driven into the wall, and the horses had been rubbed down. Luke nodded his approval, and Miguel led him back to the front door of the cottage, stepping aside with a flourish to allow Luke to enter.

The cottage was gloomy inside, but once Luke's eyes adjusted, he saw that though poor, it was clean and neat. The only smell he could detect was of something cooking, some kind of stew pungent with garlic and herbs. He'd slept in much worse conditions during the war.

"You can sleep here," Miguel announced, pulling back a curtain and pointing to a pallet on a kind of raised shelf in the corner of the room. It was large enough for two and covered in a handwoven cloth. Luke's leather portmanteau sat beside it.

He'd been offered the only bed in the house, the mother's bed. And possibly the children's, too.

"No, no, I couldn't—" he began.

"The bedding is clean, *señor*, just washed today, and dried in the sun, the mattress straw fresh and sweet," the woman told him. "And the children will not bother you—they will be quiet as mice. Or if you want, we will all sleep outside." She bit her lip and twisted her hands in her apron.

"There is no better place in the village," Miguel assured him. Four pairs of big brown eyes watched Luke anxiously.

They needed his money. Desperately.

"Very well," Luke agreed. "And I wouldn't dream of putting any of you outside." He nodded at the two little curly heads peeping out from behind their mother's skirts, and they immediately disappeared.

Luke pulled out his watch and checked the time. "Would there be any hot water?"

"He will want the hot water to make tea," Miguel, knowledgeable in the ways of Englishmen, explained to his mother and siblings.

"No tea," Luke said, running his hand over his chin. "I need a shave."

An hour later, Luke set out again for the convent, changed out of his riding clothes, freshly shaved and as neat as he could make himself in the limited conditions of the cottage. His every move had been made under the solemn gaze of two dark-eyed little girls who had no regard for the sanctity of an Englishman's curtain.

He'd sent the diminutive man of the family off to buy wine, bread, meat, and whatever else he could think of, just to get rid of him and his incessant chatter. The family could do with the food.

But now, as he made his way back up the path to the convent, Miguel joined him. "You look very handsome, *señor*. And you smell beautiful, too. You are courting one of the young ladies, yes?"

"No," Luke lied.

Miguel regarded him with astonishment. "But why else would you shave?"

"She is my wife already," Luke explained.

Miguel squinted up at him. "She is a bad wife?"

"No."

"Then why did you place her in the convent with the nuns?"

"It's complicated."

Miguel walked along beside him for a while. "My father went off and left us when I was small, when the girls were babies."

Luke glanced at the boy. "He never came back?"

"No." The boy kicked a stone over the edge of the path and paused to listen to it bouncing down the cliff.

"He was killed?"

"No, he is living in Bilbao. He found another woman he liked better than Mama. Did you find another woman you liked better, *señor*?"

"No." Luke increased his pace. The boy's innocent chatter was somehow making him feel guilty. Which was ridiculous. He had nothing to feel guilty for.

"So you have come to fetch her and take her back to England with you."

"Correct."

"Do I know her, *señor*? I know some of the young ladies in the convent. What's her name?"

He supposed it didn't matter if he told the boy her name. "Señora Ripton."

"Isabella Ripton?" Miguel's face split in a grin. "But she is my friend." And then his smile faded and he stopped dead. "You put Isabella in the convent and left her? She has lived in that place since before my father left my mother."

The accusation in the boy's eyes irked Luke.

Dammit, why was everyone looking at him as if the mess was all his fault? He was supposed to be the *hero*, dammit! First he'd saved her life and then he'd married her. He hadn't *had* to marry her. It had been the only certain way to protect her from a forced marriage to her evil cousin Ramón. It hadn't been for his own advantage in the least.

Somehow that had been forgotten and he'd become the man who'd abandoned his wife. And he hadn't. Or he had, but not intentionally.

Well, yes, intentionally, but it had been *for her own good.*

But how did you explain that to a ten-year-old boy?

Or, indeed, to a girl of almost twenty-one. He rang the bell at the gate of the convent.

Five

❧

"*B*lessed saints!" Dolores stopped stock-still at the entrance to the dining hall. She turned and said to Alejandra, "He *is* as beautiful as an angel."

Alejandra was staring over Dolores's shoulder. "Madonna, yes! A beautiful *fallen* angel. That mouth, those eyes, those cheekbones. So stern looking and yet somehow . . . wicked." She sighed.

Immediately there was a faint scuffle as the other girls pushed forward, trying to see Isabella's very real husband.

"Girls!" Sister Ignazia said, and when they did not immediately respond, she said in a warning voice, "Young *ladies*! Do I assume from this unseemly behavior that you have no wish to dine this evening?"

"No, Sister." They hurried into the dining hall in relative silence, darting avid glances at Isabella's husband.

"Do you think he would be stern in the bedchamber?" Alejandra whispered.

"Who cares?" Luisa giggled.

"Ooh, I do like a masterful man," Dolores said with a dramatic shiver.

Isabella clenched her fists. He was *her* husband, even if he didn't want her.

Lieuten— No, Lord Ripton stood behind his chair at Reverend Mother's table, in formal garb and looking handsomer than ever. The only man in a room full of women, he was the center of attention. Bad enough the other girls were fluttering and whispering and giggling as they eyed him across the room, but even *nuns* were straightening their wimples and smiling at him.

And he, Isabella thought darkly, was perfectly comfortable with the fuss. This was to be her future. The man of her dreams, adored by every woman who saw him. And kind with it, so she couldn't even hate him.

"Look, even Sister Gertruda is making up to him," hissed Luisa. "I thought she hated men."

Isabella watched as Sister Gertruda, normally a thin-lipped, humorless martinet, stood beside Lord Ripton, chatting animatedly. He listened with grave attention, nodding and making short responses, but his gaze wandered across the room to the knot of girls, his dark eyes sifting through them one by one.

Sister Josefina had decreed that their normal convent garb would be worn, no fancy dresses or hairstyles, no frills, perfume, or paint—on pain of punishment—so from a distance and at first glance, the girls would be hard to tell apart.

Isabella felt it the moment he first saw her—a faint prickle of awareness rippling over her skin. Reverend Mother noticed her arrival, and gestured to Isabella to join herself and Lord Ripton at table.

"Bring him over and introduce us after dinner," Alejandra ordered as Isabella left. "I want to meet him."

"Oh yes." Paloma sighed and fluttered her lashes. "I want to meet a fallen angel."

"Mmmm, I want to hear him speak, even if it is in English."

"How long is it since any of us talked to a man who isn't a priest?"

"I'll try," Isabella snapped, and she marched across to join her husband. Everyone had gone silly. He'd turned all their heads.

His dark eyes seemed to take in everything, but he said nothing, only murmuring a quiet greeting. His deep voice shivered down her spine.

The room fell silent while they all waited behind their chairs, then Reverend Mother gave the signal, and with a loud scraping of chairs everyone sat down.

Reverend Mother then said grace. It was a long grace and in Latin, and Isabella was so keyed up she couldn't concentrate. She'd never been much interested in Latin anyway, so much of it was just mumble. She glanced at Lord Ripton and to her shock found he was watching her, his gaze dark and intense. She immediately squeezed her eyes shut. Was he a godless heathen like Papa that he didn't close his eyes at grace?

Reverend Mother finished grace; then, just as everyone was about to reach for their food, she said, "We welcome Lord Ripton who joins us at table this evening."

They put down their cutlery and waited. "As you all no doubt have heard, he has come to collect his wife Isabella who has been with us these last eight years." She smiled at Isabella. "A most *eventful* eight years, may I say." A ripple of amusement passed around the room.

Isabella stared at a knot in the grain of the wooden table, silently willing Reverend Mother to say no more about her time at the convent. He didn't need to know any of that. And besides, the food was getting cold. Not that she was hungry; her stomach was in knots.

Why did he keep staring at her? She passed her hands over her hair, smoothing it down. Her hands were shaking. Stupid. It's not as if anything could change. She was fated to this man. He was fated to her.

A life of solid contentment.

Reverend Mother went on, "Lord Ripton tells me he plans to leave first thing in the morning, so this will be Isabella's last night with us before embarking on her new married life in England. We wish her well." Everyone raised a beaker or glass—most drinking water, but Reverend Mother, Lord Ripton, and some of the older nuns drinking wine—and drank to Isabella and Lord Ripton.

Isabella forced her lips into what she hoped looked like a happy smile, then drank. All those faces beaming at her and Lord Ripton. All that joyful goodwill. Her mouth tasted of bile. It was all a charade, a farce. He didn't want her. It was nothing but a horrid mistake.

She sat wedged between Reverend Mother and Lord Ripton, pushing her food around her plate. It was a sin to waste food—and God knew there were enough times during the war when they'd been desperate for it—but she couldn't bring herself to swallow a mouthful of stew.

She broke off a small piece of bread and tried to chew. It wedged in a hard lump halfway down her throat. She drank from her beaker and managed to choke it down.

Luke forced himself to drag his gaze off her. He couldn't believe the difference in her appearance. The clothes were dreadful, of course—drab, concealing, and coarse—but their plainness suited her better than all those frills. And now he could really see her.

Not a little ugly duckling in a flock of swans, but something entirely different.

Her skin was palest ivory, and smooth, with a delicate flush that had been concealed by the garish rouge she'd worn before.

She'd abandoned the fussy, elaborate hairstyle. Her hair was now plaited in a simple coronet around her head, the thick plaits silken and glossy. She must have just washed it, for it seemed damp. Tiny curls clustered around her temple and nape.

The unfussy hairstyle revealed the elegant line of her head and neck and framed her face perfectly. She was not conventionally pretty—not pretty in the least, actually. With high cheekbones, a pointed chin, a commanding little nose bequeathed to her by some Roman ancestor, and golden eyes that met his with a mixture of shyness and defiance, she was something far more interesting than pretty. He couldn't take his eyes off her.

He was *married* to this slender, stunning creature in the dreadful clothes.

He wanted to touch her, to see if that ivory skin was as soft and silky as it seemed. Her cheekbones gave her a faintly haughty look, and her nose was bold and commanding.

But her mouth—oh Lord, what a mouth . . . He hadn't noticed it before, when it had been painted in a small cupid's bow. Now he could barely drag his gaze from it. Au naturel, her lips were like rich, ripe berries with the bloom still on. Plump, luscious, edible.

He must have moaned, for Reverend Mother turned to him with a look of faint inquiry. He managed to clear his throat and regarded her solemnly.

"So tomorrow you two will leave us," Reverend Mother said. "Where do you plan to go, Lord Ripton?"

Isabella turned her head to look at her aunt, and Luke noticed a tiny, velvet mole, just below the delicate whorls of her left ear. His mouth dried.

"Lord Ripton?"

He glanced at Reverend Mother. "Go?"

"On your honeymoon."

Honeymoon? He hadn't even thought about a honeymoon. This was to have been a duty. "We'll make immediately for England, to my home there."

Reverend Mother glanced at the silent girl between them. "I'm sure Isabella is looking forward to seeing her new home, aren't you Isabella?"

Isabella made some sort of sound that might indicate assent, and the nun went on, "And I'm sure she'll enjoy being out in the fresh air. She is very fond of fresh air."

"Indeed?" Luke glanced at Isabella, noticed her mouth and immediately forgot what he'd been going to say.

"You have hired horses, I presume?"

Luke blinked and, with an effort, brought his attention back to the conversation. "Yes, I hope Isabella won't find the journey too wearying." It was easier to conduct a conversation with the nun than with his wife. She was seemingly the quiet type—he had no complaint there; it was restful—and it was easier to maintain a civilized conversation without being . . . distracted. It was most disconcerting.

"It will be a long time since she last rode a horse. No doubt she'll be very stiff at first."

"Oh, but—" Reverend Mother began.

"A horse?" Isabella looked up. "What kind of horse?"

He glanced down at her, surprised. "Just a hired horse; nothing very special. It took me some time to find a suitable mount. Reverend Mother, you were saying?"

"Suitable?" Isabella frowned.

"Quite suitable," he assured her. He turned back to the nun. "Reverend Mother?"

But Reverend Mother had either forgotten what she was going to say or had thought better of it.

"You don't plan to spend any time in Spain?" she asked. "Isabella mentioned your late uncle owned several Spanish estates in Andalusia. I presume they now belong to you."

"Yes, however—"

"Excellent. You will wish to visit them, since you are in Spain now."

Luke said nothing. He did not wish to visit them in the least. He addressed himself to his stew.

Reverend Mother frowned slightly. "You will want to see how they fared during the war, surely?"

Luke drank some of the thin, slightly acid mountain wine.

Reverend Mother took off her pince-nez and gave him a governessy look down her long nose. "Things are a little . . . shall we say 'unsettled' in Spain at the moment, Lord Ripton. It would be as well to consolidate your ownership."

Luke stiffened, irritated by the gratuitous advice and implied moral lecture. He had an agent to check that sort of thing for him, but he had no intention of justifying himself to anyone, let alone a bossy nun, even if she was now his relative by marriage.

"I need to return to England," he said brusquely. "I have an engagement there I must meet." And he wouldn't spend a single night more in this godforsaken country than he had to.

"It seems a shame not to—"

"A very important engagement," he said in a final note. "Tell me, I noticed when I arrived here the walls of the convent had been damaged. Were you attacked?"

He'd intended it as a simple change of subject, but beside him, Isabella's aimless stirring of the food on her plate stopped.

Luke went cold. The attacking of convents and churches had not been uncommon in the war. In postrevolutionary France the church was no longer regarded as holy, and nuns and monks and priests were simply men and women. Nuns had been raped and murdered, churches looted.

Reverend Mother's thin mouth twisted with contempt. "French, and some deserters who'd joined them. Rabble. They'd heard rumors of a treasure here. Treasure!" She snorted. "We are a simple order. Our only treasures are our girls."

As she talked, Luke relaxed. Her tone was merely indignant, with no echoes of past horror. Isabella sat quiet as a rabbit, pretending not to be there.

"I gather you managed to hold them off."

"Yes, although if—"

Isabella coughed. Reverend Mother glanced at her and said smoothly, "Fortunately they were persuaded to leave."

"My friends would like to meet you, Lord Ripton," Isabella said abruptly.

"You must call me Luke," he told her.

She turned to the nun. "Do I have your permission, Reverend Mother?"

The nun nodded, and Isabella jumped up, taking her plate to a sideboard.

The moment was lost. He'd probably never find out what happened, but he didn't care. It didn't do to stir up old memories.

He watched as Isabella carefully scraped her dinner into a pail—presumably there were pigs or chickens somewhere—and stacked her plate and cutlery. She seemed to have recovered from her upset and now appeared to accept her fate with good grace. As he'd hoped, her training in the convent had made her into a docile and obedient young woman.

The intense attraction he felt for her was the icing on the cake.

He sat back, satisfied, watching as she hurried across to the far end of the table where the schoolgirls sat. She was very slender, her figure, under the thick, concealing convent clothes, girlish rather than womanly.

"She's very thin," he observed. And underdeveloped for her age. The Spanish girls he'd known were lush and curvaceous. "She's not ill, is she?"

"We're all thin here," the nun said dryly. "We almost starved during the war, and the country has been slow to recover. Trust me, Isabella has the appetite of any healthy young creature."

Her reference to Isabella's healthy appetite caused Luke to think of quite another sort of appetite. His body stirred at the thought. It was disconcerting, feeling the early stages of arousal while sitting at table with a middle-aged nun. But something about the way Isabella moved . . . appealed.

Begetting an heir was not going to be a duty after all.

What was she saying? Isabella's expression looked quite severe as she spoke to her friends. One of them, a ravishingly pretty girl, glanced at him and said something. They all laughed except Isabella. She seemed one of them . . . yet not. A little apart.

The other girls quickly cleared away their plates and hurried toward him in a gaggle, smoothing down their hair and eyeing him in a flirtatious, fluttery manner that made him sigh. Not so different from the girls in London, then. Young, sheltered, and silly. Any remaining fears that attackers had invaded the convent faded.

He stood and bowed politely over each girl's hand as Isabella introduced him. Then under Reverend Mother's benevolent eye, the girls pelted him with eager questions.

"Have you traveled far to come here?" They spoke in slow, clear Spanish, watching him as if they might need to repeat the question.

"No, just from the village down the road," he said in easy, idiomatic Spanish. Gales of giggles, as if he were a famous wit.

"But they said you were English," the prettiest one—Alejandra?—said in surprise, and glanced at Isabella as if she'd lied to them.

"I learned Spanish when I was a boy," he explained. "I spent several summers on my uncle's estates in Andalusia." They oohed and ahhed, as if this was somehow clever of him.

He supposed most girls raised in a tightly disciplined and isolated female environment would overreact to a male presence. They acted younger than they were.

Not that Isabella was giggling or flirting. In silence she watched her friends making up to him, asking no questions herself, taking no part in the conversation. Watching over them—or perhaps she was watching over him—like a small, plainly dressed hawk.

"Do you have any brothers?" This from the intense-looking one. Dolores? The others craned forward, breathless, hanging on his every word.

He shook his head. "Only sisters."

"How many?"

"Three."

"Are they married?"

"Yes, two are married; the youngest, Molly, is making her come-out this year."

"How old is Molly?"

"The same age as Isabella."

"So *old*!" they exclaimed in surprise. "Do all girls come out so old in England?"

"No, they are usually eighteen or nineteen," he explained. "Molly's first come-out was delayed by the death of my uncle and postponed again the following year because of an illness. This year she is hoping it'll be third time lucky."

"Is she pretty, this Molly?"

"Very."

"Are all your sisters pretty?"

"Yes, they are." His oldest sister was a famous beauty. And as bossy a female as he'd ever seen.

"When you go to England, will you and Isabella live in London?"

"Part of the time. I have a house in the country and would prefer to spend most of the year there." He glanced at Isabella. "We will, of course, come to London for the season."

"The season in London!" they exclaimed. "Isabella, you are so lucky!"

He glanced at her again, and she gave a polite, noncommittal smile. Catching the exchange, the one called Alejandra asked, "Has Isabella changed much since you saw her, Lord Ripton?"

"Somewhat," he said dryly. "She's grown up." This produced a gust of feminine tittering.

"Perhaps you and Isabella will spend part of the year in Spain, as you did when you were a boy. Perhaps she can visit us."

"No." They looked startled. He must have said it more brusquely than he'd intended. "I won't be returning to Spain again."

"But—"

He glanced at Reverend Mother. "That's enough, girls," she said immediately. "Lord Ripton and Isabella have a long journey ahead of them tomorrow—"

"And a long reunion tomorrow night," the frizzy-haired one said, causing an outbreak of fresh giggles.

"Luisa!" Reverend Mother said sternly, and the girls immediately put on solemn faces. "Bid Lord Ripton good night; he is no doubt weary of your silly chatter."

One by one, they bade him good night, Isabella waiting to the last.

Reverend Mother rose. "Good evening, Lord Ripton. Isabella will show you out. I imagine there are one or two things you will wish to say to each other in private. I will see you in the morning. I hope the village accommodations are adequate." She swept from the room in a stately manner, shooing the girls still hanging around the door before her.

Luke offered Isabella his arm.

She hesitated. "Lord Ripton—"

"Luke," he reminded her.

"I don't want to go straight to England from here," she told him bluntly. "I want to visit my home first."

Luke frowned. "You told me when we first met you no longer had a home." He tucked her hand into the crook of his arm and strode toward the door.

"I don't. It's not my home anymore. But I still want to go there."

"It's a bit late to be having second thoughts about Ramón, isn't it?"

She pulled away from him, stopping dead. "Ramón! This is not about Ramón. I *despise* Ramón. I never want to see him again." She folded her arms. "But I must return to my former home."

He narrowed his eyes at her. "Why?"

She hesitated. "I need to check that everything is all right. That everyone is all right."

"There's no point in wondering about that now," he said crisply. "Besides, if it's not all right, if the place is in a mess, what can you do about it? It's Ramón's responsibility now." They emerged into the main courtyard.

"But—"

He patted her hand and said in a firm voice, "No, there's no point in going back. Trust me; it'll just upset you to no purpose."

"No, you don't understand—" A nun hurried across to unlock the convent gate and, distracted, Isabella broke off. The nun took a lantern from a hook, lit it, and handed it to Luke. She waited, smiling, ready to lock the gate after his departure.

The opportunity for a private conversation was over. Luke could not regret it. He'd said all he intended to say on the matter; there was nothing further to discuss.

He bowed, touching his lips to the back of Isabella's hand, and as mouth met skin, the desire that had been simmering in him all through dinner spiked.

She shivered, blinked at him wide-eyed, then snatched her hand back.

Luke tried not to smile. So she felt it, too.

"Tomorrow will be a long, hard ride. I'll collect you at eight," he told her. "Sleep well." For, he thought, tomorrow night she'd get no sleep at all.

*T*hat hadn't gone well, Bella thought as she slowly made her way back to the girls' dormitory. He hadn't listened to her at all.

She *had* to go back to Valle Verde. The guilt was eating away at her.

She would have to *make* him listen. It was a simple matter of respect.

She might not know how to make a man love her—from all she'd ever seen it depended on being beautiful and knowing how to flirt and flutter eyelashes. Well, she wasn't ever going to be beautiful, and she felt stupid trying to flirt—like a dog trying to perform ballet—and anyway his lashes were longer than hers.

Respect, however, was just a matter of being strongminded. Reverend Mother was not the least bit pretty, but everyone respected her—even Lord Ripton. And her predecessor, the old Reverend Mother, had been tiny and gentle with the sweetest little crumpled face, like a pale little raisin, yet even Ramón had obeyed her. Both women were, in very different ways, strong-minded. They simply assumed people would obey them, and everyone did.

Tomorrow she would look Lord Ripton in the eye, tell him firmly and clearly what she needed to do, and *assume* his cooperation.

She hoped he wouldn't demand an explanation—she would have to think of something convincing. She was too ashamed to give him the real one, and have him know what a selfish, small-minded, disloyal creature she truly was. And how she needed to make up for what she had done.

She hoped it would still be possible.

She didn't want to start her new life with the weight of Valle Verde on her conscience.

She reached the girls' dormitory, but Sister Josefina was just coming out. "Time for bed, Isabella," she said.

"Yes, Sister. Good night." Isabella headed for her own room. She'd only slept in the dormitory a few times when she'd first arrived at the convent, but her nightmares had disturbed the other girls, and eventually she'd been moved to a cell in the same wing, where she had her own little window looking out into the sky, barred, admittedly, but the fresh air and the sight of the stars had helped. She couldn't bear to be closed in, especially in the dark.

In one way she would have liked to spend her last night in the dormitory, with the girls whispering secrets and sharing laughs, and she was sure Sister Josefina, who was kindhearted and sweet, would allow it.

But in another way it was a relief to be spared the questions. After meeting him, the other girls would be full of envy for her, and excited, and would ask all kinds of questions about the man who was her husband, and she didn't think she could bear that. Especially knowing he didn't want her at all.

Besides, she had to pack.

Packing took her less than ten minutes. She'd arrived at the convent with nothing, and she'd leave with not much more. She packed a change of clothes and a few small items of sentiment: a decorative comb and a small, silver brooch—gifts from friends over the years—and a small Bible with inlaid mother-of-pearl on the cover, given to her by her aunt. It had once belonged to Papa's mother.

As for a trousseau, she owned nothing like that, nor any dowry chest full of embroidered linen like the other girls all had. Not so much as a monogrammed or lace-edged handkerchief.

She stuffed everything into a cloth bag and fastened it with a strip of leather. Not much to show for eight years. Almost half her lifetime.

Poverty, chastity, obedience: all that was about to change.

Six

〜

She was late. Luke put his watch away and resumed his pacing. Sixteen minutes past eight o'clock and still, there was no sign of Isabella. Several nuns and a couple of the schoolgirls clustered in the courtyard, waiting to say good-bye.

He was about to pull out his watch for the third time when he heard faint commotion around the corner, voices only just audible, in a hushed dispute.

"I don't care." Isabella's voice, and the sound of swift footsteps.

She marched into the courtyard. Luke's eyes widened.

"Isa*bella*!" several of the nuns exclaimed. Exasperation rather than surprise, he noted distantly. But he wasn't interested in the nuns; only Isabella.

He couldn't take his eyes off her.

Dressed in a pair of men's buckskin breeches, she strode toward him on long, long legs, the heels of her high leather boots ringing on the flagstones. He'd never seen anything like it. A white lawn shirt, a leather jerkin, and a belt completed the outfit. She held a cloth bag in one hand and carried a short, dark blue coat slung over her shoulder.

She crossed the courtyard with a loose, open stride. The breeches fitted her like a glove. The soft buckskin hugged the length of her thighs, caressing her hips and outlining every slender curve. She seemed not the least bit self-conscious.

His throat thickened.

How had he ever thought she lacked feminine curves? They were slender and subtle and they made his mouth water.

A bevy of nuns fluttered in her wake, remonstrating.

"Isa*bella*! You cannot leave the convent dressed like that!" Reverend Mother appeared in another doorway. "It is indecent."

"It's practical," Isabella argued. "We're riding."

"I don't care if you're flying! You will not leave this place dressed like that."

She met Reverend Mother's gaze and raised her chin. "I am no longer a ward of this convent." Gasps from the school-girls at her temerity.

"You are still my niece," snapped the nun, "and you will obey me. Go back inside and put on a skirt, at once."

The two women's gazes clashed. Isabella made no move.

"If I have to ride astride in a skirt my thighs will chafe," she said. At the brazen mention of thighs, there was a murmuring among the nuns and much pursing of lips.

Luke finally got his tongue to work. "You won't be riding astride."

She whirled around and stared at him. "What? I thought you had a horse." Her frown darkened. "I won't travel in a litter!"

"Of course not. I told you I'd found a suitable mount. I've brought a sidesaddle."

"A sidesaddle?" Her eyes narrowed, and Luke gestured outside to where Miguel was waiting with two horses and a donkey.

Reverend Mother swept forward. "Of course he brought a sidesaddle for you to ride. What else would a gentleman expect from a *lady*?" Her eyes bored into Isabella in silent imperative. "Now, go and remove those masculine abominations and put on a skirt at once."

Isabella looked mutinous for a moment, then with a muffled exclamation she turned on her heel and marched back the way she'd come.

Lord, but the sight of her striding away from him in those breeches, the superb curve of her backside . . . Luke could only stare. And hope his glazed look wasn't visible to his companions. His body began to harden . . . He gritted his teeth and willed it to stop. What a time and place to battle with arousal, standing in a convent surrounded by nuns.

Isabella disappeared, and a buzz of conversation followed her departure.

Reverend Mother swished forward. "Isabella can be a little . . . willful, but she is a good girl at heart. I hope you won't hold this against her. I have perhaps allowed her a little more leeway than I should have—"

"I'm not angry," he said. It came out as a husky croak.

She seemed not to hear, but went on, "During the war, things came to such a state, you see, and without Isabella's skills—" She broke off and took a deep breath. "Even if she were not my last living relative I would still say this—take good care of her, Lord Ripton. Isabella is a treasure. I know it is not immediately obvious, but—"

"I will take good care of her," Luke promised.

Reverend Mother stepped forward and put her thin, careworn hands over his. "She has a heart made for loving, that girl, and—"

He pulled his hands out of her grasp. "I said I will take good care of her. I am not in the habit of breaking my promises."

She raised one questioning brow, a mute reminder of wedding vows that he'd tried to have annulled.

He knew what she was doing—trying to do—but dammit, he was the last person to be entrusted with a young girl's heart. That kind of thing—no, never again.

He would take good care of Isabella and make sure she was safe and warm and well fed and in all material respects well cared for.

Her heart was not his concern.

He snapped the crop against his boot. Where the hell was she? How long did it take to put on a skirt, dammit? He wished to be gone from this place.

Reverend Mother gave him a searching look. "I hope I've done the right thing," she murmured.

Dammit, what did the woman expect? She knew damned well this marriage was not what either of them had intended eight years ago.

That he'd honored those original promises and come to fetch Isabella, that he was willing to make a life with her, provide for her, and get an heir on her, that should be enough. It was all he was prepared to give—all he could promise.

Whatever she had thought of Lieutenant Ripton all those years ago, he was no longer that boy. He could barely remember that boy.

Had he not—well, it was no use going down that path. What was done was done. No point in looking backward and bewailing what couldn't be changed.

He would protect and provide for her niece, honor and respect her, and that would have to be enough.

There was nothing else left in him now.

And the sooner they left this benighted country, the happier he'd be.

Finally Isabella returned dressed in a long gray skirt, the short, dark blue coat she'd been carrying now buttoned to her throat. A blue hat dangled from a string on her wrist. She handed Luke her bag, but before he could ask her about the rest of her luggage, she turned away, saying, "I'll just say good-bye to everyone."

One of the girls uttered a loud sob, and in seconds they were all at it, sobbing and embracing and uttering promises to write, to stay in touch. Even some of the nuns were weeping.

Luke busied himself strapping her bag to the back of her horse. He hated this female emotional sensibility. It made him feel helpless and at sea.

Isabella embraced each girl, one by one, and then each

nun—they were all here now to see her off. He supposed eight years was a long time. He couldn't see if Isabella was weeping or not. No doubt she was.

Luke, having made his farewells to Reverend Mother and the others, waited outside the convent gate with the horses. His riding crop snapped rhythmically against the side of his boot. He hated seeing women weep, had no idea what to do.

Lastly Reverend Mother embraced Isabella and kissed her on both cheeks. She slipped a thin gold chain over Isabella's head and blessed her solemnly. Nuns and schoolgirls crossed themselves.

With a choked sob, Isabella flung her arms around Reverend Mother's waist and hugged her convulsively. She turned, crammed the hat on her head, and marched resolutely through the gate to where Luke waited with Miguel and the animals.

"Where's your luggage?" Luke asked brusquely. Her eyes were red and her skin blotchy and wet with tears.

She scrubbed her hand across her wet cheeks and pointed to the bag tied behind her saddle. "There."

He blinked. "That's your luggage? All of it?"

She nodded and took the mare's reins.

"But I bought a donkey," Luke said, and immediately felt stupid.

She glanced at the donkey, standing patiently with Miguel. "So I see. What for?"

"For your luggage."

"But I only have this." She gestured to the bag.

"So I see." The conversation was getting ridiculous. Luke cupped his hands to give her a boost up. She placed a booted foot in his linked hands and sprang into the saddle. A slender featherweight.

She seemed comfortable in the sidesaddle, hooking her leg around the pommel and draping her skirts as naturally as if she'd ridden only the day before instead of eight years ago. Luke handed her the riding crop and adjusted her stirrup. As he did, he noticed something that made his mouth twitch. Under the skirt she still wore her breeches.

The docile and obedient bride of his imaginings was fading fast.

"What are you going to do with the donkey?" she asked.

Luke mounted his own horse. "Miguel can take him."

The boy, hearing his name, looked up. "Take him where, *señor*?"

"Wherever you like. I don't need the donkey after all."

The boy's eyes widened. He clutched the donkey's lead in his grubby fist and glanced from Luke to Isabella and back at Luke. "How much?"

"Nothing. It's a gift," Luke told him.

"A gift?" The boy's eyes gleamed, then the excitement faded. "*Señor*, my mother would not allow such a gift. You paid her already, most generously."

"They may be poor, but they have their pride," Isabella said softly to Luke. She said something in the boy's language, and Miguel turned to Luke in surprise. "Is true, *señor*?"

"Tell him it's true, Lord Ripton," Isabella said with a hint of a smile.

"It's true," Luke said, hoping it was. He had no idea what she'd said.

Miguel's face split in a brilliant grin. "What a place England must be! Thank you, *señor*, may you have many fine sons, *many* fine sons!" he told Luke enthusiastically. "My mother will be so happy. With a donkey I can collect more wood for winter. With a donkey we can carry goods to market. With a donkey I can—"

"Become the man of the village," Luke said dryly. "I have no doubt of it." He glanced at Isabella. "Ready?"

She nodded, and they set off, the convent community clustered in the gateway calling last good-byes and waving.

Miguel and the donkey ran along beside them for a short while, waving, whooping, and wishing them even more fine sons, until Isabella called to Luke, "My mare is a little fresh and needs a run. Shall we canter?" Without waiting for Luke's response, she shouted a final good-bye to Miguel and urged her horse into a canter. She had an excellent seat.

Luke followed, and in a few minutes they were alone on the narrow, winding road, heading down the mountain, leaving the convent and the village far behind.

After a while the track broadened and Isabella slowed to a walk. Luke brought his mount alongside her mare so that the horses were walking side by side.

"Not finding it too tiring?"

She gave him a surprised look. "Not at all."

They walked on in silence for a while. To Luke's surprise she didn't seem to feel the need to fill the silence with aimless chatter. Of course, it could be shyness, in which case it was incumbent on him to converse. Only he couldn't think of anything to chat about.

He pulled out a flask of cold spring water and passed it to her. She unstoppered it, drank, and handed it back to him with murmured thanks.

He was about to drink, when a question occurred to him. "What did you tell Miguel about the donkey?"

She gave a little huff of amusement. "Just that it is an English tradition for a bridegroom to give a male donkey as a gift . . ." She added with a glimmer of mischief, "To ensure a son, you understand, donkeys being . . . well endowed."

Luke, in the act of drinking from his flask, choked. She gave a gurgle of laughter and rode ahead. His demure convent bride.

More and more he was looking forward to the night.

*T*hey rode all morning, stopping occasionally to rest and water the horses and for Isabella to stretch her legs. Not that she really needed it. Her mare had a beautifully smooth gait, and the saddle fit her horse well and was comfortable.

The joy of being on a horse again, breathing in fresh, pine-crisp mountain air, did much to soothe her bruised spirit, and the narrow track forced them to travel in single file most of the time, which made conversation difficult. Far from being disappointed or bored, it gave her the luxury of being alone with her thoughts, without anyone saying, "Isabella Ripton, are you daydreaming again?"

Not that she was letting herself daydream anymore. She'd given that up. Or was trying to.

But she would have to broach the matter soon with him. She was not going to tamely accompany him to England. She had to go to Valle Verde first. But it was not a discussion to be had while on horseback.

And then there was the small matter of a wedding night. It occupied her thoughts a great deal.

"We'll stop here for luncheon," Lord Ripton said, turning off the track into a small clearing. It was a peaceful-looking place, with a stream burbling between the rocks and patches of green grass dappled by sunlight that filtered through oaks and beech trees.

Lord Ripton dismounted and went to assist her, but she slipped to the ground before he reached her. "I've brought food from the convent," she said, reaching into her bag.

"And I have food from Miguel's mother."

They made a picnic on the grass, with bread, cheese, olives, and some slices of rich, pungent sausage. Tiny birds hopped in the grass, twittering hopefully from a distance. Finches? Sparrows? She wasn't sure.

"This place reminds me of the first time we met," she said, nibbling on the crusty bread.

"I passed that place on the way here." He glanced at her and added, "We will not revisit it."

She crumbled some of the bread and scattered it for the birds. He produced an apple and sliced it neatly into eight pieces, removing the core. He cut a sliver of cheese, placed a piece of apple on it, and passed it to her, balanced on the blade of his knife. "Eat."

She took it and nibbled. It was very good, the richness and saltiness of the cheese contrasting with the sharp crispness of the apple. "Lord Ripton, I wonder, did you notice if—" she began.

"I told you to call me Luke."

He waited.

"Luke," she repeated obediently. "I was wondering about the grave. Did you see it?"

"There's no sign of it," he told her. "I stopped there briefly on the way to the convent. There is no sign of anything—only grass." He passed her another slice of cheese and apple.

"I often think of that day."

"Then stop it," he told her firmly. "It's in the past and should remain there. There is nothing to be gained from looking backward. Look to your future, think about children." He passed her another piece of cheese and apple.

He meant heirs, Isabella thought darkly, taking the proffered food. He was probably feeding her cheese and apples to fatten her up for the purpose. Like a prize mare.

She wanted children, of course she did, but first she had to settle her affairs in Valle Verde.

And he was wrong about the past. It was important. You couldn't just bury it like a body and hope grass would grow over it and make it disappear.

The past shaped who you were. It wasn't healthy to dwell in it, but you had to learn to live with it.

Sister Mary Stella, the Irish nun who'd taken young Bella under her wing when she first arrived at the convent, had taught her that. "Bad things happen," she would say, "but it does no good to pretend they never happened. If you do, they will fester and grow, and the more you try to hide them away, the more they'll rule you in secret."

Young Bella knew that was true. The nightmares came every night.

"So pull out the bad things after a bit and give them a good seeing to. Expose them to sunshine. Imagine if they happened to someone else. I promise it will look different. Then, mebbe you can let it go, and forgive yourself—yes, I know you did nothing wrong, but you can't tell me you don't blame yourself for letting it happen."

She was right. Bella did blame herself.

"We all blame ourselves, lovie; don't worry. But put the past in proper perspective and you leave the guilt behind, too. And look to the future without fear or regret." And Sister

Mary Stella would squeeze Bella's hand and say, "And I just know you're going to have a lovely future, Bella me love. I can feel it in me waters!"

Lord Ripton gave Isabella the last piece of apple and carefully wiped the blade of his knife clean. "Now, if you've finished . . ." He stood and held his hand out to assist her to rise.

"As a matter of fact, I haven't," she said and leaned back on her hands.

"Still hungry?"

"No, but we need to talk."

"Talk? Can't we do that on the road?"

"No." She waited, and eventually, humoring her, he sat down again.

"Before we go to England I need to go to Valle Verde."

"Not this again. I thought I made it clear—"

"You did, but apparently I did not make it clear enough to you. I have to go to Valle Verde because—"

"You feel a responsibility to your father's people, I know, but trust me, there is no point in your going. If you don't own the estate any longer, you cannot rectify their situation, and even if you did—"

"I could send an agent to do that job?"

"Precisely."

"Well, you're wrong."

He arched an eyebrow. "I beg your pardon?"

"You think I want to go and play Lady Bountiful to my father's peasants? I do not. Nor have I any intention of interfering with Ramón's running of the estate. Knowing Ramón, it would only make him angry and, being Ramón, he would take it out on someone else."

"So, is it something you left behind?"

"In a way."

"Then we can send someone to fetch it."

"No, we cannot." She swallowed. "It is not a thing." She met his gaze squarely. "It's a sister."

"A what?"

"My half sister." There, she'd said it.

"I thought you were an only child."

"I am. The only legitimate child. Perlita, my half sister, is the daughter of my father's mistress."

He frowned. "Your father did not make provision for the child and her mother?"

"He did." She swallowed. It was harder to admit than she'd thought. Up to now, only Father Alvarez knew her sorry tale, and that was under the seal of the confessional.

"Then what—"

It all came tumbling out then, the dreadful thing she had done. "When Papa was dying he sent the message for me to go at once to my aunt's convent. He told me to take Perlita and her mother with me, but I didn't. His message was clear, but I pretended I didn't understand it. And so I left them behind. And that was why I was attacked on the road."

"What?" He stared at her. "What possible relation could there be between leaving your father's mistress and child behind, and you being attacked?"

"I disobeyed Papa and abandoned my half sister to her fate, and that's why it happened."

"What nonsense."

She shook her head. "It's not nonsense. The men who attacked me knew about Papa's message. I told you they were after jewels."

There was a short silence as he considered her story. "What did your father's message say?"

"That I was to go at once to my aunt at the Convent of the Broken Angel—it is not the correct name of the convent, you understand, but what those who know it call it—and to take his jewels with me."

"His jewels?"

"It is what he called Esmerelda—his mistress—and Perlita. An emerald and a pearl—his jewels."

"Are you sure he didn't mean actual jewels, your mother's jewels, for instance?"

She shook her head. "No, for then he would have written

'your jewels,' because Mama's jewels belonged to me. In any case, we sold Mama's jewels to raise money to equip Papa's army."

"You sold your mother's jewels?"

"Of course." She saw his look and shrugged. "We needed guns to fight the French, and our king was a weak traitor who'd handed the country over to the enemy." She noticed his expression and added, "It wasn't so hard. I had no sentimental attachment to most of her jewelry—only the pearls. I never saw Mama wear anything except her pearls. They were a wedding present from her parents."

"Where are they now?"

"Hidden in Papa's secret safe place at Valle Verde."

"So you want to fetch them."

"No, my mother's pearls are not sufficient cause. To be honest, I don't look forward to going back there. I have no desire to meet my cousin Ramón again, and my home is no longer my home, not without Papa. But I promised Papa obedience, and I broke my promise when I fled Valle Verde and abandoned Perlita and her mother to their fate."

"You were a child of thirteen," he reminded her.

"I was responsible. And Perlita was—*is*—younger than me by two years."

"Her mother wasn't younger than you, however. She was an adult and perfectly capable of taking care of her own child."

Isabella shook her head. "She was not raised to be the son of the family," she said, hearing the edge of bitterness in her voice. "Perlita's mother is beautiful and brainless. She was entirely dependent on Papa for everything. And he passed on that responsibility to me when he left. And then, as he lay dying, he charged me with their care . . ." Her voice cracked, and he completed her tale.

"But in your fear of being forced to marry your cousin Ramón, you panicked and forgot them."

Isabella glanced away and said nothing. Fear and panic were acceptable excuses for a thirteen-year-old. Let him believe it. It was better than the truth.

"Did you make inquiries after you reached the convent?"

"Yes, my aunt sent letters to Valle Verde several times."

"And received no response?"

"No, but in wartime, letters go astray. And if Ramón received the letters . . ." She made a gesture of disgust. "Ramón would pass on nothing from my aunt. He suspected she was hiding me, but there was nothing he could do."

Lord Ripton seemed to be pondering the situation.

"Papa gave Esmerelda and Perlita a house on the estate. They must be there. Where else would they go?"

"Were you close?"

"What does that matter?" she said, a telltale defensive note in her voice. She scanned his face, trying to read his expression. "My sister's fate weighs heavily on my conscience. I *must* go." Could he not see that? He had to, surely.

"No, it's eight years since you left your half sister behind. There's no point in traipsing across Spain on a wild-goose chase. Whatever her situation when you left Valle Verde, it is long since changed, and I don't wish to delay our arrival in England any further."

"Because of this important engagement of yours?"

He looked at her. "Yes."

"What is so important that it comes before my sister's welfare?" Isabella waited. She'd bared her soul to him—almost—and he'd waved it aside as if it meant nothing. And to him, perhaps it didn't. But not to her. It was a matter of honor. And blood.

"It's not important."

"It clearly is important if you override my concern for my sister for its sake."

"I meant it's not your concern. All you need to know is that I made a promise and I intend to keep it."

An indirect cut at her broken promise to her father? Deliberate or not, it flicked Isabella on the raw. "Then I'll go to Valle Verde by myself and join you later in England."

"You'll do nothing of the sort. I won't have my wife gadding about a foreign country on her own."

"It's *not* a foreign country. *England* is the foreign country to me. You can hire guards and a duenna if you don't trust me."

"It's not a matter of trust. The discussion is ended, and you will obey me. If you're still worried about your half sister when we get back to England, I'll send someone to make inquiries. Now, let us continue on our way. I intend to reach the town of Berdún before nightfall." He rose to his feet and held out an imperious hand to assist her.

She knew it was childish, but she refused to take his hand.

They packed up the remains of their luncheon and washed their hands and faces in the mountain-cold stream. Again, Isabella recalled bathing in that other stream that dreadful day, and how Lieutenant Ripton had come and lifted her out of the freezing water and wrapped her in his shirt and comforted her.

It was hard to believe he was the same man.

The second half of the day passed more slowly. They still rode in silence, but it was the result of constraint.

Bella brooded over his brusque dismissal of her need to go to Valle Verde. She wasn't happy about it at all, but the more she thought about it, the more she had to accept that for him, a bastard half sister was of little significance.

And that his engagement in England was obviously very important.

If she didn't share his priorities, that was her affair.

*I*n the late afternoon, a light drizzle set in. Isabella made no complaint; she just pulled out the blue hat and a gray woolen cloak from her bag, put them on, and kept riding. Luke was not so sanguine. The hat offered little protection. The misty rain caught in the tiny curls that framed her face. Droplets clustered on her lashes. The cloak was old and threadbare and was soon sodden.

What the hell was her aunt thinking, letting her embark on a long and difficult journey with such inadequate clothing? It was taking poverty and simplicity too far.

"Stop," Luke told her, and with a puzzled look, she reined in her mare. He reached over, yanked Isabella's cloak off her, and tossed it into the bushes.

"What are you doing? That's my cloak. You can't—"

He pulled off his many-caped greatcoat and held it out to her. "Put this on."

"But—"

"Don't argue. It's warmer and drier than that blasted threadbare thing you were wearing."

"But what about you?"

"I'm used to being out in all weather." He rolled the sleeves up for her. "Now button it, all the way up." He watched as she buttoned it tight to her throat, then nodded and led the way onward.

They rounded a bend, and a small cluster of buildings came into sight. "The village of Biniés," Luke told her. "We'll spend the night here."

"I thought you wanted to get to Berdún tonight."

"You've ridden all day and you're cold and wet and tired." She glanced at him. "You're wetter than me."

"I'm used to it," he said brusquely. "Even in so small a village, there's bound to be an inn of sorts, though it might be a little spartan. We'll find a room and wait out the rain." And he had plans for the night that would warm them both, most thoroughly.

She hesitated, and then said, "Two rooms, please." Her skin was moon-pale and wet with rain.

He reined in his horse and stared at her. "*Two* rooms?"

She moistened cold, berry-dark lips. "You said this would be a marriage of convenience." She looked nervous, but her chin was braced and resolute. "Well, it is not convenient for me to share a bed with you . . . yet."

She was punishing him, Luke thought, for his refusal to let her go on a wild-goose chase after her half sister by her father's mistress.

But he was damned if he'd venture into the wild hills that had harbored the worst experience of his life. Bad enough he'd had to come to Spain to fetch her. That had stirred up all kinds of unwelcome memories. But to return to the hills where Michael had died so horribly . . . And all Luke's fault. No.

Besides, her tale was nonsense as far as he could tell.

What man would expect his thirteen-year-old daughter to take care of his adult mistress and her illegitimate child? Provide for them in his absence, perhaps. But escort them across a war-ravaged country? Preposterous.

The man should never have let her know about them in the first place.

Luke was damned if he'd let it drive a wedge between them. This marriage had already started on a rocky and unorthodox footing, but he was determined to make it work. And bedding her well and often figured large in his plan.

Two rooms be damned. He opened his mouth to tell her so and noted the white-knuckled grip of her reins. He glanced at her mouth. She saw him looking and swallowed.

Oh hell! It was nerves, bridal nerves. What the hell was he thinking, planning a night of passionate lovemaking on the first night they were together?

She'd been attacked as a child. And had spent the last eight years locked up with a bunch of nuns. She was probably terrified of the wedding night.

He glanced at her again, all big, dark golden eyes and gorgeous, vulnerable mouth. Of course she was scared of him; scared of what took place between a man and his wife in the bedchamber.

For one long, enticing moment he entertained the thought that it would be better to get it over with done with, show her there was nothing to fear, introduce her to a world of pleasure . . .

One glance at her white face and the set, tight look around her mouth, and he relented.

It was his own desire talking, not her needs.

Dammit!

He'd promised her friendship, and forcing a frightened bride to his bed was not at all to his tastes. He looked at her beautiful mouth with more than a pang of regret. Perhaps later he would introduce her to the pleasure of a kiss. It would be something, at least. And who knew where it might lead?

"It's not spite," she said, surprising him. "When we get to England, I promise you I will do my duty as a wife."

Do my duty. That settled it. His body might ache for her, but *do my duty* killed any desire he had to bed her tonight.

When he finally made love to her, he vowed, duty would be the last thing on her mind.

They found a small tavern that could accommodate travelers. It was simple and rustic but very clean. "Two rooms," Luke told the tavern keeper.

Seven

❧

*B*ella's bedchamber was small and, to her eyes, charming, nestled high under the narrow eaves with whitewashed stone walls and a sloping ceiling. It had a bare wooden floor with a coiled rag rug, a small cast-iron stove in the corner, and a squashy-looking bed with a bright red coverlet. Best of all it had two small dormer windows that looked out across the tiled rooftops and down into the valley, though at the moment the view was just a glimmer of wet rooftops and a haze of rain.

It was as far from her bare, narrow cell at the convent as she could imagine.

Lord Ripton had ordered hot water and a tub to be brought up to her and a fire to be lit in her room. It glowed merrily, throwing out the heat. Bella hung up her damp clothing to dry in front of the fire and slid into the gently steaming water of the bath with a blissful sigh.

I will take good care of you, he'd said, and it was true.

It might have made her feel more special if Lord Ripton

had not also seen that their horses were well rubbed down and given a hot mash, and their tack dried, cleaned, and oiled.

Lord Ripton took good care of all his possessions.

Bella Ripton, stop miserating over nothing, she told herself. He could be the kind of husband who beat an unsatisfactory wife. He could be a poxed old *vizconde*. Instead he was handsome, kind, and took good care of her. And his horses, and that was good, because she loved horses.

If he was also impersonal, stubborn, and autocratic, that was nothing to complain about. She had no reason to feel melancholy. Or even wistful. If she did, it was only because she was tired.

And because for years she'd been spinning foolish, impossible dreams about him in which he performed brave and gallant deeds, all for the love of Bella Ripton.

Not for *duty*.

The solution was clear. Stop dreaming and get on with her life, her *real* life. With her real husband, not some impossible make-believe one.

She finished bathing and changed into her other dress. She'd just shaken out her damp plaits and was kneeling in front of the stove, drying her hair, when there was a knock on the door.

"Come in," she called without getting up.

She heard the door open, and then nothing. She twisted around and peered from beneath the curtain of hair. Lord Ripton stood on the threshold of the room, staring. A bottle and two slender wineglasses dangled from his hand.

"Did you want something?" she asked.

He collected himself and stepped inside, closing the door. "You won't want to dine in the public area, so I've ordered dinner to be served in my room in fifteen minutes. I hope that will be sufficient time for you. I brought you some of our host's own brew, a kind of homemade sloe brandy; aniseed with a hint of coffee and vanilla. It's different, but very warming." He half filled the glasses and passed one to her.

"Thank you." Bella put her glass on the tiled hearth that surrounded the small cast-iron stove. "I just need to finish drying my hair. I'll join you in a moment."

He paused, then said, "I'll wait." He sat down on her bed and watched her.

With him in it her little bedchamber was suddenly a great deal smaller. Bella felt very self-conscious. He watched with silent intensity as she ran her fingers through her hair, separating the clumps to help them dry more quickly. It had gone so curly with the damp, a comb or brush would only make it worse.

Dinner to be served in his room? Why? It would make it a very intimate meal. He hadn't been at all pleased with her insistence on two rooms. Was this a ploy to get her alone with him? To seduce her? A delicious frisson, a mix of nervousness, excitement, and awareness, skittered across her skin.

She bent low to dry the underneath, and as she was curtained in hair, the scent of convent soap surrounded her. She'd washed her hair the night before. Now she felt a pang of homesickness.

Ironic when for so long she'd been desperate to leave the convent.

"Is the drink not to your liking?" he asked, his deep voice sending a tingle down her spine.

Startled from her reverie, she picked up the glass and quickly drank. She coughed at the bittersweet aniseedy taste of it as it burned its way down.

His mouth twitched in what was almost the beginning of a smile. "Not used to drinking?"

"No, we always drank water, except at Mass, of course," she admitted. The rich, sharp liquid pooled in her stomach, warming her blood, and she felt suddenly ravenous.

Her hair was almost dry, so she twisted it into a knot and thrust a couple of pins into it.

Outside, the rain intensified, beating lightly against the windows. Her stomach rumbled. Had he heard?

"Good thing we stopped when we did," he observed.

She hoped he was talking about the rain. "Yes, thank you. It was very considerate of you."

She picked up a shawl, but he took it from her. He stood behind her and wrapped her in it. His arms encircled her. He'd shaved. The faint scent of his cologne water enveloped her.

"Ready?" he asked.

"Ready." It came out in a squeak. The brandy, she decided.

*L*uke was glad he'd been able to arrange the private dinner. In such a small village tavern, he wasn't sure they'd be able to manage it, but the landlord and his wife bustled about happily—nothing was too much trouble for an English milord and his wife. The stableboy carted a small table upstairs to Luke's bedchamber, and the landlord waited on them personally while his wife cooked.

It was a remarkably fine dinner, too, for such a tiny, remote place: vegetable soup, hare stewed with figs, a mutton pie, and an omelette filled with salt cod and herbs. Isabella ate everything set before her with relish, and he was reminded of what Reverend Mother had said: she did indeed have a healthy appetite. It boded well for his plans . . .

The candlelight danced lightly across her face, caressing her full, dark lips, turning her eyes into pools of mystery. She ate in silence, but he could look at her face all night and not be bored.

Luke drank a local wine with his dinner, finding it dry and very much to his taste, but after one sip, Isabella had grimaced and set it aside. He gave the landlord a silent signal, and the man nodded and returned in a few moments, telling Isabella his wife had sent up some of her very own sweet apple cider for the young lady.

Isabella tasted it with a caution that would have amused Luke if he wasn't focused entirely on the way her mouth seemed to caress the glass. She liked it, gave the man a dazzling smile, and sent thanks and warm compliments to his wife.

Would she ever smile like that at Luke?

Her hair, twisted high on her head, curled around her face in a riot of feathery tendrils, clustering around her temple and nape. Loose in the firelight, it had been a gleaming, silken waterfall of darkness against the pale delicacy of the skin at her nape, a dozen shades of ebony twisting between her slender fingers like a live thing.

He'd longed to plunge his fingers into that thick, silken mass, place his mouth against that tender nape. Instead he'd sipped the liqueur, the taste of which would forever remind him of her. Unexpected combinations: dark, yet sweet and sharp. Cool on the outside; a slow burn within. Firing his appetite.

This unexpected, powerful desire for her was a gift. He might not be able to offer her his heart—he had nothing, less than nothing, to give—but honest, unfettered desire was, in Luke's view, a far better substitute.

She wiped her plate clean with a crust of bread and gave a satisfied sigh. "Thank you, Lord Ripton, that was delicious."

"Luke," he reminded her.

The landlord, beaming, removed the dishes and replaced them with a bowl of walnuts, a plate containing two kinds of cheese, and a dish of quince paste. He also brought the bottle of homemade brandy and two more glasses.

Luke poured himself a glass of the brandy and, when she nodded, a half glass for her. The landlord left them alone. Luke sipped the drink and cracked open walnuts for her, and Isabella made little morsels with a slice of cheese, topped with quince paste or walnuts.

The rain had died down, but wind whistled around the eaves. The fire in its small iron box threw out a surprising amount of heat. They were warm, replete, and relaxed.

Next step: the seduction of his wife. He stared at her mouth, slick with hot, spicy liqueur.

She passed Luke a slice of hard cheese topped with half a walnut. "When we go to England, will we go straight to your home in the country?"

He forced himself to concentrate on conversation. It, too, could seduce. "London, first. I have a house on Grosvenor Square. You'll need new clothes, from the skin out. An orgy of shopping. You'll enjoy that." He shouldn't have used the word "orgy."

She gave him a doubtful glance. "Mmm. Will Molly be there?" She nibbled on a slice of sheep's cheese topped with quince paste.

He watched her eat it. Salt-sweet, soft, and addictive. He swallowed, then realized she'd stopped chewing and was looking at him with an expectant air.

"Eh? What was that again?"

"Molly," she prompted. "Will she be in London, too?"

"Yes, finally." He found himself telling her about how Molly had had quite a lonely time of it while their mother was in mourning and Luke was away at school, and how, while Luke and his friends were away at the war, Molly had written to them all—cheerful, funny, affectionate letters that lifted their spirits.

"You're very fond of her, I think."

"Of course, she's my sister."

She glanced away, suddenly silent, and he knew she was thinking of her own sister. Dammit. It wasn't the same thing at all.

"Molly's my baby sister," he told her, trying to gloss over the awkward silence. "I am less close to my older sisters. They're both quite bossy. Thankfully, they have husbands and families they direct most of their energies toward."

"You said at the convent that Molly is to make her come-out soon."

"Yes, that's right."

"And is there to be a ball?" A tiny jewel of quince paste quivered at the corner of her mouth.

Luke stared at it hungrily. "Of course, on her birthday, April 4th. She and my mother have been planning it for months."

"It's not very long till April 4th. You might not get back to England in time." Her tongue slipped out and swept the quince paste away.

Luke answered without thinking. "No danger of that. I promised her faithfully—" He broke off. "There is plenty of time," he finished stiffly.

But the damage was done.

"That's your very important engagement, isn't it?" she said quietly. "Your sister's ball." Her eyes glittered.

He knew it was too late, but he found himself saying, "It's one of several important engagements, but yes, I promised her when she was just a little girl that I'd be there to dance at her first ball. I don't break promises if I can possibly help it."

"And a dance with your sister is more important than the safety of mine." She folded her napkin deliberately and rose. He moved to pull her chair back for her, but she raised her hands and recoiled as if to repel him. Her eyes were burning. "Good night, Lord Ripton," she said coolly and swept from the room.

Damn, damn, damn!

Luke poured himself another glass of liqueur. There was no point going after her. Luke knew when a woman was so angry, soft words would not smooth over the situation. Especially since he had no intention of backing down.

But dammit, what on earth had possessed him, letting slip the reason for his desire to get back to England? The only reason he was prepared to admit to, at any rate.

He wasn't even going to think about the real reason.

Fool that he was, he'd been so lust-mazed, staring at that beautiful, ripe mouth of hers and thinking about kissing her, he'd let his sister's ball slip to the one person who it would matter to. Damn and blast!

He drained his glass and prepared for bed.

She was angry now, but in time she would forgive him. Or at least get over it. Once she was in London, distracted by a whirlwind of shopping— No.

If Molly was missing, no amount of shopping could distract him. Nothing could.

But he could appease her. He'd hire men, reliable, trustworthy men who would discover her sister's whereabouts and report back on the situation. And if the sister needed help, if she needed rescuing, or money, or assistance of any sort, Luke would provide it. She could even come and live in England if Isabella wanted her there. Whatever was necessary.

As long as Luke didn't have to do the searching.

Bad enough he'd had to return to Spain to fetch Isabella. He was not staying a moment longer than necessary.

Every sight, every scent, every sound of Spain was a reminder of things he wanted to forget.

So that was his urgent appointment! A ball! A dance! Bella punched her pillow. A *dance* was more important than her sister!

She was very worried that the rumors were true. And if Ramón *had* kicked Esmerelda off the estate, and moved Perlita into the main house and forced her to become his mistress, then Bella was partly responsible.

Ramón couldn't have Isabella, so he'd taken her sister.

For revenge? As a hostage?

She didn't know. But it was her fault that Esmerelda and her daughter had been left vulnerable and unprotected.

She hadn't left them behind out of fear and panic. Nothing so excusable. Or forgivable.

It was jealousy, pure jealousy. And spite.

Now she was filled with remorse for what her thirteen-year-old self had done.

She lay in the wide, soft bed, high under the eaves with the wind rattling the shutters, and thought about the child she'd been. She hadn't realized how lonely she'd been until she went to the convent and had girls her own age to talk to.

For most of her life she'd been Mama's main companion, and then, after Mama died, there was only Papa. She'd adored her father and thought herself the apple of his eye. Until she'd seen him with Perlita.

She curled around the soft pillow, remembering the day she first learned about Esmerelda and Perlita, his second, secret family, tucked away in the next valley.

It was the year after Mama had been killed. In the months following, Papa had taken Bella with him everywhere. The country was in a desperate state, he'd said, and the royal family had betrayed them all. Soon he would have to leave to fight in the mountains, and the younger men would go with him. While he was away, the estate would be Bella's responsibility.

He'd taught her to shoot, to hunt, to survive in any situation, for if enemy soldiers came again, she was not to stay in the house as Mama had done; she was to take to the hills and hide there. He'd taught Bella as much as he could about the management of the estate, instructing her, testing her, working her remorselessly.

Bella didn't mind. She missed Mama desperately, but Papa had never paid her so much attention in her life, and she adored being so important to him. She worked and studied and practiced hard, pushing herself to exhaustion to please him.

And please him she did—often. She would never forget the day he'd patted her head and told her she was almost as good as a son. Her heart had swelled with pride. *Almost as good as a son.* Praise from Papa was rare.

She lacked beauty, Papa told her, but with his training and Mama's fortune she would make a good wife for his heir. Back then, his heir was his brother's son, Felipe.

Felipe, Papa said, was a shiftless wastrel, but harmless. He would get sons on her, and she would run the estate as Papa had taught her, and the future of Papa's line would be assured.

Twelve months, Isabella thought, curled up in the bed in the village inn; a year she'd lived in glorious ignorance, Papa's little girl, thrilled to be almost as good as a son.

And then he'd come home that time, from Barcelona. He usually brought her something when he'd been away—often it was sweets, one time it was a book on how to keep accounts, and once, on a never-to-be-forgotten day, he'd brought her a pretty pink ribbon for her hair.

This day he'd dumped his bags in the entrance and gone straight into his office to consult with his foreman. Isabella waited outside, listening to the rumble of male voices. She was impatient to greet him, hoping he'd brought her something.

Papa's bags were right there. The flap of one was open. Bella was tempted to peek.

What she saw took her breath away—a golden-haired china doll, the most beautiful thing she'd ever seen in her life, dressed in a pink velvet dress, with real lace, so beautiful it almost made her cry.

Last time Papa had brought her a riding crop, elegantly tooled, and of course, Bella had been delighted, even if it was the kind of thing you gave a son. And she did love riding.

But this gloriously beautiful doll was for a daughter, a most beloved daughter. She didn't know what thrilled her most—the beauty of the doll, or that Papa had thought to bring her something so lovely, so special. It made all her hard work worthwhile.

Every detail of the doll was perfect, even down to tiny oval pink fingernails on her dimpled china hands. Her shoes were of palest pink leather, fastened with tiny pearl buttons, and she wore white stockings made of silk. She even wore a necklace made of tiny seed pearls—just like Mama's pearls, now Bella's.

The doll's eyes were bright blue, with long lashes made of real hair. The doll seemed to smile at Bella, like a friend, like a sister. She hugged the doll to her. She'd always wanted a sister. She would call the doll Gloriana.

She lifted the dress to see what the doll wore underneath— and heard a sound at the door. Someone was coming. Quickly she thrust the doll back into Papa's bag and hurried away.

She would have all the time in the world to play with her doll.

She'd changed into her prettiest dress and waited until dinnertime with barely suppressed excitement.

"Have you been a good girl, Isabella?"

"Yes, Papa." She felt almost sick with anticipation.

"I've brought you something from Barcelona. Do you want to know what it is?"

Her hands were shaking. "Yes, please, Papa."

He'd handed her a parcel, square and heavy, too small to be the doll.

"Well, go on, open it."

She unwrapped it. It was a book; *Equus*, on the care and treatment of horses. Puzzled, she glanced at her father, thinking perhaps he'd played a trick on her and would produce the doll in a minute. "Is that all, Papa?"

He laughed, and for a moment Bella thought he had played a joke on her, because Papa didn't laugh very often. "No, of course it isn't all. Now where did I put it?" And he started patting his pockets.

And Bella had laughed with him, laughing too loudly in relief and delight that Papa had joked with her, when normally he was so serious.

"Ah, here it is." He pulled from his pocket a small twist of paper.

Bella's laughter died. She eyed the brown paper twist. She knew what it contained, and it wasn't a doll.

"Thought I'd forgotten your sweet tooth, did you?" He gave her the little packet of boiled sweets. "Now, come and give your father a kiss and then run along upstairs with your treasures."

Bella kissed his cheek and murmured her thanks. He smelled of cologne water. He'd shaved. Dimly she recognized he'd changed into his going-to-church clothes. But it wasn't Sunday, and anyway, Papa was a reluctant churchgoer at best, only attending on special occasions.

She didn't run upstairs as she'd been told, but crept off to the side and watched, as Papa had his favorite horse brought around from the stables. He mounted, then one of the servants passed up two large parcels tied with string. One of the parcels was the exact size of a doll.

Without quite knowing why, Bella slipped out to the stables and saddled her own horse. Hanging back at a distance, she followed her father into the next valley and watched him ride down a track to a small cottage set into the lea of the hill; it was a pretty cottage of whitewashed stone, with bright geraniums flowering at the windows and in pots by the terrace.

Strangely, though it was quite close to home, Bella had

never visited this valley. She'd ridden with her father over almost every inch of the estate. Or so she thought. Who lived here?

She waited by a copse of birch trees, watching as a servant ran out and took the reins and the parcels while Papa dismounted. Then from the front door burst a pretty little girl. A year or so younger than Isabella, she was dressed all in pink and white. She ran toward Papa, long, glossy ringlets tied with pink ribbons bouncing down her back.

To Bella's utter astonishment, Papa scooped up the little girl and swung her, squealing, in a wide arc. And then he kissed her warmly on each cheek and set her down.

Papa had never swung Isabella around in her life. And if Bella had ever squealed in that vulgar way, she would have been scolded for it.

A woman hurried out, also very pretty and beautifully dressed. Papa embraced her, planting a kiss full on the woman's mouth. The kiss went on forever.

The little girl must have thought so, too, because she tugged Papa's sleeve impatiently. Papa would hate that, Bella thought with a spurt of satisfaction. She waited for Papa to put the mannerless child in her place.

But to her amazement, Papa laughed—actually laughed at being so rudely interrupted—and patted the child's head. He took the parcels from the waiting servant and gave one to the woman and the other to the little girl.

She sat straight down—down on the grass in her pretty pink and white dress! And nobody reprimanded her for it! She ripped open the parcel and gave a squeal of delight and pulled out . . . Gloriana.

Hugging the doll tightly, she jumped up and ran to Papa again, and he picked her and the doll up, laughing as she planted kisses all over his face. All over his face, and yet Papa was laughing.

Then, holding the little girl in one arm—even though she was far too big to be carried—he slipped his other arm around the woman and they all went into the house together.

Like a family.

Bella watched with burning, bitter eyes. She felt sick, furious, betrayed.

And she hated the horrid pretty pink and white creature who'd stolen her doll.

And her father.

*P*apa returned home late the next day. And when Bella ran to greet him as that little girl had, he frowned and told her it wasn't dignified to run like that, and had she been a good girl and studied her book? No hug or even a kiss, just a pat on the head.

One of the servants must have told him how Bella had asked about the people who lived in the white house in the next valley, because Papa called her into his study and explained that the lady and her daughter were relatives.

Bella didn't believe him. Relatives visited. They didn't hide away in the next valley. Not that she cared who the lady and the little girl were; she still hated them.

It was only later, when she was twelve and Papa was leaving to fight in the mountains, that he told her the truth; that she was old enough to understand that many men had mistresses, and no doubt her husband would keep one, too, but she was not to worry about it.

Such things were never discussed or even acknowledged by ladies in polite society, and she should never mention Esmerelda or Perlita to anyone other than himself. If it was ever necessary for him to mention them in a letter or message, he would refer to them as his jewels—his emerald and his pearl.

Bella must have looked sour at that, because Papa had taken Bella's hand and explained that a mistress and any children she bore were, of course, to be looked after—it was a man's duty to do so—but they were not a man's *true* family. Perlita, the little girl, was her half sister, but Isabella was more important to him than Perlita could ever be.

Bella didn't believe his assurances. She'd seen the hugs,

the kisses, and the doll, and over the years there had been many other presents—she'd made a point of sneaking a peek into his bags whenever he returned, and the things he brought Perlita were always much finer than Bella's gifts. She knew which daughter was Papa's duty and which daughter received his love.

But she promised to do her duty by Esmerelda and Perlita and to make sure they were well looked after in Papa's absence. Promised faithfully.

*A*fter a fitful night's sleep, Luke woke to a chilly gray dawn. Under normal circumstances he would rise, break his fast, and continue on his journey, but now he had Isabella to think of.

Yesterday had been a long, hard day for her, emotionally as well as physically. Leaving her home of eight years would have been a wrench, and she'd be stiff and sore from riding all day. He'd let her sleep as late as she wanted.

And with a good night's sleep and a hearty breakfast inside her, she might be in a better mood.

She would put on a tantrum or two, he felt sure, but he'd remain firm. He was the husband, after all, and her role was to obey. Another three or four days' travel and they'd reach San Sebastian, and from there, depending on the winds, they could be back in England in as little as a day.

He lay in bed, dozing for another two hours, and at nine o'clock he rose, washed, dressed, packed up his things, and went downstairs. He ordered breakfast—a proper English one with eggs and ham and thick fried slices of the spicy local sausage. One could not ride for hours on a couple of rolls and coffee.

Luke finished his breakfast, had a third cup of coffee, and glanced at his watch. Time she woke. He called for the landlady. He'd send her upstairs to wake— No. He rather fancied the idea of waking Isabella himself, seeing her all warm and sleepy from her bed.

The landlady came in. "*Sí, señor?*"

"Another breakfast, please. The same again, only this time on a tray."

She beamed. "Another one, *señor*? You must be very hungry."

"It's for my wife." Luke jerked his head upstairs.

The woman followed his gesture with a puzzled expression. "Your wife, *señor*? But she has already eaten."

"Already eaten? When?"

"Before she left, *señor*. She drank a cup of coffee and took some *jamon* and bread and apples for her journey."

"Before she *what*? When was this?"

"Just after dawn, *señor*." The woman faltered at his expression and twisted her apron between worried fingers. "I hope we did no wrong, *señor*. She said to let you sleep, that you knew where she was going."

"I do indeed," Luke growled. Valle blasted Verde.

"I did think it was odd, so young a lady traveling alone without guards or duenna, and dressed the way she was, but . . ." She shrugged. "The English are different from us." She crossed herself in thankfulness.

"Have my horse brought around," he snapped. He took the stairs to his room three at a time and shoved open her door, just to check that the story was true. Empty. The bed was pulled up tidily, and a folded scrap of paper lay in the center of it. He snatched it up.

Dear Lord Ripton—

Dammit, how many times did he have to tell her to call him Luke?

I apologize for leaving you like this. Please believe that I have every intention of honoring my marriage vows—

Luke snorted.

—but as I have told you repeatedly, I have a duty to my half sister, just as you feel you must keep your promise to your sister, Molly. I go now to Valle Verde to do what I must. After that I will join you in London.

How the hell did she imagine she was going to manage that? She had no money that he knew of.

Please do not worry about me. My father taught me how to live off the land and survive in the mountains, as the peasants do. Yours truly, your obedient

—no, she'd crossed out "obedient"; she had that right, at least—

wife, Isabella Ripton.

Luke crushed the note in his fist.

Live off the land as the peasants do? Over his dead body.

He grabbed his portmanteau—thank God it was already packed—and stormed back downstairs. She had three hours on him, but his horse was faster and stronger, and with luck he'd catch her up before the end of the day.

He slammed down a small pile of coins to pay for their accommodations and flung open the front door. And stopped dead.

Half the village seemed to have accompanied the groom that had brought his horse around. They stood waiting, grinning, nudging each other, and watching him for all the world as if he were the circus come to town.

And then he saw why and swore.

Damn her, damn her, damn her! The cunning little vixen!

"Fetch me another saddle," he snapped.

The groom grinned. "Nothing else in the village, *señor*. No other saddle, no other horse, only donkeys." A chorus of happy agreement from the villagers. "Only donkeys."

Luke swore again, long and bitterly.

The chorus of comments that followed all agreed that it was wonderful to hear an Englishman with such excellent command of Spanish, even if his Andalusian accent was unfortunate.

He tossed his portmanteau to the grinning groom to tie on, then realized that mounting this horse was not going to be as simple as it usually was. And that everyone was waiting to see him struggle to do it alone. "All right then," he growled. "Which one of you bastards is going to boost me up?"

There was a press of bodies as his rustic audience scuffled and shoved, each villager wanting to be the one to boost the English milord into the lady's sidesaddle.

Legs tucked neatly in front of him, Luke rode off in pursuit of his wife with as much dignity as he could muster.

Which was none at all.

He was followed by a tribe of hooting urchins, with cheers and laughter coming from the watching villagers.

He'd strangle the wench when he caught up with her.

If he didn't break his neck on this blasted contraption first.

Eight

❧

Cold morning mist stung Isabella's cheeks, clinging to her lashes and settling like a veil of gleaming silver beads on her horse's rough coat. They were on the cold side of the mountain where the sun had not yet touched. Fog hung thick in the valleys, motionless.

They trotted along the narrow stony track that skirted the hills. Bare winter trees etched stark, then softly blurred by the mist. The silence was almost eerie, broken only by the occasional soft scuttle of a startled creature diving for cover, or a sudden beating of wings.

She was alone, on top of the world.

Freedom. She breathed in deep lungfuls. The pure, chill air bit into her. She shivered, drew Lord Ripton's greatcoat closer around her, and urged her horse a little faster. It would be better when she was in the sun again.

She felt a small twinge of guilt at taking his greatcoat as well as his horse, but he'd thrown her cloak away and given her this to wear, so what else was she to do? His coat was warm and soft and smelled faintly of horse, and of him, some clean, masculine fragrance. Disturbingly pleasant.

The morning sun gilded the tips of the hills across the valley. At the convent they'd be finishing up morning prayers and filing silently in to break their fast. Eight years, the same breakfast: convent-baked bread and fresh cold water from the spring. Only the freshness of the bread varied. And in the darkest days—thankfully well behind them now—the quantity.

If the bread was stale, Dolores would again recall her halcyon days at the convent in Aragon where the nuns made delicious cakes and custards with the yolks of eggs given to them by the local winemakers, who'd used the whites for clarifying wine.

Dolores would start describing the cakes, and then Luisa would tell her to be quiet, she was only making them miserable. Then Alejandra would start on about chocolate and how uncivilized it was to start a day without it. And then one of the sisters would tell them to be quiet, that morning was a time for contemplation of the day, not chattering about worldly things.

Isabella smiled, thinking about them all, and how each day was the same, variations on the same daily theme. She'd probably never see any of them again. How strange that thought was. The convent had been her home for eight years; the same people day in, day out, the same routine, the same food, the same conversations until there were days she was ready to scream.

She'd been so desperate to leave, she'd never thought of the convent as home. Only now she'd left there forever did she begin to realize it.

Now she had no home at all.

Valle Verde? No, that wasn't home. It didn't belong to her anymore, and she didn't belong there.

She belonged nowhere.

Legally she belonged with Lord Ripton. Her home was with him.

Whither thou goest . . . Another pang of guilt. Surely the

Bible had something to say about saving sisters. But she could think of nothing. *This is what comes of not paying attention in class*, a nun said in her mind. *A bad pupil and a bad wife.*

She wasn't really his wife. Not yet. Not until the marriage was consummated. And she wasn't running away from him, just seeing to her sister first.

If he hadn't been so unreasonable . . .

What kind of priorities did the man have? The welfare of an admittedly unknown and illegitimate sister-in—all right, *half* sister-in-law—or a dance!

A *dance*! It beggared belief.

She thought about his sister. The dance might be a frivolous reason to Isabella, but it wasn't to Molly. Her first ball, her first dance, her come-out party. It was special.

It wasn't the dance that was important; it was the promise he'd made to his sister, his beloved younger sister.

A man who didn't take promises lightly.

Isabella had made her own promise, even if her sister wasn't beloved.

Love, honor, and obey.

She would honor those promises, too, she made a silent vow. She *would* be a good wife. Just not yet.

She rounded a bend, and a small group of birds gathered around the remains of some creature erupted into the air with a violent flapping of wings. Startled, her horse plunged backward. One of his rear hoofs slipped, and he scrabbled desperately for purchase on the loose, stony ground of the narrow track.

Bella gripped on with her thighs and flung herself onto his neck, forcing him forward and down. For two long, breathless seconds she feared they would plunge down the steep slope into the ravine, but then he found his feet and moved on, emitting a few loud, indignant-sounding snorts.

Bella heaved a sigh of relief and straightened, her heart still pounding. She couldn't have done that sidesaddle. Not so easily.

On this side of the mountain the morning sun shone bright and warm. The sun was well up. About now her husband would be discovering his only option was to ride sidesaddle.

He'd be furious, that went without saying, but would he come after her, or would he do what she'd suggested in her note, and go on to England? And would he try to ride her horse?

She smiled. Lord Ripton wouldn't be caught dead riding with a lady's saddle. No man would.

He'd comb the village and find there was no other horse, let alone a saddle—the groom had assured her there were only donkeys in the village, not even a mule, and she couldn't imagine Lord Ripton on a donkey, not with those long legs of his.

He'd either have to send to the next town for a saddle or ride bareback, which she very much doubted he would. Bareback was all right for short distances and emergencies, but a whole day bareback would be very hard.

Whatever he did, she had an excellent head start, and though she didn't know the roads very well, all she had to do was keep heading east, and the mountains and the sun told her where east was.

Valle Verde was about two days' ride from here, she guessed; three if she'd miscalculated. The land immediately around her might be unfamiliar, but the mountains were in her blood. It was so good to be out from behind the high convent walls, with nothing between her and the horizon.

She wasn't sure where she'd sleep tonight. Perhaps she might find a barn or a derelict building. She was a little nervous about the prospect, but Papa had taught her how to live off the land, she reminded herself, even if it was more than eight years ago.

What would it be like, living in England? The thought of it was more unnerving than the possibility of having to sleep under a bridge. But she'd always dreamed of going to England. Mama was half English, after all, and Bella had vague memories of a tall, black-bearded English grandfather who'd given her a small dolphin statue cunningly carved from whalebone and told her marvelous stories. He'd died not long after Mama had died, Papa told her.

She shivered. Almost every one of her relatives was dead. Apart from horrid Ramón, and a few distant cousins she'd never even met, there was only Reverend Mo— No, Aunt Serafina in the convent, and Perlita.

Was that why she was so desperate to find Perlita? She hardly knew her half sister. She'd hated her for most of her life. And yet now she was risking everything to find her.

Why? Family feeling? Or guilt and atonement? A little of each? Bella didn't know. Mama used to say Bella should always try to listen to her heart and do what she thought was right. Mama, who had listened to her heart and married Papa— and where had that got her?

Right or not, all Bella knew was that before she started her new life as the wife of Lord Ripton, she had to make sure Perlita was all right. She was determined to be happy with Lord Ripton, to build a good life in England and make him a good wife, and she couldn't do that with Perlita on her conscience.

And that, thought Bella bleakly as she rounded the mountainside into full, bright sunlight, was the answer to her question.

R iding sidesaddle took a bit of getting used to, Luke decided, but as long as a man didn't mind looking ridiculous—and the applauding peasants were far behind him now—it wasn't so bad. Surprisingly comfortable. More secure than he'd expected— He caught himself up on that thought. Had he really believed all this time that riding side-saddle was precarious, even a little bit dangerous?

He had, and yet he'd never questioned the necessity for it, even though his mother and Molly rode sidesaddle—and his wife. The people whose safety he should care for most.

The worst thing about it was the difficulty of remounting. He'd stopped once to relieve himself, and getting back up was much more awkward than it should be—he was sure he made a ludicrous sight—and he wasn't hampered by a long-skirted riding habit. If Isabella had been riding sidesaddle she might have been stranded without anyone to boost her up.

The thought mollified his anger with her. Slightly.

If by some miracle he found her—and please God it was soon and she was unharmed—he'd teach her a lesson she'd never forget. Run away from him, would she? Two bedrooms indeed! Never again would she trick him thus. When he caught up with her it would be one bedroom, and one bed.

He'd show her who her husband was, and by God, she'd learn to obey him as she'd vowed to do. Just one day into their marriage and she had him careering all over Spain—sidesaddle!—on a wild-goose chase!

A hare burst from beneath a bush and went bounding across the stony ground, causing Luke's horse to shy. Bringing it under control was trickier than usual. Normally he controlled a mount with his thighs, but on sidesaddle it was all about reins and whip.

What if a hare startled Isabella's horse and she fell? Out here in the mountainous wilderness she could lie injured and helpless for days with nobody any the wiser. And wolves still roamed these mountains.

He shoved the thought from his mind. He'd learned years ago the futility of worrying about things he could not control.

She was making for Valle Verde, he knew, but by which route? He'd chosen the quickest way through the mountains, cutting along the edge of the escarpment, the roughest and most dangerous route. With luck she'd taken the more well-traveled, slower, longer, and less dangerous route. Either way, he hoped to intercept her before nightfall.

He knew these mountains, had crossed and recrossed them during the war. His perfect Spanish and his dark hair and eyes were a boon to the gathering of local intelligence, and a large part of his job had been liaison with the various bands of Spanish guerrillas.

Some of them were little better than bandits, terrorizing the local population as much as they terrorized the French; stealing, murdering, raping—all in the name of patriotism.

And from all accounts some of them hadn't disbanded after the war ended.

The mountains—as always—offered endless opportunities to lawless men.

And lawless women.

He urged the mare faster and hoped to God Isabella had taken the safer route. If she hadn't . . .

Accident, bandits, wolves—the number of possible dangers she faced made his blood run cold. The last time she'd found herself alone in these mountains . . . No, he wasn't going to think about that—though dammit, *she* should have! No blasted common sense!

If—when—he did find her, he'd school her, dammit, and teach her what those blasted nuns had failed to. Obedience to her husband.

A small flutter of white caught his eye, something pale moving at the base of a precipice. Fear sliced through him. Isabella?

He leapt from the horse and scrambled to the edge of the drop for a closer look, his heart thudding in his chest. Wordless prayers came from a place he hadn't realized was still in him.

He hung over the edge, straining to see. The pale thing moved again . . . and a small tan and white goat wandered out from the shadows, nibbling at the grass as she went.

Tension flowed out of him in a gust of relief.

He collected the mare and remounted. The moment had shaken him more than he wanted to believe. How could one small, disobedient scrap of femininity have the power to make him feel so . . .

He cut off the thought before he could complete it. Feel? He barely knew her.

Women simply didn't have that power over him anymore. He'd learned his bitter lesson seven years ago, and he wouldn't make the same mistake again. Since then various women had tried to worm their way into his affections, and he'd never had any trouble resisting them.

He'd always had a strong sense of responsibility; that was all. She was his wife, and it was his duty to protect her.

It was duty, nothing less. And nothing more.

*T*he farther east Luke rode, the more familiar the territory, and the more his spine prickled.

The war was over, he reminded himself. It was years ago. Everything had changed.

And so had he. The trick was to remember that.

As a boy he'd loved this country. His memories of boyhood summers in the vineyard were tinged with golden magic. Running wild in the fields and forests, having his pick of his uncle's fine horses, swimming in the hot summer sun, learning to hunt with falcons and hawks, and his first, tentative forays into the glorious and intoxicating world of girls.

In those days Spanish girls were the embodiment of all his ideas of feminine beauty, with their lush curves, golden skin, dark eyes and hair, and full, red lips. English girls seemed somehow pale and uninteresting by comparison, and everything about England—the land, the food, the life—had seemed anemic to him then.

Of course it was just the difference in the life he lived. England was school and duty and gray skies, and home was a grieving, newly widowed mother. Spain was freedom and sunshine and adventure.

Luke paused, took off his hat, and wiped his brow, scanning the miles of rolling hills below the fault line. No small figure on a black horse with one white foot. No sign of anyone.

High above the valley a hawk floated effortlessly, making slow circles above an olive grove. Wondering what prey the bird was intent on, Luke looked down at the ancient, twisted trees, and without warning he remembered the evening where the silent peace of an olive grove was shattered as twenty men rose up from their hiding places like wraiths in the night, slaughtering the handful of French troopers who'd camped there, as well as a couple of local peasant girls who'd joined them for the night. Traitorous whores, the guerrillas called them.

Luke had been raised to protect women, but it all happened so swiftly there was nothing he could do.

The next day he'd walked through the silent camp, the morning sun gilding the still, dead faces. He'd heard Napoleon was drafting boys as young as twelve into the army, and now he saw the rumor was true. Not one of the soldiers looked a day over sixteen; some were just boys. And the girls—perhaps fifteen or younger.

So young, so dead.

He'd thrown up in that olive grove, a thin stream of vomit steaming on crisp, dewy grass. The guerrillas had laughed at his weak English stomach.

Now, gazing down at the ageless olive grove, Luke recalled the clammy horror of that morning once again.

He itched to be gone . . .

Once he'd felt a part of this country, felt more at home here than he did in his own home. Now he couldn't bear to stay a moment longer than he had to.

He couldn't simply blame it on the war. He'd always known the bloodthirsty, almost savage violence that lay beneath the surface. It was a hot-blooded, quarrelsome land.

The England he knew currently wore a smooth veneer of civilized behavior, but then he'd never seen England conquered, its people ground beneath the heel of a ruthless invader. He prayed he never would.

But England's wars with Scotland, in his grandfather's day, were hardly civilized. His grandfather would never talk about it, but from everything Luke could gather it was cold savagery, a bloody and pitiless process of annihilation. And the aftermath . . . the clearances . . .

Wars did that to people, to countries, stripped off their polite, civilized veneer. Skin-deep . . . Absently Luke rubbed his shoulder. The hard part was replacing the veneer, trying to regain some semblance of civilization once you'd gazed into the black depths of the human soul . . . your own soul. Trying to forget.

It was easier in London. The dreams were not so frequent, and when they got too bad he could always find some distraction, an entertainment of some sort, a race . . .

Here, everything conspired to remind him, to stir up memories he'd tried to obliterate; the jagged lines of the high harsh mountains, the scent of wild thyme and oregano, and of the wind blowing through the juniper pines, the sight of a cluster of whitewashed, red-tiled houses perched on a hillside, the clank of bells on sheep and goats—even the taste of wine, warm and squirted straight into his mouth from a leather flask, and the aroma of a bubbling stew, rich with tomatoes and peppers and garlic.

Each carried the essence of Spain. Each tasted bitter to him now.

But it wasn't the war, wasn't the slaughter in the olive grove or any of a dozen or more ghastly incidents he'd witnessed in his years at war.

Luke was under no illusion: this was a purely personal antipathy, and he knew exactly where it originated. And with whom. He hoped the bitch had long since received her just deserts.

*T*he sun was sinking low in the sky, casting long shadows from the mountains and streaking the high threads of clouds with lilac, pink, and touches of gold. Luke was despairing of finding his wife before dark, when a movement on the road far below him caught his eye: a small figure on foot, leading a black horse with one white foot. Thank God. Thank God.

Luke rode down the mountainside as fast as he dared, crashing through the scrubby undergrowth, ignoring the whippy branches that smacked him in the face and body, stinging and scratching him. He didn't care; he just wanted to get down to Isabella and see for himself that she was all right.

But when he reached the road that wound along beside the

river at the base of the valley, there was no sign of Isabella, no sign of anyone at all.

He scanned the way in both directions, but the road was silent and empty. Not even any raised dust to show if someone had raced away. Where the hell was she? He was certain the small figure leading the horse was his wife.

Then, "Oh, it's you!" a familiar voice exclaimed from behind a clump of beech trees, and Isabella emerged, leading his horse.

Luke swung his leg over the pommel, leapt to the ground, took two long strides, and seized her by the shoulders.

She stiffened, bracing herself for whatever was to come.

Luke, having rehearsed the Speech to an Errant Wife a dozen times, honing it to withering perfection, found himself unable to recall a single word. He stared down at her, gripped by uncharacteristic indecision. He didn't know whether to hug her, shake her, or strangle her.

Or kiss her.

There was a long pause.

She tilted her head and looked up at him. "You mastered the art of the sidesaddle very quickly. The speed with which you came down the side of that mountain was *very* impressive. I don't suppose you even fell once, did you? I mean this morning." The minx sounded almost hopeful.

"No," Luke ground curtly. Not the slightest speck of guilt or even apology in her voice or attitude.

Her eyes were a clear honey brown and thickly fringed with short, dark lashes. They seemed to draw him closer. He carefully loosened his grip on her and stepped away. It was imperative that he establish and maintain control of this situation, and he couldn't think straight when she was looking at him like that and he was touching her.

The moment he released her, she shook herself, like a little cat who'd stepped in water. She gave him a tentative smile. "I thought you were a bandit at first."

He wrenched his gaze from her mouth, stepped back another pace, and found himself staring at her long legs and slender female curves.

Perhaps it was the artlessness of her response, or perhaps it was that she was perfectly safe and well when all day he'd been imagining her facing some disaster.

Or perhaps it was the sight of her standing in the middle of a public road clad in nothing but a pair of buckskin breeches, boots, a white cotton shirt, and a leather jerkin. Easy—and tempting!—bait for any blackguard who happened upon her.

"Where the devil is your skirt?" he snapped.

"In my bag. I thought it would be safer and more convenient to travel as a boy."

"As a *boy*?" She couldn't possibly be that naive.

"Yes, a boy traveling alone is much less remarkable than a lone woman."

"You don't look the least bit like a boy."

She smiled. "Not to you, perhaps, but then you already know I'm not a boy."

"God give me strength!" he muttered. "You look nothing like a boy."

"But I do. I've worn these clothes for years, and nobody has ever suspected I was anything but a boy."

"Traveling in the land of the blind, were you?"

"Of course not."

"Dress-ups in the convent? And the nuns told you that you looked just like a boy?"

"No, it wasn't a game. There were times when—" She broke off. "Reverend Mother sometimes allowed me to go outside the convent dressed this way, among ordinary people. They all took me for a boy."

He didn't believe her. "Why would Reverend Mother allow you to take such a foolish risk? Besides, she was scandalized when she saw you in those breeches yesterday."

"Because she saw your face when you saw the breeches."

Luke had no doubt of it. She probably saw the raw lust he'd felt, too. "You say you've had these breeches for years. When did you last wear them?"

She frowned. "Three or four years ago. But they still fit perfectly well."

He snorted. "A lot tighter, I'll wager."

She bridled. "Are you saying I'm fat?"

He rolled his eyes. "I'm saying you look *nothing like a boy.*"

"I don't agree. The girls in the convent were forever telling me I looked like a boy. I barely have breasts." She gestured, but he refused to even glance down.

He was not going to be drawn into a discussion of her breasts. He knew for a fact she had them; he could see their gentle curves even beneath the leather jerkin. Her stupid school friends were blind.

She continued, "The fact is—"

"The fact is, you *willfully* disobeyed me, you look *nothing* like a boy in that attire, and I could *easily* have been a bandit!" Why the devil was he explaining it to her? He never explained himself in the army. He gave orders and people obeyed.

Men obeyed.

"But I haven't seen a soul," she assured him blithely. "And when I thought you were a bandit, I hid—quite successfully, you have to admit. You wouldn't have known I was here if I hadn't called out to you."

"I saw you from above," Luke grated.

"Yes, and I heard you crashing through the underbrush from miles away. So—"

"If I *had* been a bandit, and your horse had snorted or made a sound? What then, eh?"

"If you'd threatened me, I would have shot you," she said calmly.

"What?"

"Shot you. With this." She reached behind her and pulled out a pistol concealed in the waistband of her breeches. He recognized it from eight years before.

"Is it loaded?"

"Of course! What use is an unloaded pistol?"

He glared at her, still seething, trying to ignore the sight of her in those breeches, the way the soft buckskin clung to her shape. "What if I'd been two bandits—or more? Bandits ride in bands, you know." He'd lost ground and he knew it. One should never argue with a woman. One should simply order. Or demand. He tried to retrieve his authority. "How dare you run off and leave me!"

"I didn't leave you," she said indignantly. "I merely parted from you temporarily. I promised faithfully to join you in England as soon as I'd found my sister. Didn't you get my letter?"

"That's not the point."

"No, the point is my sister is in the hands of a vile bully. Would you leave Molly to the mercy of a man like my cousin Ramón?"

He wouldn't, of course, but he was not going to be distracted. He returned to the issue in question. "You left without my permission."

"But when I asked, you refused, so what else was I to do?"

"*Obey* me! As you vowed to."

"When did I—oh, you mean the marriage vows. I was only a child then—"

"Nevertheless they are legal and binding."

"*You* were all ready to break them."

"I was not."

"You were going to annul them."

"As. We. Agreed. At. The. Time."

She shrugged, clearly unimpressed, and turned away.

Luke clenched his fists, wrestling with a wild impulse to turn her over his knee and spank her backside. Her naked backside. He stepped forward.

"Do you have a knife?" she asked.

Luke blinked. "Knife?"

"A hoof pick, by preference, but failing that, a small knife will do. My horse has a stone in his hoof and I can't get it out."

"*Your* horse?" he said with withering sarcasm.

"Our horse, if you prefer."

Her matter-of-fact tone infuriated him. She'd shown absolutely no remorse for her actions. He prowled toward her. He'd show her once and for all—

"Don't forget the knife," she reminded him and bent to lift the hind hoof of the lame horse. The supple buckskin stretched tight over her bottom like a second skin.

Luke stopped dead. His mouth dried.

There was a reason why women were not supposed to wear breeches, and he was staring straight at it. It wasn't possible for a man to think of anything else when he was confronted with . . . with that. It was almost worse than if she were naked.

Almost. He repressed a moan.

Averting his eyes from the delectably infuriating sight, he drew a penknife from his pocket and bent to the task of removing the stone from the horse's hoof.

He cleaned the hoof and removed the stone, then swapped the two saddles over. It was getting chilly by then, so he pulled his greatcoat out of her bag and tossed it to her with a curt, "Put it on."

A look crossed her face as if she might argue, but then she capitulated and shrugged herself into it.

It covered her almost to her ankles, and as she buttoned it, he felt a little of his tension ease. He strapped his bag and hers to the lame horse, then remounted the mare.

He held out his hand to Isabella. "Up behind me."

She gazed up at him, a mutinous expression on her face. "I will not give up the search for my sister. I'll come with you now because I have no choice, but I tell you to your face, I'll run away from you again if I have to."

He gave her a hard look. "You are welcome to try."

Without a word she took his arm, placed her boot on his stirrup, and swung up behind him. He felt her warmth at his back, then she slid her arms around his waist. He stiffened but didn't say a word.

He'd bandy words with her no longer. Tonight, when they were in the privacy of the bedchamber, he'd administer her first lesson in being a satisfactory wife.

Actions spoke louder than words.

* * *

*I*t was almost dark and the moon was rising, like a pale slice of lemon. They were riding east. Did he realize it? Bella wondered. She'd expected him to turn around and go back the way they'd come.

East was the way to Valle Verde.

She said nothing. If he'd mistaken the direction, she didn't want to let him know.

They moved at a steady walk, the lame horse slowing them down. She rode with her arms around his waist, her cheek resting against his back. He was warm and strong, and despite his anger with her, she felt very safe.

He'd been furious, but he hadn't beaten her. She openly disobeyed him, left him, and yet he'd barely touched her, only gripped her shoulders quite hard, glared at her, and then let go.

According to the teachings of the Church, husbands had the right to beat disobedient wives, and when he'd grabbed her like that, she was sure he was going to shake her till her teeth rattled. At the very least. But he hadn't.

A small bubble of hope blossomed inside her. He hadn't wanted to be married to her; had tried to annul the marriage. He could have left her to her fate, and yet he'd come all this way after her.

Despite the impression she'd tried to give him, she was under no illusion of the dangers involved in her journey back to Valle Verde. Better he thought her young and naive than that she assessed the risks and found them acceptable.

Travel in Spain was as dangerous now as it had been in the war—maybe more so, because it wasn't as easy to tell whose side anyone was on. She'd scanned the road ahead, glanced frequently back the way she came, and checked the hills above her. She'd skirted around towns and villages rather than ride through them, and hidden from every traveler before she could be seen, taking constant reassurance from the pistol at her waistband, even as she prayed she wouldn't have to use it.

A husband who truly wished to be rid of an unwanted wife would have washed his hands of her and let her risk herself.

Luke Ripton had ridden after her, made a long, rough, and difficult journey through unknown territory, sidesaddle, risking ridicule, as well as danger. It might only be a strong dislike of being disobeyed, but still, Bella couldn't help but see it as a positive sign.

She hugged him tighter, breathing in the smell of him. She remembered it from when she was a young girl, when they'd first met. He'd ridden to her rescue then, and he was still doing it now.

The moon was higher now. Its cold light silvered the rooftops and turret of a building that looked familiar. As they rode closer, she recognized it.

"El Castillo de Rasal!" she exclaimed.

"Eh?"

"That castle—it's the Castillo de Rasal, the home of the Marqués de Rasal," she said excitedly. "I did not realize we were so close. The *marqués* is—was an old friend of my father's. I've known him since I was a little girl. We can stay the night there." She felt a surge of pleasure at the prospect of seeing someone from her past after so long. The *marqués* had always been very kind to Bella.

"He might not be ali—home."

He'd been going to say the *marqués* might not be alive, she thought. "It doesn't matter. His servants will remember me and offer us hospitality, I know." Her stomach rumbled. "He keeps a very fine cook, too—the *castillo* is renowned for it."

He didn't respond.

Bella burbled happily on. "You can't see them in the dark, but the estate has very fine vineyards—the wines of Castillo de Rasal are drunk all over Spain. I came here several times with my father when I was young. The *castillo* is a medieval castle, you understand, very ancient and inconvenient, though parts of it are quite beautiful. You will enjoy seeing it in the daylight." She rubbed her cheek against his coat. "You know, I thought I would have to sleep tonight on the ground, or under a bridge, and instead we will sleep in a castle."

She felt him stiffen. "Under a bridge?"

"I had no money for an inn."

He snorted but said nothing more. They came to a tall stone gateway.

"That's the driveway," Bella said. "Turn off here."

He took no notice. They passed the gateway.

She hit him lightly on the shoulder. "Stop! You missed it! The turnoff is back there."

"We're not staying there."

"But why not? I told you, the *marqués* is an old family friend. He'd be delighted to see me again, I know it."

"No."

Bella could hardly believe her ears. "But why not? It's a wonderful place to stay."

No answer.

"The *marqués* will be very disappointed to have missed me—" she began.

"Did you write to him to expect you?"

"No, but—"

"Then he'll have no reason for disappointment."

Really, there was no cause for such churlishness. He should be grateful to be able to visit a *marqués* and stay in an ancient *castillo*. "*I* will be very disappointed," she told him.

"You'll survive it. We'll stay in the inn at Ayerbe. It's only a couple of miles farther."

"But why stay in a village inn when we could stay in a castle?"

He ignored her.

There was no point in arguing. The man was as stubborn as a rock. Bella thumped him crossly instead. He made no sign he'd even noticed.

*F*eeling the thump between his shoulder blades, Luke smiled to himself. She'd learn.

He had no doubt they'd be welcomed with open arms at

Castillo de Rasal, and would be wined and dined in a manner fit for a king, but he was damned if he was going to spend his first night alone with his wife in the home of some doting old man who'd dandled her on his knee as a child.

Luke was going to settle once and for all who wore the breeches in this family, and he wanted no witnesses to the encounter.

A soldier chose his own ground for a confrontation.

Nine

❧

"A bedchamber for me and my wife and a private sitting room."

Bella swallowed. Luke had barely spoken a word to her for the last half hour. He'd given curt orders to the stableboy at the inn concerning the care of the horses, and now he spoke to the landlord, a tall, strapping fellow with a huge mustache.

"No private sitting rooms, *señor*. You can eat here." The landlord gestured to the public dining area. "Or my wife can bring you your supper on a tray." At his words, the curtain covering the doorway behind him twitched and a round-faced woman with brilliant, almost scarlet hair piled high looked out and scowled.

"No, we'll eat here," Luke said without even consulting Bella. He leaned forward and murmured something to the landlord, a question she didn't catch. In the mood he was in, it would do no good to ask, she was sure.

The man gave him a startled look, glanced at Bella curiously, then nodded. "*Sí, señor*, I shall arrange it." He sounded bemused. What had Luke asked of him?

"Good. Now, my wife is waiting for her dinner."

The landlord bowed and snapped his fingers, and minions went scurrying to clear a table for them—the best table near the fire.

Luke seemed to have that effect on people, Bella thought. An unconscious air of command, coupled with his height and good looks.

The contrast between this and their arrival at the inn last night couldn't be clearer. Then, Luke had shown deference and concern for her after their long trip. Now, apart from the hand that lightly gripped her elbow, he acted as if he were unaware of her presence.

Her own fault, she acknowledged. Angering her husband was one of the risks she'd considered when she chose to defy him. Whatever happened between them this night, she'd face it with dignity. She hoped.

The relief that he hadn't beaten her in the road was giving way to thoughts that some men brooded on their wrongs and took their time about revenge. The dish best eaten cold . . .

She wondered again what he'd asked of the landlord.

He led her to the table, seemingly unaware of the sea of faces watching them with open curiosity. She'd removed her hat, and her coronet of plaited hair made it obvious to all that under the greatcoat, she was a woman. Bella felt the hard male glances slide over her, assessing her femininity. She held her head up and pretended not to notice.

Luke pulled out a chair and seated her with her back to the room, then sat opposite. He called for wine and ordered supper. It was warm in the dining room, and Bella began to unbutton the coat.

"Leave it," Luke told her.

"But—"

"Do you really think this is the place to test your theory that you look like a boy in those breeches?"

She flushed and subsided.

Wine arrived, and Luke poured her a glass. She took it, but before she could drink, he clinked his glass against hers and said, "To our marriage." His gaze bored into her.

What did that mean? she wondered. To the success of their marriage? Or was it an ironic toast, a sort of "to-the-millstone-around-my-neck"?

His face was as expressive as a stone statue. She didn't understand him in the least. He looked like a man set to carry out some ruthless course of action, and the leashed tension in his body unnerved her.

Deciding to take his toast at face value, she sipped the wine, then seeing his expression, she drained the glass and said, "I want a separate bedchamber."

"Bad luck."

"You promised you'd give me time."

He poured some more wine into her glass. "You promised to obey, and yet I spent most of today—sidesaddle!—combing the mountains searching for your body."

She bit her lip. "I'm sorry to have worried you. Nevertheless—"

"We're married. From now on it's one bedchamber, one bed." His tone was implacable.

The first dishes arrived: tender slices of local ham, small spicy sausages still sizzling in their own juice, grilled mushrooms fragrant with thyme and other herbs, gleaming black olives, and fresh, crusty bread.

Hunger, salted by years of convent austerity, swamped her. The food smelled delicious, and she only just remembered to murmur a quick grace before diving in.

"What did you ask the landlord to do?" she said as she served them both some mushrooms.

"Are the sausages to your liking?" he asked. "They're a little spicy."

"I love spicy food," she told him. "In the convent our food was mostly very simple and very bland. The landlord?"

He speared a sausage. "You'll see."

He was a stubborn man, but to her surprise, the prospect of sharing his bed wasn't at all . . . objectionable. Far from it.

Sometime during that last ride in the moonlight, riding pressed against his broad, strong body, her arms wrapped around his waist, inhaling the scent of him and warmed by his heat and strength, her body had decided: this was her husband.

Their marriage might have been a mistake, but it was a mistake she, at least, could live with. If he didn't love her, so be it. Mama had made herself miserable pining after Papa, yearning for him to love her, and he never had.

It was a waste, Bella decided; a waste of a life. She wouldn't make the same mistake.

She watched Luke tear a piece of bread apart with long, elegant fingers, then eat it, his face partly shadowed in the dim light, his eyes dark mysteries, the blade of his cheekbones gilded by lamplight . . . A strong jaw, dark with rough stubble.

He was one beautiful man. And he was hers.

Or he would be, tonight. Excitement thrummed.

The rest of the meal arrived: roast lamb with potatoes, chicken stew in a rich sauce of red peppers and tomatoes, and a salad of boiled green beans tossed with a lemony dressing. It was a feast fit for a king. Or a queen.

Bella ate till she was full to bursting, tasting something from each dish, then going back for more. Everything tasted delicious; the lamb was melt-in-your-mouth tender, and the potatoes were baked crispy-skinned and golden. The chicken stew was rich and full of the flavors of her childhood.

They ate without speaking, but it was not an awkward silence; each of them was intent on the meal. From time to time Luke would refill her glass or pass her some bread.

Occasionally, in the passing or pouring, their fingers brushed, and each time, Bella's pulse leapt.

She wasn't sure what this night would bring, but she longed to become a wife, instead of a half wife. And to finally know. She was woefully ignorant of the relations between a man and his wife. It was ridiculous.

Luke drank the last of the wine, and she watched his strong, tanned throat move as he swallowed. She knew how horses and dogs and chickens procreated, but as for what she was expected to do on her wedding night . . .

It was supposed to hurt, but only if you were a virgin, and since she wasn't . . .

Since she wasn't a virgin she hoped she would enjoy it. Some women did, she'd heard the girls whisper. Most didn't. Only bad girls liked doing it.

Bella thought of all the many times she'd been in trouble. Would she turn out to be a bad girl in this, too? She certainly hoped so.

She mopped up the last of the chicken and pepper sauce with a crust of bread, wiped her mouth, and sat back in her chair with a sigh of satisfaction. "That was heavenly. I don't think I've had such a delicious meal in, oh . . . I can't remember."

"Yes, the food here has always been very good."

Always? "You've been here before?"

"Once or twice," he said indifferently. "Years ago in the war."

"Then you knew we were traveling east."

He gave her a dry look. "The moon made that fairly obvious."

So he had realized they were traveling toward Valle Verde, not away from it. Did that mean he'd decided to let her go to Valle Verde after all? "So tomorrow, will we—"

"*Señorita?*" A touch on her shoulder.

Bella looked up. A rather dashing-looking gentleman of about thirty stood by her chair. "*Sí?*"

He bowed. "You are the daughter of the Conde de Castillejo, are you not?"

"I am," Bella breathed. Without thinking, she held out her hand.

"Don Francisco Espinoza de Cadaval at your service. I had the honor of fighting under your father's command. I was there when he died. It is a great pleasure to meet you, *señorita.*" He raised her hand and kissed it so ardently, she could feel the tickle of his thin, elegant mustache.

Chair legs scraped abruptly on the floor as Luke stood. "You're mistaken," Luke said in a harsh voice. Bella and Don Francisco looked at him in surprise.

"She's not *señorita* anything. She's my wife, Lady Ripton, and we are about to retire for the night. Come, my dear." He held out an imperious hand to Isabella.

"Oh, but I would like to—"

"Now, Isabella." His dark gaze bored into her, and she reflected that she'd probably defied him enough for one day already. And that a public dining room was not the place for a dispute with her husband.

Don Francisco took one glance at Luke's face, took a step backward, and bowed gracefully to them both. "Good evening, then, Lady Ripton. Perhaps in the morning . . ."

Bella gave him a warm smile to make up for her husband's rudeness. "Yes, that would be—"

"I doubt we'll have the time. We'll be departing very early." Luke took Bella's hand, pushed past Don Francisco, and led her from the room.

"Really, there's no need to be so boorish."

"There's every need. You have no idea who that man is."

"I do, too. He was one of my father's men."

"I heard who he *said* he was. He could say anything and you'd believe him."

"He was with Papa when he died," she said. "I would have liked to talk to him, to hear more—"

He stopped abruptly and swung her to face him. "The two men who attacked you when you were a child were your father's men and had been with him when he died, too, and look how well that turned out."

She bit her lip and looked away.

His voice softened. "I'm sorry, I didn't want to remind you of it, but . . . you're too trusting for your own good. Terrible things happened in this country while you were in the convent."

"Before then, too," she said in a low voice, thinking of Mama.

"I know." His hand closed over hers, warm and comforting. "But although Napoleon is defeated and there is a Spanish king on the throne again, things are still unsettled, and that's what you don't understand. Spain has broken into a thousand factions, and without reliable knowledge, you cannot know who that fellow is and what he might want from you."

There was some sense in what he said, but Bella didn't like the idea of treating everyone as an enemy until proven otherwise. "How do you know what Spain is like now? You've been in England for years."

"Trust me, I know. It was my job to know," he told her. "And when situations change, so do men's alliances. Even if that fellow was your father's right-hand man, that's no guarantee of where his loyalties lie now. Men do what they can to survive."

"So do women," she reminded him.

There was a short pause, then he said, "I don't propose to discuss it any further. I know a great deal more than you do about the situation in this country, and the dangers of trusting people you don't know, so while we are here, you'll do as I tell you."

"I'm not a child."

There was a sudden silence. His gaze intensified. Bella glanced away, feeling suddenly too warm. The clatter of pots and pans came from the kitchen, the clink of glasses and the sound of a woman reprimanding someone. From the public area the deep murmur of masculine voices drifted. Luke's gaze slipped over her, and for a moment she fancied she could hear her own heart beating.

"No, you're not," her husband said, his voice deep and low. "And it's time we both acknowledged that. Now, it's late. Time we went to bed."

Time we went to bed. The phrase wiped every other thought from her head.

They slowly mounted the stairs. Her hand was cold; his was warm. The wine hadn't relaxed her at all. In fact, she was tenser than ever.

* * *

*T*he bedchamber was small and contained only one large bed, a chair, a large looking glass on a swivel stand, and a tiled wash table bearing a large, brightly painted jug of water and a mismatched bowl. There was no wardrobe, only a row of hooks to hang clothing on. The only other item in the room was a small enamel stove. Apart from a coiled and plaited rag rug in front of the fire, the floor was bare, though clean and well waxed.

Bella glanced around, wondering what arrangements the landlord had made at Luke's behest. Lit the fire? Warm water in the jug, perhaps? Nothing as sinister as she'd first imagined.

Foolish what your imagination will produce when you're tired and hungry and cross.

Luke opened the stove and fed the fire with chopped logs from the box beside it. He lit half a dozen candles and the shadows receded.

A knock on the door sounded, and the landlord entered with a bottle and a couple of glasses on a tray. "My wife thought the lady might enjoy these," he said, indicating a dish of caramel-ized almonds, and though Bella was already full from dinner, she could not resist sneaking one before the man had even put the tray down.

So it was only brandy Luke had ordered when they ar-rived. She might have known.

"Please thank your wife," she told the man. "I'm very fond of candied almonds." She took another.

Luke slipped the man a coin and followed him to the door, locking it after him. He turned, and the look in his eyes sent a shiver straight to the pit of Bella's stomach. "Come here."

She swallowed the last of the nuts, tasting nothing, and approached him.

"Are you warm?"

She nodded, suddenly breathless. Tonight she would go from being a bride to a wife . . .

He began to unbutton the greatcoat she still wore. One button . . . two . . . three . . . His eyes burned into her. He slipped the coat off her shoulders and tossed it over the chair.

He put his hands on her shoulders, and she swayed forward, thinking he was going to kiss her, but instead he turned her around. She found herself facing the long looking glass.

"What—?"

"I had the glass brought in especially for this. Look."

Puzzled, she looked. All she could see was her own reflection and Luke's standing behind her. He stared into the looking glass over her shoulder. What was she supposed to notice?

It was eight years since she'd seen herself in a big glass like this, and she'd changed somewhat. Her skin had improved, and her hair was darker and quite glossy in the candlelight, but she'd still never be a beauty. Or even pretty. She looked quite a lot like Mama, actually. Oh well. Nothing new there.

She glanced at his reflection, all stark angles and shadows in the candlelight. He wasn't looking at her face or his, but staring into the looking glass with an odd, brooding expression. Like a starving man gazing through a rich man's window. A feast he could not have.

Miles away, she thought. Another time, another place. Another woman.

His gaze clashed with hers in the looking glass and she felt suddenly scorched.

"Well?" he demanded curtly.

"Well, what?" She tried to turn, but his hands forced her to remain facing the looking glass.

"Is that what you think looks like a boy?"

"Oh." In the looking glass her cheeks pinkened in the candlelight. She gave her reflection a critical look. She had grown in the past few years, she had to admit. The fit of the clothes was not as loose as it used to be, but compared with her friends at the convent, she was still quite skinny and flatchested. She didn't look exactly like a boy, but neither did she look very womanly. "Most people don't examine you up close like this," she began.

He made a small exasperated sound.

"And when my hat covers my hair—"

He gave her a little shake. "You would still look nothing like a boy!" He dropped his hands to her waist. "Do boys have waists like this?"

She swallowed and gazed into the looking glass at the big hands encircling her waist.

"And what about here?" His hands dropped to the slight curve of her hips. "Have you ever seen a boy with hips like these?"

Bella couldn't reply. She could only stare, mesmerized at the hands moving slowly in the candlelight, feeling the heat of his palms as they slid over her hips, the heat of his body at her back.

His hands caressed her lightly from the swell of her hips to her waist and back. "Boys have no waist, no hips; they're all straight up and down, not . . . curved," he murmured. "Boys are skin and bones, not . . . flesh."

Her breath caught in her throat as his hands traveled slowly up her body, softly shaping the curve of her hips, the dip of her waist, and higher. His touch was featherlight, and she was fully dressed in layers of clothing, yet she was achingly aware of every infinitesimal movement.

He smoothed his palms over the leather jerkin she wore. "Boys' chests are flat . . . hard . . . bony." His breath was warm on her ear. "Even in this ugly leather jerkin, you don't look the least bit flat or bony." His hands brushed lightly over the garment, barely touching her, but the tips of her breasts tingled as if she were naked.

She moistened her lips. "But the girls in the convent—"

"Were ignorant young ninnies. And they weren't looking at you with the eyes of a man. A man is attuned to the shape of a woman, even when it's subtle and hidden beneath layers. A man would take one look at you and know that under this . . ." He swiftly undid the bone buttons down the front of the jerkin. "He would find this."

He drew the two halves of the jerkin front apart to reveal the white shirt she wore beneath. Her breath came in jagged gasps. She wore a chemise under the shirt, but even so, you could see the hard points of her nipples and the faint shadow of aureole around them.

He cupped her breasts in both hands, and she gasped as he passed his thumbs lightly over her aching nipples, just once, but it was as if he'd touched a heated knife to her. She bucked under the impact and lurched back against his body.

He dropped his hands to steady her. She tried to turn in his arms, to kiss him, to do . . . she wasn't sure what.

"I'm not finished yet." He was breathing hard, but his jaw was set. "I want to make sure you understand fully." He turned her sideways and ran one hand over her bottom. "See this? There isn't a male alive with such a lush, feminine backside." He cupped one of her buttocks, and Bella's knees almost buckled. "Mouthwatering," he muttered, as if to himself.

He turned her again to face the looking glass. His hands gripped her hips; his fingers pointed toward her center. She was resistless as a doll, her mind and body trembling from the effect of his words, his touch.

She felt smoking hot, ready to burst into flame like paper held too close to the fire, not touching, but heated beyond bearing.

"As for here . . ." He placed his palm on her stomach and slid it slowly down. "Here you are wholly and entirely female." His big, warm palm covered her crotch and cupped her firmly.

Bella arched involuntarily, leaning back against him. Her legs trembled, almost too weak to stand, but he didn't let go of her and didn't move.

One powerful arm was wrapped around her, holding her upright in front of the looking glass. The other clasped her firmly and brazenly between her legs.

"Breeches do not a boy make." His mouth was so close to her ear she could feel every breath. His voice was deep and shivered through her to her very bones. "In fact, these breeches outline your femininity with loving faithfulness." He released her crotch, and she felt suddenly cold, but then one long, masculine finger moved, tracing a slow vee shape at the apex of her thighs, down one side, up the other. And then slowly along the line that bisected it.

She trembled helplessly in its wake.

He stood almost side by side with her now, his left arm supporting her, as he slowly stroked his finger back and forth between legs that would barely support her. He was hardly touching her, but it was as though his fingers left trails of fire.

Her gaze drifted away from the sight of his hands and his fingers slowly working . . . magic . . . stealing all her control . . . teasing her apart at the seams.

She could see the difference so clearly now: the vee shape in her breeches, the hard bulge of his. She stared at that bulge, trying to make out the exact shape beneath the cloth.

With an effort she dragged her gaze away and looked at him, wanting to beg for something . . . anything . . . she didn't know what.

And was riveted by the expression in his eyes.

She wasn't the only one mesmerized . . . burning.

He was wholly unaware of her regard; his attention was entirely on her body. His eyes devoured her even as his hands roamed over her, unraveling her . . .

Unraveling him . . .

And then his hands stilled, and his gaze snapped up, meeting hers. There was a brief, frozen pause, then a shutter of smoked glass crashed down behind his eyes and he was suddenly hard and distant and . . . cool.

He put his hands on her shoulders and gave her a little push away. "And that—" His voice grated harshly, and he stepped back and cleared his throat. "Let that be a lesson. Breeches or not, you look nothing like a boy."

She blinked at his sudden coldness. Her eyes dropped to his breeches, to the hard, masculine bulge.

He saw her looking. He clenched his jaw and turned sharply away from her. "Get changed for bed," he said as he headed for the door. "I'll be back in ten minutes." After he'd left she heard the key turn in the lock.

No escape possible.

She gave a halfhearted, shaky laugh. Escape was the last thing on her mind.

*B*ella wasn't sure how long had passed when she suddenly realized she was still standing in front of the mirror, gazing into it with her arms wrapped around herself and a foolish smile on her face.

He'd said he'd be back in ten minutes.

She flew into action, ripping off her boots, stockings, and breeches. She opened her bag and pulled out her nightdress. The polished wooden floor was freezing and chilled her bare toes, so she undressed standing on the small rug in front of the stove. In seconds she'd stripped off the rest of her clothes and pulled the nightdress over her head.

For the first time in her life, she wished she'd been good at embroidery. All the other girls had made beautifully embroidered nightclothes. Hers was plain cotton.

Still, if he'd desired her in breeches and a leather jerkin, he might not care about a plain cotton nightdress. She felt suddenly cold and wanted to dive into the bed, but she couldn't resist a quick glance in the looking glass.

Her hair! Swiftly she pulled out the pins that held her braids in place, and unraveled the plaits and finger-combed her hair. She should brush it, but she was sure ten minutes had elapsed, and she didn't want to be caught unready for him.

Another glance in the looking glass and she wished she hadn't looked. Before, he'd shown her someone who was mysteriously attractive. Now there was plain old Bella Ripton again, in a white cotton nightie that made her look sallow and swamped any feminine curves she might have had. And her hair was a Medusa of dark snakes instead of a woman's glory.

"Oh, Mama," she sighed. "Why couldn't we have been born pretty?"

Her feet were freezing, so she risked another moment or two on the rug next to the fire. She stood toasting herself, pulling the nightdress up to warm her bare bottom. When she heard footsteps in the corridor outside, she hit the bed in a flying leap.

She dived under the covers and waited.

The footsteps faded away. It wasn't Luke. But he wouldn't be long.

Bella lay between the cold sheets, shivering a little and hugging herself to get warm, though the cold was only external. Inside she was still hot and excited and . . . melty.

For so long, everyone—even her husband—had treated her as a child. Finally she was about to become a woman.

Who knew he could make her feel like that, just by talking . . . and touching . . . and looking?

She waited. Her insides were a mass of warm butterflies.

*L*uke had let himself out of the back door of the inn and gone for a quiet walk to cool down. So much for his intended lesson.

How had it spun so quickly out of control?

When he'd asked the landlord to provide a large mirror, Luke had planned to give his wife a short, brusque lesson; whatever she looked like in the past in those breeches, she did not look like a boy in them any longer. He'd envisaged it taking a moment or two. He would point out the obvious, and she would understand.

But she'd been inclined to argue the point, and Luke felt compelled to show her how false her assumption was.

And then . . .

He shook his head. How could he have let things spiral away from him like that?

Lord knew—well, it didn't require omnipotence—any idiot would know where it would have ended up had Luke not happened to glance at her face and caught the gleam of triumph, of female power, in her eye as she saw how in thrall to her he was. His *body* was.

Luke would be in thrall to no woman, not even his wife.

The village street petered out into a simple dirt track leading up into the wilderness. He stopped, gazing up at the looming dark of the hills, at the star-sprinkled velvet of the night, and breathed sharp, cold air deep into his lungs.

A guitar played somewhere close by. The scent of peppers and roasting meat floated on the breeze.

It was this place, this blasted country; that was all. Things he'd kept locked away, under control, were being stirred up. Disturbing his equilibrium—yes, that was it.

The last few days, memories and sensations had risen up to assault him at every turn. Isabella herself had unwittingly started the process. The circumstances of their meeting, his weakness for a woman in distress, his damned compulsion to play the hero.

But it wasn't her fault she'd unleashed his demons.

She wasn't the demon who haunted him.

She was just his innocent bride who'd been attacked as a child and spent the next eight years in a convent. And he'd treated her like a . . .

He turned on his heel and marched back the way he came. No harm done. He hadn't bared an inch of her skin, and it would do her no harm—in fact probably it would do her a lot of good to feel the pleasures of arousal.

Not that the pleasures of arousal were doing him a lot of good. He grimaced and adjusted the fit of his breeches. Not all that pleasant. But it was different for a woman.

As long as he didn't pounce on her—and he wouldn't—his self-respect would remain intact.

He wouldn't touch her again like that until they were in England. He'd promised her time to get used to him, and she would see she'd married a man of his word. She might not be a virgin but she needed time to get used to him, to accustom herself to the idea of having a man in her bed, in her body.

In England, that green and pleasant land, his emotions were not raw and jagged and edging out of control but safely stored away in the dark. Yes, he'd seduce her in England, gently, carefully, as a gentleman should.

Luke would not allow the demons of his past to contaminate his marriage. Or his bride. He returned to the inn, calm, cool, and firmly in control of his body and his marriage.

He'd been gone longer than ten minutes. He knocked quietly before unlocking the door, so as not to alarm her. As he entered, she sat up, lustrous dark tresses spilling over pale shoulders, a siren by candlelight. Damn.

"I thought you'd be asleep by now," he said.

"No." Her eyes were huge.

"I won't be long." He turned his back on her and quickly stripped to his undershirt and drawers. He normally slept nude. No chance of that tonight. Or any other night until they reached England, he reminded himself.

He blew out the candles and climbed into bed, careful not to touch her in any way. "Good night, Isabella."

"You're going to sleep?"

"Of course." His body ached for release.

"But I thought . . ."

He clenched his jaw. He knew what she thought. Damn him for a fool. "I promised you time," he reminded her. "I keep my promises."

Silence followed, and just as he was starting to hope she'd fallen asleep, she said, "I'm glad you came after me, today."

What did one say to that? "Good," he said crisply. And then, before she could turn it into a conversation, he said again, "Good night."

The truth was, it was too damned intimate, lying there side by side in the dark, talking. He never shared beds with women. Not to sleep. And certainly not to talk. It was unexpectedly . . . companionable.

"In what direction will we ride tomorrow?"

He thought about not answering, pretending to be asleep, but in the end said, "We're only a day and a half away from Valle Verde, so we might as well go on."

She gasped. "But I thought—"

"You were right," he admitted. "If Molly was in the hands of some villain, nothing would stop me from rescuing her. But if your sister isn't at Valle Verde, I warn you now, we're turning around and going straight to England. I won't go on a wild-goose—"

"Oh, thank you, thank you!" She hugged his back.

He stiffened. "Don't do that!"

"But I was just thanking—"

"Unless you want this to be your wedding night—" He ground out the words. "Stay on your own side of the bed."

There was a long silence. Finally, Luke thought, she'd settled for the night.

And then her words came out of the darkness, soft and low, but very, very clear. "I wouldn't mind."

Ten

❧

The words hung in the stillness of the night. She wouldn't
mind?

Luke's body reacted before he could think of a thing to
say. Well, of course it did; it had been primed all evening.

For a moment or two he battled with himself. Why not?
They were married, after all. Why deny himself if she didn't
mind? His body was on fire for her. All he had to do was turn
over. There she was, warm, beautiful, and willing, there for
the taking.

He repressed a groan. Could he get any harder?

But begin as you mean to go on. His earlier resolutions
came back to him.

Her warm, soft body lay a breath away. He could smell the
enticing, intoxicating scent of her, in the room, in the bed.

She wouldn't mind.

He closed his eyes, trying to block out her gentle siren
call.

He would not fall in thrall to a woman again.

"No." He ground out the word. "Go to sleep."

"Oh," she said in a small voice. And then, after a moment, "Good night then." Did she sound . . . disappointed? The bed-clothes shifted as she turned on her side, away from him.

He didn't move. He couldn't move. "Good night." Aware of how curt he sounded, compunction pricked him, even as the part of his brain that strove for control applauded.

From the outside, marriage had seemed so simple.

He closed his eyes again and tried to sleep. Beside him Isabella shifted and wriggled. And shifted again.

They were so far apart in the bed they weren't even touching, but Luke was achingly aware of every movement.

She made little noises in her throat and thrashed her feet around. What the hell . . . ?

After a minute or two, he'd had enough. "Go to sleep," he ordered.

"I'm trying."

"It might help if you stopped wriggling around."

"I can't help it," she said. "I think . . . Ouch! Something's biting me. Biting my legs."

Bedbugs? But nothing had bitten him. It was a ploy, he thought. Some feminine ploy to get his attention, to punish him, to torture him further. Though it was his own fault he was feeling tortured, he had to admit.

He got out of bed and turned up the lantern. "Let me see." He flipped back the bedclothes and bent over her legs. Sure enough, he could see half a dozen little red marks. And a black spot that jumped.

"Fleas!" he exclaimed. "Dammit, there are fleas in this bed!"

"I told you something was biting me." Isabella jumped out of the bed and peered over Luke's shoulder at the sheets. "What'll we do?"

"Get the blasted landlord to change the blasted bed!" Luke strode to the door, flung it open, and shouted for the landlord. Isabella grabbed his greatcoat, shrugged it on, and waited on the mat beside the stove.

In a moment the landlord came hurrying up dressed in

trousers pulled hastily on over a striped nightshirt. He was followed by the improbable redhead, dressed in a bright pink flannel nightgown and shawl. Short, plump, and with her crimson hair pinned up haphazardly, she folded her arms and regarded Luke with disapproval. "*Señor?*"

He glared at her husband. "There are fleas in this bed, dammit!"

The woman sniffed. "Never! Not in my inn!"

"*Sí, señor*, this is a very clean inn—" the landlord assured him.

"The cleanest inn in all of Aragon!" his wife said, her black eyes snapping with anger.

"No fleas, no bedbugs," the landlord finished.

"Rubbish!" Luke was outraged. "They've bitten my wife and I saw one for myself. Look!" He grabbed the landlord by the arm, dragged him across to the bed, and pointed. "Fleas!"

Then he turned to the wife. "And you, look at my wife's feet!"

The woman sniffed again and marched crossly over to where Isabella stood, disbelief radiating in every inch of her small person. She bent down, made an exclamation, and bent lower.

"Fleas, Carlos!" she said in an outraged voice. "Fleas, in *my* inn!" She jumped, pressed a finger to her own ankle, then squished the trapped flea between her thumbnails. She peered at Isabella's bare feet, and then at her own slippered ones, and then at the rag rug. "They're in this rug!" she exclaimed suddenly. "Carlos, come and see."

"Carlos, open the window," Luke snapped.

The landlord, caught between his wife and Luke, chose to obey Luke.

In an instant Luke rolled the flea-ridden rag rug up and hurled it out the window into the street below.

Isabella clapped and danced restlessly on her toes, hopping from foot to foot.

The fierce little lady turned on her husband. "I *told* you not to let that man bring his dogs inside the other night, but oh no, you were impressed by a title, bowing and scraping and accepting his bribes—and look where it's got you! Fleas in *my inn*! Look at the lady's poor feet!"

The man bent to look and she biffed him over the head. "Modesty!" she hissed. "You don't stare at a lady's bare feet! Don't you know anything? Bitten to pieces she is, poor lady, and what must she think of this place?"

Luke suddenly realized why his wife was moving about so oddly. She was still being bitten, dammit. Luke picked her up and held her against his chest.

"What are you doing?"

"You were hopping around. I assumed you were still being attacked."

She smiled. "My feet were cold, that's all."

"Oh." But he made no move to put her down. The floor was still cold, after all. And she couldn't wait in a flea-ridden bed.

"Aren't I too heavy?"

He snorted. She was a featherweight.

"I want another room," he informed the landlord. "With clean sheets and fresh bedding. And no rugs. Now!"

The man's wife spoke for him. "A thousand apologies, *señor*, but this is a small inn and there is no other private bedchamber, only the public room, which is not suitable for a gentleman and lady such as yourselves. But I will put this right, be assured."

She went to the doorway, put two fingers in her mouth, and emitted an earsplitting whistle. In seconds servants came running.

"Get rid of this mattress and bedding," she ordered. "To the stables with it. You, fetch the gentleman a fresh mattress. You, clean sheets, the ones off the line this morning, and fresh bedding. And you—" She stabbed a finger at a sleepy-looking maidservant. "Mop the floor. Boiling water, steep in it a handful of sage, two of lavender, and one of mint, leave for five minutes, then strain and use it to mop the floor with."

While they scrambled to do her bidding, she turned to Luke and Isabella. "My deepest apologies for the inconvenience, *señor*, *señora*, but last week my idiot of a husband allowed a gentleman to bring his hounds inside." She darted an evil look at her husband. "Against all my rules. This is what happens when I go to visit my sister!"

"He assured me they had no fleas—" the big man almost tearfully protested.

"Pfft! Have you ever seen a dog without a flea?" she said scornfully and turned back to Luke. "The dogs must have slept on that rug, and the fleas have bred in the warmth. Never mind, it will be all clean and good again in a few minutes and Carlos will bring you some of the best brandy, *señor*, and maybe some hot chocolate for your lady."

Carlos disappeared, and the servants removed the old mattress and bedding and carried in a fresh one.

"Wool stuffing," the landlady told Luke and Isabella. "New washed and dried in the sun. And the same with the sheets and blankets." She gave Isabella a smile. "Now then, my lady, you let your good man take care of you while I fetch some salve to take away the itch."

"Perhaps I could wait on the chair," Isabella suggested.

Luke stood her on the chair. There could still be fleas on the floor.

She sat, drawing her knees up to her chin, and waited wrapped in his greatcoat. She looked like a little street urchin in his too-big coat, with her bare, bitten toes poking out.

The maid arrived with a mop and steaming bucket. Under her mistress's supervision she thoroughly mopped the floor while the other servants shook out the clean sheets and bedding.

In minutes the bed was made up, the floor gleamed, and the room smelled of lavender and mint. The landlady handed Isabella a small jar of ointment, saying, "This will help with the itching. Sleep well, my lady. Once again, my apologies, *señor*. Now, out, out the rest of you, the gentleman and lady wish to sleep." She swept everyone from the room. As the door closed behind her, they heard, "And Carlos, you can explain to me why I should not make you sleep in the stable on that flea-ridden mattress?"

Isabella giggled. "Poor Carlos, do you think she'll carry out her threat?"

"Serves him right if she does," Luke growled.

Isabella unstoppered the jar and cautiously sniffed the contents. "Not bad." She began to apply the ointment to her bites.

She twisted awkwardly to reach the back of her thighs. "Do you want a hand with that?" Luke asked her.

"Yes, please."

She gave him the jar, turned her back, and raised the hem of her nightgown, revealing slender, creamy limbs that caused his mouth to dry.

"Behind my knee," she said, and he dipped a finger in the mix and dabbed it on the small red mark at the back of her knee. Her flesh was silky and tender there, and he stroked it under the guise of applying the ointment.

"Can you see any more?" she asked and lifted the nightgown higher, almost to her bottom.

He wanted to run his hands up her legs, caress her softness, but he'd made a resolution and was determined to stick to it.

"That's it," he said. His voice sounded hoarse. He replaced the stopper and set the jar down on the washstand. "Now, perhaps we can finally get some sleep."

But he knew before she even turned around on the chair to face him, before she said, "Thank you," in that soft voice, that he'd lost the battle.

She turned and swayed toward him. Or did he sway toward her? He didn't know. All he knew was that his arms wrapped around her almost of their own accord, as if separate from his will.

For a long moment he held her, pressing his face against her stomach, breathing in the scent of her through the cotton nightgown. He felt her fingers in his hair, caressing him, and he carried her to the bed and laid her down on the sweet-smelling sheets. Her hair spread out over the pillow, a tangle of twisted darkness, like the feelings seething inside him.

He kissed her then, a gossamer touching of lips at first,

barely a taste—she was an innocent, he had to remember to go slowly—but she made a little humming noise deep in her throat, twined her arms around his neck, and drew him closer.

Heat surged through him. He speared his fingers through the glorious mass of her hair and ravished her mouth with slow, soft kisses, while she returned kiss for kiss, enthusiastic little baby bird pecks.

The sweet clumsiness of those kisses forced a bridle on his rampant desire. No virgin, his bride, but an innocent nonetheless. She knew nothing about lovemaking.

He teased her lips apart, and as their tongues tangled, she grabbed his shoulders and shivered against him. He deepened the kiss. The taste of her flickered like flame along his veins.

She returned caress for caress, an eager, giving pupil.

He sucked on her full lower lip, and she writhed and clutched his arms with urgent fingers. Her nipples, under the cotton fabric, were hard little points. He brushed lightly across them, and she arched and made a sound deep in her throat. He brushed again, and again, rubbing his knuckles over them, and she shuddered and gasped.

He kissed and nibbled his way past the fragrant hollow in the base of her throat, to the shadowed valley between her breasts. Further progress was barred by a series of fine ribbons tied in dainty knots. His fingers were clumsy. She helped him undo them.

He reached for the hem of her nightgown, and with a complete absence of maidenly bashfulness she helped him pull it up and over her head, and she was bared wholly to his gaze.

The sight of her, naked, a slender ivory flame against the rumpled white sheets, took his breath away. Her eyes were wide, dark, and aroused, burnished gold in the candlelight, watching him looking at her. He must have stared too long, too hard, because she looked a little anxious and a slow flush rose to darken her skin. Her hands came up to shield her nakedness.

"No, don't," he whispered, preventing her. "You're beautiful."

For a second it looked as if she'd weep, then she turned her head away and her eyes fluttered closed. She looked so beautiful he had to kiss her again. And again.

The small moment of stiffness dissolved as she melted in his embrace again, responding with an honesty and whole-heartedness that pierced his heart. There was no guile in her— well, there was plenty; she was as full of tricks as a bag of monkeys, but not in this, not here, not now. Whatever she felt, she showed.

He ran his palms over her warm, silken skin, brushing the dark triangle of curls at the base of her belly, over her stomach, tracing the lines of her ribs—she was thin, so thin he ached for the deprivation that made her so. She quivered beneath his touch. So warm, so responsive.

He cupped the sweet, small breasts and teased the nipples with his thumb. She gasped, and then he lowered his mouth to one breast, caressing it with lips and tongue, and sucked, biting very gently. She jerked and gave a small high scream and then fell back, panting, her eyes dark and sleepy-looking with desire.

He unfastened his drawers and kicked them off. She reached for his undershirt. "No," he said and stopped her questing hands by capturing them and pressing them back above her head on the pillow, holding them one-handed. Before she could query him, he covered her mouth with his, plundering her, devouring her.

He nudged her legs apart with his free hand and stroked the satiny skin of her inner thighs, running his hand up to the warm center of her, barely touching her and then moving away . . . teasing, enticing.

He stroked her between the legs and found her hot and slick and ready. He inserted a finger. With each pull of his mouth on her breast, he felt the answering pulse deep within her. He found the tiny slick nubbin in the folds of her sex and stroked. She gave a jagged gasp and her eyes flared in shock. Her trembling limbs opened in wordless demand.

The scent of her arousal fired his senses. He should take the time to bring her to orgasm first, as he usually did with women, but urgency, red-hot and explosive, drove him now. He couldn't wait a moment longer. He positioned himself between her thighs. She wrapped her legs around him and clung on tight, kissing his jaw, his neck, sliding her palms beneath the undershirt along his back, over his buttocks, eager, aroused. His bride. His wife.

He was hard and aching, and the strain was starting to tell.

Thank God she wasn't a virgin, he thought, as he positioned himself at her entrance and thrust deep.

She stiffened and screamed. And not in a good way.

He was too far gone to stop. His body thrust of its own accord, pumping once, twice, into her stiff little body, and then the world exploded.

When he came to himself he withdrew from her, aware she winced with his every movement. He glanced down and, with a dull feeling of inevitability, saw a smear of blood. Her face was pale, her eyes dark and distressed. Tarnished gold. "You're a virgin!" he accused.

"I . . . I can't be." Bella shuddered. How could it all end so horribly? One moment she was having the most blissful time of her life, and now she was in bed with a hard-eyed stranger. Naked. She gathered the bedclothes around her, covering her nakedness, burrowing away from his accusing stare.

"Obviously you're not a virgin now. But you were." His voice was caustic. His hard, dark eyes stabbed her.

It didn't make sense. She'd never questioned that she wasn't . . . But the evidence was there, the red smear of blood on the sheets. She'd have to get the stain out before the landlady saw it. It would be so mortifying after the fuss they'd made to get clean sheets.

"Well?" The hard voice intruded on her thoughts.

"Well, what?"

"Do you have an explanation?"

"For what?"

"I was told you weren't a virgin. And yet . . ." He gestured at the sheet.

"I didn't know! It's not my fault." She flung him an angry,

wounded look. "What kind of bridegroom complains about his bride's virginity, anyway?"

He clenched his jaw and looked away.

So she said it for him. "One who thinks he was trapped into a marriage."

"*Thinks?*" His lip curled.

She punched his shoulder. "I was trapped into it, too, you know!"

"You?" he snorted.

"Yes, me. And I'm the one who's stuck with a bad-tempered Englishman who's going to take me away to a foreign country where it rains all the time and I don't know a soul."

His jaw dropped.

"You're not that big a prize, you know," she raged, tears—angry ones—blurring her sight. "I was an heiress before you married me! I could have had any man in Spain, almost."

He frowned, an arrested expression on his face.

"Don't look at me like that. Don't you dare look at me like that! I know I'm not pretty, but with my mother's fortune, I could have married well. Very well!"

Her mother's fortune was substantial. There were bonds and land and various investments—a manufactory of some sort and a woolen mill. Bella had an idea there might even be a ship or two, for her mother's grandfather had been a ship captain, and English, so most of the investments were in England.

Papa used to rant about it. It infuriated him that the fortune was so huge but he couldn't get his hands on any of it. After Mama died it was kept in trust for Bella, until she turned twenty-one, or married.

That was why Papa had quarrelled so bitterly with her grandparents and banned them from Valle Verde. Her grandparents had died soon afterward. She'd been so sad when Papa told her, because they'd died alone, without family. As she was now.

She glared at the man who was her husband. "I didn't need to entrap anyone into marriage, let alone a horrid, suspicious Englishman. And besides, it was your idea to marry me! I was only thirteen. What did I know?"

His mouth tightened.

"Yes, all right, I know I agreed to it. I was even happy about it, God help me for a naive fool. Saving my fortune from Ramón—so generous of you! Besides, I wasn't the one who denied the annulment. I didn't even know about it."

He made an exasperated sound, and she wanted to hit him again. "I know you don't believe me, but I didn't."

"But you must have told someone—"

"That I wasn't a virgin? Wrong! Reverend Mother told *me.*"

"*She* told you?"

"Yes." She scrubbed at her eyes with angry fists. "When I was first at the convent, I used to have bad dreams, nightmares about . . . you know, that day. I kept waking up screaming, and it upset the other girls, so they moved me to a room by myself."

"Go on."

"Reverend Mother—well she wasn't Reverend Mother then, just my Aunt Serafina—she asked me about my dreams and what happened that day, and I told her." Her mouth wobbled, and for a horrible moment Bella thought she might burst into tears, and she was damned if she'd give him the satisfaction. "And then she said it was a good thing I was married because I was no longer a virgin. That that man who attacked me had *known* me—in the Bilical sense, you understand—and therefore . . ."

He gave her one of those long, enigmatic looks she was starting to hate.

She made a frustrated gesture. "Well, how was I to know any different? They never tell us anything! I knew how horses and dogs and chickens did it, but when I asked Mama about it she was horrified and told me we weren't animals and it wasn't like that between a man and a woman at all." She broke off, frowning. "But it is like that, isn't it? Only face-to-face and lying down."

He said nothing.

"But I didn't know what being a virgin meant until you hurt me just now. I mean, I knew it was supposed to hurt, but that man in the forest hurt me, too. They never said what kind of hurt it should be."

Still he said nothing; only watched her with that steady, unnerving gaze.

"So I didn't lie. Or try to trick you."

There was a long silence, and she waited for him to say it was all right, that he understood, that he didn't blame her for the mistake. But all he said was, "It's late and we have another long day's travel ahead of us. We'd better get to sleep."

And then, as if nothing had happened, as if her world hadn't just been shattered, he pulled on his drawers, passed her her nightgown, blew out the candles, walked around to the other side of the bed, and climbed in.

And then there was silence.

Bella was incredulous. "Is that all you have to say?" she said after a few minutes of lying tense and expectant in the dark.

"Good night," he said politely, as if she were anyone, not the wife he'd just accused of entrapping him.

In fury she punched him on the back. And even then he said not a word.

Bella turned away from him. She curled up on the very edge of the bed, not wanting to touch him. And then the tears came, slow and silent, dripping down her face and soaking into her scrunched-up pillow.

She fought them, refusing to make a sound. She would not give him the satisfaction.

*L*uke lay in the darkness, his body sated, his emotions churning.

He didn't give a hang whether she was a virgin or not. What he cared about was the lies. He couldn't abide lies, especially from a woman. And especially from his wife.

And he had not blasted well married her for her fortune!

Had she lied or not? It was the one thing he couldn't forgive in a woman, deception of that sort. Some women did that, entwined themselves and their bodies around a man's heart, and while he was exposed and vulnerable and trusting, they lied, luring him, deceiving him, playing him for a fool . . .

If Isabella had done that . . .

He turned over in his mind all that she'd told him.

He supposed if anyone would be ignorant of the relations between men and women, it would be a nun and a young girl. Why were women kept so ignorant? He didn't understand it. Boys talked about it all the time. He'd supposed girls did, too. But perhaps girls' ignorance was to keep them from worrying about the perils of childbirth. Though that didn't make sense. Everyone knew women could die in childbed. Women bore all the serious consequences . . .

Isabella could have conceived his child this night.

Whatever the tangled web that had led to his marriage, it was well and truly consummated now. He couldn't walk away from it—and her—now. Even if he could, he wouldn't, he realized in surprise. Whatever her part in this—and he was inclined to think she was as innocent as she'd professed—she was his.

That decision made, he closed his eyes and prepared to sleep.

He was so aware of her in the bed, the sound of her breathing, the scent of her wrapping around his senses. He frowned. Was that a sniffle? He listened intently.

Her breathing was jagged, uneven, shuddery.

She was weeping; his bride was weeping silently in the dark.

He wanted to turn over, to reach for her, to draw her against him, to murmur that it was all right, that she was forgiven. He didn't move. "Are you crying?"

"No."

He turned over to face her. "You're upset, I know, but—"

"Upset?" She sat up in bed and confronted him. "Most bridegrooms would be delighted to discover their bride was a virgin. I don't know what it's like in England, but in Spain a bride brings her virginity to a marriage as a pledge of honor, a sign of p-p-purity." In the fading light from the fire he saw a couple of tears roll down her cheek. She dashed them away with an angry gesture and continued, "They don't have their horrid, stupid, suspicious husbands accusing them of being a v-virgin as if it was something to be ashamed of!"

"I didn't accuse." But he had, he knew it.

She shoved him away. "Oh, go to sleep. Just go to sleep! I don't want to talk to you."

He'd planned to do just that, but now, seeing her weeping, fighting the tears instead of using them as a weapon against him . . . He hadn't just upset her; he'd hurt her. And seriously offended her sense of honor.

He'd never considered women having a sense of honor. He hadn't considered a lot, it seemed. But though the circumstances of his marriage were far from satisfactory, he couldn't hold his anger with her, not seeing her like this.

"I apologize," he said stiffly. He wasn't used to making apologies. But he had to admit she'd come to her marriage a virgin, and he hadn't appreciated that as perhaps he should. No perhaps about it, he realized suddenly. He was glad he'd been her first. He just wished he'd known.

"I'm sorry. I didn't mean to impugn your honor. Of course I'm pleased to find you untouched. It's the same in England as here, and I am very grateful, and proud that—"

She made a frustrated sound. "Oh, don't lie to me! You're not proud in the slightest. You're still cross and you think you've been tricked. Well, Lord Ripton, I didn't lie, and you got yourself a bride with no stain on her honor *and* a fortune into the bargain, so you can take your stiff-necked, halfhearted apology and . . . and . . . choke on it!"

She lay back down, the line of her spine rigid and unforgiving.

*M*orning finally came, and if he had not slept well, the same could not be said for his bride, Luke thought. Somewhere in the wee small hours her breathing had evened out and he knew she finally slept. Only then could he relax.

Not that he was relaxed at the moment; he'd awoken fully

aroused. Under normal circumstances he'd wake her slowly and erotically and they'd make love again.

Now . . . He shook his head and willed his erection away. His marriage . . . Only a couple of days and yet anything that could go wrong, had. Lord knew what she'd spring on him next.

He slipped out of bed and pulled on his breeches, shirt, and boots. With any luck he'd be out of the room when she woke.

"Where are you going?"

He turned. She was sitting up, looking sleepy and far too enticing, with her hair tumbled around her shoulders and her nightgown half undone. Under his gaze—or maybe it was just the morning chill—her nipples peaked, and he felt his cock stir in response.

She saw where he was looking and pulled the bedclothes up to her chin. "Are you leaving me?"

"No, just going to send for hot water and order breakfast. I want a proper cooked breakfast, not a bit of bread or pastry."

"And us?"

"I now accept it was an honest mistake born of ignorance," he told her.

She regarded him steadily for a moment, then gave a brisk little nod. "Very well then, I forgive you." She climbed out of bed and marched toward the washstand, the hard little points of nipples swaying beneath the cotton.

"You forgive *me*?" Her imperious attitude amused him. Surely he should be the one forgiving her. He watched her nipples bobbing their way across the room and realized he already had.

"Yes. Now go and order your big greasy English breakfast. I will have churros and hot chocolate."

A short time later Isabella came downstairs with the long skirt of her riding habit looped neatly over her arm. She looked fresh and neat, and there was a lithe spring in her step that belied the long days of travel behind her. And the long night.

The landlady came hurrying out to inquire after her, and Luke heard Isabella reassuring the woman that her bites no longer itched and that the ointment was most effective, and yes, of course all was forgiven.

The question was, did she mean *all*? Time would tell.

She joined him at table with a tentative smile. "Did you order my churros?"

"I did indeed, and chocolate, as you desired." He decided to test the waters. "Our landlady is so mortified by the mishap last night she would give you whatever you asked for, including the head of her husband on a platter."

Isabella laughed, a delicious gurgle of mirth. "I would say, *especially* the head of her husband on a platter. Poor Carlos. But she'll forgive him." She arranged her napkin and added, "He adores her, of course."

"He does?"

She nodded. "Oh yes, it's obvious."

The landlord—head intact—arrived with Luke's breakfast of ham, eggs, sausages, and coffee. His wife followed with a napkin-lined basket of churros, piping hot and golden, and hot chocolate, thick and dark and very sweet.

The landlord hovered, seemingly inclined to linger and talk, but his wife steered him away, saying gently, "They want their breakfast, Carlos, not a conversation."

Isabella only had eyes for her breakfast. She regarded the churros with such greedy pleasure, Luke couldn't repress a smile.

She noticed. "What?"

"Years of gruel in the convent?"

She laughed. "Just bread, usually stale. And never with hot chocolate." She dipped the end of the churro in and sucked the chocolate from it with such a look of bliss on her face, he almost groaned aloud.

Tonight he would show her all the pleasures of the marriage bed. And this time it would end very differently.

Luke addressed himself to his breakfast. Isabella didn't hold a grudge; he had to give her that. She was a fighter—he liked that about her, too. He liked that she'd ripped into him when she thought he hadn't given her her due. She was angry and she'd told him why. No having to guess. No petulant miffs and silent, female sulks. She'd given him an earful and a couple of angry thumps. Open and straightforward.

And now it was over. Thank God.

He watched Isabella licking sugar from her fingers. She wasn't at all the quiet, conformable bride he'd expected. He was very glad she wasn't. One thing was certain: he wasn't going to be bored. She would lead him a merry dance—a huff of laughter escaped him—she already had.

She tilted her head with a quizzical look. "Something funny?"

"Just wondering if you knew how to dance."

She shook her head. "Only country dances from when I was a child. Dancing wasn't taught in the convent. Is it important?"

"No, I'll teach you."

"I look forward to it," she said softly, and the look in her eyes told Luke she really had forgiven him for accusing her of entrapment. Something loosened in his chest.

He put his napkin down and pushed back his chair. "If you've finished, we'd better get moving."

*H*is bride was good company on the road, too, Luke discovered. She made observations here and there, but they were interesting ones. She wasn't like some women he knew, thinking it their role to fill a silence—any silence— with aimless chatter. Nor was she the sort who expected a fellow to entertain her.

With Isabella, sometimes they rode in silence, other times they'd talk. It was easy, effortless. A bit like traveling with his friends, only more interesting, because he never knew what she'd say.

She asked him about his family, and he told her about Mother and Molly and Molly's come-out, which had been delayed so many times. "You'll like Molly," he finished. "She's fun and very sweet-natured. Everyone likes her, and she'll like you, I know."

Isabella pulled a wry face. "Maybe."

"You doubt it?"

"She probably had one of her friends lined up to marry you. She won't be at all pleased with you bringing home a foreign wife who isn't even pretty."

He shook his head. "Molly isn't like that. As long as I'm happy with you, she'll be happy, too."

"Then that's the question, isn't it?"

Before he could respond, she broke into a canter and forged ahead of him. He raced after her, caught up, and cantered alongside her until their horses began to tire. When they slowed to a walk, he leaned over and caught hold of her bridle, bringing them both to a halt.

"Molly will like you."

She gave him a wry look. "Even though I'm difficult and disobedient and quarrelsome?" She wasn't talking about his sister's opinion.

He smiled. "I'm not exactly a bundle of laughs, myself."

"You were quite lighthearted when I first met you" she said softly. "Not during the fight, of course, but afterward, when we were traveling."

He shrugged and looked away. "People change." He signaled his horse to walk on.

They walked in silence for a few minutes, then she said, "So you don't think Molly will mind me being difficult at times?"

He didn't respond. Did she think he was foolish enough to give her carte blanche?

"Reverend Mother used to say I gave her more trouble than all the other girls in the convent."

"She told me you were a treasure to be cherished."

Isabella turned an astonished face to him. "Truly? Reverend Mother said that?" She considered it. "Aunt Serafina Reverend Mother? About me? A treasure? Are you sure?"

He found himself smiling again. "She did. She told me to take good care of you."

"Well!" She was clearly astounded. A little smile played on her face. Then she shook her head. "Why is it that people only tell you the bad things to your face, never the good things? She never once called me a treasure. A plague, yes, a pest, an imp of Satan—" She broke off, clearly feeling she'd said too much.

He laughed. "Perhaps she thought praise would ruin your character."

She shook her head. "No, I've received very little praise in my life. I still get into trouble all the time."

He laughed again. "Why am I not surprised?"

She gave him a quick smile. "In my own defense, and looking back in time, there was no pleasing Papa." A wistful expression passed briefly across her face. "No matter what I did, I was never good enough."

"Why not?"

She grimaced. "I should have been born a boy."

He thought of the way she'd looked in those breeches, the beauty of her naked on the bed, the eagerness with which she'd made love to him, and said firmly, "Now there I have to disagree."

She gave him a half smile. "Very gallant, sir. But Papa preferred Perlita. She is very pretty, very feminine." She spoke lightly, but there was real pain underneath.

Luke frowned. Again, that comment that she wasn't pretty. It was partly true—she wasn't what the world called pretty— but that was far from the whole story. Her features were too bold, too unconventional for mere prettiness, but she had the kind of looks that compelled a man to stare. Luke could hardly drag his eyes away from her.

"As for prettiness," he began.

She cut him off. "Please don't offer me empty compliments," she said briskly. "I know what I look like, and I cannot change it."

"But—"

"No." She gave him a fierce look.

A defensive look, he saw. It was a touchy subject. Why, he didn't understand, but he could appreciate touchy subjects. He had a few himself. But there was more than one way to storm a battlement. Though now was not the moment.

"So as a child you were very naughty?"

She gave a gurgle of laughter. "Oh, I like the 'as a child.' For that I thank you, even if you have probably perjured your soul. But the truth is, as a child I was painfully good. I was so hungry for Papa's approval. But it never did me any good. He could not see me, I think. Only the Mama in me, and he did not love Mama." Again that wistful expression, then she shook her head, as if to clear it of unhappy memories, and went on, "And in the convent, everyone there was trying to please God in every way, and He never showed any approval, either. So in the end I decided not to try to please anyone, but to do what I thought was right, myself." She added with a mischievous look, "That's what you get for leaving me there for eight years."

Luke laughed. "Minx. So if you run me ragged, it's my own fault?"

"Exactly." She smiled. "It's lovely to hear you laugh, Luke. For a while there I thought you'd forgotten how."

Eleven

&

They rode in silence for some miles, then stopped beside a stream for lunch. The landlady had loaded them up with food for their journey: wine, bread, ham, thick wedges of pepper and potato omelette, half a chicken, and some oranges. They attacked the feast with zeal and, afterward, lay in the sun, soaking it up.

Luke had decreed they'd move on in half an hour. Now he regretted saying so.

Isabella lay on her back in the grass, one knee bent, the other leg resting across it in a boyish pose. Her breeches and boots were clearly visible, but since there was nobody else to see, Luke didn't mind.

In fact, he wouldn't mind baring a little more of her. He got up, stretched, and sat down beside her.

"If you were any kind of civilized man, we could have a proper siesta," Isabella murmured sleepily.

"No rest for the wicked," he murmured, watching her leg rock slowly back and forth. He remembered the way she'd trembled at his touch.

He rolled over onto his front, ending up lying thigh to thigh with her. "I know something better than a siesta," he murmured and stretched a lazy hand toward the buttons of her jerkin.

She pushed his hand off and moved a little farther away.

Shy, Luke thought. Perhaps it was too soon in the marriage to think about making love in the open air. "Tell me about the breeches."

"What about them?"

"You said Reverend Mother let you outside the convent dressed as a boy. Why?"

She let out a huff of amusement. "She didn't precisely let me, not at first." She wriggled around so they were facing each other and regarded him with a look of rueful mischief he was beginning to recognize. "I used to sneak out."

His lips twitched. "Why do I find myself strangely unsurprised?"

She wrinkled her nose. "Well, I hate the feeling of being shut in. And the convent was built to keep people out, not keep them in—the nuns *want* to be there. And some of the girls who are educated there would make valuable hostages. So it's not a prison. But it was for me."

Eight years, he thought.

"At first I used to go out just for an hour or so—"

"Doing what?"

"Oh, just sitting and breathing in the night, looking at the stars, or, if there was moonlight, walking and running. You're not allowed to run in a convent—'Glide, young ladies, glide!'" she mimicked. "It was easy, because I didn't sleep in the dormitory with the other girls, so nobody noticed if I wasn't in my bed."

"So how did Reverend Mother find out?"

"It wasn't for ages, and it was all my own fault. Food got very scarce during the war. The convent was down to bare bones, and I was starving and sick of having nothing to eat except watery soup with three lentils and a weed in it. So I started setting traps."

"Traps?"

"Snares. Papa taught me to live off the land." She paused. "You don't believe me, do you?"

He murmured something polite, but she wasn't deceived. She jumped up. "I'll show you." From her bag she drew a spool of thread. "Twisted silk, which means it's very strong. Your knife, please?"

Fascinated, he passed it to her.

"You do it like this, except of course you'd choose a better spot than this. And you cut these." She cut two forked sticks. "Dry, or the sap can make them stick." She selected a thin whippy branch from a nearby bush. "And then you bend this down and fasten it like this." She pinned it in place with one of the forked sticks. "And now you position this here . . ."

He watched her small, competent hands fashioning a noose and setting up the snare. No lady of his acquaintance would do—or know how to do—such a thing. He made the mistake of saying it aloud.

Instantly she looked away and said in a flattened voice, "I warned you I often do the wrong thing."

"I meant it as a compliment."

She eyed him doubtfully. "Truly?"

"Truly. I think you're a remarkable young woman."

She flushed and ducked her head, as if unused to even such minor compliments. But her mouth curved enough for him to know she was pleased.

He watched her dismantle the snare, and when she finished, he patted the ground beside him. She frowned a little but sat down again, hugging her knees to her chest. She seemed somewhat nervous of him. Perhaps she'd read his mind.

All through her recital and demonstration he'd been imagining peeling those clothes off her. A girl who hunted alone at night could surely be persuaded to make love in the grass.

"You haven't finished the story. Reverend Mother?" he prompted and was pleased when he saw her relax.

"The first time I tried, I caught two fat hares," she said, unable to hide the pride in her voice. "I left them in the kitchen along with a pocketful of pine nuts. Nobody knew where they came from." She grinned wickedly. "The cook thought it was a miracle, that our angel had sent them to save us—the angel over the gate, you know. The one who looks like you."

"Like me?" He was revolted. "I do not look like an angel."

She laughed. "You do; everyone says so." Before he could argue the point she continued, "So after that I went out hunting and foraging every night. But my dresses were a problem— they kept getting caught on things and would tear and get dirty. So I got some breeches and boots from a house in the village. Don't look at me like that—I didn't steal them."

He spread his hands in mock innocence, claiming dryly, "I didn't say a thing."

"They were her son's—he'd been killed in the war, and I traded them for—" She broke off.

"For?"

She gave him a guilty look. "For a bit of the gold chain you gave me on our wedding day. I traded it all in the end, for various things we needed. But I kept the ring; you know that." She drew it from the neck of her blouse. It dangled from the twisted silk thread, glinting in the sun.

He nodded, recalling the shock he'd felt when he discovered she'd worn his signet ring for eight years. He'd almost forgotten about it. Now he felt only possessiveness.

She tucked the ring back and continued her tale. "But after several days of the miraculous appearance of hares and rabbits and birds' eggs and squirrels—"

"Squirrels?"

"We were starving," she reminded him. "Squirrels are small but good eating. Of course, cook never admitted the squirrels, but once it's in a stew, you can't tell what it is. Anyway, one night Reverend Mother caught me sneaking in again. She was waiting in my room. Oh, the penances I had to perform . . ." She pulled a face. "But she let me out again in the end."

"It was that or starve?"

She nodded. "My contribution wasn't much, but it made the difference between us starving or not."

"No wonder she called you a treasure."

"I suppose that was it. Food is important."

"I meant the courage it took," he said softly.

"Courage? There's nothing courageous about setting a few traps."

No, Luke thought, but there was a deal of courage in a young girl roaming the mountains alone during wartime, foraging and hunting for food for her friends.

She was surprise after surprise, this wife of his.

She lay on her back in the grass, squinted up at the sun, and heaved a sigh. "I suppose it's time to leave."

Temptation stirred anew. There was nobody around for miles, so privacy shouldn't be an issue. And she loved the outdoors. What better place? "It's so pleasant in the sun; let us delay awhile. I'll show you what married couples do during siesta," he murmured and reached for her.

She jumped as if he'd bitten her, and scooted away, sitting up straight. "As to that, I don't think we should engage in . . . um, marital relations again until we get to England."

"What?" He sat up.

"Another two weeks cannot make any difference to you."

Two weeks? It damned well could. He'd thought perhaps her time of the month had come upon her, but two weeks?

"After all, you left me at the convent for eight years—"

"Is that what this is about? Retaliation for those years?"

"Retaliation? No, of course not. I just meant you obviously weren't in a hurry to get an heir then, so another few weeks won't matter now."

"Get an heir?"

"Yes, it's the main purpose of it, isn't it—like breeding horses?" Her eyes dropped and she added, "I would rather not do it for a while, if you don't mind." Her hands rested in her lap, but they were tightly knotted.

Luke stared at her, perplexed. He couldn't give a hang about an heir. When he'd taken her to bed, an heir was the very last thing on his mind. It was all her, and the need to possess her, taste her, enter— Oh, of course! That was it. Damned fool that he was, he'd been in such a hurry, he'd frightened her off, if not for life, for at least a couple of weeks.

He must really have hurt her, damn him for a clumsy oaf.

"No," he said. "We will not wait until we get to England." The longer they put it off, the more her anxiety would grow.

"But—"

He said in a gentler voice, "I was clumsy last night. If I'd known you were a virgin, I would have been more careful, slower, gentler. It will not hurt the next time."

She frowned, turning his words over in her mind, then her chin came up and her fingers curled into fists. "So you intend to force me?"

"No, of course not." He'd never forced a woman in his life.

"Good, because if you tried, I would fight you."

His brows rose at her tone, but all he said was, "I give you my word I won't force you."

"Good, then we shall wait until—"

"I have no intention of waiting."

"What? But you just said—"

"I won't force you." He gave her a slow smile. "I won't need to."

She frowned, considering his words, then sudden outrage surfaced. "You'd *drug* me? I have heard of such wickedness."

"Don't be ridiculous. Of course I wouldn't drug you! Good God! No, I promise you'll be wide awake and you'll give full consent."

She eyed him suspiciously. "Why would I do that?"

"I'll seduce you." He had no doubt of it. Yes, she was skittish now, but last night she'd responded with natural, unfettered sensuality—until he'd bungled it, entering her with more desperation than finesse. It went against his honor as much as anything. He prided himself on his bedchamber skills. He hadn't treated a woman so clumsily since he was a green and eager youth. He had no idea how his loss of control had happened last night, but he was damned sure he wouldn't let it happen again.

She narrowed her eyes at him, then shrugged a shoulder as if she didn't believe him and said with airy insouciance,

"You are welcome to try." She started packing up the remains of the picnic.

His lips twitched. The minx, throwing his own words back at him.

*T*hey reached the town of Huesca just as siesta time was ending. The streets were already filling with people all heading in the same direction, and when they reached the center of the town, they saw why.

"It's a market." Bella turned eagerly to Luke. "Can we stop and look? I can't tell you how long it is since I've been to a market."

Luke could see she was dying to dive into that throng. "Come on, then," he said. "Let's go shopping." He'd planned to buy her a cloak, and this might be an opportunity.

"Shopping?" Her eyes sparkled. "What shall we buy?"

"We'll have to see what's available, won't we? But first let's stable the horses and find a room for the night."

They found one eventually, a private room in an inn off the central square, probably the most expensive accommodation in town, but the town was full because of the market, and nothing else was available. After a wash, a change of clothes, and a drink, they stepped out onto the square and plunged into the crowd.

Isabella's eyes were everywhere; even the humblest stall was of interest to her, and Luke was reminded again that she'd been shut away from the world for eight years. She smelled the fruit, sampled everything that was offered to taste, and examined the animals from geese and pigs, to cages of bright parrots and a box of kittens. She cooed at the latter with such delight that he had to inform her that they could not travel with a kitten.

"I know. It's just that they're so sweet."

Isabella moved from stall to stall. She was friendly to a fault, examining the goods and exchanging greetings and banter with the stall keepers. And she fingered the fabrics and eyed the ready-made clothes with ill-concealed covet-ousness.

"Would it fit you?" Luke asked when she lingered over a simple dress in a glowing dark red.

"Really?" She turned to him in surprise, and seeing he meant it, she examined the dress more carefully, then held it up against her. "I think so," she said breathlessly.

"Would the *señorita* like to try it on?" The stall keeper's wife came forward. "We have a private place here, very safe." She indicated a cubicle draped in fabric set up against the cart at the back of the stall.

"*Señora,*" Luke corrected her. He examined the cubicle, nodded, then stood guard outside as Isabella and the woman stepped inside.

"What do you think?" Isabella stepped out through the curtain.

The dress was cheap, simply made, and old-fashioned to one accustomed to London society, but he could see she loved it, and indeed it suited her. The dark red was perfect for her dark coloring, and a simple decoration of pale yellow piping gave it a smart, jaunty air that suited Isabella's personality.

"Very nice," he said.

"It's a bit loose here." Isabella plucked at the bodice.

"The *señora* just needs a corset," the woman murmured.

"A corset? She isn't fat!" Luke exclaimed indignantly.

The woman tsked indulgently. "The *señora* is as slender as a reed, to be sure, but a corset also helps here." She cupped her own substantial breasts.

"She doesn't need—"

"I'd love to try one," Isabella said at the same time. And without waiting, she and the stall keeper's wife disappeared again behind the curtains. The woman yelled something to her daughter, who thrust a bundle of white things through the curtains.

Luke waited. Rustling sounds and murmurs came from the curtained cubicle.

"Now how do I look?" Isabella pulled back the curtain.

Luke stared. And swallowed. Instead of a loose neckline that hinted at gently shadowed curves beneath, two silky puffs of breast rose impudently above the neckline. A dress that was perfectly acceptable before now looked . . . mouthwatering.

His mouth was hanging open, he realized suddenly. He shut it with a snap that jarred his teeth.

"Well?" Isabella gave him a speculative look.

He ran his tongue over parched lips. "You don't need it," he told her. "It looks . . . ridiculous."

"Ridiculous?" Her eyes narrowed to two gold slits. She glanced down at her neckline then let her gaze drift slowly over him, from head to toe, lingering at his groin for what felt like minutes. Luke felt her gaze like a slow, hot caress. He felt his body stir.

He raised one brow. "Playing with fire, wife?"

She met his gaze, blushed, tossed her head, and whisked herself back behind the curtain. "I'll take two," she said. "My husband will pay."

Luke smiled to himself. He was not the only aroused person here, but he was the only one who recognized it. *You are welcome to try*, indeed. Come the night, she would discover the consequences of her reckless invitation.

Luke had never yet lost a challenge.

The stall keeper emerged from the cubicle with a knowing smile and, while Luke was waiting for Isabella to emerge, showed him another dress, the same size and style but in a patterned fabric in blue, white, and café au lait. "This would suit the *señora* perfectly," she told him.

"Wrap it up as well."

They wandered on through the market, investigating every stall thoroughly. They bought small custard-filled pastries made by nuns. They bought cinnamon-candied nuts, dried apricots, and fresh dates. Isabella found some scented soap that she said didn't smell anything like the convent soap, and Luke bought her a pair of cat's-eye earrings that exactly matched her eyes.

"I know what you're doing," she said as she happily inserted the earrings. "But it won't work."

"What am I doing?" He untangled a tendril of hair from one earring.

"Hah! So innocent. You think to seduce me with gifts."

He shook his head. "I don't need gifts to seduce you."

She gave him a speculative look, laced with challenge. "What will you use, then?"

He gave her a slow smile. "Me."

*H*is utter confidence secretly thrilled Bella, even as she tried to toughen herself against it. However many dark, smoky looks he gave her, whatever words he used to try to entice her, she would not couple with him. Not tonight.

She needed more time. Time to prepare herself, arm herself, before she lay in his embrace again. Last night he'd hurt her, badly.

Not her body. She didn't care about that small, transient hurt. All girls, all women experienced that when they first lay with a man. It was a rite of passage. If anything she was glad of it, glad to have gone to her marriage bed a virgin after all.

And the first part . . . the kissing, the touching . . .

In all her girlish imaginings, she'd never even dreamed anything so sweet. And yet so affecting.

Her insides quivered, just thinking about it. His hunger for her. His tender urgency, his slow, careful . . . worship. *With my body I thee worship.* It unraveled her, dissolved every doubt, revived every dream she'd ever had of this man, this marriage. She was filled . . . exalted . . . flooded with love.

And then . . .

She felt small and sick and cold, remembering.

His words, his response had cut so deep. The anger in him when he realized she'd been a virgin, the bitter realization he'd been trapped into an unwanted marriage. Deceived.

He'd managed to swallow the most hurtful words, but sensitized to him as she was, she'd felt his rage. It radiated off him, as tangible as heat, as scathing as ice.

She'd opened herself up to him, heart, body, and soul, and then, when she was at her most exposed and vulnerable—

"Would you like a cake?" Luke asked, pointing to a cake seller passing with a tray of wares.

Bella shook her head. "No, thank you." They continued on through the market.

No sign of that rage now. He'd harnessed it, buried it, hidden it behind a layer of gentlemanly politeness. Putting the best face on it. Even his vow to seduce her was a way of making up for the previous night. Kind and thoughtful, despite everything—and that threatened to unravel her, too.

She should be grateful for it. She was. It was just . . .

Bella Ripton, building castles in the air again. And if he happened to knock this one down—which of course he would—fool that she was, she would probably start building another.

But it was time to grow up, time to stop dreaming impossible dreams.

A crate of puppies caught her eye. Three soft, caramel fluffy ones and a small brindle mutt with a squashed-in face, lopsided ears, and a patch over one eye. "Hello, little pirate," she said and bent to pat him.

"Don't even think about it," Luke told her. "You can't take a puppy to England with you. Besides it's an ugly little mutt."

"I know, but so sweet-natured." The puppy blissfully wiggled his soft little body, wagging his tail and licking her fingers with frantic excitement. So loving; so eager to be loved. She gave him one last pat. "Good luck, little fellow. I hope you find someone to love you." They moved on through the market.

Most marriages had nothing to do with love. They were practical arrangements, alliances of family, a consolidation of wealth. And for children.

Bella needed to do what her husband had done; accept an unsatisfactory situation and make the best of it. And she would. She had every intention of making this a good marriage, to make him—and herself—happy.

She stepped back to let a couple with three children pass, two little girls and a boy. The children were dressed in their Sunday best, their hair newly washed and shining. The father carried the littlest girl on his shoulders, not seeming to mind the small fists clenched in his thinning hair.

Yes, she would build a family with Luke Ripton, and they would be happy, like that family, and would love their children. And that would be enough. She would make it be enough.

But first she needed to find a way to go on, to give herself to him night after night, and somehow protect her reckless, tender heart from the knowledge of his indifference. She'd be a fool to keep opening herself to that kind of hurt, and there was no denying the man had the power to hurt her.

It wasn't Luke's fault, she acknowledged. He'd never pretended to love her, never suggested there was even a possibility. It was all her own doing. Spinning dreams out of straw.

She bent to look at a crate of chickens, brown and glossy, clucking vigorously.

She'd read too much significance into him coming after her, worrying about her safety. Imagining he cared. It was obedience he cared about. He'd been an officer. A wife could not be allowed to disobey.

And that lesson in front of the looking glass . . . For the first time in her life she felt special, feminine, almost pretty. She'd misread that, too. It was obedience again. She was not to wear breeches.

And the lovemaking . . . The man kissed like a dream . . . made her feel things she never imagined were possible. But it was just something she had to get used to. She had to learn to give herself without craving more, to enjoy what was offered—his body, not his heart. And not feel shattered and empty afterward.

She could do it, she was sure. It was simply a matter of becoming accustomed to him, to his shaved-to-the-bone good looks, to that slow, glinting smile that caused her heart to flutter. Every single time.

"Watch out," he murmured in her ear and held her back as a donkey piled high with rolled-up carpets was led through the crowd.

She would get used to the dark rumble of his deep voice, she told herself. Eventually it would not send a warm, delicious shiver through to her bones. And his protectiveness was his husbandly duty. Just because it made her feel warm and safe and . . . cherished didn't mean he loved her. It was the novelty of it, that was all, she told herself firmly.

She watched him cleave a path through the crowd, tall, unconsciously arrogant, oblivious of all the looks and sighs he was getting from the women and girls he passed. Bella was far from unaware. It would be her lot in life, to watch other women desiring her husband. And he wasn't even trying.

He even fascinated the little ones. In front of them a woman carried a tiny girl with dark curls and huge brown eyes. The child watched Luke solemnly over her mother's shoulder. Bella glanced at him to see if he'd noticed.

His expression was as stern and graven-angel as ever, and for a moment she thought he hadn't noticed the child, but then she saw one dark blue eye drop in a slow, deliberate wink. The little girl stared. And then tried to wink back. She blinked both eyes. Luke winked the other eye. The little girl's face screwed up as she tried to copy him. She squeezed both eyes shut then pushed one eye open with her fingers.

Luke chuckled. The little girl kicked off her shoe, and before Bella could move, Luke picked it up and fitted it matter-of-factly on the child's foot. Her mother thanked him effusively, as charmed by him as her daughter was.

Bella watched, her heart awash with love. That was the trouble. There was no resisting the man.

A fist closed around her heart. How could she bear it, loving him so much and receiving only kindness in return?

Just like Mama, only Papa hadn't even been kind.

"Just what I was hoping for." Luke's voice interrupted her thoughts. He steered her to where a pile of cloaks lay draped over a trestle table. He lifted one up. Made from warm merino wool and dyed a bright scarlet, it was lined for extra warmth and had a hood edged with soft black fur. Bella let the silky fur trail through her fingers.

"Mink," the stall keeper told her.

"Rabbit," Luke and Bella said in unison. They exchanged looks and laughed.

"Try it on," Luke told her and draped the cloak around her. It was soft and warm and buttoned down the front to hang in elegant folds around her ankles. He stepped back and inspected it, then adjusted the hood. His fingers brushed cool against her skin. Warmth pooled in her stomach.

Luke gave a brisk nod and, without waiting for her response, began to bargain with the stall keeper.

The chill of the evening was whispering down from the mountains, so Bella kept the cloak on. She loved it, loved all the gifts she'd received. Loved the man who'd given them.

I don't need gifts to seduce you. He was right.

She enjoyed the shopping so much, but no amount of gifts could endanger her heart. It was the man himself.

But the happiness bubbling up inside her was a warning, and when he turned and gave her a slanting white grin, her heart gave such a leap, it hardened her resolve.

She would not make love with him. Not tonight. Not until her feelings were more under control. Or until they reached England.

Night fell, and while some parts of the market closed, others opened. Lanterns and burning brands spilled pools of golden light across the cobblestones, turning the market square into a place of warmth and shadows. The smell of cooking spiced the chill night air.

Luke and Bella ate smoky grilled chicken from one of the stalls, almost burning their fingers on the crispy-skinned, tender pieces. They nibbled on salty roasted nuts and sweet pastries and drank dark and mellow wine from grapes grown in the valleys below.

A fight broke out near a tavern. The burning brands were fading. One by one they started to smoke. Bella struggled to hide her yawns.

"I think that's our signal to retire," Luke murmured in her ear.

Bella nodded. She was very tired. She'd been spinning the evening out as long as she could, delaying the moment when she'd face him across the bed and tell him no. And then try to resist him.

They left the market area and strolled down quiet, dark streets. Passing a shadowy alley, Bella heard the sound of music and the rapid staccato steps of boot heels. At the end of the alley, light flickered, beckoning.

"Someone's dancing. Let's see," she said and tugged Luke toward the music.

"You're just putting off the inevitable." His voice was dark, smoky chocolate. It lapped enticingly at the barrier of her willpower. "There's no reason to be nervous, Isabella."

He had no idea. "I want to see this," she said, stubbornly.

He gave a lazy shrug and allowed her to lead him down the alley, the tiger indulging the tethered goat.

In a derelict courtyard a ragged band of gypsies was gathered around a fire. The light of the leaping flames caught in the bright, tawdry finery of the gypsies. Silence fell. One or two gypsies glanced their way, but nobody moved.

"It's finished—" Luke began. At the same instant, a guitar sobbed a single, imperative chord, and the silence took on a new quality. A woman began to sing, a throaty, mournful song in a language Bella did not know. She sang alone, unaccompanied but for the occasional guitar notes, lifting her blind, impassioned face to the night sky, singing of love and of pain and of death.

The hairs stood up at the back of Bella's neck as she listened. She might not know the words, but she could feel the emotion. The woman's voice throbbed as it rose and fell in a wailing, hypnotic rhythm, pouring out her tale of passion and betrayal.

She finished on a long, sobbing note that scraped across Bella's nerves, it was so full of raw pain.

And then there was silence. The firelight danced with shadows. The cold air pressed around her. She could feel Luke standing at her back, a solid masculine warmth down the length of her body.

For a long time nobody seemed to move. Then a single loud clap sounded. Then another. One pair of hands. One man. A slow, emphatic clap! *Clap! Clap!*

Bella was about to join in the applause when Luke's hands

came over hers. "Wait," he murmured. He drew her back against him.

The guitar strummed a chord. *Clap! Clap!*

The man who was clapping stalked slowly, dramatically, into the pool of firelight. His hair was long, untamed, and streaked with silver. It rippled down his back like a lion's mane. *Clap! Clap!* His clothing was ragged, but he bore himself as proudly as a king. *Clap! Clap!*

The music started. The man flung his arms up in an imperious gesture—*clap! clap!*—stamping his heels slowly in a tense, deliberate rhythm. A hypnotic beat. Bella found herself breathing in time.

He danced for himself alone, this man, tossing his head, his lean body arched like a drawn bow, tense, graceful, and controlled. His boot heels drummed a primeval rhythm. Explosive. Intensely masculine. It caught the beat of Bella's heart.

The music grew faster and faster. The dancer turned and twirled, like the sparks from the fire whirling in a spiral toward the darkness, building to a crescendo. He arched, his face raised to the sky, his arms braced, erect. His mane of silvered hair rippled down his back as his heels thundered, his hard, powerful thighs pounding like a machine. Bella's blood pounded, too.

Then a gypsy woman stepped into the pool of light. Dressed in a low-cut red dress, a black bodice tightly laced over it to frame generous breasts, she wore a fringed black embroidered shawl tied tightly around her hips.

She raised her arms high above her head and stamped her feet, twice. Imperiously.

The male dancer flung back his head and stared at her down his long, proud nose.

The woman lifted her skirt coquettishly, rapped a provocative tattoo with her heels, and flung the male dancer a look of pure defiance. Then she, too, started to dance.

The man gave her a long, brooding look, then stalked around her as she continued to dance. His heels stamped out an implacable rhythm. Dominant. Possessive. *I am your master.*

She sent him provocative looks over her shoulder but continued her defiance. Suddenly he snaked out an arrogant arm and seized her, jerking her against his chest. For an instant, she gazed up at him from under her lashes, then she flung his arm off and twirled away, her heels tapping out a counterpoint to his. He followed, surrounding her.

Bella watched breathlessly.

He seized the woman around the waist and pulled her hard against him. She arched gracefully backward, her head almost touching the ground, her fingers trailing the cobblestones. The guitar moaned and throbbed.

The woman pouted at the man, silently daring him to do more. He bent and brought his lips to her throat, but she wrenched herself out of his grip in a swirl of skirts. But she did not run away, Bella saw. She danced around him, proudly, teasingly, daring him to take her if he could. She was willing to be conquered. But she wouldn't come easily.

He watched, brooding, following her every movement, his heels drumming in an almost unbearable intensity. How could anyone resist him?

In a sudden movement he seized her again and hurled her to the ground. Bella gasped, but he had the girl safe in his grip. It was a lesson.

The gypsy girl lay sprawled in a pool of light, sultry eyed and proud, but she was his; anyone could see it. Slowly, sensuously, in utter masculine command, he drew her up his body, showing her who was master, promising her ecstasy. She rose as sinuous as a snake, twining around him, possessive, proud. Claimed, but not conquered.

The guitar strummed a long vibrating chord, and it was over. The dancers stood like statues, sweat pouring off them despite the chill of the night. The crowd began to applaud. But it wasn't over, Bella saw. The two dancers stood motionless, their gazes locked, chests heaving. Then the man threw the woman over his shoulder and they disappeared into the night.

Someone else started singing. Bella barely noticed; she was still entranced by what she had seen. She'd heard about these gypsy dances, but she'd never seen one, never seen anything like it. She felt hot, breathless, liquid, and hollow inside.

Luke pulled her toward him, turning her toward the exit. "Time for bed." His voice sounded hoarse. He was breathing hard, as if he'd been dancing, too.

"Wasn't that magical?" she breathed. A warm, delicious shudder rippled through her. "I've never seen anything like it."

For a long moment he didn't respond. He stared down at her, his gaze locked on hers in an echo of the dancers' performance. Then with a groan he lowered his mouth to hers.

The kiss was so unexpected Bella had no time to marshal her defenses. It was neither tender nor gentle, but a bold, confident possession. His mouth was hot, demanding, his blood fired by the dance. As was hers. It ravished her senses and sapped her resistance.

His big hands slid over her body, along her spine, molding her to his hard body, creating a heated, hollow ache deep inside her.

Warnings flickered faintly in her mind. Like fireflies before a storm, they faded under the searing onslaught of his mouth. Intoxicating, the sharp, smoky, hot-buttered taste of him, the scrape of his dark-stubbled jaw against her skin. She couldn't think, only feel, only taste. And give herself wholly to the moment . . . and the man.

She gripped the lapels of his coat, pulling him closer, lifting herself greedily for better access to his seeking, hungry mouth. She wanted to climb his body like a gypsy girl, to twine around his hard masculine torso, to be wrapped in his powerful arms and borne off into the night . . .

A scrape of stone in the alley, footsteps, and the acrid smell of tobacco brought Luke to a sudden, shocked awareness of what he was doing. In one swift moment he broke the kiss and thrust Isabella behind him against the wall, placing himself between her and the rest of the world.

What the hell had he been thinking, kissing his wife in public in a strange Spanish town? Oblivious of everything except the sweet taste of her. Never mind that it was dark and they'd been standing in the shadows. It was criminally negligent. Anything could happen.

Senses on full alert, Luke scanned the surroundings for signs of danger. Behind him Isabella breathed jagged gasps of air.

Two men loitered at the entrance to the courtyard, smoking, speaking in low voices. He watched them, braced for trouble, knife in hand, but they did not move. They continued talking and smoking, then one of them gave a raspy laugh and some of the tension seeped out of him. They had no interest in him and his wife.

He scanned their surroundings again. A rat scuttled along the gutter and disappeared down a drain. Other than that, nothing.

"Let's go." Taking Isabella by the arm, he marched her away. Nothing had happened, but the incident had shaken him all the same. Never before had he forgotten himself so completely that he became unaware of his surroundings. And to do so in Spain, source of so many of his nightmares . . .

"Slow down," she said, tugging on his arm.

He glanced down at her.

"Your legs are longer than mine." She was almost running to keep up with him.

He moderated his pace.

"Thank you."

They wound through narrow, dim streets. Luke scanned the shadows and tried to think of something to say. Conversation was required. He couldn't think of a thing.

Isabella was silent, too. She was warm on his arm, their hips bumping from time to time as they walked. The taste of her was still in his mouth, like wildfire in his blood. Her response had been so open . . . The eager seeking, the lithe, slender body molding to his. He'd felt quivers pass through her with every thrust of his tongue.

His body was still afire for her.

They passed some high barred gates and a dog barked. In the light of a lantern hung outside a doorway he caught a glimpse of her face. She seemed deep in thought, a slight frown puckering her brow.

Having second thoughts?

He quickened his pace. She didn't object, but her frown deepened. He didn't care if she was having second thoughts. Her seduction was a foregone conclusion.

"I want a bath," she said when they reached their lodgings. Her face, framed by the silky dark fur of her hood, was flushed. Her mouth, full, moist, and purely edible, was a darker shade of scarlet than the cloak she wore.

They climbed the stairs to their bedchamber. "You don't need a bath." Luke tamped down his impatience. She was putting off the inevitable. It would do her no good. The more she tried to avoid being bedded, the more determined he was to bed her. He had no intention of letting his clumsiness turn her off bed sports.

Besides, she was as aroused as he was by those dancers. He could smell it on her, had tasted it in her kiss. His body thrummed with awareness, expectation.

"I do. I've been riding all day. And I'll be seeing my sister tomorrow."

"If she's there."

"She is. I'm certain of it. And I want to look my best." She wore that stubborn expression; the one he was fast getting used to.

It occurred to Luke that he could use this bath to his advantage. "Very well, if you must," he said and rang the bell to order a bath to be sent up. He sprawled on the bed, sipping a brandy while servants brought in a tin bath, towels, and cans of steaming water to their bedchamber. He'd start by offering to scrub her back, and then . . .

"If you please," Isabella said when the servants had gone. She stood holding the door half open.

"I'm not going anywhere," he told her, swirling his brandy around in the glass.

She folded her arms. "I'm not having a bath while you're here."

Luke sighed. Convent-bred modesty. It would take time to

rid her of it, he supposed. He drained his glass and glanced at his pocket watch. "I'll give you fifteen minutes."

To fill in the time, he strolled back to the marketplace and prowled around it impatiently. Most of the stalls were packed up and gone. All that was left were a few carts and people camped for the night with their animals.

"A gift for your ladylove, my lord?" a cracked old voice came from the shadows.

Luke ignored it. A gift wasn't what he wanted to give Isabella. Besides, she was his wife, not his ladylove.

"A pretty shawl for a pretty lady," the old woman continued, shaking out a folded Spanish shawl. It was beautiful: heavy cream silk, deeply fringed and lavishly embroidered with flowers. Bright, but not garish. Isabella would love it.

"How much?"

She named a sum that was double what it was worth. Luke snorted.

"For your bride on her wedding night," the old crone said, black button eyes gleaming in her walnut wrinkled face. "Her *true* wedding night." As if, somehow, she knew.

Feeling vaguely superstitious, Luke paid for the shawl without haggling. He returned to his lodgings, climbed the stairs, and opened the door quietly, hoping to find his wife still in the bath. His body thrummed with anticipation.

The room was in semidarkness. His nostrils twitched and he frowned. What was that smell? Sweet, but . . . He shuddered. Roses, dammit. He could smell roses. He glanced around the room, his hackles rising. But there was nothing, no sign of—

In a dish on the washstand sat a small cake of soap, the soap Isabella had found at the market. He hadn't thought to check it. He approached it gingerly and sniffed. Rose-scented. Faugh! It was enough to choke a man.

He opened the window and threw the offending soap as far as he could, then washed his hands clean of the stink. He returned to the open window and took several deep breaths of clean air. It was cold, but better fresh air that froze than the warm stink of roses. He left the window open.

He turned to his wife, who'd lain quietly in bed the whole time, not even commenting on him throwing her soap out. His body wasn't quite as aroused as it had been before the soap incident, but that was all to the good. He planned to take things slowly.

"Isabella?" He leaned over her.

She didn't move. Feigning sleep, he decided. It would do her no good.

He unknotted his neckcloth and paused to watch her breathing. A deep, even rhythm. Dammit, it was no act. She'd been yawning the last couple of hours.

First she'd refused him, then she'd fallen asleep on him. Luke could hardly believe it. He wasn't used to female rebuffs; couldn't ever recall receiving one. And no woman had ever fallen asleep on him, not before he'd made love to her.

He stared down at her peaceful, sleeping face, and a spurt of ironic laughter escaped him. Round one to his wife.

He quietly stripped down to his undershirt and drawers. Her hair was spread out over the pillow. He carefully gathered it up, lifted it out of the way, and placed it so he wouldn't lie on it and pinch her. He slipped into bed and lay on his side, facing her.

Damp tendrils clustered around her hairline. He leaned forward to touch his mouth to her pale, velvety nape, and his nostrils twitched. Dammit, she smelled of roses. She stirred and muttered something in her sleep.

He turned his back on her and lay on the far edge of the bed, but still the faint scent of roses reached him. He picked up his shirt, draped it over his face, and tried to sleep.

Twelve

❧

*L*uke tried to resist, to get away from the vile thing, but he was tied hand and foot, trussed like an animal for slaughter, and all he could do was thrash his head and spit defiance.

Arrgh! The blade bit again, searing hot, icy cold. He clenched his teeth against the scream that threatened to burst from him. The smell of blood mingled with the stench of roses.

Roses, always roses, whenever she was here. La Cuchilla. He'd lost track of how long it had been . . .

"Don't struggle, my pretty." Her voice, so warm and caressing. "Give yourself over to the pain. Find the pleasure in it." She leaned over him, frowning in concentration. Her breasts in the low-cut gown were inches from his face.

Exquisite agony with each slow, deliberate slice of her blade, the blade for which she was named: La Cuchilla. "It's art," she told him. "You should thank me. Your friend was not so lucky." She smiled as she sliced into his flesh.

"Michael? What—" He bit down. The intense pain took

him to the edge of fainting, but he would not . . . give in . . . Not . . . give . . . her the satis . . . faction . . .

"Stubborn boy, aren't you, my love?" The husky tones were almost seductive as she carved another slice in his flesh.

"Where's Michael?" he managed to gasp.

"Dead."

Dead? He gave her a wild look and she smiled. "Yes, pretty boy, you failed. Your friend is dead. It was all for nothing . . ." She leaned back and examined his shoulder, then nodded. "I think that will do. This one is good, n'est-ce pas, *René?"*

"Sí, Rosa." A man's voice.

Rosa. La Cuchilla. Luke tried to fix it in his swirling brain. It might be important. If he survived this.

She took a handful of something. Black . . . sand? He squinted at it in the dim light. Some new torture?

She saw him looking. "Salt and ashes, dear boy. Nothing but salt and ashes. It is the final touch. I like to leave my favorites with a little gift, a small memento." She applied a handful of the blackened salt to the open cuts on his chest. "Something to remember me by."

The salt bit into his lacerated flesh, and Luke's scream finally escaped . . .

"*L*uke? Luke, wake up! You're dreaming, Luke." She held him by the shoulders. The scent of roses filled his nostrils. "Bitch!" He shoved her away as hard as he could and—

Woke, gasping to the gray light of dawn. His wife was sprawled backward on the bed where he'd thrown her. He groaned and closed his eyes. Black tentacles of the nightmare still twined through his consciousness, clinging, pulling him down. His heart was thumping, his palms cold and sweaty with fear. He took deep breaths and tried to calm himself.

"Luke?"

He opened his eyes. She knelt at the foot of his bed, watching him anxiously.

"I'm sorry," he croaked. "It was just—"

"A nightmare, I know." And before he knew it, she had her arms around him, murmuring softly that it was all right. And reeking of roses.

"Sorry," he said, and pushed her abruptly away. He shot out of bed.

"What is it?" She got out of bed and followed him.

"No! Don't come near me!"

She stopped dead, her eyes dark with worry. "Why? What's the matter? What have I done?"

He closed his eyes briefly. "Nothing. It's just . . . the smell of roses." He shuddered. "I don't like it." More like can't bear it.

She gave him a puzzled look. "I see. Would you like me to—?" Her eyes widened when she noticed the rose-scented soap gone from the dish. She glanced at the open window. "I see. I'm sorry. I didn't know."

"It doesn't matter."

Her brow wrinkled in concern. "Did you hurt yourself?"

He realized he was rubbing the spot just below his left shoulder and snatched his hand away. "No." Noticing her arms were wrapped around her body, he added, "You're cold. Get back into bed."

"I'm all right," she said quietly. "The question is, are you?"

"Yes, of course, it was just a stupid dream." He spoke brusquely, but he couldn't help himself. He hated having exposed himself to her like that. "Now get back into bed before you freeze."

She straightened the bedclothes and climbed onto the bed. "Are you coming, too?"

"No." He pulled on his breeches and boots. "Go back to sleep. I'm going for a walk." Grabbing the rest of his clothing, he let himself out of the bedchamber.

He stamped his way through the quiet streets, soft and whispering with morning fog. He was embarrassed to have caused such a fuss. How much had she heard? Futile to wish she'd never witnessed it. And now that she had, she'd be asking questions. It was what women did, he thought bitterly.

* * *

When Isabella came down to join him for breakfast later that morning, Luke noticed damp tendrils of hair clinging to her nape and temples.

"I had another bath," she explained. "Our landlady thinks I am mad." She dimpled. "That or she suspects you did something truly strange to me last night. I asked for her plainest soap. Is this all right?" She extended her wrist for him to smell.

He sniffed. Plain soap and scent-of-Isabella. His senses stirred pleasantly. He gave a gruff nod, touched by her simple acceptance of what must appear to be something ridiculous. "Perfect, thank you."

A pot of chocolate and a basket of pastries arrived. Isabella shook out her napkin, picked up a pastry, and said, "Who's Michael?"

"Nobody." A sharp jab of guilt caused him to correct himself. "No, not nobody. He was our friend. He's dead."

"He died in the war?"

"Yes." Luke addressed himself to his breakfast.

For a few minutes they ate and drank in silence. Then, "You said, 'our friend.'"

"We were at school together—Gabe, Harry, Rafe, Michael, and me. And we all went to war together, too." He sipped his coffee, strong, hot, and black, just the way he liked it. "Gabe, Harry, Rafe, and I came back."

"And you were dreaming about Michael's death this morning?"

"It sometimes happens," he said curtly. "I'm sorry to have disturbed you."

She waved his apology away. "I didn't mind. I have nightmares, too, sometimes. They moved me out of the dormitory and into a cell of my own because I kept waking people up."

He remembered her telling him, but discussion of nightmares had already made him uncomfortable enough, and he had no desire to extend the conversation. That business was in the past, where it belonged. He changed the subject. "I hired a carriage."

She looked up in surprise. "To take me to Valle Verde?"

He nodded and finished the last of his ham. "I didn't know

if your sister rides as well as you. Easier if you do find her to take her away in a carriage. It's ordered for half past nine. You said it would take two hours to get there."

Her eyes lit up. "That's a wonderful idea, Luke—thank you. And yes, two hours, more or less. And I've asked the landlady to change all the bedding so there will be no smell in the room if you want to take a nap while I'm at Valle Verde—"

"What do you mean? I'll be there with you."

She frowned and looked perturbed. "No, no, you can't go. I have to go alone."

"You're not going anywhere alone, and certainly not to Valle Verde."

Her eyes narrowed. "Don't you trust me? Do you think I'll run off on you?" Two pink spots appeared in her cheeks.

He shrugged, deliberately provoking her. "For all I know you might make a habit of it."

"Oh, don't be ridiculous." She glared at him, opened her mouth to argue, and glanced around the room at the other diners. "We will discuss this upstairs."

"We won't discuss it at all," he told her. "There's nothing to discuss."

She made a frustrated sound but refused to say another word in public. He could tell from the expressions that flitted across her face that she was marshaling various arguments to convince him.

She had a snowball's chance in hell. But it would be quite entertaining to watch her try.

"You know it's too dangerous for you to go to Valle Verde," she told him the moment they returned to their room and shut the door. "I don't know why you're being so stubborn about it."

The bed had been stripped and the bedclothes removed. Luke sat on a chair by the window, crossed his legs, and leaned back. "Whither thou goest, I will go."

She narrowed her eyes at him. "Ruth was a widow, not a husband. Husbands don't follow wives."

His lips twitched. "What a very short memory you have, my dear."

She flushed. "Be serious. You know I have to go. It's important."

"And I haven't forbidden you to go. But nothing you have told me of your charming cousin Ramón—"

"Second cousin. Twice removed. And he's not charming; he's horrid."

He said flippantly, "Clearly whoever removed him didn't do a very good job. And an improperly removed horrid second cousin is not someone I will allow you to visit alone."

"But I must—"

He made an impatient exclamation and sat up. "You told me your father told you to flee from Ramón; that he was a brute, a bully, and a thug."

"He is. He's a vile beast."

"And you imagine I'd let you visit a vile beast on your own?" Luke snorted.

She wrung her hands. "But if he sees you, Ramón will want to kill you."

He sat back and returned to flippancy. "Doesn't like visitors, eh? Too bad. I'm going."

"You don't understand. Ramón will do anything to get his hands on my fortune. He'll kill you to make me a widow."

"Will he now?" Her anxiety on Luke's behalf was quite touching.

"Yes! And then he will force me to marry him!"

He raised a lazy brow. "Really? He could do that? I'm impressed. I've been able to force you to do very little. You're quite remarkably stubborn."

She stamped her foot. "Oh, will you be serious? You cannot come to Valle Verde with me. I utterly forbid it."

He smiled. "You forbid it?"

"I do. Because if you go to Valle Verde, he'll kill you."

Luke yawned. "He is welcome to try."

*I*sabella glowered at Luke from the seat opposite. She'd been jumpy and nervous and bad-tempered the whole way. She peered out of the window of the carriage for the hundredth time and said, "We're almost there. Just over the next hill."

Luke nodded.

"It's not too late to change your mind," she told him.

"I know." They'd been over this a hundred times, too. He wasn't letting her go to Valle Verde without him, and that was that. He had no intention of arguing.

"You're a very stubborn man, you know," she said crossly.

He gave a faint smile.

They passed the last mile in silence.

"The gates need painting," Isabella observed as the carriage drove through the entrance to the Valle Verde estate. "And the stonework needs repair."

Luke leaned back against the comfortable squabs and watched her. Dressed in her new cream and blue dress and wearing that impudent corset that pushed her breasts up, she looked so delicious that it had been all he could do not to while away the journey by making love to her. But she was nervous and jumpy, and so cross with him for what she called risking himself unnecessarily, she was in no mood to be seduced.

Though Luke had always enjoyed a challenge.

But right now he was interested in her reactions to Valle Verde. Her eyes were everywhere, comparing, assessing, looking for signs of mismanagement.

The carriage jolted from pothole to pothole, and her mouth tightened. "The driveway was always smooth as silk."

But as they drove deeper into the estate, it became clear the neglect wasn't universal. The vines were well pruned, their rows neat and weed-free. Horses looked at them curiously over sturdy, unpainted fences. Nice-looking animals, too, Luke observed. Sleek and glossy.

"Ramón's built up the herd," Isabella conceded. "There look to be almost as many as before the war."

Luke's mouth twitched at her reluctant admission. "He probably stole them," he said in a comforting tone. She blinked in surprise then, realizing he was teasing her, she gave him a haughty look. Her dimple gave her away.

They passed a freshly plowed field where a dozen men

and women worked, preparing the field for planting. The strange carriage had caught their attention, and they'd stopped work to watch it go by. Clearly not many visitors came to Valle Verde.

"Oh, oh!" Isabella leaned out of the window and waved. "I know these people."

One of the field-workers gave a shout, dropped his hoe, and, with a wide grin, ran toward the carriage, waving. The other laborers downed their tools and followed, hurrying to welcome Isabella home.

Luke rapped on the roof to tell the driver to stop the carriage. He opened the door and swung Isabella down. In minutes she was surrounded.

"Little Master, you're back—"

"Welcome home, Little Master! Welcome home!"

Little Master? What was that all about, Luke wondered.

"Señorita Isabella, we never thought to see you again—"

Isabella greeted them each by name, smiling, weeping, shaking their hands, and embracing some.

"It has been too long since you came among us, Little Master," an old man said, tears in his eyes. "The true blood of Valle Verde."

"Oh, Madonna, how like your mother you have grown, little one," a motherly looking woman exclaimed.

Another woman nodded, wiping away tears with a blue rag. "The image of our dear *condesa*, the very image of her."

Isabella did not look too thrilled to hear of the resemblance, Luke observed, but she asked after each person eagerly, inquiring about their families and exclaiming over the news. She'd told him there was nothing for her at Valle Verde anymore, but she was loved by these people, he saw. And she loved them.

And he was taking her to England, where she'd be regarded as a foreigner and an outsider.

Finally, when all the personal inquiries were done, and she'd introduced him as her husband, and he'd been cautiously approved—he at least spoke Spanish like a Spaniard, even if the accent was a southern one—the talk turned to Ramón.

"He is not a gentleman, like your father, but he works hard," one man said.

"He might not be a *conde* by blood, but—"

"He's not a gentleman at all," a woman interrupted, and there was a general murmur of agreement. Beneath it, Luke thought, there was also some level of approval. Interesting. The old order was changing.

"He's a sinner and will burn in hell," another woman muttered. "Taking that girl to his bed and no talk of a wedding."

Isabella shot a glance at Luke. Her sister?

"The *conde* needs to marry money, you know that. The estate needs it." Several people glanced meaningfully at Isabella. Luke wondered if she'd noticed. Clearly Ramón wasn't the only person who thought she should have married her second cousin. Twice removed.

"No excuse for him to live in sin, though, is it?" the first woman said fiercely. She shook her head. "He's a godless man."

"As to that, the old *conde* was hardly a pillar of the Church—" The man broke off and glanced at Isabella in embarrassment. "My apologies, Little Master," he said. "I meant no insult."

She shook her head. "None taken, Elí. I know what my father thought of the Church. But now, we must hurry along, or the new Conde de Castillejo will be wondering who the people are who keep his workers from the fields."

She made her farewells and returned to the carriage, and they continued their jolting path down the potholed driveway.

Isabella sat silently, her thoughts far away, her brow furrowed.

"Little *Master*?" Luke said after a while.

She gave a rueful half smile. "A pet name."

"I guessed that much." Luke waited for the rest.

She hesitated, then explained. "My father always wanted a boy. When it became apparent that my mother would never give him one, he started to treat me as the heir. He took me out among the people with him and taught me about the running of the estate and . . . oh, and all manner of things that a boy should know." She stared out of the window a moment. "And after Mama died, he even dressed me as a boy, and that's when the people started calling me Little Master, just for fun, you understand."

He understood more than she realized, and not only her attachment to her breeches, but all he said was, "Those people love you."

She nodded. "I'd forgotten what it was like to belong." She stared out of the window, her eyes shimmering with unshed tears and added in a husky voice, "And I'd forgotten how beautiful Valle Verde is."

A large, square stone house came into view. Nine graceful stone archways flanked the front entrance, with five more along the balcony of the upper story. Poplars lined the driveway leading up to it, and an ornamental pond lay to one side.

"It's a beautiful house," Luke said.

"My family built this in the sixteenth century," Isabella told him, pride evident in her voice. "It was called El Nuevo Castillo for about three hundred years, but in my great-grandfather's day he announced that everyone must call it El Castillo de Castillejo." She said nothing more, but the lurking dimple told Luke the story wasn't over.

"And so now people call it . . . ?" he prompted.

"El Nuevo Castillo." She laughed. "People are slow to accept change in this part of the country."

"They seem to accept Ramón, all right," he pointed out gently.

Her smile faded. "They have no choice. He inherited the title and the estate. No matter that he is a vile bully and a thug, he is still the Conde de Castillejo."

Luke said nothing. The people they'd just been talking to might not love Ramón the way they loved Isabella, or respect him as they did her late parents, but neither did they give the impression they thought him a vile bully or a thug.

The carriage drew to a halt in front of the graceful line of archways. Isabella wiped damp palms on a handkerchief. "Do you have your pistol?"

"He's not going to shoot me out of hand," Luke assured her.

"You don't know that." She picked up her cloak, which she'd already folded in a bundle, and clasped it to her chest.

"I'll take that." He took the bundle from her arms, felt between the folds, and removed the pistol he knew would be there.

"But—" she began.

"You will not call on the sister whom you haven't seen for eight years with a pistol in your hand."

"But what if Ramón—"

"Leave Ramón to me." He handed her the cloak and returned the pistol to the concealed hollow in the armrest.

Servants ran out and put down the steps to the carriage. Luke descended first then turned to hand Isabella down. She descended the steps like a young matador entering the ring.

As she stepped into the sunlight there was a gasp from the waiting servants. It was a repeat of the earlier scene, with tears and exclamations of "Little Master!" and "Señorita Isabella!" She greeted them by name, hugging some, having her hands kissed by others.

"Where is Marta?" she asked, looking around for her old nurse.

"Marta has not lived here for years, *señorita*."

"And her daughter, Carmen?"

"Married a man in the next valley. Marta lives with them."

As Isabella caught up with all the news, it became clear that many of the beloved old house servants she remembered no longer worked at Valle Verde. She gave Luke a significant look. *Ramón.*

And then a sudden hush as the servants fell silent and drew back as a tall, grave young woman glided into the entrance.

No need for introductions; it was obvious who this was, even though there was not much of a resemblance between the sisters. Half sisters.

Perlita was tall and stunningly pretty, with red gold hair

smoothed back in an elegant chignon and gray green eyes fringed with long, sooty lashes.

Luke stepped back. Isabella's big moment; the reason they'd come here. He waited for the joyous reunion.

Nobody moved.

There was a long silence as the two young women eyed each other. No long-lost reunion here. Luke was reminded of two cats circling each other, hostile and wary, each one waiting for the other to pounce first—only these two didn't move. What on earth was going on?

The people of the estate edged closer, craning to see, to hear. They would have known about these two girls from the day each was born. The daughter of the mistress, now in charge of the house. The daughter of the house, now a visitor.

Perlita snapped her fingers and issued rapid orders for the carriage to be taken around the back and the horses seen to. All but the house servants melted away. Perlita was very much at home here, Luke saw; very much mistress of the house. Isabella had said her sister was nineteen, but only in years was this girl younger than Isabella. She seemed altogether more experienced, more sophisticated, and it wasn't simply her clothing.

And she did not have the manner of a helpless innocent needing to be rescued.

*P*erlita had Papa's eyes. Bella stared at her half sister, close-up for the first time in her life. Not just Papa's eyes, but his long lashes, and there was also something in the way she held her head that reminded her of Papa, too. It was an almost physical pain, seeing the resemblance. Why should she have Papa's eyes and not—

No. Bella pulled herself up. She would not think such thoughts. She was here to help her half sister, not wallow in old resentments. Perlita's looks were not her fault. Besides, having Papa's eyes only proved their relationship.

But oh, did she have to be so very beautiful? Bella could see the way Luke was looking at her. Perlita was dressed in a sophisticated green dress that exactly matched her eyes. The dress was fashionable, cut low and tight to display a lush bosom, a tiny waist, and an hourglass figure. She wore no jewelry; she didn't need to. Like her mother, she was beautiful.

Beside her Bella felt small and plain and ill-dressed. She thrust the thought aside and drew herself up. Looks didn't matter, she told herself. Character was what counted.

Hollow comfort.

Still, she wished her sister wasn't quite so beautiful. It was almost intimidating, especially with Papa's eyes staring at her with barely concealed hostility.

Nonsense, she was the elder sister, and the legitimate one, and she had every right to visit her childhood home. "How do you do, Perlita." She inclined her head stiffly.

"Sen— Isabella," Perlita responded and gave an equally stiff nod. She didn't move.

Now what? Bella wondered. She could hardly push Perlita aside and shove her way into the house.

Luke gave a soft cough and stepped forward. "And I am Isabella's husband, Lord Ripton." He bowed.

"Her *husband*?" Perlita blinked and glanced from Bella to Luke and back again. The relief in her face was obvious. She had not known Isabella was married.

"Yes, her husband. You may call me Luke, since in law, we are now brother and sister."

"Brother and sister?" Perlita echoed blankly.

"Something like that," Luke said in an easy manner that Bella envied. "Isabella and I are on our way to England, but she'd heard you were at Valle Verde and wanted to call in, to see how you were." He made it sound so casual, a mere whim. Bella was grateful.

"How I am?" Perlita gave Bella a shocked glance. "You came to see *me*?"

"Is that so strange?" Bella removed her hat and gloves and tugged her dress to straighten it.

Perlita didn't beat about the bush. "I think so, yes, seeing we've never even spoken to each other before this day."

Bella felt rather than saw Luke's reaction. She could al-

most hear him thinking aloud, *Never spoken to each other?
You dragged me halfway across the country to save a sister
you'd never even spoken to?*

Her cheeks heated. She avoided his gaze and managed to
say with an air of assurance, "Yes, but I decided it was time
we met."

Perlita's brows rose. "Why?"

Isabella glanced at the servants, avidly watching and listening, and said nothing. Perlita gave a tiny shrug, as if to
say, why not, and invited them inside.

Bella stepped inside, and memories swamped her. Nothing had changed. The arrangement of the furniture, the smell,
the cool stillness, it was all the same. Even the wall hangings
were the same ones that had always hung there, though a
little more faded. The tiled terra-cotta floors were as highly
polished as ever. Her feet itched to walk the worn patterns of
the tiles as she had a thousand times as a child; along the line
of red flowers, then onto the blue medallions, avoiding the
yellow and brown ones that looked like a lion. They didn't
really, but she'd always pretended . . .

She hadn't thought of those tiles in years, but now . . . It
was like being greeted by an old playmate. The footsteps of
her childhood.

She forced herself back into the present. The house looked
immaculate.

"Welcome to El Nuevo Castillo," Perlita said coolly.

It felt very odd to be welcomed as a stranger to her own
home.

But it wasn't her home, Bella reminded herself.

After allowing them to refresh themselves after their long
journey, Perlita led them toward the large drawing room.
Bella hesitated on the threshold. Papa's favorite room.

As if he knew how she felt, Luke slipped his hand under
her elbow. Warmed by the contact, she stepped in. It was
unchanged, too. It had always been old-fashioned—Mama
had wanted to change it but Papa always refused. It was a
man's room, with heavy varnished woodwork, studded with
silver nails, and leather-covered chairs. Even the old dueling

swords that had been in the family for generations remained crossed and mounted over the mantel, gleaming as brightly as they had throughout her childhood.

The room held a thousand memories. Even the smell was the same.

It was as if Papa had just stepped out. Bella's throat filled as the emotions she'd tried to hold back finally swamped her. Eight years since she'd been in this room. She thought she'd almost forgotten it, but now, being here . . . Her tongue thickened. She couldn't speak.

Perlita invited them to sit and ordered refreshments. In minutes tea was brought in along with a plate of small, iced cakes. It was a well run home, Bella conceded as Perlita poured.

Part of her hoped that Perlita was really only the housekeeper, here, but no . . . not in that dress.

"How is your mother?" Bella inquired politely, steadier after a few sips of hot tea.

"Married and living in Barcelona," Perlita said. She waited until the servants had gone and said bluntly, "Why have you come here?"

"Because I was worried about you."

"Worried?" Perlita arched her slender brows. "About me?" She gave a snort of disbelief.

"It's true." Bella set her cup aside and took the plunge. "I had heard you were . . . living with Ramón. I was concerned."

"You have no need. Ramón is good to me." Her eyes narrowed. "And why is it any of your business what I do, anyway?"

It was very hard, having Papa's eyes glittering at her with hostility and suspicion, but the very fact they were Papa's eyes gave Bella heart. "Perlita, I know we don't know each other, that we've never spoken, or even met, but I've known about you since I was a little girl, and you've probably always known about me. I've lost everyone and—" She broke off. "You're my sister and I've come here to meet you. And to see that you are all right."

There was a long silence. Perlita stared, her face pale as marble and, despite the fire, looking just as cold. Then her mouth quivered. "I n-never thought I'd ever hear you say that."

"I always wanted a sister," Isabella said softly. "I was so lonely as a child."

Perlita pressed her lips together and shook her head. "You hated me. You used to watch our house from up on the hill, spying on us."

"I know," Isabella admitted. "I was jealous of you."

Perlita's jaw dropped. "Jealous of me? But you were the daughter."

"So were you," Isabella said. "And you were the daughter he loved."

Perlita shook her head. "He never once called me his daughter. I was always his little pearl or his pretty one, or simply Perlita, but never, *never* did he call me—or even refer to me— as his daughter. Not once."

Isabella blinked, puzzled. "But he loved you."

"He was fond of me, a little." Perlita shrugged. "But you were the one he truly valued."

Isabella's jaw dropped. "Valued? Papa never valued me. I was never good enough. Nothing I did was ever good enough."

The two girls stared at each other, struggling to come to terms with the very different view each had of their shared past. Beside Isabella, Luke sat quietly, absorbing the implications of what each was saying. He was no stranger to the tangle of family connections and misapprehensions.

A clock on the mantel chimed, and Perlita started and glanced at the time. "Ramón will be here any minute." She jumped to her feet, looking worried and indecisive. Isabella jumped up looking ready for a fight.

Luke poured himself another cup of tea. He felt cool and distant, as he did each time Fate ushered in danger.

Heavy steps sounded on the tiled terra-cotta floor outside. "I— I'll speak to him," Perlita said and ran out of the room.

They heard voices, low at first and then raised in argument.

"Sit down," Luke told Isabella who was pacing nervously. "Finish your tea. Have a little cake. They're delicious."

She turned on him. "How can you think of food at a time like this?"

"Do you want Ramón to know you're frightened of him?"

She gave him a startled look, then plunked down on the settee beside him. "I'm not in the least bit frightened of him," she declared and plastered a haughty, unnaturally calm expression on her face.

Thirteen

❧

The door crashed open. Ramón strode into the room. Perlita followed, hovering anxiously.

Ramón wasn't particularly tall, but he was built like a bull, with broad shoulders and a deep barrel chest. Dark, with a swarthy complexion, his face was dominated by a large nose and a thick, black mustache. He barely even glanced at Isabella. With his gaze fixed on Luke, Ramón swaggered up to him, planted his feet apart, and said, "So, you walk right into my parlor, Englishman? Are you a fool, then?"

Luke politely rose to his feet saying pleasantly in English, "And a Fee Fi Fo Fum to you, too, sir."

Behind him he heard Isabella choke.

Luke continued in Spanish. "El Conde de Castillejo, I presume? I am Ripton, Isabella's husband. How do you do?" He extended his hand.

"Husband? Not for long." Ramón made no move to shake Luke's hand.

Luke shrugged, sat down again, and bit into another cake. "These are remarkably good," he commented.

As Luke had intended, Ramón seemed nonplussed by such behavior. After a minute of glowering and some more huffing and puffing, he boomed, "You stole my treasure."

Luke took no notice.

Ramón's face grew red.

Isabella knotted her fingers anxiously.

Luke finished the cake and dusted the crumbs from his fingers. Then he glanced up and said innocently, "Oh, sorry, were you talking to me? No, I didn't steal anything." Red rag to the bull.

Ramón gave a low growl. "I meant Isabella!"

"Stop it, Luke. Don't provoke him," Isabella whispered.

Luke smiled. Isabella opened her mouth to argue, but Luke silenced her with a look.

"Well?" Ramón said in a belligerent voice.

"Yes, my wife is indeed a treasure." Luke wiped his fingers with a napkin and added in a cool, silky tone, "But she's not yours, never was, and never will be."

Ramón snorted. "You're a fool."

Luke raised a single brow. "Am I?"

"To come with your rich young wife to the lair of the wolf alone and unprotected? You must be a fool."

Isabella couldn't restrain herself any longer. She jumped up. "Stop it! Don't you dare threaten us!"

Ramón sneered and gestured to the dueling swords. "On my land I do whatever I want, little cousin. And if I want to make you a widow, I will."

"Oh, you want to fight like a gentleman, do you?" Luke drawled. "In that case . . ." The ice was beginning to sing in his veins, as it always did at the prospect of a fight.

"Luke, he's not a gentleman," Isabella said in a low, vehement tone. "He won't follow any gentlemen's rules. He has no rules but Ramón's."

"Exactly, little cousin." Ramón sneered. "Ramón's land, Ramón's rules."

"No!" She tried to get between them.

Luke gripped her firmly by the arms and moved her behind him. "Sit there and stay out of the way," he ordered. "This is men's business."

She whitened but, amazingly, obeyed.

The ice well and truly singing in his veins now, Luke strolled to the fireplace and plucked one of the crossed swords from above the mantel. "Actually she's only your second cousin, and twice removed, I believe. I intend to remove her even further, so if you have a burning desire to kill me, you are welcome to try." He flexed the long blade experimentally.

Behind him Isabella made a small distressed sound. The timbre of it disturbed Luke. He glanced at her.

His little fire-eater sat frozen where he'd put her, watching Ramón, small and still as a mouse mesmerized by a snake. Her face was pale and pinched, her golden eyes dark and filled with . . .

Luke frowned. He'd never seen her looking like that before. He didn't like it. He glanced back at Ramón, who was glowering and clenching and unclenching his fists. How could she be frightened of such a fellow? Brute force, he supposed.

He lightly drew his finger along the edge of the blade. Sharp as a razor. He tested the sword for balance, then swished the blade through the air.

And from the corner of his eye he saw Isabella flinch. She gave Luke a stricken look, bit down hard on her lower lip, clenched her hands into small fists, and resolutely looked away. With a shock he realized he was the one who'd put that look in her eyes.

She was frightened for him.

He froze. For the last seven years he'd embraced any opportunity for a fight, sought out danger, gloried in living on the edge. It was the only thing that calmed, for a brief time, the restlessness, the emptiness that gnawed at him.

But the look in Isabella's eyes . . .

The singing ice in his veins faded. What the hell was he doing?

Ramón grabbed the other sword and shifted into a fighting stance. "Prepare to die, Englishman."

Isabella rose to her feet and stamped her foot. "I won't be fought over!" But her voice was high and tremulous, and the desperate sound of it pierced Luke.

He dragged his gaze from his wife's stricken profile. Time to use his brains, stop playing this stupid game—and it was a game. But not to her. And no longer to him. He had a wife now.

He flexed the blade and said to Ramón, "You are still welcome to try. I am curious, though. How do you imagine my death would benefit you?"

Ramón laughed. "Are you stupid, Englishman? I would marry Isabella, of course. She is certainly worth fighting over."

Perlita gave a distressed little moan, and Ramón's gaze snapped toward her. "It will make no difference to us, Perla."

Perlita hid her face from him and made no response. His brows locked briefly, then he turned back to Luke and his gaze hardened. "Well, Englishman?"

"Anytime you want. I didn't realize it was Isabella herself you wanted."

"What?"

"I thought it was her fortune."

Ramón frowned. "I want both, of course. The two go together."

"Ah, no." Luke made a practice pass. The thin, deadly blade sliced the air. "There you are mistaken."

"Mistaken?"

"Yes. Isabella comes separate from her fortune." He pretended to parry. "And when I am dead she will be penniless."

"Penniless?" exclaimed Ramón. His thick brows knotted in suspicion.

"Penniless?" Bella echoed in shock. She stared at Luke. It couldn't be true.

Luke met her gaze ruefully. "Penniless," he confirmed.

"That cannot be," Ramón said. "Her mother left her a great—"

"Fortune, yes, but it all came to me when we married. There were no settlements, you see. It was a marriage made in haste." He glanced at Ramón. "Your fault, that. Ironic, is it not?" He touched the point of the sword. "Naturally I made a will straightaway. Everything, every penny I own, goes to the support of my mother and younger sister."

"Is this true?" Bella stared at Luke with her mouth open.

"On my honor as a gentleman." He met her gaze ruefully, and she saw it was true.

"But what of Isabella?" Ramón demanded.

"Yes, what of me?" Bella repeated.

"You will live with my mother and sister, of course. They will take good care of you."

Bella could hardly believe her ears. But the look in his face . . . and the oath he'd sworn. He wouldn't make that lightly.

Live with his mother and sister? Be dependent on two strange Englishwomen? She didn't want to be dependent on anyone. It was her fortune, left to her by her mother. It should come back to her.

No wonder he wasn't worried about coming here . . .

Ramón was incredulous. "Isabella will have nothing of her own? *Nothing?* I don't believe it."

Perlita said, "It's true, Ramón. Look at her face."

Ramón looked, then turned to Luke. "That's monstrous! No provision for your widow?"

"I am English," Luke said carelessly. "We do things differently. A rich widow is a target for unprincipled men." He gave a cold, two-edged smile to Ramón. "But Isabella is a treasure in herself, and no right-minded man would need a bribe to marry her." He blew Bella a kiss and raised the sword. "So, if you still want to fight for her . . ."

Bella blinked. Blowing her a kiss? His eyes were dancing. He was enjoying this!

With a sudden flash of insight, she realized that her husband wasn't going to fight at all, that for all his talk and action, he had no intention of fighting Ramón. That it was all a bluff!

"Nobody will fight for me!" Bella declared, suddenly angry. Neither man even glanced at her. She didn't know which was worse, the amused expression on her husband's face or the look of determined greed on Ramón's. She knew who she wanted to hit, though, and it wasn't Ramón.

Ramón glowered. He turned to Isabella. "Did you not negotiate the marriage settlements?"

Isabella flung him a scornful look. Of course she had not negotiated settlements. She was thirteen and fleeing from her violent pig of a cousin. To Luke she said, "So, you would leave me entirely to your mother's mercy?"

"Why not? My mother is very nice," he assured her.

She narrowed her eyes at him. Luke smiled, confirming everything she'd thought.

She bared her teeth at him in what was not exactly a smile. Oh, she would make him pay for this.

Ramón exploded. "You stupid bitch! Marrying an Englishman without thought or preparation. Dazzled by his pretty face!" He smashed his big meaty fist against the wall, making them all jump. "The money belongs here, here at Valle Verde! And now it's lost, lost to you and lost to Valle Verde."

"And lost to you, which is some compensation, at least," Isabella said.

Ramón clenched his fists. "You should have married me! This is what comes of running from your family—you marry a stranger, an Englishman!" He spat.

"Still better than marrying you!" Isabella flashed.

"You brainless little slut, he's not going to look after you. Don't you understand? When he dies you'll be penniless, no better than a beggar, dependent on the charity of strangers—"

"I'd rather be penniless than married to a pig like—"

Ramón raised his hand.

And found a sword at his throat. He froze.

"Lay one finger on my wife and you're a dead man," Luke said softly.

Ramón clenched his fists.

"I meant every word," Luke said. A trickle of blood appeared at Ramón's throat.

"Please, Ramón," Perlita begged.

He glanced at her, and the tension in his big, bull-like

body lessened slightly. "I will not touch her," he growled, and Luke lowered the sword.

Perlita flew across the room and pressed a handkerchief to the cut on his neck. He brushed her off and turned to Luke. "I do not like being threatened in my own home, Englishman."

"I do not like my wife being insulted, Spaniard," Luke returned coolly.

The two men glared narrow-eyed at each other for a long, tense moment, then Ramón shrugged. "We shall eat dinner," he announced, as if nothing had happened. "Perlita?"

"It-it's ready," she said, her voice shaking. She rang a little silver bell.

Her mother's bell, Bella noted distantly. Now she was really confused.

That blood was real. Luke would have killed her cousin if he'd made a move toward her. She'd thought it was all bluff until then, but he really had been prepared to fight for her. She should be deeply flattered. And part of her was.

But mostly she just wanted to throttle him. She'd never been so frightened in her life.

"Do you want to wash before we eat?" Perlita asked. She meant relieve her bladder. She'd been frightened, too.

"Why not?" Bella said. She was full of pent-up energy.

Perlita hesitated, her gaze drawn to the two men. Ramón stood, arms folded, feet planted wide apart, his back to the room, staring out of the window at his estate. Luke had replaced the sword and resumed his seat, one leg crossed casually over the other, and was inspecting his nails.

The sight made Bella want to hit him even more.

"Do you think they should be left alone?" Perlita asked in a low voice.

"Yes!" Bella snapped. "With any luck they will murder each other and save us the trouble."

Perlita gasped in horror. "But—"

"Oh, don't worry," Bella told her. "They won't fight. They have no reason to now. Ramón only wanted me for the money."

Perlita considered that and nodded. "Yes, of course."

Of course, Bella thought as she followed her out. With a beautiful mistress like Perlita, who would even see Bella? Not that she wanted Ramón.

Besides, furious as she was with Luke for risking himself, a tiny sliver of foolish feminine flattery kept edging in. He'd offered to fight for her. It made her melt inside, and that was confusing, too.

Never had she dreamed . . . Never would the other girls in the convent believe it: two men, fighting over Bella Ripton.

Over her fortune, she reminded herself as she washed her face. Her nonexistent fortune.

Luke was simply saving himself from being murdered for it. And if he'd explained that in the beginning, it would have saved them all a lot of trouble. And worry.

She scrubbed crossly at her already clean hands. Men! They just lived to fight.

His carelessly uttered words kept humming in her breast. *Isabella is a treasure in herself.* Even if he did not mean it, even if it was just to tease Ramón . . .

She tidied her hair and adjusted the neckline of her dress. She glanced at her sister in the looking glass. Perlita's figure was superb, her breasts lush and abundant.

Bella was very glad she'd bought the corset, even if it was a little tight. At least she didn't look like a boy.

She didn't feel like a sister, either. She supposed that would come in time, though she wasn't very hopeful. All those years in the convent when she'd thought about Perlita and worried about her, she hadn't imagined anyone like this cool, young beauty who treated her with suspicion and thinly veiled hostility.

All Perlita's earlier fright had apparently vanished. Her face, as she examined herself in the looking glass, was perfect and serene.

"You're amazingly calm," Bella commented. "Does Ramón do this often? Challenge people to fight, I mean?" Threaten to make them widows. Oh, he was despicable, her cousin.

Perlita flickered a sidelong glance. "I will not discuss Ramón with you."

"But—"

"He is good to me."

"If he was good to you, he would marry you." Not try to steal other people's wives.

Perlita gave her a hard look. "You forget who you are speaking to."

Bella touched her sister on the arm. "Just because my father—*our* father—kept your mother as a mistress does not mean it was right."

"My mother had no complaints." Perlita shook off her hand. "In any case, that was then, this is now, and Ramón and I, we are not your business." She dampened her fingertip and smoothed the perfect arch of one eyebrow.

"You are my business," Bella said quietly. "You are my sister. I have no other family, just you and my aunt who is in the convent."

"And Ramón." Perlita smoothed the other brow.

"Ramón is *not* my family," Bella snapped.

Perlita raised her perfectly groomed brows. "So vehement." She peered critically at her reflection in the glass. "Why did you come here? Really."

"I told you. I came to help you, Perlita."

In the looking glass, her half sister gave her a skeptical glance. "I do not believe you." She gave her reflection one last scrutiny. "Besides, I do not need your help. Come, Ramón is hungry and he does not like to be kept waiting." She held the door for Isabella.

Luke and Ramón waited in the hallway: Prince Charming and the Beast.

Perlita took Ramón's arm and entered the dining room ahead of them.

Luke presented his arm to Isabella in a cautious manner, as if she were a wild beast who might bite him. His eyes were dancing.

She longed to box his ears. She gave him a severe look and took his arm. "Yes, I'm cross, and do not look at me like that. My cousin isn't a man you trifle with! You could have been killed!"

His mouth curved slightly. "No need to fuss. Cousin Twice-Removed doesn't bother me."

"Fuss?" She hit his arm. "Are you blind? He's huge!"

"I'm not exactly insubstantial, myself," he pointed out, six feet of lean, hard-muscled man.

"Yes, but he's built like a bull and you're . . . you're . . ." She frowned, trying to think of the right comparison.

"A lion?" he offered. "A stallion? A stag?"

She gave what she hoped was a withering look. "No, a rat."

They entered the dining room, and Isabella almost bit back a cry. The room was so bare. Just a large, plain table and chairs, none of them matching. Where was the ornately carved dining furniture, handed down in her family for generations, and the matching sideboards?

There were dark patches on the walls. Missing paintings. Her father's pride and joy, the Velázquez, gone. And the El Greco, and her mother's favorite by Luis de Morales.

Luke held a chair for Bella to be seated. "Where are all the paintings?" she asked Ramón. "And the furniture?"

Ramón snorted. "Sold." He eyed Luke sourly, then seated Perlita. Borrowed manners, thought Bella.

"Sold? But—"

"Where do you think I get the money for this?" He waved his hand as servants brought in the various dishes for the large midday meal. "How do you think I pay my workers? Do you think an estate can run on air?" He snorted again. "No, but it can run on art."

"But those paintings have been in the family for generations."

Ramón gave Isabella a hard look. "Your father, the fine gentleman, ran this estate into the ground with his politics and his private army. And the fine gentleman's fine daughter ran off with an Englishman, taking her fortune with her. So it is left to the ruffian, Ramón, to do what he can to repair the mess, to rebuild Valle Verde into the prosperous place it should be." He fell on his dinner, shoveling in his food rapidly and without finesse.

Isabella ate her meal in silence. There was much to digest here.

After dinner, Ramón pushed back his plate and said with satisfaction, "Time for siesta." He gave Perlita a heated look.

Faint color rose to her cheeks, and she turned to Bella. "I presume you will stay for siesta."

"Yes, of course, thank you, and would you mind if we stayed the night, as well?" Bella said quickly. She pretended not to notice Luke's swift sidelong glance.

Perlita glanced at Ramón, who gave an indifferent shrug.

It wasn't the most gracious of invitations, but Bella accepted it gratefully. "I don't suppose we could use my mother's old bedchamber?"

"Of course," Perlita answered. "Ramón—" She corrected herself with a hint of defiance. "*We* sleep in the *conde*'s rooms, as is right." Confirming to her sister, in case there was any doubt, that she was more than a housekeeper to Ramón. "Follow me."

Bella knew the way by heart to her mother's suite of rooms at the opposite end of the house, but Perlita insisted on escorting them. Politeness? Or underlining whose house it was now? Bella wasn't sure.

As Perlita opened the bedchamber door, Bella's gaze darted ahead of her. A rush of relief swiftly followed. The carved dressing table with the oval looking glass was there. All the furniture was still in place: the high four-poster bed; the heavy, tall wardrobes that she once hid in as a child.

"Your mother's rooms are untouched since you left," Perlita said, noticing the direction of her gaze. "Servants go in only to clean."

"Thank you." Bella was touched that they'd preserved her mother's memory. And relieved that no one went in there.

Perlita corrected her assumption in a cool voice. "When Ramón marries, his wife will have these rooms. Until then, nobody will bother to use them. Except now, of course." She left, gliding to where the bull-like master of the house waited for her.

"A levelheaded young lady," Luke said when they were alone. "Must take quite a bit of courage to live openly with Ramón. She'll have no other society: no respectable woman would have anything to do with her."

Bella shuddered. "I don't know how she can bear him. Still, she seems to be able to handle him, like leading a bull by the nose."

Luke snorted. "It's not his nose she's leading him by." He removed his coat. "But she seems to accept her position well enough."

"She might. I don't," Bella said. "She's far too good for him." It felt strange to be in this room again, so long after she'd left her home. Even longer since Mama had died. Papa had made no move to preserve it in any way; he just hadn't bothered with it, and it seems Ramón was the same. It was clean, and there were no signs of dust, but still, it felt . . . deserted.

"How do you know? You know him as little as you do her. Which I have to say was a surprise to me. You'd never even *talked* to her?"

Bella tossed her head. "She's still my sister. Almost my only relative. And it doesn't matter that I'd never met her. It's my fault she's in this situation." She examined the ornate dressing table. It seemed untouched. She opened the small drawer at the side and slid her fingers in to release the lever she knew was there. It was trickier now. Her fingers had grown since she was a child.

"Your fault? How so?"

Bella froze. She hadn't meant to say that. She'd been concentrating on opening the secret drawer and the admission had just slipped out. She closed her eyes briefly. She'd have to tell him. He'd just risked his life for her, and she owed him the truth.

And if he despised her afterward, well, it was only what she deserved.

"I lied to you before." She took a deep breath and turned to face him. "It wasn't fear that made me leave Perlita and her mother behind. It was . . . it was jealousy."

He leaned against one of the carved bedposts, folded his arms, and waited for her to explain.

She nibbled nervously on her lower lip. "I . . . I hated her for stealing my father's love. So I left her . . . to her fate." She swallowed and finished, "And then when I escaped Ramón, he took Perlita for revenge."

There was a long silence. She was very aware of his eyes resting steadily on her, but she was afraid to meet his gaze, afraid of what she might see there.

He straightened, stretched his arms reflexively, and said in a mild tone, "You don't know it was for revenge."

Bella was slightly stunned by his matter-of-fact acceptance of her dreadful admission, but she wasn't going to argue. "Well, of course he desires her—she's beautiful—but he doesn't *care* about her. He can't." She spread her arms to indicate the faded suite of rooms. "You heard what she said, that these rooms were being kept for his wife—and she didn't mean herself. Who knows what will become of her when that happens? He'll either turn her out—and it's not as if he has any money to give her; he's sold most things of value—or he'll set her up in that little house in the next valley, the house where she was born. She'll live her mother's life all over again, Luke." She gave him a despairing look. "She's my half sister, she's only nineteen, and she's ruined. And it's my fault."

Luke said briskly, "Well, in that case we'll have to help her." He sounded so certain, she felt a little better. Her husband was a man who could get things done; she was beginning to realize that. He hadn't let her down once. Perhaps he had some brilliant plan to save her sister.

"How?"

He pulled off his boots.

She frowned. Was that it? His brilliant plan was to take off his boots? "What are you doing?"

"I didn't mean this very instant." He removed his waistcoat and hung it on the back of a chair. "We can't help her now. It's siesta."

She narrowed her eyes at him. "I thought you didn't like siestas."

He tossed his neckcloth over the chair and pulled his shirt off over his head. "Depends what else there is on offer."

She stiffened. "What do you imagine is on offer?" If he thought this was the time to seduce her, in the middle of the day, in her own mother's bed . . .

"I imagine the choice is between another delightful chat with the master of the house—and he'll be none too pleased to have his own plans for the siesta interrupted—or a nap. You did see the way he was looking at your sister, didn't you?" He winked. "I prefer the nap."

"Oh." She felt a little foolish. "Yes, Ramón has got a temper." She drew the curtains to dim the room. "He really could have killed you, you know."

"No, he couldn't." He sounded almost amused. Men were strange. "Though he's probably ruthless enough to try. He's desperate."

"Desperate?" She took off her slippers.

"For money."

"Do you think we're in any danger now?" She had a sudden vision of Ramón coming in and murdering them in their sleep. She hurried across and locked the door.

"From Ramón? No, I doubt he'd worry about revenge." Luke turned back the bedclothes. "He seems to be an eminently practical fellow. Now he knows my death would not benefit him in the least, we're safe enough."

"That reminds me—"

He unbuttoned his breeches. She blinked and turned away, fighting a blush. The question of his will was forgotten.

He padded around the bed in his drawers and an undershirt. "Do you need help with your dress?"

"No, er—"

"You wouldn't want it to crush, would you? It would be a mass of wrinkles if you napped in it. Not setting a good example for your little sister at all. Let me get those laces." He turned her around and unlaced her dress at the back. She could quite easily have undone it herself, Bella thought. She'd done it up this morning with no trouble. She shivered as his fingers brushed her bare skin.

He bent and kissed the nape of her neck.

"Cold?" he asked, but there was another, silent, question in the deepness of his voice.

This was the moment. If she said yes, he would leave it at that, she knew. They would climb into bed and lie there side by side, not touching until the siesta was over. Or she could say no. Meaning yes.

So much for waiting. She was as powerless to resist him as the tides were able to resist the pull of the moon.

"No," she said. Meaning yes.

Fourteen

❦

*B*efore she knew it he'd lifted the dress over her head and removed it entirely. He draped it carefully over a chair and then turned her around to face him.

He looked at her and his eyes darkened. There was no trace of the lightness she'd glimpsed in him earlier. It was all focused, burning intensity.

She was perfectly decently clothed in her chemise and the corset, but somehow, Bella felt . . . exposed. His gaze dropped to her chest. She glanced down. Her breasts looked almost naked, pushed up as they were by her corset. From this angle she could almost see her nipples. Could he?

Leaning against the edge of the high bed, he slowly pulled her between his thighs. "I think we'd better undo that thing," he murmured. "It looks a bit tight to sleep in." His voice was quite matter-of-fact, but his eyes . . . his eyes told a different story.

"Er, no, I'm sure it will be—" she started to mumble, but then his hands were there, reaching for the hooks at the front of her corset. He paused. Bella held her breath.

"So beautiful," he murmured, and though she knew she was not at all beautiful, in that moment she believed it, believed him. He made her feel beautiful. Very gently, he brushed the back of his fingers across the delicate skin that rose from the constriction of the white linen corset.

She shivered again.

His knuckles slid down, across the linen casing, and she felt her nipples rise, hard and aching to meet them. Back and forth his big knuckles moved, a friction that barely touched her, yet her breasts were on fire.

He bent and kissed the exposed skin and then nibbled his way up her throat to claim her mouth, and as wondrous sensations shimmered through her, she felt suddenly looser, freer.

He'd removed her corset. And then she felt a draft of air against her legs and he pulled back from kissing her a moment and tugged the chemise up . . . up . . . and over her head. She folded her arms over her breasts, feeling inadequate, wholly exposed as his dark blue eyes roved hotly over her.

"Don't be shy; you're lovely," he told her, sliding his hands around her waist and drawing her nearer. "Perfect and sweet and lovely."

A rush of delicious warmth surged through her. She leaned eagerly into him, sliding her hands around his waist, lifting her mouth for his kiss. Blindly, feverishly, she found the hem of his shirt and started to drag it up his body.

"No." He caught her hands and brought them up to his chest, pressing her palms down flat on the fabric. She felt hard little nubs under her fingers. Male nipples. Remembering the pleasure of his caress through the fabric of her corset, she lightly scraped her nails over the tiny bumps. They hardened and she heard his low growl of pleasure.

He ran his hands down her spine and cupped her bottom. "Ready?"

She nodded, gasping, not sure what he was planning, but willing to go along with it.

He lifted her, and she felt her thighs drag against a thrusting male hardness. He turned and laid her back onto her mother's high, soft bed. A heavy bulge pushed against the fabric of his undergarments. She was naked to his gaze; she wanted to see him naked, too.

She reached for his shirt again, but he caught her hands and kissed her palms, lingeringly, one at a time. She shuddered delicately, and her fingers curled involuntarily around his jaw, cupping his face, as if holding the kiss in her hand. Who knew that the center of your palm could be so sensitive?

He pressed her back on the bed, his mouth devouring her while his big, warm hands slid over her ribs, down her hips, and up again, caressing her in a ceaseless hypnotic rhythm. Wherever he touched her, hot ripples flowed inside her, gathering in a place deep within her.

And all the time she felt the hot, heavy hardness of him pressing at her center.

He cupped her breasts, teasing the nipples with his fingers until she cried out with the frustration of it, not really knowing what she wanted until his hot mouth closed over one breast and sucked, and she gasped, arched, and shuddered violently, clutching his hair and holding him close.

He paused, and her eyes fluttered open. She was dazed, gasping for air, and she saw a gleam of white as he smiled. He was panting, too, and yet he was still almost fully clothed. She wanted to feel him, feel him against her, skin to skin.

"Please," she heard herself moan. "Please."

He pulled back. "No . . . not yet," he panted thickly. His eyes burning into hers, he unfastened his cotton drawers and kicked them off.

She reached for his shirt. His mouth closed over her other breast, and she almost screamed as a kind of lightning flashed through her. She grabbed his shoulders and held him tightly, but it wasn't enough, so she opened her thighs and wrapped them around him. She writhed beneath him, wanting to get closer, aching for more.

He moaned. Kissing and nipping the soft skin of her stomach, he slowly worked his way down her quivering body until his fingers slid through the hair at the base of her stomach, and between the folds, caressing her there until she could hardly bear it.

She moaned and lifted herself, pushing against his fingers. "Now, Luke, now," she panted.

And then he parted her and placed his mouth on her and she lost all control. Her body wasn't her own. Each time his mouth moved, she quivered and shuddered with helpless pleasure. It built and built until she thought she would burst, and just when she thought she could stand it no more, he lifted his mouth off her and entered her in one long, smooth thrust.

She panted, pulling him closer, wrapping her legs tighter around him as he thrust into her again and again. With each thrust, deep convulsions racked her, and she didn't know where she ended and he began as she shattered and screamed and plunged into oblivion.

*B*ella wasn't sure how long it was before she drifted back to full awareness. She could tell by the shadows on the curtains that the sun had moved quite a bit, so she must have slept for a while.

Luke had pulled the covers over them both. She lay with her head on his chest, his arm around her.

She stretched, feeling like a very satisfied cat. And laughed.

"What is it?" Luke murmured.

"Mama was wrong," she said. "It is exactly like animals. I was like a cat in heat there, and you—" She broke off.

"And I?" he prompted. "Though I ought to know better than to ask."

She smiled and rubbed her cheek against the fabric of his shirt like the cat who ate the cream. "You were a stallion."

She felt him laugh, rather than heard it, a deep vibration of his chest.

"So, I've graduated from being a rat?"

That reminded her. "You did make provision for me in your will, didn't you?"

"Not a single penny do you receive from me," he said softly.

But she wasn't deceived. She lifted her head and looked him in the eye. "But I won't be dependent on your mother and sister, will I?"

His eyes gleamed. "No."

"I knew before dinner it was a lie." She lay back down on his chest and idly twirled a small curl of chest hair that peeked from the neck of his shirt.

He stroked her shoulder. "How did you know?"

"When you told me your mother was a very kind lady, I knew then you were lying."

"But my mother *is* a kind lady."

She could hear the smile in his voice. She tweaked his chest hair.

"Ouch!"

"So, what provision have you made for me?"

"I told you, none."

She smacked him lightly on the chest.

He kissed her. "I'll tell you when we get to England."

"Why not now?"

"Because, my dear, you are a terrible liar, and we don't want to get Cousin Twice-Removed all het up and murderous again, do we?"

"Tell me or I'll make you bald in the chest." She slid her hand inside his undershirt and encountered a patch of hard-ridged skin in the hollow beneath his shoulder. "What is that?"

He jerked her hand away and sat up roughly, spilling her back on the bed. "Nothing," he said brusquely.

"But—"

"Siesta is over." He flipped back the bedclothes, pulled on his drawers and breeches, and dragged his shirt on over his head. "Do you want to stay at Valle Verde and sort out something with your sister, or shall we leave now and kidnap her for her own good?" He grabbed his neckcloth and tied it with deft precision.

Bella sat up, pulling the bedclothes around her, watching her husband pretend nothing had just happened. What was hidden under that shirt he wouldn't take off? He wasn't shy. When she'd first met him he'd taken off his shirt in the heat. He had no problem going bare-chested then. He had a rather beautiful chest, as she recalled.

Was that it? Some hideously ugly war wound he felt he had to hide from her? What kind of a shallow person did he think she was? Did he think she didn't know that soldiers could be wounded and scarred?

He avoided her gaze and finished dressing. She could tell by the set of his mouth that he wasn't going to talk about it.

But she wasn't going to let it go. She wasn't going to go through her marriage with a man who slept in his shirt. But now was not the time.

"I'd like to go for a ride later, if Ramón will let us," she said. "I would like to show you the home of my childhood. I will ask Perlita."

She glanced at the looking glass on the dressing table and remembered what she'd been doing before Luke had distracted her. She pulled her chemise on and ran across to the dressing table.

"What are you doing?"

She slipped her fingers into the open side drawer. "There's a secret compartment and I hid them here before I left. At dinner I got such a fright realizing Ramón had sold furniture— that he would do that never occurred to me. Thank God he didn't sell this." She grimaced, trying to move the hidden lever. "I didn't know I'd be gone for eight years, and Papa had said not to risk them on the journey. Besides, I would have had no use for them in a convent."

"Use for what?"

"Mama's pearls—oh!" The secret drawer sprang open and she stared into it, dismayed. "It's empty. Mama's pearls are gone."

*L*uke made as quick an exit as he decently could from the bedchamber, leaving Isabella to dress by herself and speculate some more on what had happened to her pearls.

Luke wasn't surprised they'd disappeared. It was naive of her to imagine they'd be where she'd left them, secret drawer or not. Ramón would have gone through this place with a fine-tooth comb, stripping it of anything worth selling. The pearls were long gone, he imagined. Pity, but there it was.

He'd buy her more pearls when they got to London.

In the meantime, he needed to get away. He was starting to feel . . . he wasn't sure exactly what. A bit out of control, perhaps. Usually he liked the feeling that anything might happen, but this was different.

He walked out onto the terrace. It was lined with scraggly weeds. Ramón didn't waste a penny on anything that was not productive.

Luke breathed in the cool air sliding down from the mountains. Times like this he almost wished he'd taken to cigarillos, as so many men had during the war. He imagined it would be a soothing thing to be able to step outside and blow a cloud. A kind of declaration of privacy.

But he hadn't picked up the habit. And his privacy . . . well, the less said of that the better. It was very much under threat.

Luke strolled along a pathway that led around the back of the house. Stupid idea to come to Spain on his own. He should have brought a companion, or at least a manservant, someone to keep them from being alone together all the time. He should have hired her a maid.

He could do that now, hire someone from Valle Verde, someone she could talk to, someone from home. Brilliant idea. He strode along, feeling better.

It would help if he could keep his hands off her, he thought. But he couldn't. Her slender, lissome body, all silken skin and warm, responsive eagerness. He recalled the feeling of her limbs twining around him, the blind rapture of her face lifted to his as he entered her, the feeling as her body closed around him and clenched tight . . . He groaned. He was ready, right now, to turn, march back to the bedchamber, and bed her all over again.

Control. He needed more control.

It wouldn't be so bad if it was only her body that obsessed him, but she had an . . . allure about her that he couldn't resist; an honesty, a zest for life that entranced him.

And she was very good company. He enjoyed talking to her almost as much as bedding her. Almost.

God, he couldn't recall the last time he'd lost control so completely with a woman. Lost all awareness of who and where he was. Never before . . .

He shoved the thought aside.

Luke walked past the stables. He would have liked to go in, see what was happening there. Ramón had an eye for good horseflesh, he could see, but a man's stables were private. One needed an invitation.

He walked on. There was a spring in his step that hadn't been there for . . . he didn't know how long. And the bouts of restlessness and gloom that had plagued him ever since . . .

His headstrong little wife kept him busy, that was all. Careering all over the country.

His nightmares, too, were less severe. Isabella woke him almost as soon as they started. She seemed to know, even in her sleep, that he was dreaming again.

All this time he'd never realized the solution was not to sleep alone. Simple, really.

In many ways marriage suited him surprisingly well. It was just a little too . . . intimate.

He could still almost feel her fingers touching that damned scar. Blast it. She'd see it eventually. And then the questions would start. Stripping him bare.

Behind the stables half a dozen women sat around by a trestle table laughing and chatting as they stripped the husks from cobs of maize. They smiled at Luke and bobbed their heads. Luke greeted them and walked on, his thoughts miles away.

He'd had a wound once that had been treated and bandaged and left to heal. The bandage had become glued to his wound. It had been quite all right; there was no pain, just some throbbing, which was quite bearable, and a faint smell, but only if you sniffed it up close.

Finally Rafe and Gabe insisted he remove it. It was crusted on, part of his flesh. He'd tried soaking it, but it wouldn't come off. Luke was all for leaving it as it was; no harm, it would eventually fall off of its own accord.

But Rafe had fetched a physician, and the fellow had taken one look and ripped the bandage off, painful, tearing the old wound open again and releasing a flood of pus.

The healing had to start all over again, and yes, exposed to the air it healed quickly, but to this day Luke was sure if left alone it would have healed by itself. And far less painfully.

He wasn't going to let anyone rip off his protective covering again. Not even his wife.

Especially not his wife. She still had . . . illusions.

Vanity, thy name is Luke, he thought ruefully. But he'd deprived her of her home, her country, and any choice in marriage, and he didn't want to rid her of her last illusions about her husband.

Vanity? No, he decided. Cowardice.

So be it. A man was entitled to his privacy.

He would get her a maidservant to talk to. That would put an end to this . . . galloping intimacy.

*B*ella sought out her sister and broached the matter of the pearls.

"And so is revealed the real reason you decided to 'drop in' to Valle Verde," Perlita said in a hard voice. "Those pearls."

"No, it wasn't," Bella protested. "It was just . . . while I was here, I thought—"

"You would get what you could. Well, you won't. Whatever was left in this house eight years ago now belongs to Ramón and is his to do with what he chooses."

"I did *not* come here to get what I could. Besides, those pearls belonged to me, not the estate."

Perlita shrugged. "What do you care? You are married to a rich man; he can buy you more pearls."

"It's not the same. They were a wedding present to my

mother from her mother and father. My grandfather collected the pearls himself from the South Seas."

"Too bad. You should have taken them with you when you left."

"I suppose Ramón sold them. He's sold everything else of value."

"Ramón does what he must to make the estate flourish."

"Including marrying the first heiress who comes along? And what of you, Perlita? Where will you and your loyalty be then?"

"Do not look down your nose at Ramón," Perlita flashed. "He is no different from your father—our father."

Bella was outraged. "Papa was nothing like Ramón! He—"

Perlita made a sharp gesture. "Hah! Papa married your mother for her fortune, did he not? For the sake of Valle Verde, no? It is exactly the same."

"It is not the same!"

"No, because Papa's sacrifice was in vain. Your grandfather cheated him by making sure he could not use most of the money, by ensuring most of the money went to the children of the marriage. To you."

"My grandfather did?" Bella knew nothing of this. She'd always known Mama's fortune would come to her and not to Papa's heir, but not that Papa felt he'd been cheated. He never discussed such matters with her, and she'd been too intimidated—and probably too young—to ask.

"It's why he would never let your grandparents visit."

"They didn't visit because they died shortly after Mama died."

"Did they?" Perlita said incuriously. "It's not what my mother said."

"Anyway, I would have given Papa whatever he needed—"

Perlita snorted. "He tried to get his hands on some of it during the war. I heard him and Mama talking about it. Neither you nor he could touch it. It's in some kind of trust until you turn one-and-twenty, or were married."

"I didn't know."

"I suppose, being rich and spoiled all your life, you never think about where the money comes from."

Bella gave her half sister an incredulous look. *Rich and spoiled all her life?* She'd been rich only in theory, and as for spoiled, Papa had been a harder taskmaster than the most severe of the nuns at the convent. And for a good part of the last eight years she'd lived on the verge of starvation. That's why she was all skin and bones.

She wasn't the one with the lush figure. Or the beautiful dresses. Perlita had changed into another dress after the siesta. This one was shimmering gold. It brought out the gold in her hair.

Ramón might have to sell paintings and other people's pearls to raise money for the estate, but he didn't stint on Perlita's clothing.

She opened her mouth to explain to Perlita just how rich and spoiled she hadn't been, when Perlita turned and walked onto the terrace. Bella hurried to catch up with her. "I didn't know anything about it," she repeated. She felt so foolish, discovering all this from a younger half sister.

Perlita glanced at Bella over her shoulder and asked, "Did you never wonder why Papa hated your grandfather?"

"Not really. Most of the time he never even spoke of him. One time I heard him say Mama's father was a pirate and a thief, like all the English."

Perlita curled her lip. "Because he tricked him in the marriage settlements and robbed him of his pride. Papa should have had all the money. It's why he married your mother, after all. God knows he never loved her, plain little dab of a thing that she was."

"Do not *dare* to insult my mother!" Bella flashed, her fists clenched.

There was a short silence. "I apologize. It is how my mother spoke of her. She was . . . envious." Perlita laid a hand on Bella's arm and said softly, "I'm sorry. I did not think."

Bella forced herself to unclench her fists. She gave a curt little nod, accepting the apology. It was the first time Perlita had made any gesture toward her, and she wasn't going to rebuff it.

Still, it outraged her that her father had discussed these things with his mistress in front of Perlita but never bothered to explain anything to her. No doubt because she was a *plain little dab of a thing*, too.

Perlita said, "All I know is that it galled Papa terribly that all he had was a daughter who would bring a fortune in marriage to some other man."

Bella knew that. It was why Papa had planned to marry her to Felipe. Except Felipe had died, and the heir became Ramón. And that was a very different matter.

For the first time it occurred to her to wonder why Ramón was such an impossible match for her. Despite his crudeness and lack of polish, he was still the heir.

"Papa didn't want me to marry Ramón," she said. "When he knew Ramón would inherit, he sent a message to me to go to the convent in the mountains, to escape him. Now I'm wondering why."

Perlita gave a cynical laugh. "Did you not know? They were on opposite sides, politically. Papa led his own band of *guerilleros*; Ramón remained loyal to the Crown—"

"But the Crown was held by Napoleon's brother!" Bella exclaimed, shocked. "He was a puppet!"

Perlita waved an indifferent hand. "Ramón does not care for politics. He did what he thought best for Valle Verde."

And whatever Ramón did was obviously all right by Perlita, Bella thought. She was infatuated with the man. Why, she couldn't imagine.

They strolled on, out past the pond that had once been filled with water lilies and was now choked with weeds, past the rosebushes that straggled, unpruned and neglected. Bella tried not to think about how much of the beauty of her former home was being let go in favor of what was practical. The orchards, fields, and kitchen garden were well tended and productive. She might not like the choices Ramón had made, but it was becoming clear he did care a great deal for Valle Verde. How much he cared for her sister was another matter.

"I didn't come to Valle Verde for my pearls," she told Perlita. "I came for you."

Perlita stopped and swung around to face her. "You said that before, but still I do not believe you. Why would you come for me?"

Bella took a deep breath and made her confession for the second time. "Eight years ago, when I left Valle Verde to take refuge in the Convent of the Angels, it was on Papa's orders."

"So?"

"So I should have taken you and your mother with me. It was what he wanted. And I have always felt terrible that I disobeyed—"

"He told you to take my mother and me with you?" Perlita interrupted.

"Yes."

"To a convent?"

"Yes, where you would be safe."

"With nuns?"

"Of course, with nuns. My aunt was a nun there. She is now Mother Sup—"

Perlita burst out laughing. "Lord, I would have liked to see you try. Take Mama to a convent? She would rather have died."

Bella blinked. It was the last reaction she'd expected.

"And me, I would have hated it, too." Perlita spluttered with laughter. "The clothes for a start. And then there's all that chanting and praying and kneeling."

"And sewing," Bella added balefully.

Perlita stopped laughing and eyed her shrewdly. "You hated it?"

"Every minute I was there," Bella admitted. "And most of the praying I did was to be let out." They both burst out laughing, and at the end they looked at each other with a new understanding.

"All this time, I've felt so guilty," Bella confessed. "I was angry with Papa because he was more worried about you and your mother than me. I left you behind because I was so jealous of you. I have felt so guilty about it since."

Perlita made a careless gesture. "We were children. I was jealous of you, too."

"It is the only time I ever disobeyed my father."

Perlita gave a little huff of laughter. "Nonsense."

Bella gave her an indignant look. Perlita said, "You were often disobedient."

"I was not!"

"What about the time you rode the black stallion bareback?"

"Oh." She'd been severely beaten for that.

"And when your menses began and Papa told you that you had to ride sidesaddle and must learn to be a lady and the very next day you—"

"All right, I didn't always obey Papa in every single little thing. But I still should have—"

Perlita shook her head. "What? Carried Mama and me— kicking and screaming—to a nunnery? And you a child of thirteen? The whole idea was ludicrous from the start. Forget about it, Isabella. Get on with your life."

And with those matter-of-fact words, the burden of guilt and self-recrimination Bella had been carrying all these years lifted.

Yes, she did want to get on with her life. All those years of dreaming . . .

One of her dreams was to be part of a family again. She looked at her sister. Nineteen, ruined, and in Ramón's clutches. And one day soon she'd be dumped for an heiress. It was no way for a beautiful young girl to live. Had Perlita even been away from Valle Verde?

She laid her hand on her sister's arm and said, "Come to England with Luke and me. We'll help you find a husband there."

Perlita gave her an astonished look, and Bella hastily added, "Or if you prefer we could take you to Barcelona where your mother is, or Madrid."

Perlita said nothing for a moment. She picked a sprig of rosemary and sniffed it, then crushed it in her elegant fingers. "Thank you. It is a generous offer. But I will stay here."

"With Ramón?"

"With Ramón."

Bella hesitated, then said, "A mistress, Perlita? Like your mother?"

"I love him," Perlita said.

Bella recalled the raised fist. "He doesn't hit you, does he?"

Perlita shook her head. "Never." She could see Bella still had doubts and added with a little smile, "Ramón looks very fierce—and I think he would happily kill your husband in a fight—but most of the time he is all sound and fury. Truly, with me he is always gentle as a kitten, except in bed, when he is a lion."

Bella tried not to blush at such frankness. "And when Ramón marries his heiress?"

"First he has to find a rich woman who will take him." She gave a philosophical shrug. "Not so easy since the war. Heiresses are in short supply."

"But with the title, he'll find someone, and then where will you be? In the little pink house in the next valley?"

Perlita turned and looked out toward the hills. "I was born in that house. It's not so bad."

But she was nineteen years old, Bella thought. What nineteen-year-old dreamed of living in the same isolated cottage she was born in, in the same lonely position as her mother? Even her mother was married now and living in the city.

"I always thought your mother and you must be very lonely."

Perlita said nothing.

"If you came with us—"

"No! I stay here."

With Ramón, Bella saw. "He doesn't deserve you," she said quietly.

"He's a good man, in his way," Perlita almost whispered. "He is good to me."

And that said it all, Bella thought. She loved him. And perhaps Ramón even loved Perlita. But he would marry a woman with money, just like Papa had. Making two women unhappy, just like Papa. And there was nothing she could do about it.

"Then if you are sure, we will leave in the morning. And if you ever change your mind—"

"I won't."

"If you do, the offer is always open." Bella rose on her toes and for the first time in her life kissed her half sister on the cheek. "Sister."

Perlita gave her an awkward, hurried hug and turned quickly away. Bella thought she saw the glitter of tears on her sister's long lashes, but she couldn't be sure because her own eyes were quite blurry, too.

"Do you think Ramón would mind if we rode out in Valle Verde? I would like to show my husband the place I grew up in." She also wanted to bid it a proper good-bye. When she'd fled, as a child, she hadn't realized how final her leaving would be, hadn't realized what a wrench it would be to leave this land she loved so much.

Perlita lifted an elegant shoulder. "Go where you will." Her voice sounded husky.

"Would you like to ride out with us, Perlita?" If her sister wouldn't leave Valle Verde, Bella wanted to make the most of every hour with her.

"I was never taught to ride."

Bella blinked. "Not at all?"

"Papa said I had no need to learn, that I was the sort of woman who would always be driven in a fine carriage."

As Isabella and Luke rode up into the hills, she told him what Perlita had said. "It's strange," she concluded. "Papa trained me to manage the estate and to live as a *guerrillera*, off the land, and Perlita he taught to be a lady, to expect others to take care of her."

"You are no less a lady for having unusual skills," Luke told her. Her father had a lot to answer for.

She pulled a face. "But when it came to the crunch, Papa ordered me to a convent. But I don't care," she said as if continuing some argument in her head. "I could never regret learning to ride. It's one of the joys of life, and much better than being cooped up in a stuffy old carriage. You have no idea how much I missed being able to do this when I was in the convent." And with a mischievous glance she set her horse galloping along the valley.

She took Luke all over the estate, pointing out how things had changed and commenting freely on Ramón's management, which more and more she had to reluctantly approve.

The depth of her understanding of estate management surprised him. He knew no other woman who found such things interesting. As they paused to admire a vista from one of the hilltops, Luke told her so.

She laughed. "It would have been different if Mama had given Papa a son. I would then be as ignorant as a lady should be of such matters."

"Your father must have been very proud of you."

She considered that for a moment. "Papa was not much given to praise. The best thing he ever said of me was that I was wasted as a female." There was such a look of desolation on her face as she stared across the range of hills, Luke couldn't help himself.

"I don't agree," he said. "As a man, you'd be in no way remarkable. As a woman, believe me, you're . . . unique." And he leaned across and kissed her.

It was meant to be just a light kiss, a gesture of comfort, but she leaned into him, wrapped her arms around his neck, and returned the kiss with such feeling that they both forgot where they were and almost fell off when their horses moved apart.

They laughed, a little self-consciously, but her eyes clung to his, and her mouth was damp and beautiful and slightly swollen, and before he knew it Luke had dismounted and pulled her off her horse into his arms.

Laughing, still kissing him, she slid slowly down the

length of his body, twining her limbs around him, an agonizing, delicious friction. Her body was soft and pliant, the taste of her intoxicating.

They slid to the ground, and the fragrance of crushed, new grass mingled with the scent and taste of her as he pressed her down beneath him, covering her with his body, devouring her with his mouth. He pulled urgently at her clothing, eager to peel her out of it, to reveal her lithe body with the high, perfect little breasts, but she pushed his hands aside.

"You first," she murmured, reaching for his neckcloth. She dragged it off, tossed it aside, and started on the ties on his shirt.

"No." Luke pulled back abruptly.

She lay still, the grass against her back. "Why not?"

For answer he covered her mouth with his, trying to recapture the mindless passion of a few moments before. Her question lay between them. Luke ignored it. He reached for the fastenings of her bodice.

"No." She caught his hands and stopped him. "Not until you take off your shirt."

Fifteen

❧

There was a long silence. Luke could hear some bird circling high on the wind, calling bleak and harsh.

"If you're not in the mood," he began, getting off her.

Bella caught him by the arm. "I am in the mood, but not a button, a lace, or a hook will I undo unless you show me whatever it is you're hiding." She waited. Surely it could not be such a terrible sight. And even if his wound was hideous, it wouldn't, couldn't, make him any less attractive to her. She was not such a shallow creature.

And besides, she loved him.

He didn't respond, just looked away across the hills, his profile grim and unyielding, his jaw clenched tight.

She said in a soft voice, "Luke, please don't worry. It will make no differ—"

"It's clouding over and it looks like rain. We'd better get back."

She rose, brushing grass from her skirts. "Pretending it isn't there will not make it go away, Luke. Whatever it is, it doesn't matter—"

"If it doesn't matter, why make such an issue of it?" His voice was almost savage.

"I haven't made it an issue, Luke. You have," she said quietly. "You have only to trust me."

For answer he fetched the horses. In silence he brought them back, and in silence he boosted her into the sidesaddle.

He mounted and gazed for a moment at the vista spread before them. The land of her birth. "We shall leave for England first thing in the morning. Enough time has been wasted here."

He didn't meet her eyes, and when they moved off, he rode at a distance that was too great for conversation. Bella followed, guilt and anger warring within her.

Anger won, anger that he was making such a meal of something she was sure was not so terrible. It was a handsome man issue, she supposed. Having been born beautiful, he couldn't bear now to be less than perfect.

But she was his wife. She had no quibble with him concealing his wound from the world, but she would not be stripped naked, giving up all the secrets of her body to a man who refused to take off his shirt for her.

It hadn't been easy. For the last eight years she hadn't even seen her own body—the girls had been made to bathe under a shapeless linen gown—but had she refused him when he'd wanted to strip her nightgown from her? No, even though she hadn't felt at all comfortable when he'd laid her bare, knowing she was inadequate, too skinny, and lacking the womanly curves men preferred. But she'd trusted him and revealed herself to him. Because he was her husband.

If he'd removed his shirt today, she would have happily sent years of trained convent modesty to the winds and bared herself to him and the skies and the endless rolling hills.

But would he trust her with one simple little scar? It wasn't big; she'd felt it. No bigger than her palm. But no, Mr. Too-Beautiful-for—no, Lord Too-Beautiful-for-Words wouldn't trust his wife with his one small imperfection.

It wasn't even anything to be ashamed of. A scar gained in war was a mark of heroism.

Besides, she desired him. It was all very well for him, running his hands over every inch of her skin, touching her wherever he wanted and causing her to shiver with delight.

Did he think she wanted to caress a *shirt*?

When Bella told Perlita it was their only night in Valle Verde, she nodded. "Then we will dress for dinner and make a special event of it."

Dress for dinner? Isabella washed, braided her hair into a coronet, and put on her new red dress. It looked pretty enough, but a dress bought at a town market couldn't compete. Not that she wanted to compete with her sister. Not that she could.

She looked at her reflection in the looking glass and sighed. "It will have to do."

"No." Luke, bathed and freshly shaved, looked heartbreakingly handsome in his elegantly tailored dark blue coat, buff breeches, and shining, freshly polished boots. He'd picked up a bit of color in the open air, and his cheekbones were lightly bronzed. He looked magnificent. "That dress needs something else." It was the first time he'd spoken to her since their argument in the hills.

"I haven't got anything else." Her mother's pearls would have looked perfect.

"What about this?" He placed a shawl around her shoulders. Made of heavy cream silk, it was embroidered with dark red flowers. Bella couldn't speak. She'd never worn anything so beautiful in her life.

More than that, it was a peace offering.

"Where did you—"

"Last night, after the gypsy dance, when I went out for a walk. An old crone gave me a price I couldn't resist. Pretty, don't you think?"

Bella stared at her reflection. The red flowers were the same shade as her dress, and the creamy silk made her complexion glow. She could go to supper not feeling completely inferior to her sister for once. In this shawl she felt almost beautiful. "It's beautiful," she whispered. "Thank you."

Ramón and Perlita were waiting for them in her father's study. Bella stepped into the room on Luke's arm. Perlita wore a fine gown of emerald green overlaid with gauze. She rose from her chair like a goddess emerging from the sea. Her eyes were tragic and guilt-ridden.

Bella suppressed a gasp. Her fingers dug into Luke's arm with the effort of keeping silent. He glanced at her face, then followed her gaze.

Around Perlita's neck was a long rope of pearls. Glowing, perfect South Sea Island pearls.

Ramón stood with a proprietary arm around Perlita's waist. He looked smug.

Whatever was left in this house eight years ago now belongs to Ramón and is his to do with what he chooses.

And he had, Bella saw. Perlita met her gaze and gave a small, sad shake of her head.

She hadn't known. Bella nodded and sent her sister a reassuring smile. She knew very well who was to blame. Ramón knew exactly whose pearls they were. And he was watching Luke like a wolf, waiting for him to start a fight over the pearls. Wanting him to.

Having Perlita wear them tonight was deliberate provocation.

Luke would fight him, too, Bella knew. He might have given her the shawl, but he was still wound tight from their argument on the hills. All he would need was an excuse.

Luke bent and murmured in Bella's ear. "Your mother's pearls?"

She pressed her lips together and shook her head. She would say nothing.

A servant she did not know handed around glasses of wine. She sipped hers gratefully and grimaced in surprise. It was not the smooth Valle Verde wine she knew.

Ramón was more observant than he looked. "The wine is not to your liking?"

"Not at all," she said with deliberate ambiguity. "I was just expecting it to be one of the Valle Verde vintages."

"It is Valle Verde wine."

"Indeed?" It tasted nothing like the wine Papa had made.

"Made from Valle Verde grapes, at any rate. With the size of the vineyards here, it was impractical to continue making wine at Valle Verde," Ramón explained. "To maintain the winery in a profitable state, your father should have put more fields under vines, but he preferred horses, as do I. But the vines still produce well, so I sell the grapes to a neighbor and he makes the wine and gives me a share."

"I see," Bella said politely. It was a false economy. The neighbor was a terrible winemaker.

Ramón laughed. "But why do I bother explaining business to an empty-headed woman?" He turned to Luke. "Perlita tells me you inspected the estate this afternoon, Englishman. So, what do you think?"

"It's beautiful country," Luke responded, but before he could say anything else, Perlita tinkled the little bell, giving the signal for them to go in to supper.

As dish after dish was brought out, Bella saw that Perlita had made a special effort with the meal. Every dish was one of Isabella's childhood favorites. The servants would have known which dishes, but the order to make them was her sister's gesture.

A silent apology for the pearls. Bella sent Perlita a little nod of acknowledgment and thanks.

A servant came forward with a silver carafe of wine. "I would prefer one of the old Valle Verde vintages," Bella said.

"None left," Ramón said. "I sold it all."

"Then just water for me, thank you."

His brow darkened. "What's the matter with my wine?" he growled. "Not good enough for you, my fine lady?"

She hesitated. "No," she said, deciding honesty was more important than politeness. "It's dreadful. The old Valle Verde wine was much better."

Ramón snorted. "Of course it was. That's why I sold it."

"Selling good grapes for a little money and a few cases of bad wine is poor business," she said briskly.

Ramón bristled and leaned forward. "You think so, eh?"

"I do. You'd be better off continuing to make a smaller

quantity of wine here and keeping the Valle Verde label, which you will know from your sale of the old vintages has a reputation and is worth something. It would also maintain the wine-making expertise on the estate. Once old Luis—my father's winemaker—dies, his knowledge and skill will go with him, and he is nearly seventy. When I left, he'd begun to train his grandson, but I noticed today you had Manuel mucking out the stables."

"The main income of Valle Verde now comes from the horses."

"Yes, but putting Manuel to work with horses is another false economy. Anyone can muck out stables, but Manuel, he has the 'nose' for wine." Ramón looked blank, so she added, "A winemaker's 'nose' is a talent you are born with. It cannot be taught. Manuel is completely wasted on horses." So much for not discussing business with an empty-headed woman, she thought, seeing Ramón's stunned expression.

"How do you know all this?"

Bella shrugged. "My father taught me. He knew Felipe had no interest in estate management."

Ramón glowered as he shoveled food in his mouth. He wiped his mouth with the back of his hand. "You should never have married that damned Englishman. With your fortune and that knowledge you would have made me a very useful wife."

"She will make me an even more useful wife," Luke interposed silkily across the table.

Ramón grunted. "Careful, Englishman. I can still make her a widow."

Perlita spoke for the first time. "Ramón."

He glanced at her, frowning. She met his gaze steadily and fingered the pearls at her neck, and after a moment he looked away, his color slightly heightened.

In his eyes Bella saw a fleeting glance of . . . was it shame? Surely not. She recalled what Perlita had said about the other side of her lover.

Didn't stop him being a thief.

In a different tone, Ramón said to Bella, "You are not the

simpleton I thought you were, cousin, so what will you do now you know your husband has made no provision for you in his will?"

"Keep him very healthy," she said without hesitation.

Ramón gave a snort of laughter. "Almost I could envy you, Englishman." And he glanced at Perlita and his gaze warmed. "Almost."

For the rest of the evening he engaged Luke in conversation, firing questions at him about crops and livestock and estate management in England. Luke answered with assurance and intelligence, Bella noted. He would not need her skills or knowledge.

Bella and Perlita, on opposite sides of the table, couldn't speak of anything they did not want Ramón to hear, so except when Luke addressed them in conversation, they spent most of the night in silence.

"So they *are* your mother's pearls?" Luke exclaimed after supper when they were alone in their bedchamber again. "I thought at first they were, but when you didn't react . . ."

"Yes, they're unmistakable. If I wanted to prove it, I could. The biggest pearl has a tiny mark on it where I bit it when I was a child."

"Then, dammit, I'm going to get them back for you." Luke strode toward the door.

"No!" Bella flew across the room to stop him. "Leave it, Luke."

He frowned. "But they're all you have of your mother."

She shook her head. "No, my mother is here." She touched her heart, then sighed. "Besides, I left the pearls behind eight years ago, knowing Papa was mortally wounded and Ramón was to be the new owner of the estate. I didn't think. It's my own fault I lost them."

"You were thirteen," Luke growled. "With too damn much to think about as it was. And I don't like it that that little bitch sat there smugly wearing them to taunt you." He clenched his fists. "I've a good mind to—"

"No, no, please." She grabbed his arm. "I couldn't bear it if you and Ramón fought. Besides, Perlita wasn't being smug or taunting me."

He grunted. "Why else would she have worn them? If she hadn't, we'd have been none the wiser."

"It wasn't her choice to wear them; it was Ramón's. She knew nothing about them until tonight, I'm certain. She must have asked him about them after I asked her, and then he made her wear them. She wasn't at all happy about it, I could see." She removed the silk shawl and folded it carefully.

"Swine," Luke muttered. "And she's just as bad, going along with him."

"Don't blame her. She loves him."

Luke snorted.

Bella said, "She's just a nineteen-year-old girl who's never had very much, and she's hanging desperately on to what she has. Knowing her situation is desperately insecure."

"So you're going to just give up the pearls without a fight?"

That was exactly it, Bella thought. Without a fight. Love was making a coward out of her. She wouldn't risk Luke's life for anything.

She shrugged as if she didn't care. "It doesn't matter. I've lived without them for eight years . . ." The pearls weren't worth a man's life. Any man's. Even Ramón's.

"It's not like you to give up so easily."

The pearls were her past. Luke was her future. And besides, she had better things than pearls to fight for.

She was not going to bed with a *shirt*.

She took off her shoes and began to unroll her stockings.

His eyes, dark and unfathomable, rested on her. "I'm going for a stroll before I turn in. Would you like a maid to assist you?"

"No, thank you." She'd dressed and undressed herself for the last eight years, and if her husband was going to be pigheaded and stubborn and refuse to be there to assist her now, she would manage alone.

"It occurred to me today that I've been remiss in acquiring

a maidservant for you. I'd be happy to engage a girl from Valle Verde for you to take to England." His voice lost a little of the stiffness. "She would be someone from home you could talk to in England."

It was a kind thought. Bella considered it briefly. "No, thank you. Such a girl would be lonely in a land where she had no family and didn't speak the language."

"Will you not be lonely?" he asked, as if it had only just occurred to him she was leaving everything she knew to go with him.

"I've always been lonely. I shall manage." She gave him a direct look. "Are you coming to bed?"

He avoided her gaze. "Not yet. I'm in need of a stroll."

A stroll was supposed to be a short walk. He'd been gone for ages. The candle she'd lit for him had sputtered out.

Bella sat in bed, waiting, her bedclothes huddled to her ears. She had almost nodded off when she heard the door creak open. At last.

He closed the door quietly behind him. The room was in shadows, lit only by the glow of the dying fire. He removed his coat and sat to pull off his boots. She heard first one hit the floor, then the other. He'd be starting on the buttons of his waistcoat now.

"You can light a candle if you like," she said softly. "I'm not asleep."

He paused. "No need. The fire throws enough light to manage." He removed his waistcoat and hung it on the back of a chair. He was a tidy man.

"I thought you'd be asleep by now." Next he unfastened his breeches, shoved them down, and stepped out of them. He shook them out and laid them across the back of the chair. There was no self-consciousness in him; not about his naked lower half, at least.

"I waited up for you." Now for the shirt. Would he remove it or not? Bella held her breath.

He pulled it over his head. Bella said a rapid prayer.

Then he shook out his nightshirt, put it on, and climbed into bed beside her.

Bella had to press her lips together hard to prevent her disappointment spilling out. She was determined not to nag him about it. Trust could not be forced.

He faced her in bed, his lips parted as if to say something, then he frowned, distracted. "That's my shirt. Why are you wearing my shirt in bed?"

"Work it out."

He reached for the shirt. She moved and his palm brushed against her breasts. She shivered and her nipples hardened. He noticed. His eyes darkened. "Take it off," he said softly.

She moved back a little. "Not unless you take your shirt off first."

He stiffened.

She folded her arms. "As long as you wear a shirt in bed, so do I."

"If you're going to start that again . . ." He turned away.

"But—"

"I will not discuss it, Isabella," he said in a hard voice. "If you do not wish to share a bed with me, then that's your prerogative. I shall sleep elsewhere." He climbed out of bed, gathered up his clothes, and strode stiffly from the room.

*B*ella slept badly that night. She kept waking up, thinking Luke was back, but he wasn't.

Such a short time a wife, yet already she was so used to sleeping with a big, warm man at her back, she couldn't sleep well without him. The bed felt too large, too empty, too cold.

He appeared at the breakfast table only moments after her. She was about to ask him where he'd slept when Ramón and Perlita arrived.

"Was this yours?" Perlita asked, placing a small cloth doll on the table beside Bella.

Bella picked it up. It was the doll her old nursemaid, Marta, had made her after Papa had given Perlita the doll

Bella had seen. Bella must have told Marta something about a golden-haired doll, and Marta made her one.

Bella had flung it away in a rage. She wanted a golden-haired doll from Barcelona, not a stupid homemade thing. But afterward she'd felt bad and had retrieved the homely little doll and hugged Marta.

She hadn't seen it for years, but it didn't look quite the same. It was heavier, and the hair was different—golden silk, not thick yellow wool. The doll's clothes were new as well.

Bella glanced from the doll to her sister. "I don't understand."

"I hope you don't mind. She was looking very shabby and worn," Perlita said. "So I fixed her and made her some new clothes."

Bella stared. "You made these clothes?" She examined them. The doll was dressed in traditional Aragon dress, each item finely embroidered and perfect down to the last detail.

Perlita smiled. "*Sí*, I like dolls and I like to sew. I make all my own clothes."

"You *make* them?" Bella exclaimed. Perlita made all those gorgeous dresses?

Perlita laughed. "You think Ramón would waste money on fancy dresses when Valle Verde is in need?"

To Bella's amazement, Ramón stopped shoveling food down and kissed Perlita's hand with an almost courtly air. "It's not a waste to adorn my beautiful Perla."

It was almost charming. But then he resumed stuffing food in his mouth and the charm evaporated.

The rest of breakfast passed more or less in silence. Bella had no intention of talking to her husband about the previous night with an audience present, and since they were never very talkative in the morning, nobody noticed the slight constraint between them.

After breakfast was over, it was time to leave Valle Verde. Their bags were stowed in the carriage, and everyone gathered at the front of the house to bid them farewell.

Bella said good-bye to all the servants first. It was harder than she'd thought. Even though she'd been gone for eight years, their farewells were very affectionate. "Come back soon, *señora*, and do not forget us." She was no longer Little Master.

There was only one master now at Valle Verde.

And even he managed a passably civilized good-bye, kissing her hand—he must have been taking lessons—and shaking Luke's hand in a hearty manner. No one would believe, seeing him now, that only the day before he'd offered to murder her husband.

She turned to say good-bye to her sister, but Perlita had disappeared back inside the house. "You forgot this," she said, returning with the little cloth doll. "Take it with you and keep it in memory of your foolish sister."

She hugged Bella tightly, kissing her on both cheeks. Bella fought the tears. Perlita made no attempt to hide hers.

Bella turned to get into the carriage, then changed her mind. She marched back up the stairs toward Ramón, grabbed him by the shirtfront, and dragged him aside.

"Marry my sister!" she said. "You're a stupid, thickheaded, blind fool and a disgrace, and I cannot think why she loves you, but she does, and you don't deserve her. I wanted to take her to London with me and introduce her to society—"

Ramón's face darkened. "You won't take my Perla—"

"Only because she wouldn't go." Bella thumped him angrily on his chest. "She could have made her come-out in society. She's so beautiful she would have had all the men— rich men, lords, handsome men—"

Ramón grinned. "But she chose me."

"Oh, wipe that disgusting grin off your face, you stupid, smug, self-satisfied oaf!" Bella snapped. "She's only nineteen and her life is already over—because you've ruined her. She has no friends, no relatives—only me, and I will be in England."

Ramón scowled. "She has me."

"And you think you're such a bargain, don't you? You who make no secret of wanting to marry a rich woman!" Bella poked him in the chest. "Perlita is a treasure, but you're too stupid to see it. She should be your *wife*, Ramón, building Valle Verde with you, not sitting in an empty house, seeing no one, and dressing dolls instead of having your babies. You, Ramón, are a big, fat fool. And you disgust me! I pray for the day Perlita grows up and sees you for the selfish pig you are. And when she realizes what she really wants in life, Ramón, then I will be waiting to help her get it, and she'll be out of here so fast you won't know what hit you. And then you'll only have a big house and your own stupidity for company."

Ramón glowered, his brow thickly knotted. "Little viper. Thank God I never married you."

"I thank Him for the very same thing." She wanted to hit him with frustration. Couldn't he see what he'd done to her sister? She'd come here to help her and nothing had changed, nothing.

Luke slid his hand under Bella's elbow. "Come on. You've done what you could."

Ramón waved his hand. "Yes, take her away, Englishman. You have my sympathy."

"Oh, I'm well content with my choice, Spaniard. It's as my wife said; you don't recognize gold when it's under your nose."

Bella hugged her sister one last time, saying, "Write. And come to us anytime you like," and then she marched down the steps of El Nueva Castillo and climbed into the carriage.

"Well, you got that off your chest, at least," Luke commented as the carriage pulled away.

"I should have let you kill him," she muttered. "Then Perlita would have had no choice but to come with us."

"I thought you wanted to give her the choice."

She said nothing, just stroked the little doll Perlita had given her.

"You can't rescue someone who doesn't want to be rescued."

She sighed. "I know."

"Your sister is a strong-minded young lady. Family resemblance there."

They traveled in silence for a while. "You know, I wish Perlita had stolen my pearls. It would have made it easier to leave her there."

"How so?"

"If she had them, then if and when Ramón finds his heiress, she could sell them and leave, make a new life somewhere else. That's all I really want—for her to have the choice. But since the pearls are in his possession . . ."

"She'll never leave him."

"I know." She sighed.

"No, I meant, even if she had the pearls and the choice and he found his heiress, she'd still never leave him."

"I know. She loves him." She glanced at him. "Mama always said that love was a curse."

"Your mother was right." He had the bleak, faraway look in his eyes she'd come to recognize.

The landscape slipped past. They would be back in Huesca by early afternoon.

Traveling in a carriage was nearly as boring as sewing sheets, Bella decided. Luke was about to doze off, she could tell, and she would not sit here, bored witless, bouncing around in a carriage while he slept. She poked him awake. "You can tell me now."

Luke stretched and responded sleepily, "Tell you what?"

"What provisions you made for me in your will. You said you'd tell me when we left Valle Verde, and we have. So I want to know now—and I'm warning you, Luke, I don't care how kind your mother and sister are, I won't be dependent on them."

He shoved his hands deep into his pockets and crossed his long, booted legs. "I told Ramón the truth; I left you nothing in my will."

She narrowed her eyes. His eyes were dancing. She caught a gleam of blue in the darkness and the sight heartened her. "Stop teasing." She tried to look stern.

"It's true."

She threw the doll at him. It bounced off him and hit the carriage floor with a bump.

"Ow," he said mildly. "That doll packs a wallop."

She snorted. "It's a rag doll. I know you've done something sneaky about the will, so tell me at once, or worse than a flying doll will befall you."

Luke said thoughtfully, "For a rag doll it's quite heavy."

Bella said impatiently, "Perlita restuffed it when she repaired it. She probably used sawdust or something. Now Luke, don't be so tedious—tell me."

Luke picked up the doll and examined it. "It's not sawdust. It feels like . . . pebbles or something." He took out his knife and glanced at her. "Do you mind?"

"No." She was curious, too.

He pulled back the doll's skirt and slit the stitching down her middle. He parted the seam, closed it, and tossed her the doll. "See for yourself."

Bella looked. And gasped. From the doll's stomach she drew a long string of pearls, South Sea Island pearls. "She stole them back for me."

She ran the pearls through her fingers. They were even more beautiful than she remembered, glowing with a creamy sheen. Each one was perfect. She slipped them over her head, and they went around twice, with room to spare. "Mama's pearls."

"I thought you said you didn't care about those pearls," he said grimly.

"I lied. I didn't want you to fight Ramón."

"Oh for heaven's sake—"

She looked up, worried. "They must be priceless. When Ramón finds out . . ."

"She will handle him," Luke said. "Your sister has a great deal more character than I thought. You might want to settle something on her."

"Settle something? What do you mean?"

"Some of your inheritance."

"But . . . I don't have an inheritance. You said—"

"No, I said I'd left you nothing in my will. I don't need to. You still have the fortune your mother left you."

She gaped at him, speechless. "But, how? When a bride marries, everything she owns belongs by law to her husband. I know that is true. They taught us that at the convent. Unless the bride's family negotiates settlements, and I know nobody negotiated anything for me. There wasn't time."

Luke grinned, enjoying her amazement. "Ah, but your groom did it for you. I promised to look after you, remember? Some protector I would have been if I gained your fortune through marriage one day, and was killed the next. And in wartime there was every likelihood of that."

She crossed herself. "Thank God you weren't. But I still don't understand."

"I owned your fortune—whatever it is, I still have no idea—for barely a day. When we got to the convent, I wrote out a document returning to you every penny of your mother's fortune, and anything else that you owned before the marriage, to be held in trust until you turned twenty-one. I made two copies and left one with your aunt, who witnessed it. She still has one copy. The other one is here." He drew a packet of papers from the breast pocket of his coat, selected one, and handed it to her. "That's why I left you nothing of mine in my will. You're a rich woman, Lady Ripton."

Stunned, she stared at the document. It was as he said. He'd signed everything back to her almost immediately after the wedding. She swallowed. "That is why my aunt was so sure this marriage was the right thing for me. She knew you were a man of honor. But why did she never tell me?"

Luke said dryly, "Perhaps she thought if you had plenty of money you might run off and abandon me. Any idea why she might think that?"

Bella dismissed that with a wave of her hand. "She never told me anyth—" She broke off, as a thought occurred to her. "But . . . if I were a widow—"

"You'd be a very rich one, yes."

"You fool! You crazy, reckless fool!" She flew at him and thumped him on the chest.

"What? I thought you'd be pleased."

"So Ramón *could* have killed you and forced me to—!"

"Oh, Ramón." He rolled his eyes. "Why does everyone assume that I can't handle Ramón—will you stop that, you violent little hussy? This is the correct response to learning of a husband's nobility of character." His mouth came down over hers, silencing all protests.

After a moment he murmured, "Yes, that's the kind of thing I mean. Now, let me introduce you to one of the benefits of traveling by carriage."

Just then there was a loud crack, the carriage listed to one side and slowly ground to a halt. "Problem with the wheel, *señor*," the coachman called out.

Luke cursed and released her.

Sixteen

❧

*T*hey arrived in Huesca shortly after eight o'clock. The cracked wheel, a flooded river, and even a flock of geese on the road had all contributed to a journey fraught with difficulties and delays. By the time they rolled into town, Luke was in a filthy mood.

Very little pleased him.

After some delay they found a suitable inn, but the only available bedchamber was on the top floor, and was small with a low and uneven ceiling on which he banged his head. Twice.

But he was not going to search the blasted town for another blasted room.

He was tired; he'd spent the day dragging carriages out of mud, changing wheels himself, because hired blasted coachmen had no blasted idea, and chasing geese all over the road, and he wanted his dinner. He was hungry enough to eat a horse.

"Ah, but dinner will not be served for at least another hour, *señor*."

"Blasted Spanish hours! And no, I could not be tempted with a blasted boiled egg—I want proper food, not a nursery supper!"

Bella pressed her lips firmly together trying not to laugh.

"I can see that dimple," he grumbled as the landlord fled. "Think this is all very funny, don't you, but it wasn't you who had to ruin your boots in that blasted mud."

"No," she agreed. "Nor did I slip in the mess left by a blasted goose and fall on my blasted backside in the middle of the blasted road." A choked giggle escaped her.

"So glad to have entertained you, my lady," he said with a sardonic bow. But his mood eased, and a glass of excellent French brandy hastily produced by the landlord did the rest.

By the time dinner arrived he was a lot mellower.

"We'll make it an early night," he told her. "Rise at dawn, get on the road as soon as possible. Does that suit you?"

She nodded. She was used to rising at dawn. Convents didn't encourage lazy mornings in bed, though Bella longed for one. Mama used to lie in bed until almost noon sometimes, reading novels in French and English, drinking chocolate, and nibbling on sweetmeats. It seemed the height of indulgence.

But she was tired and ready for bed, and she was weary of trying to deal with the legacy of the past—and failing. She was looking forward to her new life in England. The sooner it started, the better.

"How many days until your sister's ball?"

"Ten." He'd said it without hesitation. Didn't even have to think, to work out the days. That told her how much it was on his mind.

"Do you think we'll make it in time?"

He shrugged. "No telling. We're cutting it very fine, and there's no telling what the weather will be once we get to the coast. If the wind is in the right direction, and the tides . . . and we find a ship ready to take us straightaway . . ." He drained the last of the wine in his glass. "But if we get any more days like the last one . . ." He shook his head.

But if they didn't make it in time, Bella knew it wouldn't be the fault of the winds or the tides or anything encountered on the road. It would be her fault and no one else's. If she hadn't come on her quest to save her sister—her futile quest—they would probably have reached the coast by now, and could even be on a ship and sailing to England.

"I'll be ready at dawn," she assured him.

They climbed the stairs to their little bedchamber in silence. Bella was tired and feeling a little defeated; she'd failed to rescue her sister, and even Perlita's act of stealing the pearls for her, and the knowledge of Luke's return of Bella's fortune failed to cheer her. She wanted to fling herself into her husband's arms and make love with him.

He might have told Bella not to expect love from him, and he might agree with her mother that love was a curse, but when he made love to Bella with that slow, sensual intensity of his, it dissolved her worries as well as her bones, and she forgot everything.

Even that he did not love her. Especially that he did not love her.

Luke had married her, he'd protected her, he'd risked his life for her, and he'd made her a rich woman. He gave so much and took so little. It sounded like love . . . if you didn't know the whole story.

Bella feared it was all for honor.

On entering the bedchamber, the first thing Luke did was open his portmanteau, take out his nightshirt, and lay it on the bed.

Bella eyed it sourly. She'd dreamed of love, but he wouldn't even give her a little bit of trust.

She opened her own portmanteau and took out the shirt that she'd worn the night before. A shirtly declaration of war. Sometimes you had to fight for what you wanted. Especially with a stubborn untrusting man.

He eyed her shirt and sucked in his cheeks thoughtfully. "I think I'll get another brandy."

"You do that," she said as she started unfastening her dress. "I'll be here, in bed, waiting for you."

* * *

*H*e returned about half an hour later. Bella sat up in bed waiting for him, as promised.

She'd left a candle burning on the table on his side of the bed. He glanced at her and blew it out.

Without a word he shrugged off his coat and as usual hung it up. He untied his neckcloth and unbuttoned his waistcoat. Bella counted every button.

She was sure he was going to wear his nightshirt again, but she couldn't help herself: she was the hopeful type. Maybe in the last half hour he'd changed his mind. Maybe the brandy had given him that little extra encouragement he needed to trust his wife with whatever it was that he'd kept hidden all this time.

She couldn't imagine what it could be. He acted as if he were ashamed of it, but a war wound was not something to be ashamed of.

She ached for him to trust her.

She ached for him.

He sat to remove his boots, then his stockings. He shoved his breeches down his legs, taking his drawers with them. He folded first the breeches, then the drawers and placed them on the chair.

In the soft light spilling from the fire she could see the elegant line of his hard, horseman's thighs, his lean, masculine flanks.

He sat back on the bed and pulled the shirt over his head. She could see the broad expanse of his back, the powerful shoulders, the ridged line of his spine.

Bella wanted to scream as he carefully separated the shirt from the undershirt, shook out each garment one by one, and placed it on the chair.

He was naked, wholly naked, for the first time in their marriage.

She waited for him to reach for the nightshirt.

Some coals shifted in the fireplace, and he made a small sound of irritation and, naked in the dark, padded across to the fire. He bent and stoked it with some cut logs. In the fire-light he was all bronze and gold and shadow, lean and hard and beautiful.

Bella watched, her mouth dry.

She could not see his chest, but oh, the long, strong line of his back and those magnificent shoulders. And the firm mas-culine buttocks . . .

How could he possibly think scars would make a difference to her? Did he not understand what a fine specimen of man-hood he was? Scarred or not, he was perfect, in her opinion.

She longed to run her hands over his firm, manly flesh, feel the corded muscles of his arms, the deep chest, the perfect shoulders. Who knew that a man's shoulders could be so beau-tiful? She wanted to touch him everywhere, see all of him, as he had seen and touched her.

He padded back to the bedside, a dark silhouette limned by firelight, and . . . *No!* she exclaimed silently, as he pulled his nightshirt over his head.

She scrunched herself down into the bed.

He slid into bed and pulled up the bedclothes. "Good night."

"Good night."

Civilized people didn't quarrel, she told herself. Civilized people said polite good-nights and went to sleep as if there weren't a huge gulf between them.

She hit him.

"Ouch! What was that for?"

"You know what for," she muttered.

"I don't."

She hit him again.

"What the devil is the matter with you?" He sat up.

"I won't have you teasing me!"

"Teasing you?"

"Yes! Walking around naked, making me believe that at last you might trust me a little—but all the time you were just teasing me. Making me want you!"

He stared at her, his face unreadable and shadowed against the firelight.

"Making you want me?"

"Yes, it's not fair. How would you like it if I pranced around the room fiddling with logs, stark naked and bathed in firelight—"

"I'd like it very much."

"—and then I come back and shove myself into a huge, ugly nightshirt, covering every inch—"

"Not every inch, surely."

"Stop teasing me! Yes, every inch that counts."

"Every inch counts, believe me," he murmured. "And the inches that count most are not impeded by the shirt."

She would have hit him again, only she didn't want to make a habit of it. "It's not a joke, Luke."

"I never thought it was," he said in quite a different tone. "And if you cannot accept me as I am, I will go else—"

She grabbed him by the arm as he rose. "Don't you dare walk out on me again, for if you do, I warn you Luke, I will follow you—in my shift if I must!"

He sat back on the bed, and she released his arm.

"You say I cannot accept you as you are, but it's you who cannot accept yourself, who thinks he must hide himself from me. It's not modesty, so don't try to pretend it is. You took off your shirt without a thought when I was thirteen. I remember."

She waited for him to say something, but there was no sound in the room, only the fire hissing gently and the sound of his breathing.

"I saw you then and you were perfect," she said softly.

Still he said nothing.

She swallowed. "I have been thinking a lot about that day . . . and, and what came after it. It's my fault you couldn't get an annulment. I didn't realize what my aunt was asking me. She knew the man had cut all my clothes off me, and that I was naked, and she asked if he hurt me and I said yes, because he did. And, and then she asked me if there was blood, and I said yes, because there *was*, only . . . only not the blood she meant."

"I see."

She wished she could see his face.

"So I'm sorry. It's not much of a thanks for the good deed you did me, to tie you to me for life. I know you didn't want me for a wife, and I . . . I know a man like you wouldn't ever choose someone like me, but . . . but I'm the wife you've got, and we must make the best of it." She stared at his grim, silent silhouette, waiting for him to say it was all right, that he forgave her mistake, to repeat that he was content in his marriage.

But as the silence stretched, she knew it was just a lie he'd told to shut Ramón up.

Oh God, she was going to cry. She wouldn't. She refused to. She squeezed her eyes shut and pressed her lips tightly together.

But she must have made a sound, for he leaned forward, lit the candle, and shone it on her face. "You're crying?"

"No, I'm not." She turned her face away, scrubbing at the tears that had welled up, unexpected and unwanted. She despised tears.

There was another long silence.

"And all of this is about me removing my shirt, is that it?" His voice was quiet, but there was an unsteady note in it that caught at her heart.

She leaned forward and laid her hand on his knee. "Luke, however it happened, mistake or not, I'm your wife. I made sacred vows to love you and honor you and I promise you I will never ever break them. There is nothing you cannot show me, no disfigurement that can make any difference to me. I don't care if it's ugly or—"

"Ugly?" He gave a harsh, jagged laugh. "You think I'm hiding something ugly?" In one fluid movement he pulled his nightshirt over his head and dropped it on the floor. "There! My disfigurement! Satisfied?"

Bella stared. She couldn't believe her eyes. "That's all it is? A tattoo?" All this fuss for a little tattoo?

"It's not a tattoo." He passed her the candle and she looked closer.

"Oh my God," she whispered.

It was a scar, yet it was like no scar she'd ever seen before. In the hollow beneath his right shoulder was a rose, its petals black-edged and raised against the surface of his skin. Carved into his skin—the edges of the petals were ridges of hardened skin, stained black to stand out.

It was beautiful. And horrible in its careful, deadly intricacy.

"Who did this to you?" she whispered. Each line, each petal had been sliced into him. Who would carve such a thing into a man's living flesh?

He didn't answer. She put the candle aside and touched the rose with gentle fingertips. He flinched. She looked a question at him.

"It doesn't hurt. It was done seven years ago."

And yet he'd flinched.

It must have been agony at the time. Some men liked such things, she knew. Tattoos and decorative scars. But if he liked it, why hide it? "You chose to have this done?"

His jaw tightened and he looked away. His knuckles were white.

"It was forced on you?" she whispered in horror. "By whom?"

He hesitated, and for a moment she thought he wasn't going to answer. "A gift from La Cuchilla."

"The Blade," she whispered and looked at the cuts in his flesh. *La* Cuchilla. He'd used the feminine form but it must be a mistake, she thought. It could not have been a woman . . . could it?

He took a deep breath and didn't quite meet her gaze. "Now, if your curiosity is satisfied, wife . . ." he said in an attempt at a light, jocular tone that failed miserably.

Bella's curiosity wasn't nearly satisfied, but she could not deny him, not seeing the vile, beautiful thing engraved in his smooth, warm flesh. Done a year after he'd married her.

She pulled off the shirt she was wearing and flung it on top of his other one. She was naked beneath. She drew him down to her, covering his face with kisses, as if somehow she could make up for the dreadful thing that had been done to him.

He pressed his face against her breasts for a long moment, holding her tight against him, while a long shudder racked his body.

Bella ran her hands over his body, kissing every bit of him she could reach, glorying in him, knowing it was futile to comfort him for something done seven years before, but unable to stop herself from trying.

He gently rubbed his face against her breasts, then his mouth closed hotly over her nipple and she gasped. He teased it gently with his tongue and teeth, and then sucked hard. She arched beneath him as a deep shudder rippled through her. He continued suckling and teasing until she was squirming and writhing under him.

He slid his hand down her belly, between her legs where she ached for him.

"No," she said, and with every bit of self-control she could muster, she pulled away.

"What's wrong?"

"Nothing," she panted. "My turn."

She pushed back the covers, baring him to her gaze in the candlelight, her big, golden warrior.

She ran her fingertips lightly over his chest, learning his texture, the firm flesh, the hard muscles, exploring the small nubs of his flat male nipples. His body was hard and hot, and she loved the feel of it, the feel of him.

She bent and flickered her tongue over his tiny, hard nipples, tasting salt and a sharp, masculine flavor that was all Luke. She loved the taste of him. She teased his nipples as he'd teased her, nibbling and gently biting them, scraping her teeth over their tips, and she smiled as he shivered and arched, as she had.

She smoothed her palms over the bands of hard muscle across his belly and scratched lightly like a cat down the line of dark hair arrowing from his belly to his groin.

Her hands wandered lower, and feeling bold, she ran one

finger lightly along the hardened length of him. He shuddered under her touch. She caressed the sensitive tip, tracing one fingertip gently over the tiny bead of liquid, smoothing it over him. The hot, satiny feel of him entranced her, and her palm tightened around him.

"Witch," he groaned, but his eyes were half closed with pleasure, and he shuddered in a way she recognized. Emboldened by his obvious pleasure, she wrapped her whole hand around him and squeezed.

"Enough." His body was hard trembling with barely controlled need. "Do you want me to explode?"

He slid his hands between her thighs. "Now," he muttered.

"Yes, now, my love."

His eyes flew open, but she had not the courage to repeat it. "Now." She parted her legs and took him into her, and with a moan, he thrust and thrust, his gaze locked on hers, unbroken, until she shattered in his arms and he shattered with her.

*T*he soles of his feet burned, his vitals were molten agony, every part of his body screamed with silent pain, and until the blade cut into him he hadn't thought it was possible to feel any more pain.

But it was.

The blade sliced into his flesh in a cold, burning arc, slow and painstaking in its precision.

He stiffened, biting down hard on the inside of his mouth to stop himself from screaming. He'd rather die than scream.

Screaming was the point of the exercise.

Screaming and information.

"I do like to mix business with pleasure," La Cuchilla had murmured in his ear. And made another slice in Luke's flesh.

His body shook with the effort not to scream. He bit down on his tongue, and his mouth filled with blood.

"Beautiful." La Cuchilla took a handful of blackened salt and slowly, thoroughly massaged it into the cut, packing it under each leaf of flesh. Forming the petals.

Luke arched and shuddered against the sting of the salt.

"Ahh, you fight it, but you will love the effect, truly." La Cuchilla *sat back and waited until the pain dulled to an almost bearable level, then smiled into his eyes and sliced again . . .*

Luke screamed.

Panting, sweating, and rigid with fear, he surfaced from the darkness, his shoulder on fire, his arms and legs flailing, shamed, dirty, and desperate to escape.

"Luke, Luke, it's all right," a soft voice called in his ear. "It's just a dream. You're safe."

He thrashed around, fighting nameless things, his body afire. He turned and there, lit by a glow of candlelight, he saw her, pale and lovely, her eyes clear and golden, shining with honesty and love like a beacon in the night.

He grabbed at her mindlessly, using her to haul himself from the morass of dark horror. He seized her roughly, pushed her legs apart, and plunged himself into her soft receptive body.

She slid her fingers into his hair and closed her eyes, but he shook her hard, shouting, "No, look at me! Look at me, damn you!"

And she opened her eyes wide, shining clear and gold, and clung to him as he rode the storm, thrusting deeply into her, burying himself in her, cleansing himself in her heat and softness, driving out the demons that plagued him.

Until he shattered and was safe.

He lay there, panting, on her breast, and at last her eyes fluttered closed.

Slowly, Luke came back to himself. Through the shutters on the window he could see slits of cold, predawn light.

He was still inside his wife, still crushing her into the hard, lumpy mattress. Oh God, what had he done, using her so roughly? Grabbing her like an animal, pounding into her. Shouting at her.

Shame coiled in his belly.

He gently disengaged and moved off her.

"Isabella," he began.

She stirred sleepily against him. "Well, if that's what a nightmare does to you, remind yourself to have them more often." She stretched and twined herself around him. "Do we have time for a nap before dawn?"

"You didn't mind?"

She half opened her eyes and looked at him, a catlike smile of satisfaction curling her lips. "You want me to purr?"

It surprised a laugh out of him, and suddenly he found himself laughing and laughing. Horrified, he realized he was on the verge of tears. Laughter turned to choked sounds, and she wrapped her arms around him and held him tight as he fought the laughter-sobs that wracked him.

"Hush, my love," she murmured. "It's all right. Let it go, let it go." She drew him down to her breast, stroking his damp hair back from his forehead, and murmured soothing things until the bout of emotion had passed and he lay calm.

And was safe.

"La Cuchilla?"

He nodded.

"What sort of a person would do that to another person?" She could not believe a woman could do such an evil thing.

He didn't answer. She stroked his hair. "How did it happen?"

He shook his head. "It was just . . . something stupid. We were young and stupid."

"We?"

"Michael and I."

She waited. And he knew he would have to explain, some of it, at least. All these years he'd kept it locked up inside him, and now . . .

But if he was going to keep waking her up with the damned dreams . . .

Trust, she'd said. It didn't come easy.

"Michael was one of us, Wellington's Angels, or his Devil Riders, depending on who you talk to. Five of us from school, Gabe, Harry, Rafe, Michael, and me."

He could hear her soft breathing and the shifting of coals in the dying fire.

"Michael was the only one of us who didn't make it home."

She tucked the bedclothes more warmly around them both and waited.

"It was in 1812. Not long after our victory at Salamanca. I'd just turned twenty-one; Michael was twenty-two. The war was going well, we were young and full of the confidence of youth . . ." He sighed. "Such extraordinary confidence. We'd been at war for years, and despite horrendous casualties all around us, none of us—our friends, the five of us who'd been at school and joined the army together—had even been seriously wounded."

He lay quietly, recalling that time. Seven years ago, yet it felt in some ways like a hundred years. And in others, like yesterday. "We half believed ourselves invincible. Life was painted in bold bright colors, no shades of gray for us. It was all a big adventure; we lived for danger." He shook his head. "Such fools young men can be."

"Tell me what happened," she said softly.

"We were riders—glorified messengers, really—taking messages from headquarters, liaising between different sections of the army, delivering information, money, orders—whatever was required.

"This day we'd come—Michael and I—from an important briefing, and we'd been ordered to take messages to—" He broke off. Even after all this time, the habit of secrecy was strong. "Suffice it to say Michael was riding to meet a general and I was taking the same information to our Spanish allies in the hills."

"The *guerrilleros*."

"Yes. But just out of camp we were . . . waylaid. A stupid thing; we should have known better. A . . . a woman in distress."

"It was a trap?"

He nodded. "Next thing, Michael and I were in the cellar of a house being . . . questioned."

"Tortured," she whispered.

"He was in the next room. I could hear him . . . hear what they were doing to him. And he could hear what they were doing to me." His breathing grew harsher with the memory. "It was . . . bad." He'd thought he would die of the pain. "I wanted to die."

She held him tightly, her lips against his temple.

"But you didn't give in," she whispered, "didn't give up the information."

Luke closed his eyes. So tempting to let it pass, to let her think he was the hero she wanted him to be.

Trust, she'd said.

So he told her. "I don't know. I think I did. I don't re-member."

"What do you mean, you don't know?"

He made a helpless movement. "We were found, Michael and I, in the cellar of that cottage a week later. Michael had been dead a week by then. I was out of my head with fever. Michael's body and mine bore identical marks of torture, but he'd had his throat cut and I—I had been left with a blanket, water, and this." He gestured to the hideous rose.

"We learned soon afterward that the French had the infor-mation." Bitter shame washed through him as he forced him-self to admit, "It seems pretty obvious who talked." He waited for her response. Isabella was a Spanish patriot, the daughter of a leader of the *guerrilleros*.

She made no comment, no exclamation of horror or dis-gust, and gave no false comfort or meaningless sympathy. She just held him tight for a long time, then kissed him.

The breath he didn't know he'd been holding escaped in a long sigh.

"I've never told anyone that. Not my friends, not my fam-ily." He felt lighter already. "My superiors knew we'd been tortured, of course, and that the French had the information, but there was no way of telling who'd given it—Michael and I weren't the only ones with the same information—so no action was taken." No court-martial, he meant.

"Of course no action was taken," she said. "They saw you were a hero."

He turned his head and stared at her. Had she not under-stood what he'd just told her?

She made an impatient gesture. "It was Michael who talked, of course."

"You don't know that," he croaked.

She shrugged. "I never knew Michael, of course, but I do know you." She smoothed cool fingers across his furrowed brow and said softly, "Luke, even in your dreams you fight this La Cuchilla. You did not give in, my love, I know it, and if you were not so hard on yourself, you would know it, too. Now come to bed. It's almost dawn, but I think we both need a little more sleep before we ride on, don't you?" And she snuggled down in the bed, pulling him with her.

Luke lay in her arms, feeling empty, drained, and wakeful. So simple. Such an easy absolution. He wanted desperately to accept it, to embrace the notion that it hadn't been all his fault.

Except he hadn't told her the whole story. Not quite. Not his deepest shame.

*T*hey made a late start in the morning and reached Ayerbe as the sun was sinking low. Luke paused on the outskirts of the village. "How tired are you?"

"Why do you ask?"

"I know we'll be made very comfortable at the Inn With No Fleas, but if you aren't too tired, we could travel on another hour and call in at the Castillo de Rasal."

Bella had been looking forward to a hot meal and a bed, but at the prospect of seeing the Marqués de Rasal again, she felt her energy renewed. "Oh yes, do let us go on. I'd love to see the *marqués* again. He was my father's dearest friend, and like an uncle to me when I was a child."

Satisfied, he gave a brisk nod, and they continued on their way.

He'd hardly said a word all day. Bella had been observing him quietly. Physically there was a new ease between them, but whether that came from Luke or herself was another question.

In the darkest hour of his torment he'd turned to her instinctively, seeking her body, her comfort, to help drive out his demons . . . The dark, desperate violence of his need for her had pierced her heart. And her body still thrilled with it.

And that dreadful tale . . . He'd never told it to another soul, not even his oldest friends.

He might not love her, but instinctively, he'd trusted her.

Even his offering to stay at a place he did not know, with people he did not know, was a small sign of trust. It was an indirect apology for his refusal to let her visit there last time. The knowledge filled her with quiet warmth.

She glanced across at him, riding toward the deepening lilac sky, his face grave and drawn, like that of a man contemplating his doom. It wasn't the air of a man who'd bared his soul. Instead of exhibiting the lightness and relief she'd always felt from sharing a terrible secret, it was almost as if his shame had increased.

Still, probing now would only make him clam up further.

Bed was the place to talk. After he'd taken her, in that period when it seemed two people could get no closer, when the barriers between them were soft and transparent and the world had shrunk to just one bed, a place of sated bodies, quiet murmurs, and slow, soft touches.

She had not known that place existed.

She understood now why married women talked about when they were girls, even after a month of two of marriage. It had always seemed to her to be an affectation, a way of lording it over their unmarried friends. Now, only a handful of days into her marriage, her real marriage, she knew it was not.

She was not the girl she'd been a few weeks ago. It was not simply being part of someone else—that wasn't quite right; she was herself and he was a separate being, very separate at times. But she was a different person now, with insights into her own nature—and his—that she'd never dreamed of.

The feeling, when he took her body, of being subject to the deepest animal instincts, of letting go all that was civilized, all that was schooled . . . The power of his body as he thrust into her again and again, the strength of her as she took him in, the racking build of pleasure, the deep, sweaty joy in the act.

And the freedom of being able to let go, to scream, to bite and scratch and let out the wildness she'd tried to hide all her life, and he liked it. More than liked it. Gloried in it.

Being married was like coming out of a cocoon, splitting the old carapace, and finding the world was full of rainbow colors. And that you could fly.

She glanced across at her grim-faced husband.

Or not.

Seventeen

~

The Castillo de Rasal was an imposing stone building rising high above the surrounding landscape, a fortress that
made no bones about domination. Even as darkness fell, its
silhouette towered darkly above them, blotting out the night
sky and the stars.

Luke handed his card to the servant who answered the
door. Isabella had written something on the back. Normally
he preferred to travel as Señor and Señora Ripton—it was
wiser not to let people know you were rich—but in this case,
he brought out his title. The servant took the card, asked them
to wait, then glided away.

This was not like Isabella's former home; Castillo de
Rasal was ancient, but far from shabby. Everything that could
be polished gleamed, the entrance was lit by flaming torches,
the light catching on rich tapestries and precious metals and
flickering over gilded frames surrounding glowing works of
art. Generations of wealth were represented here.

They did not have to wait long. The *marqués* himself
came to greet them, saying, "Isabella, my dear, dear child,

what a delightful surprise. We thought you were forever lost to us. And now, look at you, all grown up and the image of your dear mother."

He was more than sixty, a tall, spare, handsome man with silvering dark hair, a scimitar of a nose, and a small goatee. He embraced Isabella, kissing her on both cheeks and giving her a warm hug, before turning to greet Luke.

"Isabella's husband? How very pleased I am to meet you, dear sir." He gave Luke a searching look. "You have a treasure here, Ripton, I hope you know."

"I know it, sir." Luke glanced at Isabella, who was looking flushed, glowing, and, to Luke's eyes, utterly beautiful.

The *marqués* caught the exchange and smiled. He clapped Luke on the back. "Excellent, excellent, I'm glad to hear it. Come in, come in, dinner will be put back half an hour—no, no, you are not holding us up. My wife has been out all day and has only just returned."

"Your *wife*, Tío Raul?" Isabella exclaimed.

He smiled. "Yes, my dear, I remarried several years ago. An old fool, you might say, but wait till you meet her. She has just gone up to change and is never speedy in these matters, so there is plenty of time for you two to wash and prepare yourself. And no need to dress for dinner. We shall be quite informal here tonight, *en famille*." Quite disregarding the fact he was in formal satin knee breeches, silk stockings, and a beautifully cut coat. "Now, run along with Pedro here. He will show you to your rooms and see to your every need." He beamed. "Little Isabella, all married and grown up. Such a pleasure, my dear."

Alone in the sumptuous bedchamber allotted them, they changed out of their riding clothes. Looking far too delicious in her chemise, corset, and stockings, but entirely unaware of her effect on him, Isabella brushed out her hair, while Luke shaved in his underwear. They'd handed her red dress and silk shawl and Luke's coat and shirt to Pedro for ironing.

Luke wished they'd had an hour before dinner. What was it about that corset?

"I wonder who Tío Raul married? He's been a widower as long as I can remember."

Luke wiped the last of the lather off his chin and dried his face. He had little interest in the new *marquésa*.

Isabella started to rebraid her hair in her customary coronet. It framed her face perfectly. "He fought Napoleon, you know. When Papa died, the *marqués* took command of Papa's *guerrillero* force."

Luke was surprised. "Those *guerrilleros* led a hard life. It couldn't have been easy for an—"

"Don't dare say an old man." She laughed. "He'd never forgive you. Particularly with a new wife, who from the sounds of things might be quite a bit younger."

Their clothes came back pressed and immaculate, and they quickly dressed and went downstairs.

"Come in, come in," the *marqués* greeted them. "My wife sent a message that she will be a little delayed and that we must start without her." He turned up his hands in a helpless male expression. "Women, never on time. Let us go in."

He ushered them into a large dining room where the walls were encrusted with gloomy painted ancestors. The first course was brought in, a dozen different dishes, all looking and smelling delicious. "Eat, eat," he urged. "You will be hungry after your long journey." They needed no further encouragement.

"I understand you are traveling on horseback. You were an intrepid horsewoman as a little girl, but now . . ." He paused delicately. Wondering if Isabella's husband was a careless brute or simply strapped for cash, Luke decided.

"We're in a hurry," Isabella told him. "My husband has an important engagement in England, and it is quicker to travel on horseback than in a carriage. Besides," she flashed the *marqués* a quick grin, "I enjoy it. For too many years I was shut up in a convent, and the one time my husband made me travel in a carriage I was so bored. I cannot tell you what a joy it is to gallop over the hills in the fresh air."

And the cold and the wind and the rain, thought Luke. Without complaint.

The old gentleman laughed. "You haven't changed, dear child. Now, tell me, how did you two meet? I can't say I approve, an Englishman taking my little Isabella out of Spain."

Isabella stilled, her face suddenly pale. Did she really imagine Luke would tell her beloved *marqués* the dreadful circumstances that had brought them together?

"It was a chance encounter," Luke said easily. "One of those things. One meeting and that was it. My fate sealed." As soon as the words were out of his mouth he realized how she would take them. He hadn't meant that, not at all. He'd meant it to sound romantic.

The *marqués* nodded. "It was like that for the *marquésa* and me. We met a year ago, in Madrid. She'd had a terrible war, poor girl. Lost every one of her family, as with so many of us." His glance embraced Isabella in acknowledgment of her own loss.

He lifted his wineglass. "But we must rebuild, must we not? To Spain, and to rebuilding."

They drank the toast.

"Toasting me? How kind," purred a sultry voice. A woman in her midthirties glided in, dressed in a dark red dress cut low to frame a magnificent bosom, cinched tight at a narrow waist, and sleek over voluptuous hips. Hair, black as a raven's wing, was drawn back in an elegant coiffure, highlighting perfect skin, delicate cheekbones, and full, rouged lips.

No secret why the *marqués* had married her.

The scent of roses emanated from her perfect body.

Luke's gorge rose.

"Ah, my dear." The *marqués* rose to greet his wife, and Luke rose with him, jerkily, shoving his chair back so roughly that it almost fell. A servant caught it.

The *marqués* performed the introductions. Luke barely heard a word.

He couldn't think. His skin grew clammy. From the other side of the table he heard Isabella give a meaningful cough. He didn't so much as glance at her.

"Delighted to meet you, Lord Ripton." The *marquésa* held

out her hand to him. Luke made no move to take it. He stared at the elegant, outstretched hand as if it were a cobra.

The lustrous dark eyes widened, then narrowed. They caressed his face, drifted down his body and up again, then came to rest just below his right shoulder. The rouged lips curved in a tiny smile.

She laughed, a rich contralto chuckle. "So delightful that I can still have that effect on a young man."

Luke stiffened. She was toying with him. Incredible. She had no fear he would denounce her.

Did that mean the *marqués* knew who his wife really was?

"Isabella, we're leaving," he snapped.

"*What?* But Luke—"

"Now!"

"No. It's the height of incivility—"

In English, he said, "It's her, the person I told you about."

"What person? What are you talking about?"

"The one who did this." He touched his shoulder.

Her eyes widened. "La Cuch—?"

"Don't say it," he cut her off sharply, keeping a wary eye on the *marqués* and *marquésa*. "Do *not* say the name," he repeated, still speaking English. "There is danger here, and you must get away."

It took her a moment to absorb what he was telling her. "It was this woman who did that frightful thing to you? I cannot credit it." But though she was incredulous, he could see she believed him. She stared at the *marquésa* in horror. "But we must tell the *marq*—"

"No! He knows. Now do as I tell you and get up and leave the table, quietly and quickly."

She shook her head. "You're wrong. I've known him all my life and he is a man of honor. He cannot possibly have knowingly married La Cuchilla."

Damn! She'd said it. Now the fat was really in the fire.

"La Cuchilla?" the *marqués* exclaimed. "What is this about La Cuchilla?" He rose to his feet, his brow furrowed with confusion. Or was it apparent confusion? Luke wondered.

In two strides Luke was beside his wife. He pulled her to her feet and pushed her behind him. "We're leaving now," he told the *marqués.* "Don't try to stop us."

"I wouldn't dream of it, my dear fellow," the *marqués* said, holding up his hands pacifically, "but I have no idea what you're talking about. What's all this about La Cuchilla?"

Luke glanced from the man to his wife and back again. Was it an ingenuous effort to lull him into a sense of safety? Could the man really not know? No, a Spanish patriot who'd commanded a guerrilla force would surely know La Cuchilla. And that being so, he'd have every reason to kill anyone who knew it.

"Isabella, come," Luke said, taking her arm and keeping himself between her and the *marqués.*

But Isabella was having none of his protection. She stepped forward and said to the *marqués,* "My husband recognizes your wife, Tío Raul. The *marquésa* was once a French agent known as La Cuchilla. She tortured young men for pleasure."

The *marqués* stared, then shook his head. "No, no, my dear, that cannot be right. I've heard of La Cuchilla, of course—who in these parts has not? But she died several years ago."

"Died?"

"She was caught and hanged by patriots. A well-deserved death for a witch and a traitor."

"Then they hanged the wrong woman," Luke said grimly. "Because the real La Cuchilla is sitting there, at your side."

The *marqués* looked at his wife.

She gave him a look of faint bewilderment. "The poor young gentleman is mistaken, of course, my dear. Perhaps his ordeals in the war have left him . . . confused. Or perhaps he has me mixed up with another woman."

The *marqués,* relieved, nodded. "Yes, that must be it."

"He is *not* confused," Isabella insisted. "If he says you are La Cuchilla, then you are."

"Isabella!" the *marqués* exclaimed. "My wife cannot possibly be—"

"She is," Luke said. "She tortured and killed dozens of men."

"La Cuchilla did, yes," the *marqués* agreed. "But not my wife. La Cuchilla operated in the north, and was seen back and forth across the border, but I met my wife in Madrid. The first time she had ever been this far north was when she came here, on our honeymoon."

"So she said," Luke said.

The *marqués* drew himself up. "Sir, you are offensive. A case of mistaken identity is forgivable, but to insult my wife, in my own home . . ."

"It's not a case of mistaken identity, Tío Raul," Isabella intervened hotly. "My husband was himself tortured by La Cuchilla. Do you think he would then mistake another woman for her?"

The *marqués*'s dark brows snapped together over his beak of a nose. "You were tortured, sir?"

"I was," Luke said stiffly. He loathed admitting it.

"And yet you survived," the *marquésa* said softly. "An odd kind of murderer, this La Cuchilla."

Luke stared at her. Was he meant to be grateful she'd spared his life?

Isabella flung her a look of hatred. "Show him, Luke."

Luke tried to hush her with a look, but she ignored him and pulled open the neck of his shirt. "There," she said, exposing the carved rose.

There was a hiss of intaken breath as the *marqués* saw the design. He gave his wife a troubled look. "Rosa?"

"Show me." The *marquésa* sauntered over and reached for Luke's shirt with a single polished fingernail.

He stepped back, rigid with loathing. "Touch me again, you witch, and I'll kill you."

She swiveled to face her husband and gave a helpless feminine sigh. "I don't know what he's talking about, my dear, and if he won't even show me the pretty design . . ."

"*Pretty design?* You know *exactly* what he's talking about! You carved that vile thing in my husband's flesh!" Isabella said furiously. "You think you can wriggle out of it because Tío Raul and my husband are too gentlemanly to put a woman to the test. But I'm no gentleman!" And snatching up a carving knife from the table, she grabbed the *marquésa* around the neck and placed the blade against her cheek.

"*Isabella!*" Luke and the *marqués* exclaimed in unison.

"Put the knife down."

"Isabella, child, this is madness. Rosa is my wife!"

"Raul, help me! She's insane!"

Isabella ignored them all. "Now, *marquésa*—tell us the truth, or I'll carve a 'pretty design' on your cheek. Of course, I'm not an artist like you, but perhaps I could manage a B for 'bitch,' or an M for 'murderer' . . ." She pressed the cold edge of the blade against the smooth damask cheek.

The woman shrieked. "Raul, Raul, I beg of you!"

The *marqués* made a halfhearted move to help her, but Luke grabbed him by the arm, murmuring, "Leave it. Isabella won't hurt her, but if you interfere, someone really will get hurt." And it might be Isabella.

The *marqués* heard him and made no further move.

The *marquésa* heard him, too, and braced herself to fight.

"Make no mistake," Isabella murmured in her ear. "I'll happily carve your cheek into mincemeat."

The rouged lips curled in a sneer. "You haven't the guts, little sheltered bud of the aristocracy."

"Oh, haven't I?" Isabella said silkily. "I might not be old like you, but I lived through a war, too—and I killed three men. Now I know that's nothing by your standards—they were all vile pigs who were attacking a convent—but believe me, I would have no trouble at all killing a vicious she-wolf who tortured and maimed my husband, murdered his friend, and"— she glanced at the *marqués*—"deceived a kind and noble patriot who deserved better. Why wouldn't I carve my initials into your face?" She pressed the blade against the smooth cheek. "Now talk."

The *marquésa* said nothing.

"That poor woman who was hanged in your place, was it a lucky case of mistaken identity?"

The woman's eyes flickered with brief scorn. Both Luke and the *marqués* saw it.

"Ah," Isabella said. "So you arranged for her to die in your place. Very clever."

"Rosa." There was a world of horror in the *marqués*'s voice.

"See, he knows it now, so you might as well admit it: you are La Cuchilla."

There was a long silence. Isabella pressed the knife deeper, and the woman hissed, "Yes, yes, very well, yes. But it was a long time ago."

The *marqués*'s breath gushed out. Luke released him, and the *marqués* sagged onto a chair, looking suddenly old.

"Raul," the *marquésa* pleaded. "It makes no difference to you and me. We all did things in the war that we want to forget. Raul?"

He stared at her a long time. Then he said, "I married La Cuchilla," in the oldest, weariest voice. He buried his head into his hands.

"Raul, please . . ." He didn't move, and the *marquésa* knew she'd lost him. Lost everything. Her claws rose. Isabella moved the knife. Bright beads of blood appeared in a line across the pale cheek. Her eyes glittered hatred and she hissed with fury, but she did not move.

"You tortured my husband?"

"Yes."

"And his friend. You murdered his friend."

She snorted. "Michael? He was no loss to the world."

"He was a loss to his family and friends."

The woman looked at Luke and said deliberately, "Michael was a nuisance. A dead bore."

It was an odd thing to say. Bella glanced at Luke. His face was stark and drawn, his fists clenched.

"Why do you say that?" Bella asked.

Silence.

"Was it because Michael gave you the information?"

The woman's lush lips thinned in a sneer. "Every detail."

"Is that why you murdered him?"

"No, I cut his throat to stop his whining," La Cuchilla said coldly. "I despise weaklings."

"Did my husband give you any information?"

"No. That one took twice the punishment and said nothing."

"And that is why you left him alive?"

She gave an infinitesimal shrug of her elegant shoulders. "He was beautiful and brave—a worthy enemy. Why would I kill him?"

"Why would you carve that, that *thing* into his flesh?"

"My pretty rose?" La Cuchilla smiled. "A whim. A little something to remember me by."

A whim? To painfully brand a young man with a mark that she knew would shame him for the rest of his life? Luke would have seen it every day of his life since, a reminder that he had betrayed—or believed he had betrayed—his country and his friend.

It was pure, cold-blooded evil. Bella's hand shook visibly with the desire to plunge the knife into the woman's black heart.

But she couldn't bring herself to do it. She'd found out all she needed to know. Luke now knew what had happened. Perhaps now he could forgive himself. Not that he had anything to forgive himself for. He was a hero. With a sob, Bella flung the knife away, pushed La Cuchilla aside, and dived straight into Luke's arms.

He hugged her tightly. "You crazy, crazy girl! To put yourself in such danger!"

"I had to. Neither you nor Tío Raul would ever hurt a woman, even one such as she. I knew the threat to destroy her beauty would make her talk. The beautiful ones are always the vainest."

The *marquésa* pressed a white lace handkerchief to her cheek. It came away smeared with blood. She stared at it, and her face twisted with hate. "For that, you ugly little stick, you will die!" She produced a small, deadly looking pistol and aimed at Isabella.

The *marqués* yelled a warning. Luke turned, saw what was happening, and shoved Isabella behind him, protecting her with his body just as the pistol went off. The ball slammed into him and he crashed to the floor.

The *marqués* moved. A knife flashed through the air. La Cuchilla staggered, the blade buried deep in her throat. She gurgled horribly, clawing at the knife, then slowly sank to her knees and toppled over. Her blood spread in a crimson pool across the white marble floor.

"*H*ow bad is the injury?" the *marqués* asked. The body of his wife had been removed. There was no sign of blood on the smooth marble floor. Bella didn't ask what had been done with the body. She didn't care. All her concern was for Luke.

"A flesh wound only," Doctor Lopez said. "He was very lucky it struck where it did. As far as I can tell, no bones have been damaged. Bone fragments are the worst, but I believe he will recover, as long as there is no infection." The doctor, a surgeon-physician, had arrived almost immediately. He lived on the estate, the *marqués* said. A good man, very experienced with wounds of all kinds. The war, you understand.

Bella clung to her husband's hand, unable to take her eyes off his face for even a minute. "He's still unconscious."

"Be grateful for it," the surgeon told her. "It will spare him the pain when I remove the ball." He drew out a long pair of silver tongs, inserted them carefully into the hole beneath Luke's shoulder, and began to grope around inside.

In an extraordinary act of fate, the bullet aimed at Bella had pierced Luke through the center of the rose carved into his skin. It was nothing but a mess of blood and torn flesh now.

The surgeon probed, Luke groaned, even in unconsciousness, and Bella's stomach lurched. She clutched his hand to her breast and prayed silently.

"Almost there . . . just . . . yes." Doctor Lopez drew out the ball. He sprinkled sulfur powder into the wound and looked at the *marqués*. "Gunshot wounds are poisonous. I ought to . . ." He glanced at the fire and then at Bella.

"Ought to what?' she asked.

"Cauterize the wound. It is the accepted practice, but—"

"But what?"

"It is not pleasant for ladies to watch." He took out a long metal implement and placed it in the fire to heat. It was like a bent poker, with a drop-shaped metal end that was, Bella realized with a sick feeling, about the same size and shape as the hole in her husband's body. She shuddered.

"It will not be pleasant for my husband, either." She took Luke's other hand. "Do it. Quickly, while he's still unconscious."

The *marqués* came to stand behind her and placed his hands on her shoulders. "Your father would be very proud of you, my dear."

The surgeon carefully lifted the cauterizing tool from the flames and tested it by sprinkling a few drops of water on it. They sizzled. When he judged the temperature was right, he said, "Hold him still."

The *marqués* held Luke down by the shoulders. Bella closed her eyes. There was a hissing sound and a ghastly smell of burnt flesh. Luke's body jerked.

For a moment Bella thought she would faint. She clung tightly to Luke's hand, determined not to leave him, even for an instant, and after a moment or two the dizziness passed.

"It's done." The surgeon bent over the wound, examined his handiwork, and nodded. "It looks good. Smother it with fresh honey and cover it lightly with clean gauze. Keep it clean and let the air get to it as much as possible. If there's no infection, he should be fully recovered in a couple of weeks."

If . . . Bella thought. How would they know?

"He may have a little fever," the doctor continued. "Give him willow bark tea and such like—the usual treatments. And plenty of rest for the next few days."

Bella nodded. The convent had educated all the girls in the treatment of illness.

"Don't look so worried, my dear. Your husband is a strong, healthy fellow," the *marqués* said in hearty reassurance. "And if Doctor Lopez says he will recover, he will, never fear. The good doctor looked after us during the fighting. He lost fewer than most."

"How very reassuring," said Bella faintly.

* * *

*T*he first thing Luke was aware of was pain. His shoulder was on fire. His mind was fuzzy. And there was something he was supposed to . . . *La Cuchilla*? He could smell sulfur . . . burned flesh. . . gunpowder. The usual nightmare?

It all came back to him in a flash. La Cuchilla had pulled out a gun. . . and shot at— *Bella?*

His eyes flew open. "Bella!"

There she was, sitting on the edge of the bed, holding his hand, looking pale and worried but otherwise undamaged. At the sight of her sweet, anxious face, something in his chest clenched like a fist. He tried to sit up. "Did she hurt you?"

She pressed him back against the pillows. "Hush, don't move. You'll hurt yourself."

He scanned her body frantically. "Dammit, did she get you?"

She smoothed his brow. "No, my love, I am unhurt. It was you she shot."

My love. The words, as well as the knowledge she was unhurt, seemed to ease the burning in his shoulder. And the ache in his chest. "That's all right, then."

"It's not all right," she began indignantly.

Luke scanned the room. "Where is the she-devil?"

"She's dead." Bella glanced at the old *marqués*.

He stood behind Bella, looking gray and somehow shriveled. "Lord Ripton, I apologize, most sincerely, for the actions of my wife." The old man's words were both formal and sincere, but underneath, he was shattered.

Luke's anger that Bella had been endangered drained away. How could he blame this dignified old man for doing exactly what Luke had done? "Not your fault, sir," Luke managed. "Destiny. Always gets you in the end."

So she was dead. An end to it, at last.

"I killed my wife—no." The old man corrected himself heavily. "I executed La Cuchilla myself."

Not his wife: La Cuchilla. The simple statement held a great deal of pain. And humiliation. He'd loved his wife, but she'd betrayed him and he'd killed her. And now he was grieving.

Bella placed her hand over the old man's. The *marqués* withdrew it with quiet dignity.

Pride. It could lead a man into the worst of mistakes, or carry him through the unthinkable.

"I'm sorry," Luke said. He was tempted to lie back, close his eyes, let it all float away, but the stench of the past was bitter in his nostrils, and if he didn't explain now, he suspected he never would. Besides, he owed an explanation to his wife and the old man. Luke had set the whole disaster in motion by coming here. He struggled to sit up. It was more difficult than he thought. He was weak as a kitten and every movement swamped his shoulder with liquid fire.

"Later. You need to rest," Bella insisted.

"I'll rest better once I get this off my chest." Luke had heard confession was good for the soul. He hoped it was true.

"Very well, but make it quick. The doctor said you should rest." She fussed around him for a moment, arranging pillows behind him, fetching him a glass of water, and making sure he was comfortable.

"It didn't happen quite the way I told you," Luke admitted when she was finished. "Michael and I both knew La Cuchilla seven years ago. Knew her quite well, in fact."

"You *knew*—"

"This was long before we were captured and tortured. We had no idea she was La Cuchilla, of course. We knew her as *Señorita* Martinez, Rosa Martinez, a Spanish lady. Michael was in love with her." He met Bella's gaze and added, "We both were. At least we thought so at the time." Looking back, he could see it wasn't love at all, but a heated, heady brew of lust, well spiced with danger and rivalry.

Luke grimaced. "We were young men at war, far from our homes and our families. We were young, impressionable, and lonely. And she was very beautiful."

"She is still beautiful—or was." The old *marqués* crossed himself. "And she was very, very charming."

Bella gave an unimpressed sniff. "So everybody fell in love with her. Go on with the story."

Luke might have smiled at her caustic tone, but the prospect of confessing what he'd done weighed heavily on him. "Michael wanted to marry her. He'd actually proposed to her, had even spoken to his commanding officer, seeking permission to wed."

"And you? Did you want to marry her, too?" Bella asked.

Luke shook his head. "No, not at all. I desired her, of course." A cool statement for the white-hot blaze of lust Rosa Martinez had incited in him seven years ago. "But marriage never occurred to me—well, she wasn't the kind of woman one marr—" He broke off and turned to the *marqués*. "My apologies, sir. I meant no offense."

"None taken, Ripton. I knew Rosa was no innocent when I married her." He made an expressive gesture. "Truth to tell, when a man gets to my age, he prefers a woman of some experience."

Luke acknowledged the statement. He could appreciate that now. "She was experienced even then," he said. "We were no match for her. Michael was determined to marry her, despite his commanding officer's orders to the contrary. And I . . ." I was a fool for lust, Luke thought.

"And you?" Bella prompted.

Luke closed his eyes briefly. "Rosa chose me. She made it very clear she preferred me to Michael and she did everything she could to encourage my attentions." From flirtatious behavior to plain speaking to . . .

"What did you do?" Bella asked.

"I tried to stay away from her."

Her brows rose. "Even though you desired her and she wanted you?"

"Yes, of course. It was a point of honor. She was my friend's beloved, and he had honorable intentions toward her—marriage, no less. So I tried to have nothing to do with her."

"Rosa wouldn't have liked being refused," the old *marqués* said. "Especially by a handsome young man."

"She didn't," Luke admitted. He ran a hand across his chin. "She redoubled her efforts. She used Michael to try and make me jealous, tried to play us off against each other." He glanced at the *marqués*. "She kept building up Michael's hopes and dreams, talking about their future together, but all the while, her attentions were aimed at me. And then, one night . . ." He swallowed. "One night . . ." It was damnably hard to spit out what he'd done.

"She seduced you." The *marqués* said it for him.

Luke nodded. "I woke up one night and she was . . . there, next to my bed." Dressed in a black velvet cloak and wearing nothing under it. "I tried to send her away, but . . ."

"No man could have," the *marqués* said bluntly. "Don't blame yourself. How did the other boy react when he found out?"

The old guilt swamped Luke. "I should have told him, but . . . I couldn't. It would have been like—I don't know—like kicking a puppy. Michael was a believer. A dreamer. He thought Rosa was a saint, but he was the saint. He put women on a pedestal, to be worshipped from afar. He'd never even had a woman before: Rosa was his first." Luke shook his head. "So I couldn't tell him, couldn't bring myself to tell him of the double betrayal, his friend and his betrothed."

"So Rosa told him," the *marqués* said.

Luke nodded.

"How?" Bella asked. "When?"

Luke looked at Bella. "I told you about the day we rode out after the briefing. It was Rosa we met on the road in apparent distress, so of course neither of us thought twice about stopping. In moments we were captured and the next thing we were imprisoned in a cottage. And being questioned about the information we carried," he explained to the *marqués*. "We carried messages in our heads for the allied command."

"And that's when she told your friend?" Bella asked.

Luke nodded. "Yes, but only during the—while she was—"

"Torturing him," Bella said grimly.

Luke nodded. "She used it to torture him—oh, she used her knife with wicked skill, but she also described what she and I had done together. In great detail." His eyes were bleak and somber. "That's the real reason Michael gave in, why he told her what she wanted to know. Because he had no will to resist. Because between us, La Cuchilla and I broke Michael's heart." His voice was harsh, scalding with self-recrimination, as he added, "I might not have betrayed my country, but I sure as hell betrayed my friend."

Luke couldn't bring himself to look at his wife or his host, knowing the condemnation he would see in their eyes.

"Of course you didn't." Bella slid her arms around him and rubbed her cheek gently against his chest. "That evil bitch was the one to blame, not you. You were her victim as much as Michael."

Luke blinked. Absolution didn't come as easily as that, surely?

"Exactly!" the old *marqués* said. "You only think that because your friend died and my w—La Cuchilla killed him. As she had killed many a good and true man before. That's what she did, my boy. It was her particular skill, to find men's weaknesses and exploit them. She was Michael's weakness, Michael was yours. She tortured you both, that day, remember? And she didn't only use her blade on you, either."

Luke stared at the old man, struck by the truth of the old man's words, yet still unwilling to believe.

The *marqués* continued, "If it hadn't been you, she would have seduced another of Michael's friends—and of course you were seduced, do not pull that face at me! Who was just twenty, still wet behind the ears, and who was thirty and had no doubt had more men than you'd had hot dinners?" He patted Luke's arm. "A pair of young, idealistic boys would have been putty in La Cuchilla's hands. Don't blame yourself over such a thing. Look at me, I am old and consider myself a man of the world, but I am just as foolish. More so—I married her." He gave a humorless laugh. "To tell you the truth, I am heart-sore, but also . . . embarrassed." He shook his head. "To marry my mortal enemy . . ." He contemplated his folly for a moment, then said as an afterthought, "And let me tell you, a young man's heart doesn't break so easily, not over an unfaithful woman. Perhaps, since you say your friend was young and naive, it was a painful awakening, but it would have happened anyway. It was inevitable." He grimaced and added, "And better before the wedding than after it."

He leaned forward and poked Luke firmly on his uninjured shoulder. "So cease this self-recrimination, young man, else it will poison your life. Terrible things happen in war, but the war is over. The dead cannot be brought back, but in the matter of La Cuchilla, justice has at last been done. Your friend is dead, but not at your hand or by your will, and he is revenged and will be at peace now. And you, my boy, are alive—spared again this very day! And you have this lovely young wife, so do not waste the gift that God has given you—live well and be happy." He rose to his feet and said wearily, "Now, I must be off. I must bury my wife." There was both grief and acceptance in his voice.

After the *marqués* had left, Luke, dazed, turned to Isabella. "I've always blamed myself for Michael's death. Now I don't know what to think."

"Don't think," she told him. "Sleep. You will feel better in the morning."

Luke, exhausted by his injury and his admissions, obeyed and soon slipped into a deep, dreamless sleep.

*L*ater that night the fever started. Bella sat up with Luke all night, feeding him willow bark tea and sponging down his heated flesh.

As she sponged, she thought about the story he'd told. Two young men's lives had been destroyed by that woman. Almost destroyed.

Luke felt such guilt over his betrayal, but even Bella, with her limited experience of life, could see that an eager and impressionable young man would have no chance against the wiles of a clever and beautiful woman. Witch.

The rose carved into Luke's flesh was a constant reproach. A brand of guilt.

It was too late to save Michael, but as she tended Luke's feverish body, Bella vowed she would make the rest of Luke's life as happy as she possibly could.

* * *

*L*uke's fever passed quickly, and in two days he was well enough to insist they continue on their way.

Bella, of course, gave it a flat veto. "It's ridiculous to think you can travel yet. Riding is out of the question! You'll open up that wound again, and then it will get infected and—and, people *die* from such infections, Luke!"

The *marqués* had intervened. He owed them a debt, he insisted. If it was ever discovered that he, a known patriot, had married a notorious French agent, a traitor, and a torturer . . . No, no, and no! That woman was never to be mentioned in the Castillo de Rasal again. He had wiped the whole unpleasant incident from his mind.

The old gentleman was putting a brave face on it, Bella thought. Deep down he was grieving. His wife's betrayal had cut deep. He had been intensely humiliated, and yet . . . he loved her.

Love is pain.

The *marqués* was also, Bella suspected, only too glad to get rid of herself and her husband; reminders of his grievous mistake in judgment, as well as witnesses to his killing of his wife, so when Luke had proved so stubborn about traveling on, the *marqués* had seized on the excuse and pressed his best traveling carriage on them so Luke could travel in the utmost comfort. He'd provided a coachman and grooms and two outriders and had sent riders on ahead to arrange the change of horses with minimum delay.

Apart from sleeping overnight at various inns, they'd traveled almost nonstop for four days. Bella was weary of it.

Luke was dozing again. He'd spent a good part of the journey sleeping. It was good for his recovery, she knew, but carriage travel, even in a well sprung, comfortable carriage, was so dull. She'd attempted to read one of the books the *marqués* had pressed on her as a parting gift, but the carriage bounced so much, trying to concentrate on the print made her feel ill.

They hit a pothole, and Luke grabbed a strap with his good hand. Good, he was awake.

"I've done a lot of thinking in the last few days while you've slept, Luke, and I've made a few decisions."

"Sounds ominous," Luke said with a faint smile. There was a new ease to him since they'd left the Castillo del Rasal. A lightness. As if he'd started to forgive himself. Not that he talked about it, or probably ever would, but she was hopeful.

"It's not quite that, but you might not like what I've decided to do," she said seriously. "It concerns my mother's fortune."

"Your fortune," he reminded her.

"Yes, exactly," she said, leaning forward. "It is *my* fortune, isn't it?"

"Yes."

"And I can do with it whatever I want, and you won't try to stop me?"

He considered that for a moment. "I suppose it depends what you want to do. If it seems to me unwise or imprudent, I will voice my opinion, possibly quite strenuously."

"But you won't actually stop me?"

"I can't stop you," he said. "It's your fortune."

Bella could still hardly believe it. For so long she had owned nothing, and before that she hadn't had any choice in any of her life. But this man, this beautiful wonderful man had signed away all his rights to her fortune—and though she had no exact idea of the extent of it yet, she knew it must be substantial.

"I've decided what I want to do with it—part of it, I mean, not the whole."

"I see."

"I'm going to give some of it to the other girls in the convent." And before he could say anything, she rushed on, "You see they're all stuck there because they have no dowries and their families are too proud to admit it or to let their daughters marry men not of their class. It's such a waste. They'll end up having to become nuns and nobody should be a nun unless they want to! And they're my friends."

He nodded. "So you're going to give them a dowry? All, what is it, six of them? That's quite a sum."

"I know, but you said I could spend—"

"I'm not arguing," he pointed out gently.

"Oh. Good. But that's not all. I want to give a share of the fortune to Perlita."

"Perlita?" He stared at her, dumbfounded for a moment, then burst out laughing.

"What is so funny?"

"After all the trouble we went through to keep Ramón's greedy paws off it! You know she'll give it all to him, don't you?"

She grinned triumphantly. "Ah, but it will be Perlita's dowry. Ramón will only get it if he marries her."

"And if he doesn't marry her?"

"He will," she said confidently. "He loves her. He's only considering marrying someone else because he's desperate to bring Valle Verde back to its former glory. And I want that, too, for it was once my home and I love it. So . . ." She tilted her head and gave him a quizzical look. "What do you think of my plan?"

"It's an excellent solution to all your worries."

"My worries?"

"You have a tendency to fret about other people's welfare," he told her. "This way you'll only have one person to fuss over."

She frowned. "Who?"

He leaned forward and tugged her out of her seat and onto his lap. "Me."

"Luke! Your wound."

"Treat me gently," he murmured.

Eighteen

❧

"I've never seen so many people in one place." Bella's head swiveled left and right as the carriage Luke called a "yellow bounder" wove through the crowded streets of London.

They'd landed at Portsmouth that day, and raced across the country at a speed Bella could barely believe. They'd only just arrived in London. It was the night of Molly's ball.

"Grosvenor Square on our left," he pointed out. "Have you ever eaten ice cream?"

"No, but—"

"I'll take you to Gunter's, then. You'll like it—damn!"

"What is it?"

"I'd forgotten about the dinner."

"What dinner?"

"The dinner before the ball. I'd hoped to introduce you to my mother before the ball, but she's giving a dinner beforehand and her guests are arriving already. See all those carriages lined up ahead? That's my mother's house. Your house, in fact. It actually belongs to me."

Bella glared at him. His mother's house? He'd completely

ignored all her protests. "I told you, Luke, I'm not going to your sister's ball. I don't have anything to wear. This is my best dress and look at it!" They both studied her red dress. It was looking sadly the worse for wear. "Even a housemaid wouldn't wear this."

He dismissed it with a gesture. "I know that. I'd planned to get Molly to lend you a dress." He pulled out his watch and consulted it. "But we're running later than I'd hoped. There won't be enough time for the maids to adjust it."

"Adjust it?"

"Yes, Molly is plumper than you. And a bit taller, too." He narrowed his eyes at her in calculation. "I have it—Nell!"

"Nell?" She knew who Nell was; the wife of one of Luke's closest friends, Harry. But her lack of dress wasn't really the problem. It was a useful excuse, that was all.

Bad enough to be shabbily dressed in the heart of fashionable London, but on top of it all, Bella was as nervous as a mouse about meeting Luke's friends and family en masse.

The foreign girl who trapped their darling into an unwanted marriage. The shabby foreign girl. But Luke was oblivious.

"Nell and Harry will be staying at Lady Gosforth's. You'll like Lady Gosforth. A right old tartar, but underneath she's got a heart of gold." Before Bella could say a word, Luke stuck his head out of the window and shouted directions to the postilion.

"How do you know this Nell would be willing to lend me a dress?"

He snorted as if the idea of Nell's refusing was ridiculous. "Nell's more your style, too. She's an elegant little thing. You'll like Nell. She's like you, a horsewoman to the fingertips." He sat back and then gave a crack of laughter.

"What?"

"I can't wait for my friends to meet you."

"Why?" she asked suspiciously.

"I told them to expect a demure and obedient little convent girl, someone who'd been patiently sewing samplers all these years."

She snorted.

He laughed again. "Exactly! They're going to *love* you."

She smiled and gazed out of the window. Of course it would be nice if his friends loved her, but she really didn't care. There was only one man she wanted to love her, and he was oblivious.

They reached Lady Gosforth's town house, but to Luke's dismay they found that Nell, Harry, and Lady Gosforth had already left for the pre-ball dinner. Even Lady Gosforth's dresser had gone out for the evening.

"However, Cooper, Lady Nell's own maid, is upstairs, Lord Ripton," Lady Gosforth's butler said. "Would you like me to summon her?"

"The very thing, Sprotton. Fetch her down at once," Luke said, and in a short time a pretty, young, smartly dressed maid-servant appeared.

Luke explained what was wanted. Cooper looked at Bella and her eyes lit. "Oh, sir, I think I have the very thing. And no, miss, I mean m'lady, Lady Nell wouldn't mind a bit. In fact when we got the dress home, we decided the color wasn't quite right on her. It'll be perfect for you, miss, trust me." She ushered Bella upstairs and Luke went around the corner to his lodgings to change.

In thirty minutes, Cooper did what Luke had failed to do in several weeks of marriage: convinced Bella of the benefits of having a good maid.

Bella stared at her reflection in the looking glass. "It's a miracle," she breathed. If the girls in the convent could only see her now. Less than half an hour, and yet nobody would have guessed that Bella hadn't spent half the day primping.

Cooper laughed. "No, m'lady, but it's a fact that this dress suits you better than it ever did Lady Nell."

"It's the dress and the magic of Cooper," Bella insisted. The dress, in green and bronze silk, fitted her perfectly, as did the corset designed for the dress. She didn't look skinny any-more; she looked . . . slender. And elegant. Even fashionable. And with a delicious hint of bosom.

Cooper had done something magic with her hair, too,

braiding it in an elegant variation of her usual coronet, and weaving in bronze and green and cream ribbons.

A whiff of the hare's-foot over her complexion, the merest breath of rouge on her cheeks and lips, and Bella barely recognized herself. It was about as far from the way she'd looked when she'd met Luke at the convent as it was possible to be. Thank goodness.

"Now for a shawl," Cooper said, opening a chest.

"What about this?" Bella produced her cream silk shawl.

"Oh, m'lady, it's gorgeous," Cooper breathed. "I'll just press the wrinkles out of it, and it'll be perfect."

"And . . . pearls?" She took out her mother's pearls.

"Perfect, m'lady, just perfect. You look an absolute picture, if you don't mind me saying."

Bella took a deep breath before she began the descent down the stairs. Dressed like this, she felt up to any gathering of friends and relatives. She hoped Luke approved.

She was a third of the way down when Luke appeared at the foot of the stairs. Bella almost stumbled. He'd always looked handsome, but now, freshly shaved and dressed in full formal evening dress, he looked utterly magnificent.

She must have made a sound, because he looked up. And froze.

She forced herself to keep walking. Absurd to be so nervous of her own husband looking at her, but . . . They weren't butterflies in her stomach; they were sparrows. Whole flocks of them, circling and dipping.

His eyes, a deep, glittering blue, devoured her. He didn't say a word, but the look in his face . . . it made her chest thicken and her heart pound.

For the first time in her life, she felt—no, she *knew* she was beautiful.

Sprotton had sent away the yellow hire carriage, and Lady Gosforth's landau awaited them. Luke handed Isabella up. "You know," he said, as the carriage moved off, "there's something I've neglected to tell you."

"Oh?" It sounded important.

"Yes. It occurred to me just now when you came down the

stairs looking more beautiful than any man's wife should look."

"Oh."

"I should have said it a long time ago."

"Oh?" It was ridiculous; she couldn't think of a single thing to say. Her heart was beating so fast. The carriage slowed. Were they there, already?

"Yes, back on the boat. Or the carriage. Or even before that, at Castillo de Rasal." He frowned. "Possibly even at Valle Verde. Or at Ayerbe in the Inn With No Fleas—" The carriage stopped. He looked out of the window. "Ah, we're here. I'll tell you later."

She grabbed his wrist. "Don't you dare tease me like this, Luke Ripton. Just tell me now!"

He looked at her, a little smile playing around his lips. "It's not urgent. It'll keep."

"Luke!"

His voice deepened. He leaned forward and drew her into his arms. "It's just this: I love you, Isabella Ripton. I have for I don't know how long. It might have been at the convent, or later at—"

A servant pulled the carriage door open. "Lord Ripton, you're home!" the man exclaimed joyfully.

Luke chuckled and pulled back from the kiss he'd been about to give her. "See, I said I should tell you later."

Bella was too stunned to move. "You love me?" she repeated blankly.

The servant gave her a startled glance, looked at Luke, grinned, and promptly began to close the carriage door.

"No." Luke stopped him. He took Bella's hand. "Come, my love, they're all waiting for us. I sent a note around. Dinner has been put back."

She followed him in a daze. He loved her? Or was that just something he said to make them all feel better about the marriage? He'd said it in front of his servant, after all.

Oh, it didn't matter. He loved her; he'd said so. She didn't care if it was a ruse or not. For tonight, she'd just believe it.

Tonight she felt beautiful and her husband had told her he loved her. It was enough.

She entered the house in a daze, and she spent the whole evening in a daze. She met dozens of people. His family were all natural beauties. She was the ugly duckling among them, but tonight she didn't care. He loved her.

His friends were all tall and amazingly good-looking. Not as good-looking as Bella's husband. And he loved her.

Somehow—she had no idea how—she got through the dinner. And then the orchestra struck up the first waltz. Luke had promised the first waltz to his little sister, Molly. It was a long-standing promise, and Bella was glad he was able to honor it, even if she had to resign herself to sitting out the dance with Luke's mother.

She could manage some of the country dances—they were similar to dances she'd learned as a child—but she didn't know how to waltz. Luke had tried to give her a lesson in waltzing on the ship coming over, but the sea wasn't exactly smooth and it had been one-two-three-stagger, one-two-stagger.

She sat with Luke's mother and Lady Gosforth and watched Luke and Molly twirling around the floor. She vowed to learn as quickly as possible. It looked like fun.

And then it was the second waltz. Luke's friend Harry bowed and led Molly out onto the floor. Molly was glowing with happiness. She didn't just have one big brother; she had four.

"My waltz, I believe," Luke said and bowed before Bella.

"No," Bella said, and then realized it sounded rude, and Luke's mother was right there, watching. "You know I can't waltz."

"You managed perfectly well on the ship."

"It was only once, and it was all one-two-stagger, because of the waves," she explained to his mother. She turned back to her husband. "I can't, Luke. I'll make a complete mess of things."

"Nonsense," Luke said briskly. "All you need to do is trust yourself to my lead." He glanced at her face and laughed.

"Oh well, one-two-stagger will do nicely. It's so crowded nobody will notice. And if they do, we shall set a trend. Come, wife, you vowed to obey me. At least make a pretense of doing so in public." He took her hand and almost dragged her onto the floor, ignoring her arguments, teasing her, and laughing.

Lady Gosforth, seeing Lady Ripton's face, broke off from the comment she'd started to make. "Oh my dear, whatever is the matter?"

Lady Ripton's gaze was fixed on her son and his wife. Her eyes were filled with tears.

"Is it the little Spanish gel? Has she upset you?" Lady Gosforth began.

Lady Ripton shook her head. "Look at my son," she whispered. "Look at him, Maude."

Lady Gosforth lifted her lorgnette and peered at Lady Ripton's son. "What? Looks a damn sight better than he's looked for years, if you ask me."

"Exactly. That little Spanish girl—" Lady Ripton mopped away a fresh surge of tears. "Look at him, Maude—he's laughing. He's teasing her. He's dancing. That dear, dear child has brought my son back to me." She sobbed happily.

"My dear, yes, I see it," Lady Gosforth murmured.

"All the boys came back changed. Harry and Gabe and my dear Rafe—you know as well as anyone the darkness they brought back from the war."

"All had demons riding them," Lady Gosforth agreed. "Wild to desperation, every one of 'em."

"And Luke was the worst. But over the years, I've watched each one of those boys settle down, fall in love, become . . . happy. But not my Luke, never my Luke." She wiped her eyes. "And when he told me he'd married a foreign girl when he was just nineteen and she thirteen . . . Of course I expected the worst. I've been so deeply distressed about the whole thing—well, you know all about it. But look at them, Maude. Just *look* at my son and that wonderful girl."

On the dance floor Isabella was twirling lightly in Luke's

arms as if she'd been doing it all her life, gazing up at her husband, her hand clasped against his heart. And Lady Ripton's tall, beautiful son was gazing down at his little Spanish girl with a look in his eyes that brought fresh tears to his mother's eyes.

"She adores him," Lady Gosforth commented.

"And he adores her," Lady Ripton sobbed. "The dear girl."

"Y ou were going to tell me something," Bella reminded Luke that night as they were preparing for bed. Her first ball had been magical. Luke's friends and relations had welcomed her with open arms. The men had danced with her, their wives had befriended her, and Luke's mother embraced Bella whenever she saw her. She still felt like dancing.

"Will you look at that," Luke exclaimed softly under his breath. He'd just removed his shirt and, as was his usual habit, had peered under the gauze bandage that covered his wound.

"Show me." Bella hurried over.

Luke slowly lifted the bandage off. With it came the dried scab of the wound. Beneath lay new skin. Shiny pink skin, a little puckered. He was scarred, yes, but there was not a hint of a rose anywhere to be seen.

"Oh Luke . . ."

He picked her up and carried her to bed.

"M uch later she stirred in his arms, stretching languorously. "You were going to tell me something."

"Hmm?"

"In the carriage. You started but we were interrupted." She was hungry for the words.

He pulled her close to him and rolled over so she lay on top of him, naked, skin to skin. "You want all the gory details, do you?"

"Yes." She kissed his chest. "Every. Last. One." She punctuated it with kisses.

He thought for a moment. "I'm utterly and totally besotted with you."

She frowned. "Besotted? That means drunk."

"Drunk, intoxicated. In love with."

She kissed him again. "I prefer the last one."

"I love you Isabella Mercedes Sanchez y Vaillant Ripton, with all my heart and soul. You are the light of my life. Almost literally. You saved me, you know."

"What from?"

"From the darkness within me."

"It was not your darkness, and anyway"—she kissed the fresh pink scar—"it's all gone now."

He kissed her long and thoroughly and then said, "And?"

"What do you mean, and?"

"Haven't you got something to say to me?"

"But you know I love you. I told you ages ago."

"A bare ten days ago."

"Hah, so you do remember."

"I have a terrible memory." He smiled. "Say it again."

He was as hungry as she was for the words, Bella saw. She kissed him, moving lower each time. "I. Love. You. Luke. Ripton."

"I like your punctuation. Do it again."

Epilogue

❦

"You don't mind, do you my dear?"

"Not at all," Bella assured her mother-in-law. "I am very happy to marry Luke again. I made those first vows as a child and did not really understand what I was promising." And Luke had made his assuming he could get them annulled. "To pledge myself to your son as an adult, in full knowledge of what these sacred promises mean, will make me very happy."

"And besides, you were married in a tiny village church with no family or friends whereas—" Lady Ripton broke off. "Oh my dear, I'm sorry. I did not think."

Bella smiled mistily. "It does not matter. I have been without family for a long time."

"You don't mind about the church? St. George's Hanover Square is the most fashionable church, and it's where all my children were christened and confirmed. But it's not Catholic."

Bella smiled. "I don't mind. Papa was an atheist and, while Mama was quite religious, I was educated in a convent . . . the Inquisition—faith by fear?" She shook her head. "No, a church is a church. It makes no difference to me."

"Excellent. Now, put on your shawl. It's still a little chilly outside." She adjusted Bella's shawl and inspected her. "There, so lovely you look. Such a shame your own mother could not—No." She broke off, dabbing at her eyes. "We will not cry and come to your wedding with red eyes."

Bella touched her mother's pearls. "I know. Mama has been very much on my mind. She was cynical about love, but at heart she was a romantic and she loved weddings. She would have loved to be here. She would have been happy for me."

"Of course she would, and I'm sure she's with you in spirit—oh dear." She dabbed again at her eyes. "Now come along, we don't want to be late. Who's giving you away?"

"I don't know. Luke said he'd arranged it, but he didn't tell me who."

"It will be one of the boys," Luke's mother said. "Gabe or Rafe or Harry. Such excellent friends. Ready?"

Bella made one last inspection of herself in the looking glass and nodded. She walked down the stairs arm-in-arm with her mother-in-law. "Good heavens," Lady Ripton exclaimed. "Visitors? At this hour and on such a day? Who can have admitted them? We must send them away."

In the hallway Molly stood talking to an elderly couple, a tall, distinguished-looking man with silver hair and a neat white beard, and an elegantly dressed little white-haired lady. She looked up as Bella descended and clutched the man's arm.

Bella's footsteps faltered. That little lady . . . it couldn't be . . . Mama with white hair?

She stopped on the last step, breathless.

"I see you're wearing your mother's pearls," the man said in a deep, husky voice.

She knew that voice. "Grandpapa?"

"You look beautiful, Isabella," Bella's grandmother said. "The image of your dear, dear mother." Her voice cracked with emotion.

"I thought you were dead," Bella whispered, embracing them.

"Oh, my darling girl." Her grandmother hugged her tightly.

"We thought the same of you," her grandfather said gruffly.

"But how . . . how did you know? And find me on this day of all days?" Bella asked when they'd recovered enough to speak.

"Lord Ripton tracked us down," Bella's grandfather told her. "Said he thought I might like to give the bride away."

"Oh yes, please." Bella wept and hugged them both again.

*I*t was a beautiful wedding, Bella was sure. Much more beautiful than the first time she'd married Luke Ripton. There were flowers and elegant clothes and fashionable guests and music.

But she didn't remember this one any better. She was too full of happiness to notice anything. Anything except the blaze of love in her husband's eyes as she walked down the aisle toward him.

"Love isn't pain, Mama," she whispered. "It's joy."